THE DEVIL'S CUT

HARVEY BENNETT THRILLERS

BOOK 18

NICK THACKER

CHAPTER 1
MARAYU

700 YEARS *Ago*

Islands of Puerto Rico

Marayu squinted at the horizon, salt sting in her eyes, wind whipping her braided hair against her cheek. The predawn sky glowed gray above the frothing waves that battered the reef off the coast of her island home.

She was perched in the bow of a narrow dugout canoe, scanning the water for signs of trouble. A dull roar rose behind her, where the surf pummeled the breakers. Storm winds gusted in fits, carrying the tang of brine and the faint promise of rain.

In all her seventeen seasons, Marayu had never seen the reef so restless so early in the year. She tightened her callused fingers around her paddle and glanced over her shoulder. Ohatí — her closest friend and brother-in-arms — balanced on the stern, gaze sweeping the sea as if he expected an enemy war canoe to materialize any second.

Her mind flicked back to the wounded stranger they'd dragged aboard just three nights ago. He'd been half-dead, moaning about raiders who'd "burned villages" and "taken everything." Marayu had listened to his delirious rambling, heart pounding. Usually, the Yukayan reef safeguarded their shores from invaders — sharp coral pillars and shifting channels made landing nearly impossible unless you knew the precise paths.

But storms could rewrite that labyrinth overnight. Sometimes entire reefs crumbled. Sometimes they rose in new, jagged formations. Sometimes a fresh sandbar emerged, wide enough to harbor an invading force.

Her mother used to say the island was alive. Not just the coconut palms and flamboyant trees, or the shoals teeming with parrotfish, but the land itself — a living being, shaped by hurricanes that battered them each season. Marayu grew up believing it. She felt it now, that pulsing energy beneath the waves. It unnerved her.

She guided the canoe closer to the reef, forcing down her dread. This patrol was her duty as one of the lead scouts under Cacique Caguax. When she was younger, she'd dreamed of it: gliding along the reef's edge at dawn, armed with spear and courage. Now that dream felt heavier. She couldn't quite banish the memory of that stranger's blood seeping into the water.

A sudden swirl of foam rose to her left, and she braced for the canoe to tilt. Beneath the surface, the coral shimmered with uncanny light in the gathering dawn. Sharp ridges jutted like broken teeth. She could almost imagine them shifting at the Watchers' command — those ancient sea-spirits Behique Azurína always spoke of in her midnight chants.

Ohatí cleared his throat. "Marayu, you feel that?"

She turned her head, heart thumping. "What do you mean?"

He shrugged, adjusting his grip on his paddle. "It's like the reef's not settled. The currents are off." His face was grim in the half-light. "Too many swirling eddies. And I keep thinking I hear drums."

Marayu listened. The wind keened, but beneath it all, she sensed... something. A far-off thrum that might have been the thunder of distant waves, or the echo of enemy war drums. The hair on her arms rose.

"We should go back," she said. "Caguax will want us to report if we sense anything strange."

Ohatí nodded. Together, they angled the canoe away from the reef. The swirl of currents tried to pull them back. Marayu set her jaw, digging her paddle hard, ignoring the protest of weary muscles. She'd been at sea for hours, and the rising gusts stung her cheeks, but she refused to falter.

If war was coming, she could not show weakness. Not to the clan, not to the Watchers, and certainly not to the men who'd kill them all if they found a way through the reef.

By the time they returned to the Yukayan village — a cluster of palm-roofed huts on a rocky bluff overlooking the ocean — the sun was up, painting the sky in streaks of pink and gold. The sea breeze carried the scent of cassava bread baking, a sure sign of breakfast. Normally, that smell lifted Marayu's spirits, but not today. As she and Ohatí beached the canoe, the hush of the onlookers told her they already suspected bad news.

Cacique Caguax himself strode toward them across the packed earth of the plaza. He was tall, his braided hair streaked with gray, his broad shoulders draped with a cotton mantle. By his side walked Behique Azurína, who leaned on a carved staff etched in wave-like designs. More villagers clustered behind, waiting.

Ohatí raised a hand in greeting but wasted no time. "Cacique," he began, voice tight, "the reef's changing again. Currents are swirling near the southwestern pass. It's wide enough that an enemy canoe might slip through if they're skilled — maybe more than one."

A ripple of murmurs passed through the watching villagers. Marayu stepped forward, clearing her throat. "The water felt unsettled, like a storm's forming. I can't say if it's next week or next month, but we all know hurricanes come when the Watchers command them."

Caguax's eyes flicked between them, unreadable. Then he nodded, turning to the crowd. "We've survived storms and threats before. But now we have word of raiders scouring the coast. We must prepare." His voice grew louder. "All warriors, gather your weapons. Strengthen the beach defenses. Scouts, stay on watch day and night."

He paused, then lowered his tone. "And the rest of you — pray. If the Watchers see fit to unleash another great hurricane, it may be our best chance at driving off any invasion."

Behique Azurína tapped her staff, the hollow thunk of wood against earth echoing. "I'll prepare an offering," she said softly. Her sharp gaze slid to Marayu. "I want you at the ceremony."

Marayu bowed her head. She'd never refused Azurína before, but an uneasy knot formed in her stomach. Offerings to the Watchers were never trivial. The old tales spoke of ancestors who sacrificed prized possessions — or worse — to appease the sea-spirits. Marayu hoped Azurína wasn't planning something quite so grim.

CHAPTER 2

CARLOS

Off the Coast of Culebrita, Puerto Rico

Carlos Ortega clung to the side of the *El Tiburón*, gasping for air.

He hauled himself up the short ladder, his arms trembling from the effort of his dive, and his wetsuit clung to his body, soaked with saltwater that dripped onto the boat's worn wooden deck. The Caribbean night pressed in around him, vast and oppressive, with the moonlight reflecting off the surface of the water in shifting patches of silver.

A warm breeze stirred the air, bringing with it the faint tang of fish and seaweed. Gentle waves slapped at the hull, a rhythmic sound that ordinarily might have soothed him. Tonight, it only heightened his dread.

I should never have gone this far, he thought, blinking seawater out of his eyes as he steadied himself. He clutched a waterproof bag to his chest as though it contained his very soul.

But what choice did I have... ?

The deck felt small and precarious under his feet, as though it might tip him back into the dark sea at any moment.

He caught a glimpse of the boat's captain at the helm, a man whose real name Carlos had never actually learned. They had agreed on a price, that was all. Now the captain glared at him, his expression tight with anxiety. The overhead light near the wheel cast harsh shadows across his face, making him look older than he probably was.

"You find anything?" the captain asked in Spanish, voice low, as though speaking too loudly might draw unwanted attention. His words cut through the gentle nighttime sounds: the quiet hum of *El Tiburón*'s engine, the distant cry of a seabird, the mild slosh of water against the hull.

Carlos, breathless, tried to gather himself before replying. He raked a hand over his close-cropped hair, which felt matted and heavy with salt. "Sí," he managed. "I found it."

"What? What is *it*?"

Carlos smiled, a wry grin on his face. "Proof."

The captain's eyes slid down to the satchel in Carlos's grasp. His gaze flicked back up almost immediately, as if whatever lay inside might burn him if he stared too long. "We should not have gone near that place," the captain muttered. "They call it *El Cementerio de los Contrabandistas* for a reason. Ships go down there and never come back. You think you're the first to go poking around?"

Carlos exhaled, feeling a dull ache spread through his shoulders. "I had... to see. After the hurricane came through, people started talking." His voice trembled with residual excitement and fear. *I had to find proof,* he thought. *I had to.*

A hurricane swept through the area last year, and the massive reef system and the shallow waters surrounding it — always a popular diving spot — had been hit hard. The sea life calling the reef home moved back in quickly, but the sands had shifted, creating new channels through the reef, forcing tour operators and guides to relearn the safe routes.

But the hurricane had done more than mess with the tried-and-true routes through the coral kingdom. It had uncovered a few shipwrecks that had previously been buried under dozens of feet of sand. For centuries, unlucky boats had found the reefs and perished there, creating a graveyard of watercraft of all shapes and sizes.

There was one ship in particular that had caused a stir in the small diving community. Just a rumor, no one had found definitive proof of its existence, but it was said the ship had been found on accident, shortly after the hurricane had terraformed the ocean floor.

He opened the top flap of the bag with shaking fingers, careful not to reveal too much just yet. He could still picture the twisted remains of centuries-old ships down below, their timbers covered in coral and strangled by algae, as though the sea had swallowed them whole and refused to let go.

The captain shifted uneasily, tapping the throttle to keep *El Tiburón* steady. Though the boat was small and worn, it had good bones — a dependable craft for coastal fishing. That reliability was why Carlos had chosen it in the first place. Now the captain looked ready to turn around and gun the engine for the nearest port. He probably wanted nothing more than to forget tonight.

Yet they both knew it was too late for that.

Carlos closed the satchel again and glanced over his shoulder, scanning the open water. The night was deceptively peaceful. The moon, though bright, seemed to illuminate only the immediate vicinity, leaving a vast expanse of ocean in darkness. He remembered diving among the reefs earlier, shining his flashlight on ghostly shapes half-buried in silt. He had never seen anything like it — ship after ship, from different eras, interwoven in a watery tomb.

He shivered. "I saw the old wrecks," he murmured. "And more. Something that shouldn't exist."

The captain shot him a nervous look. "If it's truly older than the Spanish... what does that mean?"

"It means," Carlos said, "we're talking about a civilization that predates everything we know about the Caribbean. Before Columbus. Before the Taíno. Maybe something even more ancient."

A gust of warm air ruffled his hair, and for a moment, the only sounds were the faint hum of the engine and the gentle lap of waves against the hull. Carlos lowered himself to the deck, exhausted from his dive. He set the satchel beside him and pressed a hand against his chest, feeling the heavy thud of his heart. He couldn't shake the feeling that they weren't alone out here, that eyes were watching from the darkness.

"I don't like it," the captain said, voice shaking just enough to be noticeable. "Whatever you found, it's cursed. Look what happened to the other ships that went down there."

Carlos forced a laugh, though it came out ragged. "You believe in curses, Captain?"

"Yes, damn it," the man hissed. "Sometimes it's not about whether you believe. It's about how the sea... punishes those who go where they shouldn't."

Carlos couldn't argue, not entirely. Part of him wished he could toss the artifact and the bag overboard and pretend this night had never happened. But he couldn't. He'd risked everything to come here, to find evidence of a lost world. He pulled the zippered sack closer, curling protectively around it like a dragon hoarding treasure. He wanted to ask the captain about local legends, about rumors of an "ancient curse," but the man's posture suggested he was already at a breaking point.

Shaking his head, Carlos stood. His wetsuit squelched with each step as he wobbled toward the helm, scanning the horizon again. The ocean looked empty. Still, the hairs on his arms stood up.

We shouldn't stay out here long. He swallowed. *Just get back to shore. I'll take the find to someone who can interpret it properly...*

He was about to speak when a sudden flicker of movement caught his eye. It came from the edge of the boat's spotlight, a faint glimmer of reflected moonlight. Carlos squinted, taking a step closer to the side. The captain noticed and turned the wheel slightly, angling the boat so the spotlight stretched across the water. For a fleeting second, Carlos thought it might be a dolphin or some drifting debris. Then he realized it was much larger — and it moved with intent.

"Captain," he said, voice cracking. "There's something out there."

The captain cursed under his breath. "Turn off the light. Maybe they won't see us."

But it was too late. Carlos reached for the switch, only to freeze as the shape came into full view: a sleek, black Zodiac boat, gliding across the surface without any running lights. Even from a distance, Carlos could see several figures aboard, silhouettes that radiated calm menace. One of them lifted a hand in their direction.

CHAPTER 3
MARAYU

700 YEARS *Ago*

Islands of Puerto Rico

That night, after hastily gulped rations, Marayu joined the clan in the center of the village. A large fire crackled, sending sparks into the humid air. Drums pounded, resonating in her chest. She slipped through the gathering crowd, weaving past friends and elders. Ohatí caught her eye from across the circle, eyebrows raised as if to say, *Stay alert.* She nodded back.

Caguax stood near the fire, his expression lit by dancing flames. Behique Azurína raised her arms, the swirling tattoos on her forearms rippling with the motion. From a small leather pouch, she scattered powdered shells onto the embers, releasing a burst of white smoke. The drums deepened, and the villagers fell silent.

Azurína's chant began low, guttural, a series of words passed down through generations. Marayu couldn't decipher the old language precisely, but she felt its power. Her skin tingled. the Watchers. The ancestors. All invoked in a single breath.

Then Azurína reached out, motioning Marayu closer. Heart hammering, Marayu stepped forward. She'd never been called to the center during a ceremony before. Her every nerve buzzed with apprehension. She met Azurína's eyes — dark and intense — and knelt as directed.

"Place your hands in mine," the behique murmured.

Marayu obeyed. Azurína's fingers were cold despite the heat of the flames. Slowly, Azurína guided Marayu's hands over the brazier, not quite touching the coals but close enough that the scorching heat licked at her palms.

"Watchers of the deep," Azurína called, voice rising, "hear us. The storms may come to tear and to reshape. We do not resist; we only ask that you spare our children. Let the wrath of wind and wave fall upon those who would desecrate our shores."

A swirl of wind whipped the fire, sparks grazing Marayu's face. She squeezed her eyes shut. In that instant, she heard something that sounded like a distant conch horn, echoing in the night. She shuddered.

When she opened her eyes, Azurína withdrew. The old woman seemed drained, sweat beading on her temples. She turned to the assembly. "the Watchers have accepted our plea," she said quietly. "But we must be ready. The storms that rewrite our island can just as easily devour us if we lose faith."

Marayu slowly rose to her feet, stepping back into the crowd. An uneasy hush swallowed the village. The hush of people uncertain if the Watchers' fury would protect them — or if they'd be collateral damage.

The days blurred into a tense routine. Marayu split her time between patrolling the reef and drilling with the other warriors. She'd grown proficient with a spear as a child, but now her moves were sharper, more desperate. She couldn't banish the image of marauders pillaging the shore if the reef gave them passage.

Ohatí joined her on every patrol. They were rarely alone — Caguax sent others, too — but it helped to have his familiar presence at her back. She remembered the first time they'd snuck away from chores to fish near the lagoon, still children. He'd teased her for flinching at a reef shark's silhouette. She'd teased him back for squirming whenever a jellyfish brushed his ankle. Now, they faced dangers that dwarfed those old memories.

One oppressive afternoon, Marayu guided her canoe around a newly formed sandspit. The sky was dull bronze, the air so thick she felt she might choke on it. She glanced at Ohatí. "It's like the sea is holding its breath."

He nodded grimly. "Storm's coming for sure. Maybe a big one."

She stared out at the hazy line where ocean met sky. A memory pricked her mind: her grandmother's tales of the Great Surge decades ago, when an entire spit of land near Culebra had vanished under walls of water. Houses were swept out to sea, farmland destroyed. But in that same event, a new islet appeared miles away, formed by displaced sand and coral. *the Watchers demand a sacrifice,* her grandmother had said. *But they grant a gift in return.*

Would that same cataclysm repeat soon? The thought made her spine prickle.

Ohatí inhaled sharply. "Look."

She followed his pointing arm. A flotilla of canoes glided along the horizon — too far to see details, but enough to spark alarm. Not Yukayan canoes — those were smaller, narrower. These vessels were broad, each carrying many rowers. Possibly the war canoes they'd been dreading.

Marayu felt a surge of cold dread. The wind carried the faint thrum of distant drums, an unmistakable war beat. They needed to report back immediately.

She pivoted the canoe, adrenaline throbbing in her temples. This was it. The invasion. And with the storm so close, everything would converge — human conflict and the Watchers' fury — one unstoppable wave of chaos.

They made it to the bluff by dusk, delivering the news. Cacique Caguax called an emergency council in the open plaza. Smoke from cooking fires melded with the perfume of tropical blooms, a deceptive calm for the storm-charged night. Warriors clutched spears and clubs, their expressions grim. Behique Azurína prepared another mixture of herbs, but Marayu noticed her hands trembled as she sprinkled them onto a brazier.

Caguax's voice boomed. "So it begins. The enemy fleet is coming from the west. We believe they'll attempt the southwestern channel — our reef's weakest point. Our advantage is that the Watchers might tear them apart if they venture into those waters at the wrong tide."

He paused, gaze flicking to Marayu. "But we can't rely on that alone."

Marayu lifted her chin. "We'll engage them in the shallows before they land."

Ohatí spoke up, eyes reflecting torchlight. "If they make it through the pass, we funnel them into narrow channels. That's where we strike hardest."

Caguax nodded approval. "Half our warriors will hold the beach. The other half will use canoes to herd them onto the reef. Even if the Watchers don't unleash a hurricane tonight, the swirling currents might do enough damage."

A rumble of thunder punctuated his words, as if the sea itself concurred. The assembled warriors exchanged uneasy glances. The plan was straightforward, but the risk was colossal: if the storm arrived in full force, the Yukayans could be swept out to sea alongside their enemies.

But better that, Marayu thought, *than to surrender and let them burn our homes.*

CHAPTER 4
CARLOS

Off the Coast of Culebrita, Puerto Rico

"Down!" the captain barked.

A staccato burst of gunfire ripped through the stillness, and Carlos heard bullets whizz past. He threw himself flat, pressing his body to the deck. The captain yelped, returning fire with a small pistol he'd picked up, but his shots went wild, spraying sparks as they ricocheted off the sea. Another gunshot answered, abrupt and cruel. A sharp cry tore from the captain's lips, then he fell silent.

Carlos stayed prone, feeling his heart pound so violently he thought it might burst. Warm blood dripped onto the deck near his head. He couldn't tell if it was from the captain or from some stray wound of his own. *Get up. Move. Fight. Something.* But fear paralyzed him.

He crawled a few feet, toward the dive vest laying on the deck. His scuba gear was nearby, but he wasn't sure he could make it all the way there.

The spotlight flickered crazily as *El Tiburón* swung in a slow circle, engine still running but helm unmanned. The boat rocked under the weight of a new presence. Carlos caught a glimpse of black boots landing on the deck. Slowly, he raised his eyes and saw one of the intruders — a tall man in dark clothes, wearing a tactical vest and night-vision goggles. The man held a silenced pistol, its barrel still exuding a faint wisp of smoke.

Carlos's gaze darted to the helm. The captain lay slumped over the wheel, his eyes open and unseeing. Blood soaked his shirt. A nauseating wave of grief and guilt churned in Carlos's stomach. *He didn't have to die.*

Another figure appeared behind the first, also dressed in black, also armed. This second figure kneeled and swept the deck with a narrow beam from a flashlight. When it fell on the waterproof satchel, they pointed. The tall man nodded once and advanced, crossing the short distance in two strides.

Carlos tried to scramble back, dive vest in hand, but he had nowhere to go. The tall man seized his arm, yanking him upright with chilling ease. Carlos's breath caught in his throat, and his legs refused to support him.

"Where is it?" the tall man asked in Spanish, voice cold and devoid of emotion. "What did you take from the water?"

Carlos couldn't speak. He just shook his head, wide-eyed. The man jerked his arm again, nearly popping it from the socket. Carlos let out a ragged cry, fighting the urge to faint. Another wave of terror crashed over him when he saw the second figure retrieve the satchel, carefully opening it to inspect its contents.

A flashlight shone on the stone fragments, the unknown relics from El Cementerio de los Contrabandistas. Carlos watched the second figure nod in confirmation to the tall man. *They found the main piece,* he realized, heart sinking. *They know what I took.*

"Please," Carlos managed, voice trembling. "I —"

The tall man gave him a contemptuous glance before raising his pistol. He pulled the trigger without a word. Carlos felt a sudden, searing pain tear through his chest. His world tilted; the deck rose to meet him. He saw the black Zodiac drifting alongside *El Tiburón,* the men passing the satchel between them as if it were a mere package. The gunman stepped over Carlos's collapsing body, not even looking down.

Blood pooled beneath Carlos, warm against the cold sea air.

Get to the gear, he told himself. *Get overboard, and maybe you can get away.*

El Tiburón rocked, its helm unmanned and its engine sputtering. The tall man and his companions vanished back into the Zodiac, moving with the same fluid efficiency they had arrived with.

Carlos took the opportunity to pull his bloodied, beaten body back toward his gear. Moving was excruciating, but he had to get his gear on and into the water — the men might come back to ensure he was dead.

He growled in agony, slipping the mask over his head. Thankfully, he could easily slide into the water off the back deck where there was no railing, and with a final burst of adrenaline-fueled energy, he did just that.

The men returned then, and he heard voices as he slipped beneath the lapping waves. He held his breath — not because he needed to, but out of fear.

He listened, wanting to swim deeper into the reef and the wrecks that might provide a bit of safety, but he also wanted to hear what they were saying.

The voices rose as one of the men discovered Carlos missing. He heard *"into the water"* and *"can't return unless it is finished."*

Carlos didn't need to hear more. He turned and dove, forcing his wounded lungs to provide just a bit more support, just a little longer.

Then he heard it. A splash, a man entering the water above him.

They're coming for me.

CHAPTER 5
MARAYU

Islands of Puerto Rico

When darkness fell, lightning flickered at the edge of the clouds. Marayu's heart pounded as she took her place in a canoe with Ohatí and two other warriors.

They wore simple chest wraps and carried bone-tipped spears, short bows, and a meager supply of arrows sealed in hide quivers. She could barely see the lagoon's boundary beyond the gloom, but she felt the swell of black water rocking them.

Ohatí breathed, "Here they come."

Marayu peered through the gloom. At first, she spotted only faint torchlight dancing across waves. Then a row of canoes emerged, close enough that she glimpsed shapes of men. They advanced with chilling confidence, ignoring the jagged silhouette of the reef.

She swallowed thickly and reached for her bow. Somewhere onshore, Yukayan archers readied a volley. She heard the whistle of arrows slicing the sky, then angry shouts as the invaders scrambled to shield themselves. Lightning ripped across the clouds, illuminating the chaos in stark white.

The first foreign canoe struck a hidden outcropping with a jarring crunch. Men spilled overboard, their screams lost in the thunder. Marayu exhaled relief — they'd drawn first blood. But more canoes veered around the wreck, learning fast.

Ohatí spat a curse. "They're heading for the southwestern pass. Follow me!"

He and Marayu paddled hard, ignoring the spray that stung their faces. Another flash of lightning revealed a war canoe loaded with at least a dozen men, all chanting in a language that rang harsh in Marayu's ears. She could see their clubs and spears glinting.

"Don't let them break through!" one of the Yukayan warriors bellowed.

Marayu raised her bow, took aim as best she could in the flickering light, and loosed an arrow. It thunked into the prow, missing the rowers by inches. A second arrow soared from a comrade's bow, striking a raider's shoulder. He toppled with a cry.

But still they surged forward. The unstoppable mass of canoes reached the southwestern pass. Marayu's canoe was there to meet them, sides slamming together in the rough water. She gasped as a raider lunged, hurling a spear that whistled past her ear.

She dropped her bow, grabbed her own spear, and lunged upward, jabbing the man's torso. He howled, blood arcing into the sea. Ohatí pivoted behind her, swinging a club that knocked another raider overboard. The scuffle was raw, chaotic. Canoes pitched with every wave, making balance precarious.

Boom — thunder crashed. This time, the wind tore overhead with frightening intensity, kicking salt spray into their eyes. A swirling gust battered the wave crests, and lightning revealed a monstrous wall of cloud looming to the north. A hurricane was forming, and quickly.

All around them, Yukayan and enemy canoes clashed among the reefs. Arrows hissed, men shouted, water churned with flailing bodies. Marayu's heart pounded like a drum. She stabbed another raider in the thigh, but her spear jammed in bone. She had to yank hard to free it, nearly losing her footing.

A wave slammed the side of the canoe, drenching them. She looked up to see the war canoe with the serpent figurehead — that had to be the invaders' flagship — bearing down with savage purpose. Grim men in black and white paint rowed with iron discipline, chanting in unison.

Her stomach clenched. They were unstoppable, heading straight for the pass. the Watchers had to help, or they were finished.

From the bluff, a conch horn sounded. Marayu recognized it as the signal for retreat — she and her group were meant to pull the raiders into the reef so the shore-bound warriors could pelt them from a distance. But the swirling wind drowned out the horn's second blast. The sea roared, thunderclaps boomed.

Suddenly, a flash of lightning revealed mountainous waves rolling in from the open ocean. The storm had arrived in earnest. the Watchers were rewriting the sea.

A tremendous swell lifted Marayu's canoe, nearly flipping it. She and Ohatí clutched the gunwales, hearts in their throats. The invaders weren't so lucky. The serpent-headed canoe next to them crashed into a coral outcropping, splintering in a deafening crack. Men shrieked as they toppled into the frothing water. Another wave hammered them, swirling their bodies beneath the coral fangs.

Marayu couldn't draw breath. The wind tore at her lungs, the rain lashed her face. She glimpsed a battered group of Yukayan warriors trying to paddle out of the chaos, but a wave snatched them sideways, slamming them onto the reef. the Watchers weren't choosing sides — this storm wanted everyone.

Ohatí grabbed her arm. "We can't stay here!" he shouted, voice nearly lost in the gale. "We have to get to shallower water or we'll be dashed apart!"

She nodded, chest tight with both terror and determination. They set their paddles to the water, riding the monstrous waves closer to shore. Fallen torches flickered in the dark surf. Broken canoes bobbed among the debris. She thought of the bodies afloat, recognized that some might be Yukayan. Her tribe. A surge of grief mingled with anger.

Lightning flared again. The southwestern pass was in utter chaos. The swirling water parted for an instant, revealing twisted shapes of coral and the upended forms of at least three war canoes. the Watchers had made that place a death trap for anyone foolish enough to enter. If she and Ohatí lingered, they'd share the same fate.

They paddled with every ounce of strength, ignoring the stinging salt and howling winds. The storm battered them relentlessly, waves rising higher. Eventually, they reached the lagoon near the shore. The water grew shallower under the keel, though currents still threatened to capsize them.

Shouts echoed from the beach. Torches lit panicked faces. Yukayan warriors rushed into the surf, grabbing canoes, hauling in survivors. Marayu collapsed forward, letting them drag her onto the wet sand. She coughed, lungs burning, throat raw from salt and fear.

Ohatí staggered to his feet beside her, hair plastered to his scalp. "We... drove them off?" he gasped.

She glanced back at the raging sea. Through the sheets of rain, she could make out the remains of the enemy canoes, either shattered on the reef or flailing in the unstoppable currents. Another wave — taller than any she'd ever seen — surged in the distance. Even from shore, she felt its raw power.

"We survived," she whispered. *But at what cost?*

The hurricane raged all night, tearing through palm groves, toppling huts, flooding farmland. The Yukayans huddled in the sturdiest structures on the bluff, praying. Marayu tried to sleep but kept jolting awake, mind haunted by the battle's images: men drowned in the reef, canoes splintered like driftwood. She dreamed of the Watchers controlling the storm, weaving monstrous waves from the sky, rewriting the coastline with each thunderous crash.

By dawn, the gale abated. A strange hush fell, as if the storm had devoured every sound. The village stepped outside, eyes wide. Where once there was a smooth beach, a jagged ridge of sand now rose. And where the reef had been, large sections lay rearranged, massive coral towers collapsed or shifted, forming new channels. Debris littered the shore — both raider and Yukayan alike.

Marayu's chest clenched as she spotted fallen warriors among the driftwood. Families wailed, searching for loved ones. Many had survived; many more had not. She swallowed back tears, biting her lip hard.

A tall figure approached: Cacique Caguax, hair matted with rainwater. He looked haggard, a raw scrape on his temple. "Marayu," he said softly. "You fought bravely. Both you and Ohatí. Because of you, they didn't land in force."

She bowed her head. "We lost so many."

His voice cracked. "Yes. But we're still here, and the invaders...they're gone. Scattered, drowned, or retreated. the Watchers' storm was fierce enough to break them."

Her gaze strayed to the horizon, where battered planks and foreign bodies washed in on the tide. the Watchers had chosen to reshape the battlefield, not necessarily to spare the Yukayans but to enact the unstoppable cycles of ruin and renewal that defined these islands.

Behique Azurína limped over, leaning heavily on her staff. She surveyed the changed coastline: new sandbars, an altered shoreline. "the Watchers have rewritten the land once more," she murmured. "In time, we'll discover hidden passages or newly revealed reefs that might hold relics from older times. Such is our fate."

Marayu exhaled, gaze drifting across the devastation. Part of her felt a dark awe. As horrifying as the storm was, it was also mesmerizing — a raw display of nature's power. The Yukayans lived and died by these storms, each one erasing the old maps and forging new shapes.

Her knuckles whitened on the spear she still gripped. *We're alive.* That was all that mattered right now.

They had to rebuild.

CHAPTER 6
RAMÓN

Off the Coast of Culebrita, Puerto Rico

Ramón Mendoza stood at the port-side railing of *El Tiburón*, one hand gripping the chipped paint as he peered over the edge. He'd heard the telltale gentle splash — someone sliding off the stern of the boat.

The momentary hush in the gunfire confirmed what he suspected: their wounded target, a man named Carlos, had slipped into the water. Ramón glanced at his fellow Syndicate operatives, who traded uneasy stares. None seemed inclined to jump in after the man.

Ramón set his jaw. He had spent time in colder waters off the Strait of Magellan, training for free-dives in zero-visibility conditions. Though he'd only joined the Black Coral Syndicate a year ago, his skill in water-based ops had already earned him a certain grim reputation.

Tonight, he intended to prove himself once more.

A pair of men crouched near the boat's dim spotlight, scanning the waves for any sign of a head bobbing up. One of them spared Ramón a look that said, *We need you to handle this.* Ramón gave a curt nod, turning from the rail.

He shrugged free of his fatigue jacket, dropping it at his feet. He unzipped a knife sheath from his belt, checking the blade's edge. Satisfied, he re-sheathed it and paced toward the low gunwale. The others watched with anxious faces — some novices, others battered from the earlier firefight.

"Gear?" someone offered, holding up a battered half-mask and a near-empty scuba tank. It would take too long to secure properly, and the tank's regulator hung half-disassembled.

Ramón shook his head, letting a flicker of contempt show. *If they'd prepared better, we wouldn't have this fiasco.* But he said nothing.

He inhaled twice, deep and measured, steeling himself. Then he vaulted the rail, plunging into the black water.

The ocean closed over him with a muted *whump.* A momentary chill spiked across his skin, though the Caribbean warmth softened it. He surfaced briefly for one last gulp of air, ignoring the boat's spotlight above him. Then he submerged, letting darkness fold him in.

Beneath the surface, moonbeams cut faint ribbons through the water. Ramón oriented himself, scanning for any reflection of metal or glint of dive gear. He kicked outward, pressing deeper. The hush below replaced the chaotic noise above — he heard only his heartbeat and the distant hum of *El Tiburón*'s idling engine.

Carlos had been shot. Ramón counted on that wound slowing him down. *He can't hide for long.* Ramón's lungs felt taut with the usual burn of free-diving. He exhaled a small trickle of air, calming his nerves.

Two minutes, maybe three — he'd done it plenty of times. *Just find him quickly.*

He skirted along the reef's slope, ghostly shapes of coral heads drifting in his periphery. In the gloom, the water felt claustrophobic, heavy with shifting silt. A bullet hole or two from the earlier firefight might be leaking blood. A swirl of red might show him the way — but in low light, it was nearly impossible to see.

Then, out of the corner of his eye, he caught a flicker. A shape, a diver's silhouette, hugging the coral.

Got you.

Ramón sank to half a meter above the seabed, creeping behind a coral pillar. His lungs clenched — he had perhaps thirty seconds left before he'd need air. He tightened his grip on the handle of his knife.

The diver pivoted slightly, a short scuba tank on his back. Carlos, for sure. Ramón could see the man's labored breathing: small bursts of bubbles from the regulator. He suspected the gunshot wound was draining Carlos's strength. *He won't last long.*

But a desperate man would fight to the bitter end.

Ramón kicked off the coral, gliding forward. Ten feet. Five. Carlos twitched, sensing movement. In a burst of silt, Ramón slammed into the man from behind, hooking an arm around his midsection. Carlos's eyes went wide, a muffled shout lost in the water. Ramón jammed his free hand to the main hose near the regulator's first stage.

Slice it.

He unsheathed his knife in a fluid motion and slashed across the thick rubber.

A violent hiss erupted, bubbles surging past them in an effervescent cloud. Carlos writhed in terror, reaching back to claw at Ramón's face. The mercenary jerked his head to the side, catching a glancing scrape from Carlos's nails. *Damn him.* Ramón twisted the knife again, severing any backup line. The hiss faded to sporadic spurts as the cylinder's pressure plummeted.

His own lungs screamed for oxygen now. He let Carlos's flailing body shift, then seized the mouthpiece from the severed line, pressing it to his own lips for a desperate pull. The taste was bitter, metallic — laced with the diver's blood. But it gave Ramón a precious moment to quell the black spots dancing in his vision.

Carlos saw the act, horror contorting his face behind the mask. Ramón felt a grim satisfaction: *Your last breath is mine.* Then the mouthpiece sputtered, pressure gone. Carlos tried to kick away, but Ramón locked an arm around his thigh, yanking him back.

The two men spun into the coral-littered seafloor, scraping limbs against rough outcroppings. A swirl of red fanned from Carlos's bullet wound.

Ramón's final borrowed breath faded, chest tight. He had to finish this now. Carlos managed to land an elbow near his temple, jarring him. The knife slipped from his hand. *No matter.* He latched onto Carlos's harness, jamming an elbow into the diver's diaphragm.

Carlos convulsed, a spasm that signaled the last push of oxygen in his bloodstream was running out.

They slammed into a piece of half-buried wreckage — old timbers spiked with barnacles. Carlos's mask cracked against the beam, sending more bubbles rushing out. Ramón used the momentum to wrap his arm around the diver's throat, ignoring the man's gurgling attempts to claw free. Darkness pinched at Ramón's vision, but he squeezed with every fiber of muscle he had. *No mercy.*

Carlos's movements grew feeble. A final shudder rippled through his limbs. Then he went limp, eyes rolling up. Ramón shoved the diver away. The body drifted in place, regulator dislodged, hoses flapping. The reef's silt enveloped them in a murky shroud.

Ramón's own lungs seized, demanding release.

Without hesitation, he kicked for the surface, arms sweeping in powerful strokes. A dull roar filled his ears — lack of oxygen threatened to black him out if he hesitated. The slope angled up. He glimpsed the shimmer of boat lights above.

Focus. Surface.

His heart pounded dangerously fast.

He broke through into the night air in a burst of foam, gasping. Salt spray stung his eyes. *El Tiburón* loomed about fifteen feet away. A silhouette on deck shouted, pointing a flashlight. Ramón waved an arm, forcing ragged inhalations of the sweet air he'd been denied.

They tossed a rope ladder. Ramón grabbed it, hauling himself on board. He collapsed onto the deck, coughing up brine. The Syndicate men crowded around, some brandishing rifles, but no new threat.

"Dead," he forced out between gulps. "He's dead."

One of the other men — a tall, wiry operative named Ortiz — helped him to his feet, slinging a threadbare towel over his shoulders. "You good?" Ortiz asked quietly.

Ramón nodded, still catching his breath. Water streamed from his hair, rivulets trickling onto the blood-streaked deck. He'd done his job, no loose ends left.

Within minutes, the men tossed lines from their smaller Zodiac that had been idling alongside *El Tiburón*, waiting for quick escapes. Ortiz motioned for the mercenary to transfer over. They were done with this old fishing boat, which might be left drifting or scuttled. The remains of the firefight and its casualties would vanish under rumors and bribes. That was the Syndicate's modus operandi — no witnesses, no evidence.

Ramón nodded. He wrung out the last of the saltwater from his fatigues, ignoring the stinging cuts on his arms. The frantic moments of fighting underwater had left him scratched and bruised, but nothing serious. He checked his knife — still sheathed, though the blade would need cleaning. *Another reminder of the kill.*

The men parted to let him pass. He climbed over the side into the waiting Zodiac. Two more operatives manned the controls, armed and ready. One gave a low whistle.

Ramón kept quiet. *No need for bragging.*

The Zodiac's engine kicked in, low and powerful. Ortiz, perched near the bow, signaled to slip away from *El Tiburón*. The small craft cut across the choppy waters, leaving the battered fishing boat behind. The mercenary sank onto a bench, letting exhaustion wash over him. He stared at the black waves rolling against the hull.

Carlos's final expression still flickered in Ramón's mind — eyes wide with terror, a swirl of escaping bubbles. That silent scream haunted him even now. But like every other job, he forced it down. *This is what the Syndicate demands.* He was loyal enough not to question it.

Ortiz muttered something about heading back to their hidden cove for a rendezvous. Ramón barely listened. His ears still rang from the rushing blood in his head. He gripped the side of the Zodiac with white-knuckled fingers, watching the reflection of moonlight in the water. The crew spoke in hushed tones, content that their target was eliminated.

The outboard motor hummed a steady drone. None of them asked

Ramón for details. The open sea stretched ahead, a flicker of distant lightning unveiling the horizon. The mercenary closed his eyes for a moment, breathing the salt-tinged air deeply.

Another mission completed.

Another threat to the wreck's secrets snuffed out.

CHAPTER 7
RAMÓN

THE MEN in the Zodiac cut their engine once they were a safe distance from *El Tiburón*. The night swallowed them, as though they'd never existed. One of them turned to Ramón, speaking in a low voice. "All clear?"

Ramón nodded, passing over the satchel. "All clear," he repeated. In the dim light, he looked at the relic. He had no interest in the artifact's story or historical significance. All that mattered was that their employer — the leader of the Syndicate — wanted it.

An employer who didn't tolerate failure or loose ends.

He zipped the bag closed, placed it under a bench. "Let's go," he said. The others obeyed without question.

Within minutes, the Zodiac was at full throttle again, blending with the darkness. Behind them, *El Tiburón* bobbed on the waves like a ghostly husk, slowly drifting away from the site of violence.

In the distance, a faint cluster of lights indicated Puerto Rico's shoreline, too far to see the tragedy that had just taken place. No alarm would be raised until someone stumbled on *El Tiburón* drifting, or until daybreak revealed the boat's battered shape. By then, the Black Coral Syndicate would have vanished, leaving no traces behind except for two dead men and a grieving ocean.

In a small cove near the Culebran coastline, hidden from prying eyes by a tangle of mangroves, the black Zodiac glided ashore. Ramón stepped out first, boots sinking into wet sand. Another man hopped out next, carefully carrying the satchel. They moved with synchronized efficiency, as though they had rehearsed every step.

A battered SUV waited under the cover of thick foliage, headlights off. Two more figures stood by, one smoking a cigarette, the other checking a phone. They barely exchanged greetings. Their entire operation functioned on minimal words and maximum action. Ramón pointed at the satchel; the smoker nodded and walked forward, dropping his cigarette in the sand and crushing it underfoot.

He took the bag, opened it just enough to see the stone fragments. The beams of a flashlight danced across ancient carvings on weathered stone, miraculously well-kept from centuries of being buried in the sand. "Good," he murmured. His Spanish was thick with an Eastern European accent — his father was Cuban, his mother Romanian. "We'll send it on the next boat. Everything else is handled?"

"Sí," he answered. "No survivors."

The one with the flashlight glanced at him. "You're sure?"

A nod. "They weren't expecting us. One tried to escape into the water. We followed. Both men are dead."

"Bueno," said the flashlight man. He closed the satchel. "Come on. We need to move."

They climbed into the SUV, which rumbled to life. No headlights turned on. The driver eased it forward, passing carefully through the mangrove thicket until they reached a dirt track. Without a word, they sped away into the pre-dawn gloom. Behind them, the black Zodiac remained near the waterline, set to be retrieved later.

Meanwhile, out on the open sea, *El Tiburón* drifted. The wind picked up, rustling the torn scraps of a net hanging from the boat's railing. The sun's first rays peeked over the horizon, staining the eastern sky a soft orange. In that morning light, the battered vessel appeared almost peaceful, as if the events of the previous night had been a nightmare that left only faint traces behind.

But the truth was there, in the stiffening limbs of the captain, and in the echoes of gunfire that lingered in the salty air. The relic was gone, stolen by men who wouldn't hesitate to kill again if the prize demanded it. For them, human life was expendable, mere collateral damage on the path to profit and power.

A few hours later, a local fisherman named José spotted *El Tiburón* from a distance. He knew it well — it was his brother's boat. He'd often accompanied him on fishing excursions, taking his turn at the helm while his brother ran lines.

He squinted at the familiar shape on the water, noticing that it wasn't moving except for the natural drift of the current. Concern pricked at him. This stretch of coastline was typically busy in the morning, with boats heading out to fish or ferry supplies. A stationary craft, especially one with no visible activity, hinted at trouble.

Cautiously, he approached, calling out in Spanish, "Hola? You need help?"

When no answer came, a chill slid down his spine. He cut his engine and drifted closer, heart pounding.

I knew it was a fool's errand, he thought. He'd told his brother that taking the diver out to the reef at night was dangerous enough — and to search for the rumored ship that had apparently been unearthed after the hurricane was suicide.

No one knew the new routes through the reef well enough yet. If his brother drifted too close, they could be ensnared on the reef, or a shipwreck.

He approached alongside *El Tiburón*. As soon as he saw the blood on the deck, he inhaled sharply, crossing himself. He found his brother's body shortly thereafter. Terror gripped him as he realized both men must have been shot — the diver apparently making it overboard, and likely perishing underwater.

Horrified and overcome with grief he couldn't even begin to process, he retreated to his boat and radioed the authorities with shaking hands.

Before the day was done, the local police would come out, frown over the crime scene, and shake their heads. They would suspect pirates or drug runners, perhaps. They'd call it an unsolved homicide, lacking leads. But José knew the score — the perpetrators might know some of the local police, might even be in cahoots with them. Corruption was easy here, when money was hard to come by.

He thought about that. Perhaps calling this in was the wrong move. He *had* given them his name, out of fear that not coming clean might implicate him.

But now, he wondered if fear of retribution might keep them from pursuing the matter too aggressively.

Or if those who murdered his brother might come after him next.

CHAPTER 8

SARAH

DR. SARAH LINDGREN stood at the front of a humid lecture hall on the University of Puerto Rico's *Río Piedras* campus, brush-tipped pen in hand, a half-finished diagram of a Taíno settlement scratched onto the whiteboard. Usually, she'd have used the sleek digital projector that sat nearby, but sometimes old-school methods stirred more curiosity in her students. And curiosity, as she often preached, was the lifeblood of any anthropologist.

She set the pen down and rubbed her thumb across a faint smear of black ink on her palm. "So," she said, turning to face the rows of students, "if we accept the outdated trope that all early Caribbean peoples were just 'camping on the beach' all the time, how do we explain the existence of roads, ceremonial plazas, or complex trade networks in pre-colonial Puerto Rico and the surrounding islands?"

A murmur rippled through the class. Barely a dozen undergraduates were present — summer sessions were always smaller — but the closeness of the group brought out more honesty. One young man at the front, wearing rectangular glasses, raised his hand. "A lot of high school textbooks still gloss over Taíno settlements. They say the Taínos lived in simple huts, and that's about it."

Sarah allowed herself a warm smile. She loved these earnest questions.

"And that's precisely the misconception we'll keep challenging. Because, yes, they had bohíos — circular huts with thatched roofs — but they weren't just ephemeral campsites. They built community centers, known as yucayeques, with designated areas for cooking, crafting, and worship. We have evidence of caneyes — rectangular buildings reserved for the cacique or important rituals — and even ball courts, or bateyes, lined by petroglyphs."

She clicked to a digital slide, showing an aerial photograph of an excavated Taíno settlement in eastern Puerto Rico. "See? Stone outlines, postholes, refuse heaps, even patterns in shell middens that suggest systematic disposal — signs of a planned community."

At that, a woman in a teal headscarf spoke up from the middle row. "Dr. Lindgren, you mentioned worship. Could that worship have involved permanent shrines?"

Sarah nodded, excitement kindling in her dark eyes. "Exactly. The Taíno religious world revolved around zemí worship — zemís being figurines or idols representing gods, ancestors, or natural forces. But they wouldn't just leave them lying around in random huts. We find evidence of purposeful spaces: small altars, carved stone seats, and ritual enclaves near ball courts. Which implies architecture, not just improvised lean-tos."

She paused, letting the weight of that statement settle. "Folks, you see how that changes the narrative? Our image of these societies isn't just families squatting in a circle on the sand, but thriving communities with social structures, leadership, religious practices, and architecture."

As she said the word *architecture*, Sarah felt a familiar wave of nostalgia. Her father, Dr. Graham Lindgren — renowned archaeologist and world-traveling explorer — used to say the same thing whenever they scoured remote sites in her teenage years. *Never dismiss how creative humans are when it comes to building homes.* She remembered how proud he was that she'd followed in his footsteps, forging her own path in anthropology, fueled by the Jamaican heritage she'd inherited from her mother.

A warm breeze drifted through the classroom's open windows, carrying the hum of traffic and the sweet smell of plantains frying at a nearby food kiosk. Sarah's part-Jamaican roots had always drawn her to the Caribbean's indigenous past, a tapestry woven from multiple migrations, layered histories, and formidable resilience — especially in places like Puerto Rico, where the Taínos had left their mark in more ways than the mainstream narrative acknowledged.

"Now," she continued, stepping away from the whiteboard, "I know I've assigned you readings that focus heavily on Taíno and Igneri artifacts found in coastal dig sites. But for today, I want us to step back —"

She pulled up another slide on the projector. This one showed a mountainous region with thick forest. "This is Utuado, in the central highlands of Puerto Rico. Archaeological digs here uncovered evidence of hillside terraces for farming, plus artifacts that suggest a more permanent settlement. We're talking about entire communities built inland, not just by the shore. The soil was good for cassava, and the vantage offered protection. Does that sound like people who were merely beach-campers?"

A subdued chuckle spread through the room. Sarah caught a glimpse of appreciation on a few students' faces. She recognized that look of *I never thought about it that way*. It was why she taught — even if a career in field archaeology might have been more glamorous, guiding these bright minds felt just as vital.

A hand shot up. "Dr. Lindgren," asked a lanky woman in cargo shorts, "how did they manage hurricanes? If they built inland, I guess they'd avoid storm surges, but... those winds are no joke."

"Excellent question," Sarah said, nodding. She walked to the whiteboard, drawing a quick schematic of a typical Taíno bohío: a circular outline, conical roof. "First off, the circular design helps dissipate strong winds. Fewer corners to catch wind and rip the structure apart. They often used strong wooden posts and flexible palm thatch, which can bend. Plus, they were excellent at reading the seasons and the environment — picking spots less prone to flooding, reinforcing communal structures before storm season."

A voice from the back: "And shrines? Did they protect those specifically?"

Sarah arched an eyebrow, pressing a button to shift the slide. A new image showed a carved limestone idol partially submerged in water, discovered near a cave system in western Puerto Rico. "We find glimpses of shrines in caverns, on hilltops, even along certain reefs. The point is: these were deliberate choices. They knew the spiritual significance of those landscapes. Hurricanes might damage or transform the coastline every year, but some shrines stayed intact for generations. They'd rebuild them if they washed away, or shift them to safer locations. And in some cases, shrines were hidden in caves, protected from the wind."

She paused, her gaze traveling over the attentive faces. "The Taínos and other early Caribbean peoples didn't passively accept the environment. They adapted to it — shaping and reshaping their communities. That's a sign of resilience and continuity."

Sarah stepped back from the podium, letting the last image linger. It showed an intricate petroglyph of a coiled hurricane symbol, carved into a cave wall. The swirling lines seemed to suggest both danger and sacred power.

"All right," she announced. "Let's break for fifteen. When we come back, we'll dig into the case studies from Vieques and the Lesser Antilles. Then, we'll talk about some newly discovered subaquatic sites. If the lab across campus is open, I might even show you a few artifacts in person."

CHAPTER 9

BEN

THE SEAPLANE'S propellers whirred to a stop, and Harvey Bennett peeled himself out of the narrow seat, fighting an overwhelming sense of claustrophobia that had been building ever since they'd taken off from San Juan. Bright sunlight blasted into the cabin through the open door, causing Ben to squint as he hefted his carry-on bag over his shoulder.

This is insane, he thought, taking in the stark transition from the plane's cold, recycled air to the steamy, tropical heat outside. *Why did I let Reggie talk me into this?*

He stepped onto the small floating dock and was promptly greeted by a swirl of warm air mixed with the tang of saltwater. The breeze carried the cries of seagulls and the distant hum of outboard motors — signs of life in Culebra, Puerto Rico. They'd arrived.

Reggie hopped out behind him, all smiles and bouncing steps, as if this were the greatest day of his life. He wore board shorts, sunglasses perched on his head, and a grin that could power a small city. Meanwhile, Ben felt like a lump of bread dough left out in the sun. He adjusted his backpack and tried not to scowl too obviously.

A local dockhand rushed forward to help them with their luggage, speaking Spanish with a cheerful lilt that Ben could only partially follow.

The man gestured broadly toward the end of the dock where a cluster of golf carts waited, presumably rentals for arriving guests. Reggie nodded enthusiastically, fumbling in his pocket for a tip. The dockhand waved off the money with a smile, as if to say, "No worries, amigo," and ran back to assist the next passenger.

"Man, can you feel that sun?" Reggie asked, stretching his arms wide as if embracing the entire island. "I'm soaking it in."

Ben wiped a line of sweat from his forehead. "Yeah," he muttered. "It's about as subtle as a flamethrower."

"Come on, man, lighten up. We're in paradise!" Reggie shot him the kind of grin that usually meant trouble. "Sarah said Culebra was beautiful, and she wasn't kidding." He surveyed the aquamarine water, the palm trees swaying in a mild breeze, and the scatter of colorful buildings hugging the shoreline. "I'm already loving it."

Ben grunted. "Paradise is overrated when your skin is blistering." He could already feel his neck and arms prickling under the relentless sun. *I must look like a boiled lobster.* He reminded himself that Julie and Hope were safely up in Montana, spending a week with her parents. He had no obligations here — no rescue missions, no phone calls — just a forced vacation. *I should be grateful, right?*

Reggie elbowed him. "We just got here. Give it five minutes before you start complaining."

Ben raised an eyebrow. "I'd complain sooner, but I'm too dehydrated."

"Ha! Then let's fix that." Reggie pointed toward a small waterfront kiosk advertising fresh coconuts, smoothies, and piña coladas. "I'm getting us drinks."

"You realize it's, what, eleven in the morning?"

"Sure do. Which means it's basically lunchtime. Lunchtime in the Caribbean equals rum."

Ben sighed. He felt his shoulders slump under the oppressive heat as Reggie swaggered off toward the kiosk. A few other passengers from their seaplane milled around, some snapping pictures of the vibrant harbor, others rummaging in suitcases for sunscreen and hats. The entire place had the feel of a postcard: teal water lapping at a pristine shoreline, small fishing boats bobbing at anchor, a handful of pastel-colored cottages perched on a rise overlooking the sea.

This isn't so bad, Ben admitted to himself, though his mood wasn't quite ready to lift yet. He was an Alaska guy, used to crisp mountain air and cool summers. The humidity clung to him like a wet blanket. Still, the idea of a week with no responsibilities, no criminals, and no emergencies... that part sounded good. He just wished it was about twenty degrees cooler.

Okay, fifty *degrees cooler.*

A squawking gull swooped low overhead, making Ben duck on instinct. He cursed under his breath. "Relax, gull, I'm not after your fish," he muttered. Then he took a few steps down the dock, feeling the rough boards under his sandals.

A small group of tourists snapped photos of each other in front of the seaplane, all excited chatter. Their squeals of delight at the exotic scenery caused him to cringe inwardly.

He let his gaze wander across the water, noticing a few larger boats moored farther out. A fisherman stood on the deck of one, mending a net. Another boat was a sleek catamaran, presumably for private charters. Then his eyes landed on a battered wooden fishing vessel chugging away from the docks, its engine coughing black smoke. He shook his head. *That thing looks barely seaworthy.*

"Here you go," Reggie's voice interrupted, drawing Ben's attention back. Reggie held out a plastic cup with a tiny umbrella. "Piña colada for the grumpy Alaskan. Drink, enjoy, loosen up."

Ben accepted the cup and took a tentative sip. Coconut, pineapple, and a potent dose of rum flooded his taste buds. "That's actually pretty good," he admitted, voice muffled by the umbrella. "Thanks."

Reggie beamed, as though he'd personally invented tropical cocktails. "Told you. Now, let's get our golf cart. We've got a bungalow to find!"

They headed over to a small rental shack where a young woman behind the counter cheerfully asked for Reggie's name. He flashed his signature grin, gave the reservation details, and within minutes they were handed the keys to a bright yellow golf cart that looked like it had seen better days. A sticker on the side read "Island Cruiser #7," and the seats were patched with duct tape. Ben threw his bag in the back while Reggie fiddled with the ignition.

The engine sputtered, then roared to life. "Let's do this," Reggie said, popping the cart into gear. "Our beachside palace awaits."

CHAPTER 10

SARAH

FIFTEEN MINUTES LATER, Sarah's classroom had thinned out, leaving only a cluster of enthusiastic undergraduates lingering near the whiteboard. Their hushed chatter filled the humid air. The promise of lab artifacts had sparked excitement, and nobody wanted to risk missing the chance to see them.

Sarah glanced at the time on her phone: she had just under an hour before her next meeting. Enough, hopefully, to show them the highlights. One of the custodians — a kindly older gentleman — poked his head in, nodded to her with a polite smile, then continued down the corridor, pushing a squeaking cart of cleaning supplies. Through the open door, Sarah could see a slice of the outdoor courtyard; the midday sun illuminated the top of a flamboyán tree, whose bright red blooms swayed in the breeze.

She turned back to the small circle of students. "All right," she said, voice low and conspiratorial. "Let's go see if the lab is open. We can check out some actual Taíno artifacts — no one's going to fall asleep with a real cemi in front of them, right?"

A round of soft laughter rippled among the group.

Leading them into the hallway, Sarah talked in a warm, off-the-cuff manner about the archaeological process — how context was everything, how a single pottery shard could reshape entire theories about migration routes or settlement permanence. It was the sort of conversation she loved best: easy, informal, hands-on learning.

She keyed into a narrow corridor off the main hallway. The floors smelled faintly of disinfectant, and overhead fluorescents buzzed. At the end of the corridor loomed the lab's thick metal door, its small window revealing neat rows of steel tables inside. Sarah waved her ID card over the reader, and a green light blinked.

When the door clicked open, a rush of cool, artificially chilled air greeted them. The lab was small but orderly — four long tables, each lined with labeled plastic bins and carefully curated samples. On the far wall hung a bulletin board plastered with polaroids of recent digs, pinned side by side with typed notes.

"Welcome to our archaeology nook," Sarah said, flipping on the overhead lights. "We've got to be gentle — some of these pieces haven't been fully catalogued. The department's archivist would kill me if we broke anything."

A few students chuckled nervously. They drifted around the tables, drawn to the transparent bins filled with pottery shards, shell ornaments, and carved stones. Sarah walked them through a few highlights, pulling out each artifact with a gloved hand and describing its significance. The students listened, rapt. Sarah's voice took on a soft, reverential tone — she believed every artifact had a story, and these were no exception.

A willowy student named Valentina pointed at a jagged shard of limestone in a separate tray. "What's that from?" she asked. "It looks almost... worked, but the shape is odd."

Sarah carefully lifted the piece. It was about the length of her hand, with a few faint, parallel scratches across its surface. "We think it might be part of a ritual seat — or duho — common in Taíno ceremonial circles. The shape is unusual because it might have broken off something bigger." She angled it under the overhead light. "See these lines? Not random. A pattern that might represent swirling water. Possibly hurricane imagery, or a cosmic reference."

Another student, Miguel, stepped closer. "Hurricane imagery? Could that be symbolic?"

Sarah nodded. "The Taínos were keenly aware of storms. They personified destructive forces in their mythology — there's evidence some petroglyphs represent the spirit or deity of hurricanes. That awareness of nature's power was woven into their shrines and daily life."

Miguel's gaze flicked to the artifact. "Makes sense. A population living in the path of annual storms would absolutely respect that force."

She set the limestone shard down carefully. "Exactly."

A hush fell as they absorbed it all — the artistry, the resilience. Someone took a few quiet pictures on their phone, though Sarah gently reminded them to ask permission before posting anywhere. The hum of the AC unit filled the space, a steady backdrop.

Eventually, the conversation drifted back to the main reason they were all so enthralled: proof that early Caribbean peoples weren't merely "camping." They were building, worshipping, shaping their world.

A student in a green headband, Carmen, raised her hand, as if they were still in class. "Dr. Lindgren, can I ask... aside from the obvious stone or coral altars, do we know of any bigger architectural footprints? Like huge walls or fortifications, something that might indicate a more advanced civilization?"

Sarah stifled a smile. *Advanced?* She'd always disliked that term; these societies were advanced in ways outsiders hardly recognized. But she knew what Carmen meant: large, dramatic ruins akin to pyramids or citadels.

"The Taíno and their predecessors didn't go in for monumental stone architecture like the Maya or Inca," Sarah said, choosing her words. "They used organic materials — wood, thatch — that degrade quickly in the tropics. So we rarely see big ruins. But that doesn't mean they lacked permanence or complexity. They just took different forms."

A murmur of understanding spread. Carmen nodded thoughtfully.

Sarah turned her attention to a short, muscular student standing at the fringes — Luis, if she recalled. He'd been quiet in class but was always scribbling notes. Now, he chewed his lip, eyes fixed on the display. "Dr. Lindgren," he said hesitantly, "could we ever find, like... entire lost towns hidden in the jungle? Or maybe something was covered by a landslide?"

She hesitated, glancing around. "It's possible, sure. Over centuries, the rainforest can swallow structures. Landslides, or even new growth, can obscure roads or plazas. But in Puerto Rico, we've done quite a bit of surveying. The big finds so far are mostly in the form of plazas, ball courts, petroglyph-laden caves, smaller domestic sites. No sprawling megalopolises uncovered yet."

Luis made a thoughtful sound. "So... more like pockets, not huge cities."

"Precisely."

Sarah motioned for them to gather around a final bin on the back table. Inside it lay a handful of clay shards that had a distinctive geometric pattern. "Okay, last show-and-tell item. These came from a site near the southwestern coast, part of what was likely a mid-sized village. The pattern is repeating triangles, painted with a red dye that tested as achiote."

She paused, wanting to emphasize the significance. "That indicates a symbolic design effort — a style they repeated over multiple generations. So again, we're not talking about a random campsite. This was tradition, a sense of identity, and it spread across multiple households."

The group murmured approval. After a few final photos and whispered conversations, they started to wander back toward the corridor. Everyone seemed both energized and subdued, as though they'd just glimpsed a hidden world.

They reconvened in the lecture hall later, where the air felt hot and still compared to the lab's chill. Sarah stood near the whiteboard, fielding last-minute questions about excavation techniques and how ancient communities leveraged trade across the islands. Slowly, her gaze drifted to the clock overhead — it was creeping toward the lunch hour, and she had another obligation soon.

"All right," Sarah said, pressing her hands together. "I think that's enough archaeology for one session. You're free to go — just remember to do the reading on Saladoid ceramics for next time."

Several students thanked her, while others grabbed their backpacks and hurried off. A handful lingered. Carmen hung back, glancing at Sarah with a half-smile that suggested she wanted a private word.

"Sure, Carmen," Sarah said, nodding at her to step closer. "Something on your mind?"

Carmen smoothed her green headband, looking a little shy. "I didn't want to bring it up in front of everyone, but... see, my grandmother lives in Culebra, that little island east of Puerto Rico. She's always telling me these wild stories about 'cities under the sea' that storms sometimes expose. I used to laugh it off, but your talk about subaquatic sites makes me wonder if there's some truth in it."

Sarah tilted her head. "Cities under the sea... It's a common legend in a lot of coastal cultures. But often these stories carry a kernel of historical memory — like a settlement partially submerged after a massive storm. Why do you ask?"

"Well," Carmen said, lowering her voice, "there was that huge hurricane recently. It messed up Culebra's reefs pretty bad. My grandma swears that during the storm, fishermen spotted stone pillars jutting up in the shallows near one of the cays. Nobody's found them since, or at least nobody's talking about it." She laughed nervously. "Probably just old wives' tales, right?"

Something sparked in Sarah's mind. She'd heard rumors from colleagues: fragments of rumor, half-verified sightings of "stone lines" off the smaller islets. She'd never had time or funding to check them out. "Not necessarily," she said carefully. "The ocean can shift sandbars overnight, especially after a big hurricane. I mean, entire stretches of beach can vanish, so it's not impossible that the storm revealed something. Or reburied it."

Carmen's eyes lit up. "You really think so?"

Sarah shrugged, but her pulse quickened. "I won't say it's definitive, but that's exactly how new sites get discovered — people notice anomalies after storms. If your grandma has specifics about the location, maybe gather a bit more info. I'd be happy to hear it."

Carmen beamed. "I will. Thanks, Dr. Lindgren."

With that, she hurried off, presumably to her next class.

CHAPTER 11

BEN

BEN CLIMBED in next to him and tried not to roll his eyes. The cart lurched forward, and they rattled out onto a narrow street lined with colorful houses and small shops. Tourists in flip-flops meandered alongside locals pushing carts of fresh fruit or handmade crafts. Every window seemed to display bright tropical shirts, beach towels, and trinkets shaped like parrots or sea turtles.

They passed a small bar with a chalkboard sign reading "Fresh Grouper Today!" in shaky white letters. The smell of fried plantains drifted through the air, mixing with the heavier scent of sun-baked concrete. Ben found himself clutching his piña colada as though it were a life preserver. Beads of condensation slid down the cup, mirroring the sweat on his brow.

"Sarah texted me earlier," Reggie said as he drove. He had to raise his voice a bit to be heard over the rattle of the golf cart's engine. "She wants to meet up in San Juan at some point this week, but she's swamped with her conference. Archeological stuff. You know how it is."

Ben nodded vaguely. "Yeah, sure." He liked Sarah Lindgren — she was smart, funny, and perfectly matched Reggie's energy level, which was no small feat. *Still can't imagine how an archaeologist fits with a former Army sniper*, he thought, sipping his drink. *Then again, I suppose I'm hardly in a position to judge relationships.*

They paused at a stop sign and let a pair of cyclists pass. The cyclists waved cheerfully, and Reggie waved back like a local politician. Ben attempted a small nod. "So Sarah's the reason we're here, basically," he said.

"Partly, yeah," Reggie admitted. "But mostly it's about you needing a break. You pretend you're just chilling all the time, but I know better. Plus, Julie outed you."

Ben raised an eyebrow.

"She told me you've been running yourself ragged — reading up on declassified military and CIA reports to glean insight into whatever the Faction's doing, training for who-knows-what, *always* on alert."

Ben shrugged. The truth was that after everything they'd been through recently, including a brief romp in the Bering Sea running from Russians who hadn't gotten the memo that the Cold War had ended, he *did* need a vacation. But that didn't mean he had to be happy about the heat and humidity. "Better to be prepared than caught off guard," he muttered. *Because trouble always finds us, doesn't it?*

Reggie slapped the steering wheel lightly. "Well, now you can un-prepare for a bit. Drink piña coladas, fish, maybe snorkel. Enjoy the local cuisine, you know? Sarah mentioned there's some cool shipwreck site off the coast. Might be worth checking out."

Ben let out a small snort. "A *shipwreck*? Reggie, we're not here on a historical expedition."

"Why not? You love a good mystery. Don't you remember that time —"

"Don't." Ben cut him off before the memories came flooding back. *We agreed this was a vacation. No drama.* He steadied himself, forcing a deep breath. "Let's just see the bungalow first. One thing at a time."

Reggie grinned his characteristic face-wide grin. "Deal."

They continued puttering along the road, passing more pastel-painted buildings and open-air cafés with plastic chairs. A group of tourists lugging inflatable beach toys and snorkeling gear trudged along the sidewalk, pointing excitedly at maps. The air was thick with sunshine and possibility, almost as if the day itself was saying, *See? Nothing to worry about here.* Ben wished he could believe it.

A few minutes later, Reggie turned down a gravel path lined with palm trees. The occasional coconut hung overhead, and Ben eyed them warily — he'd heard stories of coconuts dropping on unsuspecting pedestrians. *Probably better not to stand under one for too long.* The path opened up to a small clearing where a single-story bungalow stood, painted a bright turquoise that seemed to glow under the midday sun.

"Ta-da!" Reggie announced, stopping the golf cart dramatically. "Our home for the next week."

Ben climbed out, letting his sandals sink into warm sand. Up close, the bungalow was charming in a rustic way. Salt-stained shutters, a thatched porch awning, and large windows facing the ocean. A friendly explosion of bougainvillea framed the entrance, its pink flowers in vibrant bloom.

"Not bad, Reggie," Ben admitted. "You did okay." Despite himself, he felt a small wave of relief. *At least we won't be stuck in some run-down motel.*

Reggie hopped onto the porch, fishing a key from his pocket. "Wait till you see the inside. We've got a fridge full of beer, a couple of fishing rods in the back closet, and a view that's supposed to be killer at sunset."

Ben followed, stepping into a living area decorated in a beachy style — wicker furniture with bright cushions, whitewashed walls, and a few local art pieces depicting sea turtles and coral reefs. A ceiling fan spun lazily overhead, stirring the warm air into something a bit more tolerable. Through sliding glass doors on the far wall, he glimpsed a wooden deck with a few chairs and a hammock. Beyond that, the ocean.

The cool tile floor felt good under his feet. He set his bag down, letting out a long breath. *Could be worse,* he thought, recalling past accommodations he and Reggie had endured during some of their misadventures — like the time they had to bunk in a dilapidated safehouse with no running water. At least here, he had a chance to shower off the sweat.

"The bedroom's back here," Reggie called, wandering down a short hallway. "We're sharing, right?"

Ben didn't answer.

"Okay, fine. Two bedrooms, actually, sorry to bum you out. And here's the kitchen. Ooh, a blender. We can make more piña coladas!"

Ben shook his head. "I knew I should have waited for Julie to be able to come with me. We've got a whole week of this? You're relentless."

"And proud of it."

CHAPTER 12

BEN

FOR A FEW MINUTES, they moved around the bungalow, staking out where to stash their gear, checking that the fans worked. The place was small but functional, with enough space for two guys who didn't need much more than a bed and a fridge. Reggie was quick to find the Wi-Fi password taped to the fridge and typed it into his phone, while Ben tested the water in the shower — lukewarm at best, but in this heat, he suspected the colder it was, the better.

"All right," Reggie said, clapping his hands together. "Since we've got the day ahead of us, how about we celebrate with some fishing? The ocean's right there, man!"

Ben stared at him. "I need at least twenty minutes to unwind, maybe take a quick nap. Or at least put on more sunscreen."

"What!" Reggie said. "We didn't bring the girls with us *specifically* so we wouldn't have to wait around for them to get ready."

Ben just blinked at his friend.

"Fine, fine," Reggie relented. "I'll stock the cooler with drinks. Then we can decide our next move." He looked at Ben thoughtfully. "You sure you're okay, buddy?"

Ben paused, letting the question sink in. *Am I okay?* He felt the tension in his shoulders, the discomfort of being somewhere so different from home. And the vague suspicion that trouble lurked even in paradise. But he forced a small smile. "Yeah," he lied. "Just... adjusting to the heat."

Reggie nodded, satisfied enough. "Cool. I'll be outside."

As soon as Reggie left, Ben sank onto the couch, grateful for the overhead fan. The cushions smelled faintly of coconut oil, probably from countless beachgoers renting this place before them. He closed his eyes, letting out a slow exhale, trying to let his mind drift. *This is just a vacation,* he reminded himself. *No crises. No manhunts. No shootouts.* He wasn't sure why he felt the need to remind himself of that, except that history had shown him he rarely got to enjoy peaceful downtime.

Julie said I needed a break. She insisted I come here, he thought, feeling a pang of guilt at being away from his wife and little daughter. But Julie had been adamant — she wanted Ben to decompress while she took Hope to visit her parents. As if reading his mind, his phone buzzed. He pulled it out to see a message from Julie:

> Hey honey, safe travels? Let me know when you're settled. Hope misses you already!

Ben felt a small smile tug at the corners of his mouth. He quickly typed back:

> We made it. Place is hot as Hades, but Reggie is in heaven. Miss you guys.

He considered adding a heart emoji — the youths were apparently wearing him down — but finally listened to his better, more *mature* judgement, and didn't. He pocketed the phone. Outside, he heard Reggie singing an off-key tune while rummaging through the cooler. *At least one of us is having a blast,* Ben mused.

He stood, stretched, and made his way to the sliding glass doors. The deck overlooked a narrow strip of white sand leading down to the water. Waves rolled in, lapping gently, their constant hiss a soothing soundtrack. Farther up the beach, he could see a few other bungalows scattered among palm trees, though none seemed occupied at the moment.

Okay, so this is paradise, he conceded. *Maybe if I can just endure the sunburn...*

He slid the door open and stepped outside, the heat immediately intensifying. Reggie was crouched by a small chest cooler near the edge of the deck, loading in cans of local beer and ice. He looked up with a mischievous grin. "Ready for some fishing, Captain Alaska?"

Ben winced. "Nope. Not that."

Reggie cackled. "Just trying it out. What about 'Chugach Ben?'"

Ben glared.

Reggie dusted off his hands and stood. "Fine. We'll keep brainstorming. Anyway, This wreck site Sarah mentioned — it's supposedly just a short boat ride away. Locals say it's always been a cool snorkeling spot. I figure we can check it out tomorrow, or the next day. No rush. But let's keep it on the to-do list."

Ben rocked back on his heels. "By the way, why'd she tell you about the shipwreck site? We're not really the snorkeling type."

Reggie shrugged. "Yeah, apparently it's famous for some reason. Might have some Spanish galleon remnants, or maybe something older. I don't know. She's the expert, not me." Reggie shrugged as if it were no big deal. "But I'm always game for an adventure."

Ben snorted softly. "Famous last words."

Reggie shot him a playful glare. "You say that like you expect everything to blow up. Relax. The biggest risk here is a sunburn."

"Which I already have."

"Then you're safe. No more risks for you."

Ben had to chuckle at that. He'd known Reggie for years, and while their personalities clashed at times, he had to admit that Reggie's enthusiasm *was* contagious — when it wasn't driving him crazy. The man had once been a sniper for the Army, then found his niche with the CSO, joining Ben in more than a few dangerous situations.

"All right," Ben said, stepping off the deck onto the sand. The warmth hit his toes, and he curled them experimentally. "Let's see if we can catch dinner."

Reggie whooped, carrying the cooler like a prize trophy. They strolled a short distance along the shoreline, passing an abandoned jet ski moored to a post, until they found a decent spot where the water seemed calm. Reggie pulled out two fishing rods he'd grabbed from the bungalow's closet — serviceable enough, though clearly battered by previous renters.

CHAPTER 13

BEN

THEY SET up near a driftwood log that served as a makeshift bench, and Reggie began tying lures with the efficiency of someone who'd done this many times before. Ben opened one of the beers, letting the cool fizz coat his throat. A gentle breeze ruffled his hair, the smell of salt and seaweed drifting past.

This is fine, Ben told himself, gazing at the horizon. *Normal people do this on vacation. Sit on a beach, fish, have a beer. It's not complicated.*

He cast his line out, watching the lure plunk into the water. Behind them, gulls wheeled in lazy arcs, eyeing the possibility of scraps. Palm fronds rustled overhead, providing sporadic shade. Reggie cast his own line with a flourish, then settled onto the driftwood, rummaging in the cooler for another drink.

For a long moment, neither spoke. The hush of the waves and the occasional screech of a gull were the only sounds. Ben let himself relax, just a little, focusing on the gentle tug of the tide.

"You know," Reggie said eventually, "this might be the first time we've hung out without being shot at. I mean, this month, at least."

Ben gave a wry chuckle. "Don't jinx it."

"You're the one who always says *Famous last words.*"

Ben shrugged. "Force of habit. We've been through... a lot."

"And now we're not," Reggie said quietly, reeling in a few inches of line. "We're good. Don't worry so much, brother."

"Famous last words." They both laughed, then a soft exhale escaped Ben's lips. *I hope you're right.* Out loud, he said, "I'm trying. Really. This will be a good time, man. For real."

They sat like that, content enough in the moment. The midday sun beat down on them, but with hats, sunscreen, and the occasional sip of cold beer, it became tolerable. Ben felt beads of sweat trickle down his back, soaking into his shirt, but it was strangely comforting.

Time passed in a hazy dream. Each cast of the line felt meditative, each wave's whisper lulled him deeper into a sense of calm. After an hour of minimal bites — aside from one small snapper Reggie tossed back — they decided to call it quits. Reggie packed up the rods, and Ben helped lug the half-finished cooler back to the bungalow. By then, both men's stomachs were grumbling.

"What say we head into town, find more food?" Reggie asked, wiping sweat from his forehead.

Ben nodded, hooking his thumbs under the straps of his backpack. "Sounds good. I'm not too hungry, but I'll go anywhere indoors. With air conditioning."

"Works for me. Let's rinse off, then we can drive the golf cart back."

They trudged into the bungalow, showered quickly in lukewarm water, and changed into dry clothes — light linen shirts for Reggie, a simple T-shirt and cargo shorts for Ben. The overhead fans throughout the bungalow provided little relief as they toweled off. Ben felt the heat returning with a sticky vengeance the moment they stepped onto the porch, but at least he was no longer coated in salt.

Driving back toward the center of town, they passed more small shops, a bakery advertising fresh pastries, and a stand selling grilled pinchos — meat skewers. The smell of charred pork and spices wafted through the open sides of the golf cart, making Ben's stomach growl.

"How about that place?" Reggie suggested, pointing to a modest eatery with a sign reading "La Cosecha del Mar." It looked half-restaurant, half-fish market, with open-air seating and a row of plastic chairs under a thatched roof.

Ben shrugged. "Sure."

They parked the cart on the roadside, hopped out, and found a table near the edge of the seating area. A ceiling fan spun overhead, providing a bit of a breeze.

A waitress approached, smiling, and handed them menus that listed everything in both Spanish and English. Reggie scanned the menu, eyes lighting up at the mention of fresh-caught grouper. Ben flipped through it, squinting at items like mofongo, rice and beans, and a variety of fried seafood.

"Fried plantains," Reggie said, nodding approvingly. "I'm definitely getting those. And the grouper special. And maybe a side of tostones."

Ben set his menu down. "I'll have... shrimp mofongo," he decided, partially because he'd heard of it before. He motioned for the waitress, and they placed their orders, also requesting two tall glasses of ice water. After she left, Reggie leaned back in his chair, tapping his foot to some distant salsa music drifting from the kitchen.

"You know, that local wreck that just got uncovered again," Reggie began. "Sarah said it might be near where Manny Delgado used to run tours."

"Who's Manny Delgado?

"Never met him," Reggie said. "I guess some old treasure hunter who owns a few small businesses, dive shops, that sort of thing. Basically a legend around here. Big fish in a small pond, I guess. And I think he had a thing for Sarah."

Ben's eyebrow arched upward. "That's what she said?"

"Well, that's what I got from it."

"You think *everyone's* got a thing for Sarah," Ben added.

"Can you blame them?" Reggie shot back.

Ben rolled his eyes, but smiled. "Anyway, she thought we should meet up with this Manny guy?"

Reggie shrugged. "*If* we got bored, or needed anything, she said." He paused, glancing around. "She said — and these are her words — 'he's a hoot.' I don't think we'll get bored, or need a hoot, exactly, but it might be cool."

Ben shrugged. "Sure, maybe. Let's just see how the week goes." He was too hungry to argue about potential adventures. The last thing he wanted was to dive near some wreck just for the thrill of it. But he also knew Reggie well enough to suspect that *any* mention of a mysterious shipwreck would eventually reel him in. *And who am I to stand between Reggie and a new adventure?*

"So," Reggie continued, "did you hear about that fisherman's bar at the far end of the beach? Sarah told me they serve the best local rum. We should scope it out tonight."

"Your capacity for rum and food never ceases to amaze," Ben said dryly.

"Just saying, we can celebrate our first night in paradise." He gave Ben a once-over. "And you can learn to have fun in the sun, you big polar bear."

Ben rolled his eyes, though the corner of his mouth twitched in a half-smile. "Fine. We'll see. But no bar fights."

"Aww, come on. That's half the fun." Reggie's teasing grin earned him a mock glare.

CHAPTER 14

BEN

THE WAITRESS RETURNED with their drinks — ice water and an extra pitcher to refill. Ben gulped his water gratefully, feeling the cold liquid restore some of his dwindling energy. The rum and beers from earlier had left him dehydrated, and the stifling humidity didn't help. He poured himself another glass, ignoring Reggie's amused expression. *Laugh all you want; at least I'll stay conscious.*

Their meals arrived shortly after, and the aroma of garlic, onion, and fresh seafood filled the air. Reggie immediately dug into his grouper, moaning in delight. "Dude, this is insane," he said around a mouthful, ignoring basic table manners. "So fresh."

Ben speared a shrimp from his mofongo — plantains mashed together with garlic and broth — and took a bite. The flavors were rich and comforting. *Okay, this might be worth the heat.* He found himself relaxing, letting the background chatter of the restaurant and the gentle swirl of the ceiling fan lull him.

Between bites, Reggie made conversation about local snorkeling spots and the possibility of renting kayaks, listing half a dozen "must-try" activities he'd gleaned from Sarah. Ben half-listened, content to enjoy the meal and pretend they were just normal tourists.

When they finished, they leaned back in their chairs, letting the waitress clear their plates. Reggie asked for the check, waving off Ben's offer to split it. "I got this one," he said, pulling out his wallet. "Besides, it's all CSO money. Plus, I need to butter you up if I'm going to drag you into that shipwreck dive."

Ben smirked, tossing his napkin on the table. "Still not sure about that. But thanks for lunch."

They stood and stretched, feeling pleasantly full. Outside the restaurant, the afternoon sun was less harsh, softened by a few wispy clouds. A light breeze carried the briny smell of the harbor. People bustled around them, some carrying beach bags, others lugging groceries or diving gear. The island buzzed with a casual, laid-back energy.

Reggie shot Ben a glance that was almost paternal. "You doing better now?"

"Yeah," Ben admitted, rolling his shoulders. "Food helped. So did the shade."

"Awesome. Let's head back to the bungalow, maybe crash for a bit, then we can decide if we want to do anything tonight."

Ben agreed. They hopped into their golf cart and rattled away from the restaurant, merging onto a slightly busier road that looped along the coastline. Every turn presented a new postcard-perfect view: turquoise water on one side, lush greenery on the other. They passed a small pier where children jumped off the edge into the water, shrieking with laughter. Tourists snapped photos from a vantage point near a cluster of pink bougainvillea.

I can see why people love it here, Ben thought, feeling his earlier cynicism thaw. *It's beautiful.*

At the bungalow, Reggie parked haphazardly in the sand, and they made their way inside. The interior felt surprisingly cool in comparison to the outdoor heat, the fans dutifully circulating air. Ben plopped down on the couch, letting out a contented sigh.

Reggie rummaged in the fridge, then came over with two bottles of water, handing one to Ben. "You should hydrate."

Ben snorted. "Yes, mom."

"Hey, if you pass out, I'm not carrying you."

"I weigh more than you, anyway," Ben said, cracking the bottle open and taking a long drink. He set it on the coffee table, then reclined. *Maybe we really can just relax. Just for a day or two.* He tried to recall the last time he'd gone anywhere that didn't involve chasing leads or running from bad guys. His mind came up blank.

Reggie flopped into a wicker armchair, propping his feet on a stool. He scrolled through his phone for a moment, presumably checking messages from Sarah. Then he shut it off and let out a deep breath. "So, buddy," he said, "are we actually going to fish more, or maybe snorkel, or do you just want to lounge here?"

Ben shrugged. "I'm open to something mellow. Maybe a walk on the beach in the evening when it's not so hot."

"Sounds romantic."

Ben smiled. "But if you want to snorkel, go for it. I'll watch from the shore."

Reggie rolled his eyes. "You're such a party animal." Then he grinned. "But okay, fair enough. We'll take it easy today. Tomorrow we can see about that wreck. Maybe hire a local guide or something."

Ben nodded, though a pang of unease flickered in his stomach. *A wreck dive...* On the surface, it was harmless — tourists did it all the time. But in his experience, nothing was ever that simple. He stifled the feeling and reminded himself that Reggie just wanted to see some fish and maybe some old timbers. *Don't overthink it.*

"Anyway," Reggie continued, "I think I'm gonna take a short nap. That meal put me in a food coma."

Ben lifted a hand in lazy approval. "I might do the same."

Reggie headed down the hall to the second bedroom. Ben remained on the couch, letting his eyes drift shut. The gentle hum of the fan blended with the rhythmic hush of distant waves. For the first time that day, he felt a semblance of genuine calm. No immediate threats, no pressing obligations. *Maybe I can actually get used to this,* he thought. *It's just a vacation...*

His mind wandered, flitting between images of Julie and Hope back in Alaska, to the fisherman's bar Reggie had mentioned, to the rumor of the local wreck site. He recalled Reggie's words about an "ancient Spanish galleon" or something older. *Probably just a tourist attraction with some coral-encrusted cannons.* A small part of him twinged with curiosity — an unconscious reflex that had led him on countless missions in the past.

He snorted softly. *Knock it off. You're not investigating anything here.* With that thought, he let the wave of weariness pull him under, and he drifted off into a light doze.

Somewhere in his half-sleep, he thought he heard the faint echo of gunshots — a flashback to earlier exploits. But the sound faded, replaced by the whisper of the sea breeze through the palm trees outside. *Probably just a dream,* he reassured himself. *Nothing to worry about...*

He dozed deeper, lulled by the midday heat and the faint, comforting presence of normalcy. Outside, the sun tracked its course across the sky, and island life carried on. A gentle calm enveloped the bungalow, broken only by the occasional rustle of Reggie shifting in his bed or the distant call of a gull. And for a while, Harvey Bennett could almost believe this was exactly the vacation he needed — short, harmless, and worry-free.

CHAPTER 15

RAMÓN

RAMÓN MENDOZA STEPPED CAREFULLY over the slick limestone floor, the rhythmic drip of stalactites echoing through the rugged cave. A single diesel-powered generator hummed in a side alcove, its makeshift cables snaking across wet rock to fuel the overhead floodlights. The light cast long, wavering shadows against half-buried crates, a battered table, and stacked barrels that gave the cave a surreal, pirate-like atmosphere.

Outside, through a yawning mouth in the cave wall, the ocean's steady roar drifted in — an isolated cove on a tiny offshore island Valeria Cruz had chosen for its secrecy. Ramón suppressed a flicker of admiration. *It's remote enough that no one stumbles in uninvited.* He wove around a cluster of Syndicate men, who were either cleaning rifles or scanning battered documents by lantern. Their hushed voices mingled with the incessant drip of water seeping through the cavern roof.

He finally spotted Valeria Cruz near a makeshift desk — a plank of wood balanced on crates — where she hovered over the satchel he'd retrieved, stained with brine and flecks of something dark. Ramón knew exactly what was in that bag.

Money.

Not literally, but Cruz would have some contact somewhere that could turn the contents of the satchel into cold, hard cash.

But it wasn't just about the money. He sensed there was more to it. Perhaps the contents of the old worn bag represented much more; in fact, he was sure of it. He didn't truly understand *why* this artifact — just some stale old piece of rock — was so critical, but Cruz's expression told him the bag held the key to something far bigger than she'd revealed.

Cruz glanced up, a single overhead bulb swinging on a cable, casting half her face in sharp relief. "Ramón," she said, her voice echoing off damp walls, "I was expecting you sooner."

Ramón offered a clipped nod, stepping closer. "The men said you needed me."

She rapped her knuckles on the satchel. "We've got a problem," she said quietly. "The boat captain — Ortega — he's dead. You saw to that along with the diver, yes?"

He inclined his head. "Yes. He and his friend were dealt with. Slipped overboard in the end."

Her lips formed a thin line. "Then we have a new concern. That man had a brother, also a fisherman, and it sounds like he might know something." She pulled a folded scrap of paper from the bag, scanning its contents. "Word is he's spooked, maybe asking questions around the southwestern cays."

Ramón bit back a sigh. *Another fisherman, another risk.* "You think he knows about... this?" He gestured at the satchel — *the artifact.* Proof that there was more out there. He hated how many times they'd killed trying to find it, but orders were orders.

Cruz exhaled, the tension in her stance visible. "He might, but even if it's not this *exactly*, he may suspect the rumors are true. That there's *much* more to be found out there since the weather changed the sands by the reefs. But if the captain confided in him about the diver's find — this 'cursed relic' or whatever nonsense they believe in — I can't risk him talking to the wrong people. Authorities, do-gooder archaeologists, even rival smugglers. We cannot afford a rumor chain leading back here."

The generator sputtered briefly, making the lights flicker. Shadows danced on the jagged walls. Ramón eyed the men behind Cruz: a handful of Syndicate operatives, wide-eyed in the uncertain glow, some rummaging through crate lids, others checking ammo. They all pretended not to listen, but ears perked up whenever Cruz spoke about that relic-laden satchel.

He returned his focus to Cruz. "I'll handle it," he said simply. "You want him — quiet."

Her eyes flickered with cold amusement. "Of course. If he's told no one, intimidate him into silence. If he's told others, we eliminate the entire trail. Understood?"

Ramón nodded, stepping around a puddle that glistened at his feet. "Clear. I'll pick a small team, keep it discreet. No messy bodies washing up."

Cruz pressed a palm to the satchel, as if reassuring herself it was still there. "Good. Meanwhile, I'll finalize the next move with our artifacts. We have a contact interested in buying a few of them, once they're verified. The fewer people poking around that wreck, the better."

Ramón shot the bag a sidelong look. "I still can't fathom why these chunks of carved stone are worth so many dead men, *jefa.*" He used the respectful Spanish address, but a flicker of curiosity slipped into his tone. "We're up to our necks in murders. That diver, the captain, plus others."

Cruz's mouth tightened. "Because it's bigger than you realize, Ramón. This is no ordinary relic. It's representative of something *so much* larger. Some say it predates Spanish arrival by centuries, or that it could be tied to an unknown civilization. And now that the hurricane changed the reef's geology, we've found this, proving there's even more in that reef. Enough to potentially remake our entire Syndicate."

She paused, letting the slow drip from the cave ceiling punctuate her words. He sensed there was more she wasn't telling him. *Not my job to know*, he reminded himself. But he couldn't help but grow even more curious because of the obvious withholding of information.

"I don't care about curses," She continued. "But private collectors, black-market buyers... they'll pay a fortune. I plan to harness that potential."

He stiffened. *Potential for what? Money? Influence?.* "I'll do my part."

She swept back a damp strand of hair from her forehead. "Yes, you will. The captain's brother could derail everything if he starts shouting about old wrecks and murder. Put him down or muzzle him. Your call."

A hush settled. The generator coughed again, returning to a steady hum. Outside, the surf pounded, the tide rising. Ramón glimpsed flickers of lightning in the far corner of the cave mouth. Another storm might be rolling in.

Fitting for our pirate-like hideout.

He left Cruz near the battered table, stepping toward the side passage where a few barrels had been arranged as seats. His second-in-command, Gabriel Ortiz, leaned there, arms folded. Ortiz gave him a questioning nod. "Well?"

"Another job," Ramón said. "A fisherman, the brother of the boat captain. We leave in a couple of hours, keep it quiet."

Ortiz sighed. "We keep stacking bodies." He jerked his head at the men rummaging in crates. "They're uneasy about how many locals we've offed. Some are whispering the relic is cursed."

Ramón huffed. "The boss doesn't care about curses. She wants secrecy. We deliver." He shrugged off any moral qualms. "We'll take two men with us, that's all. Don't want to spook the entire village if that's where he is."

Ortiz nodded in agreement. Then he lowered his voice. "You buy into this artifact hype?"

"Don't ask me," Ramón muttered, letting a droplet of water splash onto his shoulder. The cave's dripping was incessant. "As long as the boss pays, I do my job."

Ortiz grunted. "Fair enough."

Ramón found a corner near the cave entrance, peering out at the swaying palms on the narrow beach. The tiny island boasted a hidden cove, perfect for mooring the Syndicate's boats. They'd set up inside the cave like modern-day pirates, complete with crates of contraband, weapon caches, diesel drums for the generators, and even a state-of-the-art comms center in one of the side chambers off the main hall. Waves foamed over the rocky inlet, lit faintly by the occasional lightning flash. *An apt hideout for killers who treasure a cursed relic,* he mused.

He inhaled the sea breeze, letting the salt tang fill his lungs. The memory of that diver's watery death still haunted him. Another fisherman, dead. Now the brother.

When does it end?

CHAPTER 16

VALERIA

THE CAVE FLICKERED with oil-lamp shadows, long and wavering, like ghosts stretching over the damp stone. Valeria Cruz stood near the seawall entrance, watching as the outboard motorboat sliced toward the cove's inlet. A low fog hovered over the water like breath held too long.

Ramón had left ten minutes ago, off to handle another complication.

Now came a different one.

The boat nosed through the narrow reef passage, expertly piloted by one of her men. Seated at the bow, his dark blazer utterly out of place in the salt-soaked tropics, was a man known to her only as *Halim*. He stood before the engine even cut, his patent leather shoes somehow finding stable footing on the slippery limestone dock.

He didn't wait to be invited ashore. That, in itself, irritated her.

"Señora Cruz," he said, adjusting his cufflinks as he stepped into the cave. "I trust your location is as secure as promised."

Valeria inclined her head, arms folded. "You tell me. You're the one who showed up in person."

"I find face-to-face conversations... harder to record."

"And easier to manipulate," she said coolly.

He offered a faint smile, acknowledging the jab without confirming it.

He was younger than she'd expected — late thirties, maybe — but with a politician's composure and a banker's precision. The kind of man who wouldn't touch cash if he could help it, but still made millions flow like water.

He scanned the cave — its crates, diesel drums, fuel-stained floor. The dozen armed men pretending not to stare. Then he fixed his gaze on the satchel beside her.

"Is that it?" he asked.

Valeria didn't answer. Instead, she gestured toward the makeshift desk, and the two of them moved through the cave's humidity in silence. The idol inside the satchel rested atop a folded U.S. Navy map from the 1950s, covered in hand-scribbled markings. A crude but precise record of recent salvage dives.

She unwrapped the idol like a bomb. It might as well have been.

Halim leaned closer. His expression flickered — just for a moment — as he took it in.

Serpentine head. Abstract eyes. Inhuman hands carved in high relief. Etched symbols flaked with salt and time.

He straightened. "Authentic?"

She nodded. "Pre-Taíno. Possibly centuries older. Recovered from a wreck uncovered after the hurricane shifted the seabed near the reef. There are others — buried, scattered — but this confirms what we suspected. A whole civilization, gone unnoticed beneath your project site."

She didn't say the word. *Hotel.* He didn't need to hear it.

Halim didn't blink. "And if it's real?"

Valeria arched a brow. "Then it's protected. This area would qualify as a Class 1 Cultural Heritage Zone. That means survey teams, government oversight, and the worst thing in the world — *attention.*"

She let that hang between them. The rain outside began to hiss harder on the surface of the sea.

He turned slightly, facing the dark ocean mouth. "You assured me early interest would be... contained."

"And it has been," she said. "For now. But more wreckage is exposed every day. If we don't remove it — or destroy it — the authorities will find it. And then your little venture disappears into red tape."

"My investors do not appreciate delays," he said.

"Then they should have chosen a less historically rich target."

His gaze sharpened, but she was already turning away, rewrapping the idol in burlap.

"The Syndicate has dealt with interested parties. A salvage diver. A boat captain. A few locals," she said. "We're thorough."

"And violent," Halim added.

"Only when necessary."

He took a slow breath, controlling his expression. "And your plan?"

"Simple," she said, tossing the wrapped idol onto the desk with a heavy *thud*. "We collect everything. Every relic, every artifact, every whisper of a pre-Columbian past. What we can't sell, we sink or burn. If there's nothing left to find, there's nothing to protect."

"You believe you can erase history?"

"I believe I can bury it again, like it was buried before."

The cave fell silent again. A drop of water hit the idol's burlap wrapping like a punctuation mark.

"You realize," Halim said slowly, "this makes you complicit in cultural destruction."

Valeria laughed, dry and short. "Please. Don't pretend to care. Your company is building a monument to engineered paradise — on a reef that's been here longer than your bloodline. You're here for return on investment. So am I."

She walked past him toward a side alcove, beckoning him to follow. They stopped beside a low crate, its lid propped open to reveal dozens of smaller artifacts: carved tools, shell ornaments, rusted blades fused with coral.

"All pulled from that reef in the past month," she said. "That storm turned the ocean floor upside down. There's a vault down there — centuries old. And this is just the edge of it."

Halim reached into the crate and picked up a narrow figurine carved from dark volcanic stone. "You realize this one resembles Olmec work?"

"I know what it resembles," she said. "I also know what it's worth. On the open market, pieces like these go for hundreds of thousands. But if a government steps in, they'll sit behind glass for eternity."

She stepped closer, lowering her voice.

"And they'll stop construction. Shut everything down. Freeze every account tied to your project. Is that what your investors want?"

His hand tightened on the figurine, then placed it gently back inside.

"No," he said.

She smiled again. "Then we move forward. Quietly. Aggressively. And I'll need more funds. And extraction clearance for a larger haul. The next few days will be crucial."

"Provided there are *no more* delays?"

Her eyes narrowed. "Delays come from *outside* my organization."

He turned back toward the entrance, the sea now glowing faintly in the approaching lightning. "And if others begin asking questions?"

"Then they'll find a cave. Empty. Silent. Like it's always been."

He paused at the lip of the cave mouth. His shoes crunched over grit. "You're confident."

"No," Valeria said, eyes locked on the wrapped idol. "I'm committed."

CHAPTER 17
VALERIA

VALERIA CRUZ STOOD ALONE at the cave's edge, salt spray stinging her face as she watched the sleek black boat disappear beyond the rocks. The faint thrum of its twin outboards faded beneath the endless crash of waves, swallowed by the rhythmic percussion of water against stone. Dark clouds gathered on the horizon, promising another storm.

She didn't move. Not for a long while. The wind whipped her hair, but she remained motionless, like one of the ancient statues they'd recovered from the seafloor. Her men knew better than to disturb her when she took these moments of solitude.

The meeting with Halim still echoed in her mind. That was his way — he came, he smiled, he measured everything and everyone with those shark-black eyes. Said nothing direct, promised nothing concrete. And when he left, he took pieces of you with him, fragments of resolve and certainty that you hadn't even realized were missing until hours later.

But Halim was necessary. He was leverage. A conduit to resources and connections she couldn't access through normal channels. His Saudi money could build things, change landscapes, reshape coastlines. Make problems disappear.

Still, he wasn't the one in charge here. Not of this operation. Not of her people. Not of her. Never of her.

The men in the cave whispered when they thought she couldn't hear them, their voices carrying through the limestone passages like ghost radio. About Halim. About the shadowy foreign investors. About secret buyers in Dubai or Qatar or whatever new money paradise was trending that week. They assumed she answered to someone higher up the chain, that she was just the liaison, the mouthpiece, the pretty face put forward to handle the day-to-day operations while real power lurked in the shadows.

They were wrong. Dead wrong.

None of them knew — couldn't know — that she'd built this Syndicate from nothing but bones and blood and bitter experience. She'd smuggled weapons through Venezuelan jungles with nothing but a satellite phone and a machete before half these men had even grown a spine. She'd bribed her way through Colombian ports, ghosted through customs in Curaçao, negotiated black-market auction deals on six continents. And never once — not once — had she needed someone to tell her what came next.

This cave, this network, this entire operation? It was hers. Every dark corner, every secret passage, every encrypted channel and hidden cache. She'd carved it out of chaos with her own hands.

The Syndicate had been a mess before her — a loose collection of artifact thieves and regional smugglers, all stepping on each other's deals and getting shot for their trouble. No organization. No vision. Just desperate men scrambling for whatever scraps they could grab.

She'd changed all that. Consolidated power. Eliminated rivalry. Gave them structure, discipline, direction. The ones who couldn't adapt disappeared quietly into unmarked graves or the endless Caribbean deep. The ones who survived learned quickly that her way was the only way.

And when she introduced digital ledgers, shell companies, encrypted communications networks, and middlemen with law degrees from prestigious American universities? They'd stared at her like she was some kind of witch, conjuring gold from sand.

But it worked. God, how it worked.

The old guard had sneered at first. Called her innovations unnecessary. Dangerous. Said you couldn't trust computers and lawyers with the kind of business they did. But they changed their tune when the money started flowing in clean and untraceable, when their operations became invisible to law enforcement, when their profits tripled in the first year alone.

And now? Now they called her *La Jefa*.

Not behind her back anymore. Not in whispers. They said it to her face, with respect and just the right edge of fear in their voices. Because they'd learned what happened to people who didn't show proper respect.

She turned from the sea and walked back toward the main chamber, her boots echoing sharp and purposeful on the damp limestone. The cave system was a maze of natural passages and carved rooms, some dating back centuries to when pirates used these hidden coves. She'd expanded it, modernized it, turned it into something between a fortress and a corporate headquarters.

The latest piece of tech — a fingerprint-locked steel door — clicked open at her touch. Inside, banks of computers hummed, monitoring everything from weather patterns to coast guard frequencies. This was her real power center, not the theatrical throne room where she met with clients.

Halim was useful — she reminded herself of this fact daily — but he was also expendable. If the deal went sideways, she had two more potential buyers lined up. Not as rich as his Saudi backers. Not as clean. But hungry. That was all she needed. Hungry men made reliable partners, as long as you controlled the food.

What mattered now was time.

The idol they'd recovered from the reef wasn't just another pretty trinket for some billionaire's private collection. It was proof. A breadcrumb leading to something older and larger than any known civilization in the Caribbean. Not Taíno. Not Spanish. Something that predated both, something that shouldn't exist according to accepted history.

The moment it became public knowledge, everything would change. The reef would be shut down faster than a sneeze. UNESCO would swarm in with their clipboards and cameras. Universities would send research vessels. The Puerto Rican government would plant their flag and build fences. The whole area would become one giant protected site, crawling with archaeologists and grad students and documentary film crews.

And the Saudis? They'd pull out of the resort project so fast it would leave scorch marks on the contracts. No one wanted to build a floating paradise over sacred ground. Not when headlines would scream: *Pre-Columbian Burial Sites and Ancient Cities Discovered Beneath Coral Shelf.*

Halim's people wanted a clean slate for their project. An empty canvas to paint their dreams of luxury and excess.

So Valeria would give them exactly that.

By clearing the reef of its secrets — *all* of its secrets — before the world ever knew they were there. The artifacts would disappear into private collections. The evidence would vanish into secure vaults. And any unfortunate souls who stumbled onto the truth?

Well, the Caribbean was deep, and it kept its secrets well.

She smiled as she settled into her chair, fingers dancing across keyboards, bringing up satellite imagery and patrol schedules. Behind her, the cave mouth framed a slice of darkening sky. Thunder rolled in the distance, and she could smell rain on the wind.

Let them come, she thought. *Let them try to stop me.* She hadn't built all this by backing down from a fight.

And she would face whatever came next the same way she'd faced everything else in her life — head-on, weapons hot, with a plan for every contingency and a bullet for every problem.

La Jefa had spoken. And now it was time to work.

CHAPTER 18

REGGIE

REGGIE SHIFTED on the wooden stool, peering around the thatched-roof pavilion with a bright surge of contentment warming his chest. He'd chosen a prime spot — right near the bar, close enough to people-watch, but not so close that he and his best friend Ben were surrounded by a crush of tourists.

The place felt alive, humming with the kind of casual, carefree energy Reggie had craved ever since they arrived in this tropical paradise.

He lifted his glass of local rum and let the swirling scents of caramel and spice tickle his nose. He took in the setting: a beachside bar perched a few yards from the gently foaming shoreline, its thatched roof supported by sturdy wooden posts. Strings of colorful lanterns hung from the rafters, bobbing in a mellow evening breeze that teased the edge of the hot, humid air. Together, those lanterns cast splashes of pink, green, and yellow across the sand and wood, painting the bar with dreamlike illumination.

The slow strum of acoustic guitars drifted from a tiny stage in one corner, where three musicians tapped their sandals on the floor and played a soft, summery tune that made Reggie's heart do a lazy little dance. Conversations rose and fell around them, like small waves on the shore itself. Bursts of laughter from nearby tourists reminded him that, for once, he wasn't in the middle of some high-stakes fiasco. At least not tonight.

He turned to check on Ben. His best friend nursed a glass of rum, swirling the amber liquid with a cautious sip. Reggie gave him a broad grin — he could practically read the tension behind Ben's eyes even though his friend tried to appear relaxed. Ben was the type who never truly let his guard down, always scanning for potential trouble. Yet here, in a bar dappled with colorful lantern-light, Reggie wanted to coax him into a moment of genuine peace.

Reggie raised his own glass in a small salute to that idea, letting the rum's aroma fill his senses. "Now this," he said, projecting his voice over the lively chatter, "is what I'm talking about. Good music, cold drinks, ocean air. We've got it all, my friend." He let the words ring with an enthusiasm he genuinely felt. After all, he'd spent the entire day coaxing Ben into relaxing: a few lazy hours on the sand, a short trip into town for fresh fruit, and now, an evening of tropical drinks. That was how Reggie believed life ought to be enjoyed — without constant worry.

Ben nodded, sipping his drink. "At least the scenery is nice," he said under his breath, though Reggie caught the faint flicker of guarded appreciation in his friend's gaze. From this vantage, the ocean spread out behind them, tinted bronze and lavender by the sinking sun. Reggie spotted a few distant silhouettes of surfers bobbing in the waves, finishing their last rides of the day.

He let his eyes sweep the pavilion. Low wooden tables formed a ring around the stage, and a simple bar — just some aged planks hammered together — stood at the back, with a canopy of thatch overhead. The bartenders bustled with an easy efficiency, mixing rum-based concoctions or handing out bottles of local beer. The place wasn't fancy, but it held a relaxed, genuine charm.

Reggie noticed that a few surfers had colonized one corner, their boards leaning against a post, salt streaking their hair. Another cluster of middle-aged tourists in bright floral shirts occupied a table near the stage, laughing too loudly at jokes Reggie couldn't quite overhear. He suspected they might have downed a round or two of strong cocktails. Locals perched at the bar, sipping mojitos, speaking in machine-gun Spanish that Reggie barely followed but delighted in hearing. He adored the swirl of languages, the scents of grilled seafood, and the sensation of salty ocean breeze against his sun-kissed skin.

He caught Ben's eye again, noticing how his friend still seemed to be scanning the crowd. *Ben's never off duty,* Reggie thought. He tried to lighten the mood. "You'll adapt. Maybe," he teased, leaning back on his stool so the weight of the day's heat wouldn't press so heavily on his shoulders. "Come on, man — look at this place."

Ben exhaled, wiping sweat from his brow. "Yeah, I guess," he murmured, a half-laugh slipping out. "I'm just glad there's a decent breeze. Otherwise, I might have melted an hour ago."

Reggie grinned, soaking in the moment. *At least he's not entirely miserable.* The evening breeze, gentle though it was, cooled them slightly, stirring the lanterns overhead. The lanterns' arcs of movement mesmerized Reggie for a second, as if they were a playful reflection of the bar's easygoing vibe. He inhaled contentedly and gazed at a couple dancing near the stage. The man had a wide-brimmed hat, the woman a flowing sundress that spun with each sway. They moved to the gentle guitar chords with an affectionate calm, as though they had nowhere else to be in the world.

He turned back to Ben, letting out a soft chuckle. "Nice to see people enjoying themselves," Ben mused, following Reggie's line of sight to the dancers.

Reggie tapped his foot in time with the guitar's mellow tune. "That's the idea, buddy," he said, giving Ben a light elbow. "This is paradise, remember?"

Then, in a moment of playful mischief, Reggie nodded at the dancing couple. "You want to dance?" he asked, widening his grin to let Ben know he wasn't entirely serious. He could guess how his friend would react, but teasing was half the fun.

Ben shot him a wry look, and Reggie answered by making a dramatic fake-vomiting sound. It was silly, but it coaxed a genuine laugh from Ben, which Reggie counted as a small victory. They both needed such small moments of levity, especially after the whirlwind of stress they'd been under in recent months.

Despite his cheerful front, Reggie felt a glimmer of sympathy for Ben.

He knew his friend had a habit of staying on high alert, no matter how idyllic the surroundings. Reggie didn't blame him, but part of him wished he could shake Ben's shoulders and say, *Relax for once. No one's out to get us tonight.* Of course, he kept that to himself; Ben wasn't the type to appreciate direct scolding about caution.

A local waitress passed by, balancing a tray of rum cocktails in tall glasses garnished with tiny umbrellas and fruit slices.

He took another swig of his own rum, relishing its smooth, spicy burn as it trickled down his throat. "We've done a good job lazing around," he teased. "I'd say we earned this final beverage, don't you think?"

Ben nodded slowly. "We did. Although… " He trailed off, scanning the bar's entrance with that subtle wariness Reggie recognized so well. The wide gap in the thatched wall framed the setting sun, which was now a brilliant disc of gold sinking into the horizon. Long shadows stretched across the sand, while the sky shifted to a painting of pinks and oranges.

DUSK HAD SETTLED across the coastline, a warm palette of violets and oranges lingering on the horizon as Ramón Mendoza stepped from the small dinghy onto a half-rotten wooden pier. Three other Syndicate men — Ortiz, Lopez, and Castellanos — followed, boots landing with soft thuds. The hush of an early evening hush draped the area: not quite night, but past the vibrant glow of sunset. Overhead, the first few stars pricked the indigo sky.

They had come for José Ortega, a fisherman rumored to know far too much about what had happened to his brother at sea. The Syndicate — under Valeria Cruz's orders — deemed José a loose end. *Find him, silence him, or scare him into vanishing*, whichever ended the risk of him talking about the old wreck or the diver's discovery. Ramón hadn't questioned it; he rarely did. Obedience kept him alive and in Cruz's good graces.

A faint evening breeze rustled the palm fronds lining the shore. Ortiz flicked on a small flashlight, cupping it to avoid attracting attention. "The house should be near the big tamarind tree," he said quietly. "Green walls, tin roof, or so the boss's contact said."

Ramón gave a curt nod, letting his eyes adjust to the dim. The dull lap of waves on the sand behind them provided a soothing backdrop to the tension in his chest. "We approach quietly," he murmured. "Check if he's inside. If not, we wait or track him. Keep it simple."

Lopez and Castellanos both nodded. Dressed in dark windbreakers and cargo pants, rifles stowed discreetly, they looked more like covert soldiers than local fishermen. Which was exactly the point — intimidate quickly, vanish swiftly. That was the Syndicate's way.

They left the pier, crossing a narrow stretch of beach. The sky overhead deepened by the minute, the last slivers of dusky color draining into the west. The men advanced single file, footsteps muffled by the fine, warm sand. A dog barked faintly in the distance, but no other sign of life. In the hush of early evening, the local fisher families were likely indoors, finishing dinner or resting after the day's toil.

A cluster of modest houses soon emerged from behind a line of tall, spindly palm trees. Worn fences, chipped paint, sagging roofs — hallmarks of a humble coastal village. A single streetlamp flickered near a dusty lane, providing meager illumination. Ramón surveyed the shapes in partial gloom, searching for their target: a green-walled, tin-roofed structure near a large tamarind tree.

"Over there," Ortiz whispered, pointing to a silhouette. Moonlight revealed a wide-spreading tree above one of the houses, its trunk splitting into thick branches. The house indeed had greenish walls, though the color was hard to discern in the low light. In the front yard, a battered fishing net hung from a post.

Ramón signaled the men to spread out around the yard. Lopez slipped left, Castellanos right, while Ortiz stuck close to Ramón. They advanced carefully, scanning the windows for movement. The muffled hum of a generator or fridge might have come from inside. No direct sign of occupant.

A wooden gate separated the yard from the lane. Ramón tested it gently — unlocked. He pushed it open, the hinges squeaking softly. He winced, pausing to ensure no reaction came from within. The evening air hung thick with humidity, carrying the faint odor of fish and brine that clung to every fishing settlement. Still no sign of activity, no lamplight.

He motioned Ortiz to cover the house's side while he and the others approached the front door. The overhead power line crackled, the single lamp on the street behind them flickering sporadically. *This is too quiet,* Ramón thought, a prickle of unease creeping along his spine.

The house's front door was modest, painted the same chipped green as the walls. Ramón tried the handle — locked. He rapped his knuckles once, listening intently for footsteps or a voice inside. Nothing. Ortiz approached, offering a pry bar. Ramón inserted it at the latch, applying steady pressure. The flimsy lock gave after a moment, letting the door swing inward.

They slipped inside, rifles up in case the occupant was armed. A hush filled the living area — a small couch, a table with a scatter of fishing equipment. The gloom parted under a narrow flashlight beam. Ramón's gut tightened as he realized the place felt stale, unoccupied recently. No half-eaten meal on the table, no fresh footprints on the dusty floor.

Ortiz spoke softly, "No one's here."

Lopez stepped into a side room — likely the bedroom. "Empty," he confirmed. A quick rummage of the dresser revealed clothing, some personal knickknacks, but no occupant. A small photograph on a nightstand showed two men on a boat, presumably José and his late brother. "This is definitely the place," Lopez concluded.

Ramón cursed under his breath. "He's out. We'll check the shore."

They left the house as silently as they'd arrived, though the broken door lock remained a clue that unwelcome visitors had come. If José returned, he'd see it. But maybe that'd flush him out anyway. The four men regrouped by the leaning tamarind tree in the yard.

"Beach?" Castellanos asked. "He might be tending his nets after dusk."

Ramón nodded. "Better than waiting here. We'll fan out, check the shore and adjacent huts. If we don't find him, we stake out his place." They set off down a sandy path that angled behind the row of houses, hugging the faint edge of the settlement.

The hush of evening enveloped them again, broken only by chirping cicadas and an occasional dog's bark. The half-moon overhead bathed the scene in a pearly glow. As they neared the beach, the air took on a saltier tang. The roar of gentle waves became more pronounced.

At the shoreline, they found a handful of small fishing boats moored: battered skiffs and one slightly larger craft. All seemed abandoned for the night, sails or nets stowed. No sign of anyone working in the moonlight. The men split up to check each boat, stepping lightly on the wet sand. But none revealed a living soul.

"He's not here," Ortiz muttered. "Maybe he's out drinking or at a friend's home." He cast a wary glance at the moonlit water. "Could be gone for the evening. People around here gather in local bars or small parties at night."

Lopez knelt, eyeing footprints in the damp sand. "Hard to tell how fresh they are. Could be from an hour ago, or earlier in the day. The tide's messing them up."

A flicker of frustration gnawed at Ramón. He scanned the beach, noticing a rocky outcrop to the north. If José had come here to do something clandestine, he might be behind that outcrop. "Let's check the rocks," he decided. "If we don't see him there, we circle back to the houses or keep an eye on the roads."

They trudged north, following the gentle curve of the shoreline. The sand hardened underfoot near the water's edge, reflecting the moonlight so clearly it almost gleamed. The men formed a loose arc, rifles kept close but not brandished. The Syndicate wanted no shootouts in plain sight unless absolutely necessary.

The beach narrowed around the outcrop, where dark boulders jutted into the sea. A swirl of foam caressed their base. Ramón paused, hearing a faint scraping sound. He flicked a hand for silence, ears straining. Another quiet scrape, perhaps a foot on stone.

He inched closer, peering around the largest boulder. The moonlight revealed a hunched silhouette — someone standing near the rocks, arms folded. *Could that be José?*

Ortiz nodded vigorously, confirming the silent guess. The shape indeed matched a fisherman's build. The man — barely visible — seemed to be rummaging with something at the rock's base, maybe a hidden net or line.

Ramón breathed out slowly. *We got him.* He motioned for Lopez and Castellanos to swing wide, cutting off an escape route, while he and Ortiz advanced directly. One misstep might spook him, so they moved quietly, letting the waves mask their approach.

At about twenty yards away, the figure froze. Possibly he heard them. He spun around, the moonlight catching his face. A mustache, weathered features — José Ortega. *No doubt.*

José took one wide-eyed look at the black-clad men, rifles half-raised, and acted on pure fear. He bolted, stumbling over the rocky ground but regaining momentum with desperate energy.

Ramón dashed after him, cursing under his breath. *Again, a chase.* The fisherman scrambled around the boulders, heading inland. Ortiz barked, "Stop!" but José only redoubled his speed. The synergy of adrenaline and terror propelled him up a small incline leading away from the beach.

Lopez and Castellanos converged from the sides, but the fisherman squeezed between them, arms pumping. The men lunged, missing his shirt by inches. He pivoted onto a dirt path that wound back toward the village, the night swallowing his silhouette.

Ramón felt a surge of annoyance. *He was right there.* He sprinted, each stride jarring his knees. He refused to open fire just yet — one gunshot might alert half the village. Instead, he clenched his jaw, pushing forward in raw pursuit. The fisherman had a limp, but fear gave him speed.

They reached a slope thick with low shrubs. The fisherman tripped briefly but caught himself, scuffing one knee. A hiss of pain escaped him, yet he charged on. Ortiz, panting at Ramón's side, hissed, "We must bring him down." Ramón nodded.

Suddenly, the slope turned treacherous with loose gravel. The fisherman lost his footing. A gasp tore from his throat as he slid down a few feet, arms flailing. He twisted an ankle or bashed a knee — hard to tell, but he cried out. The mercenaries closed in, certain they had him pinned.

But with a frantic burst, José pulled himself upright, hobbling forward, refusing to be caught. The path connected to a narrow alley behind a row of small houses. Flickers of electric light glowed in a few windows, accompanied by faint voices from inside. *If he calls for help, we risk a crowd.*

Ramón willed his legs to keep pumping. The fisherman's breathy gasps echoed through the alley. Ortiz swung left, trying to corner him. José barreled right, half-limping, half-running. Another adrenaline-laced spurt overcame his obvious pain. He panted, eyes wide with panic.

The alley spilled out onto a slightly broader street. Strings of overhead bulbs illuminated a few shabby storefronts. A group of locals strolled by, giving startled looks as José stumbled into view, blood staining his pant leg from the tumble. The man half-fell against a signpost, regaining balance only to push onward. People exclaimed, "¿Estás bien?" but he ignored them, fixated on escaping.

Ramón slowed, signaled the others to keep weapons hidden. The four of them had to appear normal — not a hit squad chasing a wounded fisherman. He hung back a second, letting José move ahead into the throng. The fisherman cast one backward glance, terror flaring at the sight of his pursuers.

Lopez cursed. "If he starts shouting we killed his brother —"

"Then we're done," Ramón finished grimly. "Move."

CHAPTER 20
REGGIE

WE SHOULD PROBABLY HEAD BACK SOON, Reggie thought he heard echo in Ben's silence. Indeed, nighttime in a foreign place could be unpredictable, but Reggie didn't mind. He'd often lived on the edge, enjoying the rush of new sights and experiences.

Ben's the one who always thinks about exit routes.

For a moment, Reggie considered pressing him to stay longer. Why let the night end so soon?

Instead, he watched the man behind the guitar shift into a soft, melodic chord progression, and the small crowd near the stage murmur their appreciation. The vibe of the place reminded Reggie of countless postcards: a thatched roof near the shore, a warm breeze stirring, guests wearing bright patterns and sipping colorful drinks. He lived for these experiences — moments that made him feel connected to the wide world's simpler pleasures.

From the corner of his eye, he spotted a pair of surfers returning from the waves, boards tucked under their arms. They high-fived each other, no doubt celebrating a day of decent surf. Over by the bar, a group of local guys in board shorts chatted up a pair of tourists with wide smiles. Laughter and the clink of glassware punctuated the lively background murmur.

Reggie's chest felt full with satisfaction. *This is exactly how I pictured a laid-back tropical bar.* He turned to Ben, noticing his friend swirling the rum in his glass, still looking half-wary, half-relaxed.

"What's got the almighty Harvey Bennett all shook?" he asked.

Ben shrugged. "Reconsidering that snorkel trip."

He let out a short laugh. "Don't worry, big guy," he teased. "It won't kill you to do something touristy every now and then."

He savored that moment, letting the rest of the bar's hum swirl around them. The band strummed a final chord, then transitioned to a slower tune. People clapped politely, a wave of soft applause rippling across the tables. A local bartender whistled in approval.

Beside him, Ben cleared his throat, swirling the final bit of liquid in his glass. Reggie guessed he was about to voice some pragmatic remark about the time or the walk back to their lodging. But Reggie decided not to push. He'd let Ben handle his own pace.

An older couple ambled by, the man balancing a plastic cup brimming with a fruity concoction. The woman wore a wide-brimmed hat with a hibiscus flower pinned to it. They smiled politely at Reggie as they passed, and he returned the gesture with an easy grin. He loved how these coastal towns attracted such a range of personalities. Everyone seemed more open, friendlier.

Just then, a faint swirl of wind fluttered Reggie's Hawaiian shirt. It was loud and bright, a kaleidoscope of tropical flowers, and he knew it made him stand out like a neon sign, but that was half the fun. *Let's see Ben in a shirt like this,* Reggie mused. He wondered how much rum he'd need to get into his friend before he could ply him to try on a shirt like his.

If there's even one on this island that would fit him. He stifled a laugh, imagining Ben's face if Reggie suggested matching outfits.

The bartender behind them clapped his hands in time with the music, occasionally ringing a bell whenever someone ordered a round of shots. The clink of glassware followed, prompting cheers or laughter from various corners of the bar.

Reggie leaned back, letting the stool tilt precariously on two legs. "You see those surfers in the corner?" he said, pointing with his glass. "Think they'd mind if we joined them tomorrow? Maybe I'll talk them into teaching you how to surf."

Ben's half-lidded expression revealed amusement and mild horror at the idea. "I'll pass," was all he said, but Reggie saw the faint crinkle at the corner of his friend's eyes. He was teasing, at least partially. *I'll keep working on him,* Reggie thought.

Quietly, Reggie said, "Thanks for coming here with me. I know you'd rather be somewhere quieter." He let a gentle sincerity tinge his tone. "But... it's good to see you not wearing your perpetual frown."

Ben, surprised, gave him a faint grin. "I don't *always* frown, do I?"

Reggie spread his hands in a comedic shrug. "Only when you're conscious." Then he patted Ben's shoulder. "But seriously, buddy, we need these breaks. Could be a chance for something normal."

Ben sighed, swirling the remnants of rum. "I guess so. Normal is nice, once in a while. Still... always keep an eye open, right?"

Life didn't always hand them these slices of joy, and Reggie, for one, wanted to soak up every second. "Eh, couldn't hurt to just... *let go* once in a while, right?"

He winked.

CHAPTER 21

RAMÓN

RAMÓN'S TEAM weaved through onlookers, ignoring the questioning stares. Ortiz hissed directions: "He's heading for that side street." Indeed, José had veered left, aiming for a road that sloped down to the beach district — a cluster of open-air bars popular at night.

The road was lit with decorative lanterns, throngs of tourists and locals mingling in a swirl of music and laughter. The fisherman plowed into them, apologizing breathlessly or ignoring protests. A guitar strummed from somewhere, a competing radio spilled salsa rhythms. The synergy of the evening crowd masked the chase's footsteps.

Ramón's pulse hammered.

If he disappears in these crowds, we lose him. Or if he shouts about murderers, the entire crowd might riot or call the police. They had to intercept him quietly. He signaled the men to spread out, forming a net behind José.

But the fisherman, though injured, navigated the flow of people with surprising agility, desperation fueling him. Now they were only a stone's throw from the beach bars — large thatched pavilions strung with colorful lights, where travelers sipped rum cocktails and watched the ocean's shimmering night. Music spilled into the street, mingling with the hum of conversation.

José glanced back once, meeting Ramón's eyes across the swirl of bodies. Fear mingled with grim determination. The fisherman staggered, pain contorting his face, but he refused to stop. A few onlookers noticed the blood and tried to help, but he brushed them off.

A call of "¡Policía!" might have hovered on someone's lips, but no one took immediate action.

Ramón grit his teeth, sidling between a group of surfers. He saw Ortiz to the right, scanning for a chance to grab José. Meanwhile, Lopez and Castellanos angled from the left. The fisherman, spotting them, cut a diagonal path across the street, colliding with a fruit vendor's cart. The cart rattled, sending a few mangoes rolling. He apologized frantically, then lurched onward.

The fruit vendor yelled in confusion, halting Ramón for a heartbeat. By the time he dodged around, the fisherman was nearing the large thatched roof of a popular beach bar — the same one rumor held had a decent band most nights. Glowing paper lanterns hung overhead, a swirl of voices and music drifting out. It was well-patronized, a hub of tourist activity.

Worst place for us to do anything violent.

Lopez called out quietly, "He's going inside that bar!" A note of alarm tinted his voice. Indeed, José staggered across the threshold — an open entrance in the woven walls that faced the beach. A lively guitar strum reached a crescendo, then receded into melodic chords.

Ramón's stomach dropped. If the fisherman told people about "Black Coral Syndicate" or "murdered at sea," they'd have a full-blown panic or immediate calls to the police. Their secrecy might be irreparably damaged. But the boss demanded no more leaks.

He forced himself to remain calm. "We follow. No open guns. He's wounded — he can't last much longer."

Ortiz nodded grimly, concealing his rifle under a jacket. "We do this quietly." And then, to himself, "unless there's no other way."

They closed the distance to the bar's entrance, stepping from the well-lit street onto the sand that led up to the pavilion. The band inside shifted tunes, the hum of conversation rolling like a tide.

Ramón glimpsed José inside, already drawing alarm from patrons with his battered appearance. The fisherman half-collapsed near a wooden post, clothes ripped, blood staining his shirt. *He's about to beg for help.*

Exchanging one last urgent glance with Ortiz, Ramón prepared himself for potential chaos. "Remember — no gunfire unless we have no choice," he hissed. "We can't let him talk."

They advanced into the bar's perimeter, the music's volume rising. Raucous laughter and lively chatter reverberated off the thatched roof. People noticed José, face contorted in pain, a trembling hand pressed to his side where he was covering some sort of wound, as if he'd been impaled on a stick prior to entering the establishment. Concern spread among onlookers. Ramón's heart hammered: *He's about to reveal everything... or at least enough to ruin us.*

The fisherman stumbled deeper, ignoring the gasps of those trying to help him. Chairs scraped, a hush falling in that corner of the pavilion. Some patrons craned their necks; others stood, uncertain. A local bartender shot a worried glance, as if to call the police. *Too many eyes.*

Ramón hovered near a row of small wooden tables, scanning the crowd for an opening to seize José silently. But it was too jam-packed. And the fisherman was in the bar's center now, about to speak. A pair of foreigners, tall and broad-shouldered, also rose from their seats, concern etched on their faces. *Tourists, no doubt.*

Somewhere behind him, Ramón felt Ortiz and the others fan out, presumably searching for vantage points to intervene. The fisherman, chest heaving, parted his lips in a ragged cry. Ramón braced for the worst. *If we act now, we risk drawing every pair of eyes in the place.*

José coughed wetly, voice rising just enough for the entire bar to hear. "Ayuda... help me... " The simple Spanish plea echoed in the hush. The band's guitar abruptly stopped. Confusion reigned. More patrons gathered, forming a ring around him.

That ring of onlookers obstructed the mercenaries' line of sight. Ramón cursed under his breath, weaving closer. He managed to catch a glimpse of José's anguished face, sweat beading on his brow. The fisherman swayed, leaning on the wooden post for support.

He's on his last legs.

One or two patrons tried offering him a seat or water. Another grabbed napkins to stanch the blood seeping from his earlier injuries. The fisherman's next words might be crucial. Ramón's pulse thundered in his ears, the adrenaline spike making each second feel like an eternity.

Ramón edged forward, but a cluster of concerned tourists blocked him. The fisherman's battered voice rose, possibly naming his brother's murder, or referencing "Black Coral" or "older than the Spanish."

The mercenaries prepared themselves to do whatever was needed — including gunfire — to stop him from revealing the Syndicate.

In the swirl of panic that would ensue, they'd slip away.

CHAPTER 22

BEN

BEN OPENED his mouth to respond, but at that moment, the crowd seemed to shift. One of the bartenders stepped aside, and for an instant, he noticed a man limping in through the entrance, half-collapsing against a wooden post.

His shirt was tattered, smeared with something dark — *blood*? A hush fell over nearby tables as people realized something was wrong.

Ben and Reggie both sat up straighter. The man was short, with a weather-beaten face and a trembling hand pressed against his side. He staggered a few steps into the bar, looking wildly around.

He's hurt, Ben realized, adrenaline beginning to spike. *Badly.*

A couple of locals moved toward him, concern etched on their faces. But the man lurched past them, heading straight for the center of the bar as though on autopilot. His lips moved, but Ben couldn't hear him over the music. Then the guitarist on stage noticed and abruptly stopped playing. The sudden silence drew everyone's attention.

The man's voice rose, ragged and thin. *"Ayuda...* help me... " He coughed wetly, sagging against a table, knocking over a candle. The flickering light cast strange shadows across his battered features.

Ben exchanged a look with Reggie. *Should we help?* Reggie's eyes narrowed, and he started to stand. The other patrons stared, uncertain. A few tried to approach, offering him a chair. One local man said something in Spanish about calling the police. But the newcomer shook his head in frantic denial.

He stumbled, nearly falling, and ended up leaning heavily on a wooden post supporting the thatched roof. "They... they murdered my brother," he said in a thick accent, his voice cracking. "And... a diver. Took... something from them... " He spoke mostly in Spanish, but occasionally lapsed into halting English. At the words *murdered* and *took something*, the bar collectively drew in a breath.

Reggie's posture tensed. "Hey, pal, you need a doctor," he said, stepping closer.

The man's eyes locked on Reggie. "They — my brother... he found —" He sputtered as if short on breath, then switched to Spanish. "Lo mataron... they shot him at sea. They must have shot the diver, too." His gaze swiveled to Ben, who had now also stepped forward, trying to see if the man was stable. Blood soaked the man's torn shirt at his side.

Ben's instincts kicked in. *He's in shock, wounded... we need to call an ambulance.* But the fisherman's next words rooted him in place.

"El Cementerio de los Contrabandistas... " the man whispered. "My brother found something... older than... older than the Spanish... they took it... " His voice broke on the last word, and he staggered, nearly falling. Reggie caught him by the arm, helping ease him onto a nearby stool.

Now the entire bar's attention was riveted on them. Some folks pressed in, trying to see what was happening. Others hovered at a distance, confused or scared. The bartender hurried over, eyes wide, as though wondering if he should call the police. Several tourists looked around nervously, uncertain if this was some kind of staged drama or a real emergency.

"What do you mean, older than the Spanish?" Reggie asked quietly, trying to keep his voice calm. "Who are you talking about?"

The man coughed, flecks of red spattering his lips. "My brother, ... diver with him... went looking for a wreck, a treasure... no, not treasure." He frowned." something... *cursed*." His eyes glistened with desperation.

"He told me he was... going to prove it... but then I found his boat, *El Tiburón*. I found my brother, dead."

Ben nodded slowly. "And the diver?"

The man swallowed, then shook his head. "No, but there was blood. I believe he went overboard. Perhaps trying to... escape... the same men who came after me."

Ben stared at the wound in the fisherman's side. "We need to stop your bleeding. Do you know who these men were?"

"Police... they do nothing," the fisherman said in a rasp. "They wore... black. I know them. They are... corrupt. Or they... they fear the Syndicate. But you... you must help. Don't let them —"

His words choked off, and he slumped. Reggie struggled to keep him upright. Ben darted forward, pressing a napkin from the bar against the fisherman's side, trying to stanch the flow of blood. *Not good... not good at all.* "Hold on, man, we'll get you an ambulance," Ben said, voice firm.

But the fisherman's gaze flicked up, burning with a sudden intensity. "You don't... understand... they're looking for more. The wreck... my brother said... it's older than anything... in these waters." His tone shifted to a mere thread of sound. "He said... *El Cementerio de los Contrabandistas*... cursed..." Then his breath caught. "Black... Coral... Syndi —"

A deafening crack split the night, echoing through the bar. People screamed. A shot rang out, and before Ben could react, the fisherman jerked sideways, eyes rolling back. He collapsed off the stool, blood spreading from a new hole in his torso.

For a second, Ben just stared, heart hammering.

Then the bar erupted.

CHAPTER 23

BEN

SOME TOURISTS SHRIEKED and dove for cover, knocking tables over in their scramble. Glasses shattered on the floor, and the band members scattered, sending guitars clattering to the stage. Reggie let go of the fisherman, pivoting on instinct. "Ben, down!" he shouted, yanking Ben behind a fallen table.

Ben's mind caught up in a rush, adrenaline surging through his veins. *Someone shot him, from outside?* He peered around the table's edge. The bar's entrance was partially visible through the chaos, but he saw only silhouettes in the dying sunset glow. A second shot fired, splintering a wooden beam overhead. More screams followed. People fled the bar en masse, some ducking low, others simply running for their lives.

Reggie's eyes blazed, scanning the area for the threat. Ben forced himself to stay calm, resisting the urge to leap up and confront whoever was shooting. They needed to identify the gunman first. The fisherman lay sprawled on the sand-strewn floor, unmoving, blood staining his clothes and pooling around him. Ben's stomach clenched. *We're too late...*

The bar lights flickered, and the guitarist's amplifier screeched in feedback before cutting out entirely. Someone cursed in Spanish from across the room. Ben tried to spot a muzzle flash or any sign of a shooter. Shattered glass crunched underfoot as patrons scrambled for safety.

"There!" Reggie shouted, pointing toward the entrance. Ben caught a glimpse of a shadowy figure moving just beyond the threshold, possibly ducking behind a low wall. Reggie tensed as if to chase, but Ben grabbed his arm.

"No!" Ben growled. "We don't know how many there are." His voice sounded raw in his own ears. "Could be more outside."

Reggie clenched his jaw, eyes still locked on the doorway. "He's getting away."

"Yeah, and you might get shot." Ben wasn't thrilled about letting a murderer escape, but they were unarmed, out in the open. Another gunshot could easily put them in the fisherman's position. "We have to handle this smart."

A beat passed. Reggie nodded curtly. They both rose a fraction, peering over the overturned table just enough to see that the entrance now stood empty. Whoever had fired those shots was gone, swallowed by the twilight. The band members remained huddled behind their stage, the few remaining patrons were pinned under tables or cowering behind the bar. Overhead, the lanterns swung madly, casting jittery pools of colored light.

Ben's chest tightened as he turned his attention back to the fallen fisherman. He scrambled over, ignoring the shards of broken glass that bit into his knees. Reggie moved to help, but they both knew, almost instantly, that it was too late. The fisherman's eyes stared blankly, unseeing. Blood soaked the floor beneath him, a final testament to his desperate plea.

"Damn it," Reggie murmured, pressing two fingers to the man's neck. No pulse. "He's gone."

For a moment, the bar's chaos retreated into an eerie hush around them, leaving only the ragged breathing of survivors. *We arrived here to have a quiet drink,* Ben thought, his pulse thundering. *And now we're kneeling over a dead man.*

He lifted his gaze to meet Reggie's. In Reggie's eyes, he saw that familiar spark — indignation and curiosity mingled. Ben inhaled unsteadily. *Here we go again.*

The bartender, a middle-aged woman with tears streaming down her face, crawled up to them. "Is... is he... ?"

Ben nodded solemnly. "He's gone. We need the police, an ambulance — something."

She blinked back tears. "Sí, I... I will call them." Then she scurried toward the bar's back counter, rummaging for a phone.

Reggie stood, scanning the wreckage. The band was still cowering, the other patrons either gone or trembling behind makeshift cover. A few ventured out cautiously now, realizing the shooting had stopped. Outside, the last of the sunset gave way to deep purple skies dotted with early stars.

Ben rose too, feeling shock wash over him. He stared at the fisherman's body, remembering the man's final words: *Older than the Spanish. They took it. The Black Coral... Syndi...* The name fizzled out, but it didn't take much to connect the dots. *Black Coral Syndicate?* It sounded ominous — and consistent with rumors he'd heard about modern-day pirates in these waters.

This was supposed to be a vacation. He exhaled slowly, trying to reign in the swirl of thoughts. A wave of frustration hit him. *Why do we always land in the middle of this kind of thing?*

Reggie knelt again, checking the fisherman's pockets carefully, possibly looking for identification or a clue. He glanced up at Ben. "Nothing. Just a wallet with a few pesos, a driver's license. Name says José Ortega." He shook his head, closing the man's wallet respectfully. "Poor guy. He came here for help."

"And he got a bullet instead," Ben muttered bitterly. The sense of injustice burned in his chest. José had specifically said the police wouldn't help, that they were corrupt or too afraid to confront this Syndicate. *He came to us, random strangers, because we looked like we could handle ourselves?*

Reggie's jaw tightened. "They killed him to silence him." He rocked back on his heels, scanning the bar's entrance again. "Bet you anything that bullet was meant to keep this story buried."

Ben raked a hand over his face. A fleeting memory of the fisherman's words about his brother, a diver, and a stolen bag and artifact flashed through his mind. *Older than the Spanish... El Cementerio de los Contra-bandistas... murder.* He could almost piece together the scenario: the fisherman's brother discovered something at that reef, and now a criminal outfit wanted to eliminate all witnesses.

A shaky voice spoke up from behind them. One of the bar patrons, a young tourist with wide eyes, asked, "Is... is it safe now? Did the shooter leave?"

"I think so," Reggie answered, though he didn't sound entirely sure.

Ben looked around. More people were emerging from hiding. The bartender was on the phone, speaking rapidly in Spanish, presumably to the local police. The band's guitarist crouched near the stage, hugging his instrument as if it were a lifeline. A couple of tourists dashed out into the night, perhaps deciding that any place was safer than here.

The overhead lanterns flickered in a sudden gust of wind, casting jittery shadows across the bloodstained floor. Ben felt a visceral tug of anger at seeing such brutality in what had been a cheerful environment mere minutes ago. *He died for nothing. He was just trying to warn us... or get help.*

"Ben," Reggie said quietly, "we should go."

CHAPTER 24

BEN

BEN'S EYES NARROWED. "LEAVE? NOW?"

Reggie nodded. "The cops here might not be our friends. We don't know. That guy said they were corrupt, or at least unhelpful. And if someone's gunning for us because they think we might know something, staying at the scene could be dangerous."

A wave of frustration surged through Ben, but he couldn't argue the logic. *He's right.* They had no weapons, no backup, and no reason to trust local authorities. On the other hand, ditching the scene felt morally wrong. "But... this man is dead. Shouldn't we wait to give a statement?"

"I doubt a statement from us would help," Reggie said, grim. "Might put a target on our backs. Whoever this Black Coral Syndicate is, they clearly have no qualms about murder."

Ben inhaled sharply. A swirl of images from the fisherman's last moments whirled in his head. *He wanted us to help.* But rushing in blindly wouldn't do any good either. "All right," he said through clenched teeth, "we can go. But we should figure out what's going on before we make any moves."

Reggie stood, glancing around at the bar's chaos. The bartender was still yelling into the phone, tears staining her cheeks. Another local man had found a sheet or tablecloth to cover José's body. Tourists milled about in a daze. "Let's slip out the back," Reggie suggested, nodding toward a gap in the rear wall where crates of supplies were stacked.

Ben was about to follow when a timid voice behind him spoke, "Señor, did you... know that man?" It was the bartender, who had finished her call.

Ben shook his head. "We'd never met him before."

Her face crumpled. "He was so scared. Kept saying he was next... that no one would believe him about a dead diver and an ancient relic... " She covered her mouth, fighting sobs. "All this blood, for what?"

Ben didn't have an answer. He gently squeezed her shoulder. "I'm sorry," he said, voice hushed. "Look... the police will come. Tell them what happened. Maybe they'll do something." Even as he said it, he doubted his own words.

She nodded, eyes full of devastation. Ben felt his heart twist. Then Reggie tugged on his sleeve, and Ben allowed himself to be guided out through the back. They maneuvered around plastic crates stacked with limes and soda bottles, their footsteps crunching on bits of broken glass. Once outside, they found themselves on a narrow stretch of beach that extended behind the bar, illuminated only by distant streetlights and the lingering glow of the sunset.

The night's heat still pressed down on them like a damp blanket, though the shock of recent events made it feel somehow colder. Waves crashed softly a dozen yards away, their gentle rhythm at odds with the violence they'd just witnessed. No one else seemed to be out here — most people had fled or gathered at the front.

Ben paused, exhaling in a shaky sigh. "Reggie, this is messed up."

"Yeah," Reggie agreed, gaze scanning the shoreline. "This is exactly the kind of thing you were hoping to avoid, right?"

Ben barked a humorless laugh. "You think?"

Reggie looked sympathetic for once. "Sorry, man. Look, you want to go back to the bungalow, lay low?"

Ben's mind raced. "He was talking about something ancient, older than the Spanish... a cursed wreck... and the Black Coral Syndicate." He frowned at the memory. "He wanted us to help. This group must be serious if they'll kill someone in a crowded bar just to keep them quiet."

Reggie crossed his arms, shoulders tense. "Could be the same smugglers Sarah's read about. She mentioned hearing rumors of a criminal outfit around here. That might be them, and the same wreck."

Ben clenched his fists, then forced them to relax. *Stay calm.* "I don't want to drag us into a war," he said slowly. "But it seems we're already in it. We're witnesses, at the very least."

"Yeah," Reggie murmured. "And we've got a dead fisherman pointing us to that graveyard reef. He said his brother and a diver were murdered there... looking for something ancient, and apparently found it. This is big, Ben. The question is, do we just back off and pretend we know nothing?"

Ben looked out at the dark horizon. *I came here for rest, to escape danger... but trouble always has a way of finding us.* He couldn't shake the fisherman's last plea. *He asked for help. He died believing we might do something.*

"No," Ben said at last, his voice low. "I can't just walk away from this. I want to, believe me. But if these people think we know something already, we're targets. And if we do nothing, more people could die."

Reggie nodded, resolute. "Agreed. We can do some digging, maybe start by talking to locals off the record. Find out what the fisherman meant by *El Cementerio de los Contrabandistas.*"

"Let's try to stay under the radar until we know more."

"Works for me," Reggie said. "But first, we need to get out of here without the cops pinning us down for questioning."

They made their way along the shadowy back of the bar, stepping carefully through the sand. An overturned kayak lay half-buried near a cluster of coconut palms, its hull battered by time. Music from inside the bar had ceased entirely, replaced by frantic voices. Blue and red lights flickered at the far side, announcing the arrival of the local police.

Ben's nerves jangled at the sight of those lights dancing across the palm fronds. He stuck close to Reggie, who took the lead. They cut across the sand, then found a narrow path that wound past a collection of trash bins and an old fishing net draped over a fence. Eventually, they emerged onto a dimly lit side street that led back toward the main road.

CHAPTER 25

RAMÓN

RAMÓN MENDOZA FELT the sweat gathering at the base of his spine as he stood in the narrow alley behind the beachside bar, ears still ringing from the pandemonium that had erupted moments before. The echo of that single gunshot — fired by one of his men — lingered in his mind like a sudden thunderclap. Now he was outside, pressed against the rough stucco of a building, trying to steady his breath while the hot evening air closed in around him.

He could hear voices shouting from inside the bar, a swirl of panic and confusion surging through the open walls. The fisherman lay dead in there, that was certain. But the police, or some kind of local authority, would surely arrive soon, responding to terrified calls from staff and tourists. There was no time to linger.

He cast a quick glance at his three subordinates: Ortiz, Lopez, and Castellanos. Each one was trying to compose themselves in the shadows as well. They'd followed procedure — taking out the fisherman before he could reveal too much, before he could fully name them or the Syndicate. But in a place like this, a single gunshot in a crowded bar was the worst kind of spectacle. The last thing they wanted was a confrontation with half the tourists and local police.

Ramón clenched his jaw, scanning the alley's far end for any sign of uniformed figures or suspicious onlookers.

Ortiz was the closest, breathing hard, his right hand resting under his jacket where he'd concealed the pistol. Ramón forced himself to exhale, to restore the calm that usually governed him. The fisherman was dead — José Ortega, the man who might have undone all their carefully kept secrets.

He was a liability no longer.

Now the main objective was to vanish back to their boat, slip into the night, and return to the safety of their island cave. That was what Valeria Cruz demanded of them: immediate disappearance after ensuring no loose ends remained. Ortega's final words had been cut short, ensuring that the two large American men he'd stumbled against wouldn't learn enough to become real threats.

Ramón knew those Americans might still try to piece together what had happened, but Ortega's death was the crux. The fisherman's knowledge had died with him, that half-finished revelation about artifacts and older mysteries. No doubt the men who'd been next to Ortega when he collapsed would wonder. But they were tourists, Ramón told himself, just travelers with no real stake or insight. They wouldn't have enough to chase the Syndicate.

Even if they tried to get involved, it would be a feeble attempt at playing hero. Ramón needed to reassure his men, though, because he could sense their anxiety through the darkness.

He signaled them to follow him deeper into the alley, away from the commotion. Lights spilled out across the sand to their left, where the bar's open layout allowed glimpses of chaotic movement — people tending to the body, frantic phone calls, staff urging everyone to stay calm. A few more shouts echoed in the night, but Ramón paid them no mind. He had to focus on extracting his group. If the police arrived, they'd come from the main road, so the best route was around the backside of the block, then cutting through a side street toward the smaller pier they'd used to land in relative secrecy.

Ortiz reached him first, face drawn. "Shouldn't we have dealt with those Americans?" Ortiz asked, voice low. "They were right there. They're going to see he was shot. They might try to describe us."

Ramón shook his head, waving off the suggestion. "They didn't *see* us. And Ortega's dead. That is the crucial point. He's the one who knew what we couldn't let him say. A couple of random guys from out of town won't matter. At most, they'll tell the local cops they saw some man die. We're ghosts, Ortiz. We're not sticking around to be identified."

Lopez and Castellanos joined them, glancing nervously back at the bar. The tension on their faces confirmed they were thinking the same thing: This was messy. "They might talk," Lopez hissed. "Shouldn't we —"

"No," Ramón cut in, trying to keep his voice calm but firm. "We can't gun down tourists on a crowded beach. We'd have half the island's police after us before we ever reached the boat. It's done. Ortega was our objective. We have no reason to stay. Let's move."

The men exchanged glances, not entirely reassured, but Ramón was in charge here. He knew that killing innocent bystanders, especially foreigners, would only escalate the situation to a point Cruz herself would never forgive. Better to trust that the fisherman's partial words would remain just that — partial. Even if those big American men tried to chase the story, they wouldn't have enough to blow the lid on the Syndicate.

Not unless they were unbelievably stubborn or lucky.

He gestured for them to follow, leading the way down the alley. They slipped along the backs of more shuttered stores and one-story homes, the typical architecture in these beach neighborhoods. The low hum of air conditioners, the stray bark of a dog from a neighboring yard, the scuff of their boots against the sandy ground — these were the only immediate sounds.

The further they got from the bar's radius of light and voices, the safer Ramón felt. His heart still beat quickly, though, a reflection of the adrenaline spike from that single shot in a place full of tourists. He hated chaos, preferred a clean operation. Yet he couldn't deny that the fisherman's abrupt exit from this world was necessary.

At the corner of a small intersection, they paused beneath a streetlamp. Its flickering bulb revealed the men's sweat-slicked faces and the tension in their eyes. Ramón held up a hand, peering around to ensure no local cops patrolled. The street was empty. Only a pair of old bicycles leaned against a chain-link fence, no sign of their owners. Satisfied, he beckoned the group onward.

Ortiz tugged at Ramón's sleeve once more. "But if Cruz asks why we didn't handle every possible witness, what do we say?" he asked, voice barely above a whisper.

Ramón scowled at the question but kept his tone measured. "We couldn't gun down everyone in the bar," he answered. "We're not terrorists. We'll say Ortega died before he finished speaking. He never named us, never said enough to identify the Syndicate. Shooting more people would only create more problems. The boss didn't order a bloodbath; she wanted Ortega silenced. Our job is finished."

Ortiz nodded, though his worry was still etched across his features. Ramón understood. The group had all done some brutal tasks before, but rarely with so many spectators a stone's throw away. This felt exposed. Still, the mission was accomplished, and they had to trust that no serious leads would emerge from a couple of clueless tourists who'd only glimpsed the fisherman's final moments.

Behind them, the distant hum of another bar's music faded into the general hush of nighttime. In its place, the deeper quiet of a tropical evening took over, punctuated by the whisper of the tide. They navigated through two more side streets, weaving between modest bungalows and small, unlit shops. Here and there, a light glowed in a window, revealing a family finishing dinner or watching television. Ramón kept a steady pace, mindful of the others' footsteps behind him. They all wanted to get back to the boat before the local police blocked off roads or started searching. Time was ticking.

Finally, they reached a narrow dirt path that sloped downward to the water. This was where they had moored their dinghy near an old, disused pier. Clouds drifted across the moon, so the night was patchy with intervals of silver light and deeper shadows. Ramón led the way, scanning for any sign of watchers or suspicious movement. The path was deserted, overshadowed by a line of crooked palm trees. Each gust of warm air rustled the fronds overhead, a soft hiss that teased Ramón's ears.

He spotted their dinghy bobbing at the end of a small makeshift dock. It was basically just a few planks hammered together, half-submerged. Soggy seaweed clung to the posts. The men moved as one, stepping carefully onto the slick wood. The boat gently rocked, waiting for them. Ramón exhaled a fraction of the tension. Almost there. A clean getaway, if no one had followed them. And he was fairly certain no one had; the entire bar had been in disarray.

They climbed aboard, stowing rifles quickly under a plastic tarp. Castellanos handled the outboard motor, giving it a careful pull. The engine sputtered, then caught with a low, rumbling hum. The group cast quick glances at the shoreline, confirming no lights or silhouettes approached. Satisfied, they cast off, letting the motor push them out into open water. The reflection of a half-hidden moon glimmered on the gentle waves.

As the dinghy picked up speed, Ramón felt the wind drying the sweat on his brow. He said nothing for the first few minutes, letting the men decompress from the tension. The black waters parted under the boat's bow, creating a steady white foam that glowed faintly in the moonlight. Overhead, a scattering of stars emerged, though some were obscured by the drifting cloud cover.

Eventually, Castellanos, seated near the engine, cleared his throat. "I still think we should have done something about those Americans," he said. The breeze carried his voice forward over the motor's drone. "What if they ask too many questions?"

Ramón turned slightly, eyes still on the horizon. "They can't identify us by name. Ortega died before he spelled anything out. We're not in the local databases. And a thousand random tourists flow through that bar every night." He tried to keep his tone steady, but deep down, a thread of concern twisted. *What if they asked questions?* But he reminded himself again: The crucial piece was Ortega's knowledge. That died with him. "Besides," he continued, "two big guys from the States aren't going to unravel the Syndicate. Let them think it was just a tragedy or some local violence. They'll be on a plane home in a week or two."

Ortiz looked unconvinced, though he nodded. "If you say so. I just don't want to face Valeria Cruz's wrath if it turns into an investigation."

Ramón felt that pang in his chest at the mention of Cruz. She didn't tolerate blunders. He pressed his lips together. "We did what we had to do. If there's any blowback, I'll handle it." He let that stand as final. Inside, he wrestled with a flicker of doubt. For all he knew, those Americans might be the nosy type, but he'd handle that if it arose. Right now, their job was to return to the island cave.

With that, he signaled Castellanos to set a course parallel to the coastline, heading for a hidden cove where a larger vessel waited to ferry them to the tiny island that served as their base. The engine's low hum provided a monotonous comfort, a background note to the swirl of thoughts in Ramón's head. He gazed at the dark horizon, letting the sea breeze ruffle his hair, still damp from sweat.

CHAPTER 26

RAMÓN

THE BOAT GLIDED across calm waters, each wave a gentle rolling motion.

Ramos and his men allowed a hush to fall over them, occasionally murmuring about the day's tension, or about how close the fisherman had come to naming them. Lopez pointed out the faint glow of distant shore lights, remarking on how quickly the local police might lock down the bar. Ramón just nodded, picturing uniformed men flooding the place, demanding statements from every sunburned tourist and flustered bartender. But they'd find no sign of him and his men. They were ghosts on this water, already halfway to their hidden stronghold.

He recalled how the fisherman had nearly said too much, stumbling in front of those tourists. Another half-second of breath, and maybe the entire operation would've been compromised. That kind of near miss weighed on Ramón's mind, fueling an inward sense of worry.

Cruz believed everything was under control, but the Syndicate seemed to be spinning riskier webs lately. The artifact, rumored to be older than the Spanish, had started a chain reaction of violence. Ramón wondered how many more times they could kill witnesses in public before a real unstoppable trouble brewed.

He sucked in the salt-laced air, forcing the tension out of his shoulders. They were safe for tonight. Tomorrow would bring fresh directives from Cruz. She'd want details of how Ortega died, a blow-by-blow account of the fiasco in the bar, and possibly plans to relocate deeper into the island's labyrinthine cave system.

She hated being exposed.

And after a shooting in front of foreigners, she'd hate it even more. The best Ramón could do was present the facts plainly: The fisherman never fully identified them or the artifact. The Americans were basically clueless. That was enough to keep her from lashing out, or so he hoped.

Within half an hour, they reached the mouth of a secluded cove, its high cliffs shadowed in the moon's half-light. The engine dropped to a quiet purr as Castellanos guided them in. Here, thick foliage grew along the steep rocky walls, obscuring the narrow channel from casual observers.

They pressed forward, hugging the starboard side to avoid hidden reefs. Ramón watched the water's surface for any sign of shallow coral or drifting logs. The last thing they needed was a damaged boat that stranded them.

A faint glow from a single covered lantern signaled their allies on a waiting craft, anchored deeper in the cove. The men exhaled relief. They maneuvered the dinghy alongside it, exchanging coded signals with the lookout. Carefully, they transferred aboard a small but capable motorboat that had better range. One guard remained on the waiting craft to handle the dinghy. Ramón, Ortiz, Lopez, and Castellanos arranged themselves near the bow.

With a low growl of the engine, the motorboat set out again, leaving the cove behind. Now they'd push out to sea, heading for that tiny, virtually uncharted island that the Syndicate claimed for their hidden base. The night wind picked up, splashing them with a fine mist of saltwater. Ramón's clothes clung to him, a mix of sweat and ocean spray. It wasn't comfortable, but he felt the tension fade as the coastline receded, replaced by open sea under a half-shrouded moon.

Castellanos cut the throttle once they were far enough out, letting the engine idle while they checked bearings. Ortiz used a small GPS device. Even in the hush, the sense of relief was thick. The men relaxed, though they still carried that aftertaste of adrenaline. Lopez rummaged for a bottle of water, passing it around. Ramón took a swig, letting the tepid liquid soothe his throat. He realized he hadn't had a drink since well before the fiasco at the bar.

The conversation turned back to the Americans, the only two men who seemed interested in helping the fated old fisherman. While he didn't think that alone was cause for alarm, Lopez insisted they looked pretty big, possibly ex-military. Castellanos shrugged, uncertain. Ortiz remained quiet, giving Ramón a look that asked for final reassurance. Ramón offered the same line: "They don't matter. The fisherman was the key. Without him, no one can piece this together. If they do try, they'll hit a wall of silence."

Yet inside, a flicker of doubt persisted. *What if these Americans were the meddlesome type?*

He let that worry simmer. For now, he had no evidence they were anything more than random travelers. Maybe they'd rummage for answers, but the Syndicate had ways of shutting down prying eyes. If the boss needed, she'd post watchers in that bar district, ensuring no one uncovered the truth. Ramón forced himself to focus on the bigger picture: The artifact remained safe, Ortega was gone, and their path back to the island was clear. He'd deliver his report to Cruz and abide by whatever next steps she dictated.

After verifying their heading, the motorboat roared back to life, crossing open water in a gradual arc. The moon emerged fully for a moment, silvering the waves around them. Ramón felt the boat rise and fall with each gentle swell. The conversation among the men quieted, each lost in his own thoughts. The events of the night weighed on them — shooting a man in a bar was never the preferred approach, but it was what had to be done.

Two hours passed in that methodical transit, the ocean's darkness stretching in all directions. At last, they spied the faint shape of the tiny island — no more than a rocky mass crowned with dense vegetation. A single lamp near the hidden cave mouth flickered, guiding them in. They cut speed, carefully navigating the rocky coastline until they found the narrow inlet that gave access to the cave. The waves slapped against stony outcroppings, creating an echo that amplified inside the boat.

Ramón's chest tightened momentarily as they slipped into the cove. Memories of other nights surfaced: lugging contraband, disposing of loose ends, a swirl of secrets. Tonight was no different. They glided between the rocky walls, eventually mooring at a rickety wooden platform that jutted out from the mouth of the cave. Guards there recognized them, offering tired nods. No questions asked — this was the Syndicate's routine.

He hopped onto the platform, ignoring the protest of weary legs. The men followed, stowing the boat. A single generator inside the cave provided minimal power, illuminating the wet rock walls with a harsh, utilitarian glow. The space smelled of salt, mildew, and faint diesel fumes. Stacked crates formed partial barricades near the cave's interior, and a short corridor led deeper, where the Syndicate's main operating area lay hidden.

They trudged inside, boots echoing on stone. Ortiz asked if they'd have to give a full debrief to Cruz immediately. Ramón suspected yes. She liked updates as soon as they returned. But she might be asleep if the night was too advanced. He felt a tug of dread: Cruz rarely slept. She'd be waiting.

Sure enough, in the central section of the cave, a handful of Syndicate operatives milled about. Some glared at them with curiosity, having heard the rumor of a bar shooting. Ramón signaled them that it was done, that Ortega was gone. The men parted, letting them pass.

They found Cruz near a makeshift table, reviewing a small stash of documents under a hanging lantern.

She's a natural, he thought. He couldn't imagine her as anything but a modern-day pirate. He almost laughed thinking of her sitting behind a proper desk, hair combed, dressed in — *yeah, no sense going there*, he thought. *She's a pirate, through and through.*

Her expression, cast in the flicker of yellow light, was as unreadable as ever. She glanced up, eyebrows tight. No words of greeting, just a tilt of her chin to indicate they should come forward. Ramón steeled himself, stepping closer. The others hung back a pace or two.

He explained the basics: They had tracked Ortega, he'd fled into a bar, they'd had to shoot him before he spilled secrets. The bullet ended him mid-sentence.

They'd left the place in chaos. A couple of big American tourists *might* have glimpsed Ortega's final moment, but that was all. Cruz's lips tightened at the mention of tourists. She demanded more detail, and Ramón offered a concise version of how none of them had engaged or confronted the bystanders.

They'd simply left, knowing the fisherman had been the real threat.

Cruz gazed at him for a long, silent moment, then gave a small nod. "Messy," she said, voice low. "But Ortega's gone. That's what matters. The rest is noise."

Ramón took that as acceptance. Yet he saw a flicker of tension behind Cruz's eyes, maybe the same worry that flickered in his own chest. Another public killing was never ideal. Eventually, she dismissed them with a wave, reminding Ramón that the artifact's secrecy must remain absolute.

He nodded. The men stepped away, relieved that Cruz's initial reaction was measured. For now, they were safe from her wrath. Unless something else happened — like those Americans poking around.

As they settled deeper into the cave, stowing gear and grabbing a quick meal from the supplies, Ramón couldn't shake his lingering unease. Yes, Ortega was dead, but the entire scene felt too dramatic. One bullet in front of all those tourists, the man practically in the arms of that big American. Even if the man never recognized them, the memory might stick in his head. If by some twist of fate he dug too deep, maybe they'd have to deal with it again.

For now, though, Ramón told himself that was a remote possibility. He'd abide by the Syndicate's creed: The job was done. No need to dwell. He tried to let that logic soothe him, if only for the night.

He found a spot near the cave's rock wall, letting exhaustion wash over him. The synergy of salt-laced air and mild diesel fumes formed an oddly comforting sensation. He unrolled a thin sleeping pad, acknowledging that if trouble came, he'd have to be ready in an instant. There was a makeshift barracks deeper in the cave, just a wall in front of which some wooden bunks had been erected, but he typically liked to be closer to the exit.

He was no pirate. He could see the appeal — Cruz seemed to have fully adopted the lifestyle — but he was a bit of a holdout. Mercenary, sure. But the key was *money*. He was in it for the cash, not just the freedom.

Another day in the Syndicate's shadowy realm. Another body lost to their insatiable cause.

But the boss was satisfied, his men were safe. That was enough to end the day, even if a small voice in his mind whispered that everything was becoming more precarious with each kill.

Tomorrow, they would see what new tasks or new nightmares emerged. For tonight, at least, Ramón tried to let the gentle drip of water in the recesses of the cave lull him to sleep, ignoring the knot of worry coiling in his stomach.

CHAPTER 27

BEN

THE STREET WAS DESERTED at this hour. A single streetlamp buzzed overhead. Beyond it, night claimed the rest. The hush felt surreal after the chaos in the bar. Ben flexed his fingers, trying to shake off the adrenaline that still coursed through him.

Just a half hour ago, we were sipping rum, enjoying the music, Ben thought. *Now we're slinking around in the dark, trying to avoid a criminal syndicate.* His mind reeled at the speed of the reversal.

Reggie pointed to a distant corner where a few cars were parked. "The golf cart's that way, right?"

"Yeah, about two blocks from the bar's main entrance. Let's hope no one messed with it."

They walked briskly, glancing over their shoulders more often than they would have liked. The hush of the sleeping town pressed in on them, punctuated by the occasional bark of a stray dog or the distant rev of a motorbike. Their sandals scraped against uneven pavement, and overhead a few stars blinked indifferently.

When they reached the golf cart, it appeared untouched, parked alongside a couple of similar rentals. Reggie hopped in the driver's seat, fumbled with the key, and started the engine. Ben slid into the passenger side, scanning the street for any sign of watchers. He saw none.

"All right," Reggie said, voice subdued. "We'll go back to the bungalow. Then figure out what to do next. I'll text Sarah, just to keep her updated."

Ben nodded, exhaling. *At least we can regroup there.* He felt an uneasy churn in his gut. This entire scenario felt dangerous — and familiar, in the worst way. *We're vacationing in a place controlled by a group that kills divers and fishermen for some ancient artifact. Great.* But he kept his thoughts to himself, not wanting to stoke Reggie's tension.

The golf cart rumbled down the dark roads, passing closed shops and shuttered windows. Even the row of beachy souvenir stands they'd seen earlier were locked tight for the night, their colorful displays hidden behind rolling metal doors. Only a stray cat skittered across the path, illuminated briefly by the cart's weak headlights.

They navigated onto the coastal route leading to their bungalow, the ocean to their left a black void. The memory of the fisherman's final words looped in Ben's mind, refusing to let go. *Older than the Spanish. They took it... My brother... The Black Coral Syndicate...*

He remembered how the man had locked eyes with him, *begging* for help. Now he was dead, shot down before he could finish explaining. Rage flared briefly in Ben's chest. He gripped the golf cart's side rail until his knuckles whitened. *Why can't these thugs just leave innocent people alone?*

"We'll get to the bottom of this," Reggie said quietly, as though reading Ben's mind.

Ben cast him a sidelong glance, half-grateful, half-annoyed that Reggie seemed so sure. He forced a nod. "Yeah. But let's be careful."

The bungalow came into view, its porch light glowing softly, a misleading beacon of peace. Reggie pulled the cart to a stop, and they climbed out. The palm trees rustled overhead in the breeze, and the distant crash of waves reminded Ben of the natural beauty that had drawn them here in the first place.

They stepped onto the porch. Ben dug for the key, but Reggie held out a hand. "Shh." Reggie tilted his head, listening. Ben froze, heart thumping. After a tense moment, Reggie shrugged. "Thought I heard something."

Ben swallowed. *Now we're seeing threats everywhere.* But better safe than sorry. They quietly entered the bungalow, flipping on the lights, scanning the living room for any signs of forced entry. Everything looked as they'd left it. Still, the sense of security they'd felt earlier was gone.

Ben locked the door behind them, double-checking the windows. Reggie let out a heavy breath and sank onto the couch, rubbing his temples. "Hell of a night."

"Understatement," Ben muttered. He peeled off his sandals, feeling the grit of the day's sand between his toes, reminding him how drastically things had changed in the span of a few hours.

They stayed like that for a while, the silence thick. Eventually, Reggie spoke up. "So... we're definitely in the middle of something big." He looked at Ben gravely. "You sure you're ready for that?"

Ben rubbed a hand over his face. *I wanted to avoid all this.* But he found himself nodding. "If that fisherman's story is true, we might be the only ones who can do something. At least figure out what's going on." He paused, recalling the name that had spilled from the fisherman's lips: *El Cementerio de los Contrabandistas.*

"We need info about the Black Coral Syndicate. Locals might know more — someone who isn't scared to talk."

Ben exhaled, feeling the weight of the fisherman's death settle on his conscience. *We didn't pull the trigger, but I can't just ignore what happened.* "We'll start tomorrow," he said, though he already knew it wouldn't be simple.

Reggie nodded, stifling a yawn. "I'll grab my laptop, see if I can dig up anything. You... try to get some sleep?"

Ben barked a hollow laugh. "Sleep?" *After that? Right...*

They lapsed into silence again, each lost in thought. Outside, the ocean continued its ceaseless rhythm, uncaring about the violence that had unfurled. The fisherman's blood was still drying on that bar's sandy floor, and somewhere, the murderer was likely reporting a successful hit to the Syndicate. *We're in it now.*

Ben crossed to the window and stared out at the moonlit beach. *Trouble found us,* he thought, pressing a hand against the glass. *We'll have to find a way to handle it.* Whether that meant diving into the cursed reef or confronting armed smugglers, he couldn't say. But one thing was certain: their quiet vacation was gone.

Behind him, Reggie tapped on his laptop keys, the faint clicks echoing in the hush. Ben took a deep breath, forcing himself to stay focused, to quell the swirl of emotions. Tomorrow, they'd begin investigating. For now, he needed to calm his racing thoughts enough to rest — if that was even possible. He closed his eyes, drawing in the humid night air.

José Ortega... I'm sorry we couldn't save you.

The dark tide of exhaustion pulled at him, but he resisted for a moment, scanning the horizon for any sign of movement. Nothing. Just the moon reflecting on rolling waves. A gentle wind rustled the bungalow's porch screens. The world out there might look serene, but he knew better now.

He turned back to Reggie. "Be careful," he said quietly.

Reggie paused his typing, gave a solemn nod. "Always."

Ben stood there a moment longer, letting that single word resonate in the tension-filled air. Then he flicked off the living room light, leaving only a small lamp on. The music from the bar had long since faded, replaced by the hum of distant sirens — maybe the police. But they were too late for José.

We'll find out who did this, Ben promised inwardly, *and why.*

CHAPTER 28

REGGIE

REGGIE COLLAPSED onto the bungalow's battered couch, letting his body sink into the worn cushions. The scent of salt air drifted through the half-open window, mixing with a faint whiff of mildew clinging to the upholstery. He listened for a moment to the hush that had settled over the little house — outside, crickets chirped, and the distant waves of the Caribbean whispered against the sand. Inside, the only sound was a soft snore from the far side of the room, where Ben sat slumped in a dining chair, arms folded over his chest as if determined to stay alert even in sleep.

Reggie closed his eyes, trying to process the past few hours. He and Ben had gone from laid-back tourists to unwilling witnesses of a murder all in one night. The fisherman's face still hovered in Reggie's mind — brow furrowed, voice urgent — until that final burst of gunfire ended everything. They'd managed to escape, but not without tangling themselves in a local criminal enterprise called the Black Coral Syndicate.

He inhaled slowly, counting to four, then exhaled just as slowly. He felt a jolt of guilt. *We aren't just stumbling anymore. We're actively stepping deeper, letting curiosity and maybe empathy pull us in.* The fisherman's pleading eyes wouldn't let him turn away.

But even as Reggie tried to ground himself, his mind roamed to Sarah. She was the one who'd originally mentioned rumors of a "smuggling ring" operating in these waters. At the time, Reggie hadn't taken it too seriously — there were always stories about illicit goings-on in ports around the Caribbean. But now, after what they'd seen, he wished he'd pressed Sarah for more details. *If we'd known more, maybe we could have avoided the bar, avoided the confrontation, avoided that poor man's death...*

His phone lay facedown on the coffee table. He scooped it up, pressing the lock button to see a dark reflection of his own face in the black screen. He wondered if Sarah was awake. She was a night owl, especially on nights before her lectures at the university, often preparing slides or diving into half-finished research papers. If she wasn't up, he could at least leave a text for her to find in the morning.

But he suspected she'd be awake. She always seemed to know when something was wrong. He glanced at Ben once more — still motionless, save for the subtle rise and fall of his chest. Then he unlocked his phone, feeling a wave of relief at the familiar list of messages. Sarah's name was near the top.

He composed a message with trembling fingers:

> Hey, it's me. Long night. Remember that smuggling ring you mentioned? Think we accidentally kicked the anthill.

He paused, reread the words. Not exactly an easy confession to parse, but he didn't want to bury the truth. He needed Sarah to know they were in deeper than they'd intended. With a sigh, he hit *Send*.

He waited, the phone feeling too heavy in his grip. Outside, a gust of wind rattled the palm fronds. After a tense minute, the phone buzzed. Sarah's name lit up the screen, along with her reply:

> What do you mean kicked the anthill? Are you guys okay?

Reggie let out a short laugh, the tension easing fractionally. *She's definitely awake.* He typed faster this time:

> We're fine. More or less. Got caught in the wrong place at the wrong time, heard a fisherman talk about the Black Coral Syndicate. Then someone shot him. We bailed. Now we're lying low at the bungalow.

His heart thumped as he watched the three little dots on the screen, indicating she was typing. He could almost hear her voice in his head, that serious undertone she used when her protective instincts flared. The phone buzzed again:

> Shot him?? This is serious. Did you see who did it? Are you in trouble?

Reggie scratched the back of his neck. It was always a dance with Sarah — knowing how much to share so she understood the gravity of the situation, but not panicking her in the process. She was in San Juan, juggling a busy teaching schedule and a research conference.

He didn't want to drag her into the middle of a potential crime spree. She'd do it in a heartbeat if asked — but that was the problem. She'd do it.

> Not sure who fired the shots, but they're part of that syndicate. We're not exactly in danger right now. Probably. Just… let me fill you in once we sort it out.

A beat passed. Then another message:

> Sort it out?? Reggie, you're not cops. This is big league stuff. Let me help. I've got local contacts from the university — anthropologists, historians, even a couple folks with NGO connections. They might have info about that syndicate.

He exhaled. He loved that about Sarah — her unstoppable drive to fix things, to learn everything. But some messy street-level conflict with armed criminals wasn't her usual realm of expertise. Also, she had enough on her plate with her academic commitments. He typed a reply, choosing his words carefully:

> We'll handle it. I promise. I can't drag you into this when you're swamped with your classes and conference. Just keep doing your thing, okay?

He watched the screen flicker, then the next text arrived:

> Don't do anything reckless. If you need me, I'll drop everything. No question. Just… promise me you'll stay safe.

He clenched his jaw, an unexpected flush of warmth hitting him. The genuine concern in her words made him realize how close he felt to losing control of the situation. "Stay safe," she said, but they'd already seen a man murdered. Hardly safe. He typed back:

> I promise. We're lying low. Not about to charge in guns blazing. Miss you a ton.

He hesitated, staring at the last phrase. *Miss you a ton.* In the day's chaos, he hadn't allowed himself to dwell on the longing that welled up whenever he thought of her. But now that the adrenaline was ebbing, he felt the ache — wishing she were here, wishing she could talk some sense into him in person. Maybe just the comfort of her presence would remind him that not everything was a looming threat.

The phone buzzed:

> Miss you too. I should be done in a couple days. If you guys are still there, maybe I can head over. Or we can meet in San Juan. Just keep me posted. And for real, no heroics, Reggie. We're a team — remember that.

He smiled faintly. *A team.* That was Sarah's motto, especially when she traveled for digs or taught summer courses in the region. She believed in synergy, in combining resources. Meanwhile, Reggie had always been a bit more spontaneous — some might say impulsive. Then again, he'd usually relied on Sarah to ground him. And right now, his anchor was a phone screen with short text messages.

> No heroics, got it. Just gotta figure out what's going on. We owe that fisherman at least some attempt to find out who shot him, right?

A weight settled in his gut. The fisherman's last pleas echoed in his head: *The Black Coral Syndicate... they took... my brother...* Then the gunshots. He clenched his teeth. If they did nothing, his death would become just another statistic.

Sarah's response came in, more subdued:

> If that's how you feel, do it carefully. Keep me in the loop. I'm serious, Reggie. I can drop everything.

He pressed the phone to his chest for a second, eyes closing. Part of him wanted to ask her to come right now, help them dig for answers — she was brilliant, resourceful. But he also knew she had obligations. She'd worked so hard on her new class syllabus, and her father, Dr. Graham Lindgren, had been praising her progress. Reggie didn't want to be the reason she jeopardized her professional momentum.

He typed:

> You focus on your conference. Let me handle the dirty work. We're not alone — Ben's here.

Immediately, a self-mocking grin twisted his lips. *Right,* he thought. *Ben's here, meaning we have a buddy for moral support, not exactly a paramilitary squad.* But the two of them could watch each other's backs, gather intel carefully, decide if the risk was worth pressing forward. He tried to reassure himself, ignoring the creeping dread in his belly.

Sarah's next text read:

Fine. But keep me updated every step. Please. And… I miss you.

Reggie swallowed. He typed back:

I miss you too. We'll talk in the morning, okay? I need a bit of rest. This day has been — intense.

Understatement. Goodnight, babe. Stay safe.

He locked the phone and let his head drop against the back of the couch. The minimal overhead light in the bungalow cast flickering shadows on the wall, shaped by the rotating ceiling fan.

He took a slow breath, sorting through the conversation in his mind. He'd told Sarah they were fine, that they'd be careful. But part of him wondered if that was even possible.

One slip-up tonight had nearly gotten them killed.

REGGIE GLANCED AT BEN, who still dozed fitfully.

Outside, the wind picked up, and a gentle whoosh of rustling palm leaves drifted through the open window. The air carried the briny tang of the ocean, reminding Reggie of simpler joys — sunbathing, snorkeling, cold beers on the beach. They'd arrived expecting a relaxing getaway. Instead, they had front-row seats to an island underworld.

He tried to imagine how the Syndicate operated. Probably a well-connected group, smuggling contraband through the reefs like a pirate-style cartel. Likely with more than a few paid-off cops among their ranks. The fisherman's mention of an "ancient artifact" stuck in his mind, though. *Older than the Spanish... They took it... My brother...* That snippet of desperation hinted at more than mere narcotics or stolen goods. Artifacts implied historical or archaeological value.

Possibly something local fishermen had stumbled upon in the ocean. Possibly something that had the Syndicate killing to protect.

He sighed, rubbing his temples. *Focus, Reggie. Tackle this step by step.* They had a day or two to gather info discreetly — talk to locals, maybe bribe a fisherman or two for details. If it looked too risky, they'd bail. Right?

The question gnawed at him, and he realized Sarah's unwavering sense of justice had rubbed off on him. She'd want them to do the right thing, carefully but decisively. She'd once told him: *"Neutrality in the face of cruelty helps only the oppressor."* Those words stuck, though Reggie had teased her for quoting heavily paraphrased moral lessons.

Yet it still rang true.

Outside, the cicadas sang. The bungalow's wooden beams creaked as the wind shifted. Another wave of memory hit him: how, just last night, he and Ben had joked about lazy mornings, sipping coffee while reading thriller novels in hammock chairs. The stark shift from that carefree banter to tonight's flight from gunfire left him off-balance.

He yawned, exhaustion sweeping over him like a heavy blanket. Maybe rest would help. Tomorrow, they could act. *Better rest while we can,* he thought. The next day might bring more questions — and hopefully some answers. If the universe was kind, they'd avoid more violence.

He glanced one last time at Ben, half-convinced he should carry him to the bedroom so he'd sleep better. There was no way he could lift the guy, but his prosthetic arm might be strong enough to drag him...

Not that Ben would ever allow it. He chuckled, imagining Ben waking up to being dragged across the bungalow by Reggie.

Reggie let him be, figuring the discomfort of the chair might keep him half-ready for any night-time intrusions. A part of Reggie wanted to stay up as well, to stand guard against the unknown. But his eyelids weighed a ton.

He closed his eyes. The fisherman's pleas reverberated in the darkness. *They took him... older than the Spanish... Black Coral Syndicate...* The waves outside provided a soothing counterpoint. In that strange symphony of dread and hope, Reggie's consciousness dipped, a final swirl of adrenaline leaving his veins.

Sleep tugged at him, promising at least a short reprieve.

He drifted, feeling the tension in his shoulders loosen. Tomorrow, they'd figure something out. They *had* to. Sarah trusted him to be smart, to keep them safe. That sense of duty, tinged with guilt and compassion, was all he had left to guide him.

CHAPTER 30

SARAH

SARAH CLASPED the edges of the lectern at the front of the lecture hall, forcing a calm smile even though her thoughts were tangled in knots. The fluorescent lights buzzed overhead, making the early morning light that leaked through the tall windows seem washed out.

Normally, she loved this room — the high ceilings, the faint odor of chalk dust despite the modern whiteboard, the rows of earnest faces. Teaching gave her energy. But today, no matter how hard she tried to focus on her slides about pre-colonial Caribbean trade routes, her mind refused to settle.

She glanced at the digital clock on her laptop: 9:07 a.m. The session started seven minutes ago, and she was already behind her usual routine. That wouldn't do. She took a breath, trying to anchor herself in the present. *Come on, Sarah, you're here. They need you engaged.*

Yet images of Reggie kept drifting into her consciousness. *We got caught in the wrong place at the wrong time,* he'd texted, followed by a horrifying mention of gunshots and a shady syndicate. When she'd finally gone to bed well past midnight, her stomach was still churning with worry. She'd woken up this morning to nothing new from him. No reassurance, no updates. The silence ate at her.

A cluster of students near the front row — four of them — raised inquisitive eyes, obviously noticing that she hadn't launched into her customary lively opener. Sarah inhaled once more, then forced a smile and pressed the forward arrow on her slide deck.

"All right, everyone," she said, voice echoing in the half-filled room. "Welcome back. I hope you had a productive evening finishing the reading on Saladoid ceramics. Today, we're exploring pre-colonial trade networks among the islands, focusing on how materials like flint, cassava, and even certain ornamental stones moved between communities."

She clicked to reveal a map showing broad arrow lines arching among the Caribbean islands — Puerto Rico, Hispaniola, Jamaica, and the smaller island chains bridging them. A typical day's discussion topic. Ordinarily, she'd feel that little surge of excitement. She loved unveiling the complexities of ancient maritime travel to students who'd only ever read the surface-level, simplistic paragraphs in high-school textbooks.

But now, those bright lines on the screen only reminded her how far away Reggie and Ben were, in some corner of the island dealing with criminals. Possibly in danger.

She cleared her throat, forging ahead. "So, the Taíno — like their predecessors — were adept seafarers. They moved goods in canoes that could hold dozens of people and cargo. This facilitated economic and cultural exchanges, influencing everything from pottery styles to religious practices..."

Her own words sounded distant. She paused mid-sentence, fingertips brushing the laptop trackpad. She'd neglected to prepare a second set of slides that expanded on the religious significance. In fact, she'd been planning to refine them last night, but the texts from Reggie had shattered her focus.

A student in a teal headscarf — Yara, from her advanced discussion group — raised a hand. Sarah recognized her immediately; Yara was bright and always ready with deep questions. Right now, Sarah felt a pang of gratitude for the distraction.

"Yes, Yara?"

"Dr. Lindgren," Yara began, "I remember you mentioning in your last lecture how the Taínos built inland communities, not just coastal. Could that have impacted their trade network if storms or hurricanes reshaped shorelines regularly?"

Sarah tried to gather her drifting thoughts. "Great question," she said, forcing herself to push aside personal worries. "Yes, actually. Hurricanes and the shifting coastline absolutely played a role. Coastal routes might be blocked or altered, so traders often relied on well-known inland paths or avoided traveling during storm season. Some archaeologists argue that's why certain inland settlements developed strategic trade outposts — places to store surplus or wait out storms."

She illustrated the point by clicking to the next slide, showing photos of a partially excavated inland site in Utuado. She highlighted the relics found there — ceramic fragments, stone tools from other islands — proof of interisland connections.

Yara nodded, seemingly satisfied, and other students jotted notes. Sarah exhaled. *I've got this. Keep teaching.* She advanced another slide, describing how cyclical storms might deposit foreign debris, sometimes leading to accidental discoveries of exotic materials. The mention of storms made her mind veer to Reggie's text again: *Shot him... We bailed... Lying low at the bungalow.* Her stomach tightened.

After a few more minutes, she sensed restlessness creeping in. She needed to shift tactics. "All right," she said, stepping away from the podium. "Let's break into small groups. I'd like you to discuss how changing coastlines and frequent hurricanes could affect trade routes between Puerto Rico and the Lesser Antilles. Specifically, think about the archaeological evidence we might find — like layered shell middens or relocated pottery caches. I'll roam around and listen."

A soft shuffle of chairs followed as the dozen or so students formed clusters, leaning in to share ideas. Sarah hovered at the edges, offering the occasional pointer: *"Remember how storms can open new channels, or bury old ones."* She nodded, heartened that they were engaging. But she couldn't fully focus. She checked her phone under the table — no new messages.

Five minutes later, she paused at a group discussing the correlation between ritual objects and trade. She added a note about how items used for worship — like cemis or amulets — sometimes traveled great distances, possibly connecting spiritual practices across islands.

In mid-explanation, her phone buzzed softly. She froze, heart thudding, and pretended to check her watch instead of diving for the device.

She finished her comment about traveling amulets, then excused herself with a quick smile. At the front of the room, she ducked behind the lectern, phone in hand. The screen displayed a notification from Reggie:

> All good here. Tired. Will fill you in soon. Stay
> safe. Miss you.

Sarah let out a breath she hadn't realized she was holding. He was okay — for now. The text was brief, but it was better than silence. She typed a quick reply, biting back the urge to demand details:

> Relieved to hear from you. Be careful. We'll
> talk as soon as I'm done teaching. Miss
> you too.

She paused before hitting Send, wrestling with the desire to grill him for more info, to insist he call. But Reggie had explicitly said "tired." Probably they'd been up half the night. She pressed Send, hoping he might be sleeping now, or at least lying low.

CHAPTER 31

SARAH

SHE SHOVED the phone into her pocket, turning back to the class. The group activity was winding down, a few heads turning her way expectantly. She put on her best professional smile and clapped lightly to recapture everyone's attention.

"All right, folks! Great discussions, I'm sure. Who wants to share insights?"

She listened to their short presentations with half an ear. Most were decent — talk of how storms might rearrange entire coastlines, submerging or revealing sites, thereby altering trade. Normally, she'd be thrilled by their analysis. But her thoughts churned with *What if the the anthill they kicked is more violent than they realize? What if they're not safe at the bungalow?*

She forced her focus back as one student concluded, "So, that might explain why certain archaeological layers show abrupt changes — like a village relocates inland after a massive hurricane." Another group nodded, impressed.

Sarah nodded, her professional mask slipping as a thought struck her. "Actually, this relates directly to what the hurricane did to the coastline here in Puerto Rico. The storm's power reshaped entire sections of the eastern shore, especially around Culebra and the surrounding islands."

She pulled up a satellite image on the projector. "Look here — the force of those waves actually exposed portions of the seafloor that had been buried for centuries."

She zoomed in on the reef system off Culebra's coast. "Local divers and fishermen reported seeing previously unknown structures emerge after the hurricane passed. Stone formations that didn't match natural coral patterns." Her heart quickened, feeling the pull of adventure. *Another time*, she thought. "There's evidence suggesting an ancient community — possibly a splinter group of the Taíno — used these reefs not just for fishing, but for ceremonial purposes."

A student in the back raised his hand. "Like building underwater shrines?"

"Exactly." Sarah advanced to a slide showing eroded stone formations barely visible through turquoise water. "These, of course, weren't originally underwater. Sea levels were lower centuries ago, and these structures would have been accessible during low tide. The hurricane stripped away layers of sand and coral growth, revealing what might be the remnants of religious sites." She paused, careful not to reveal too much about what Reggie had discovered. "We're still analyzing these findings, but they suggest a sophisticated maritime culture that used the natural reef system in ways we hadn't imagined."

She clicked to another image, this one showing a partially exposed stone wall emerging from the coral. "Nature giveth, and nature taketh away. The same forces that revealed these sites could easily bury them again in the next major storm. That's why careful documentation is so crucial — and why we have to move quickly when new evidence appears."

If they only knew how quickly others were moving, she thought grimly, remembering Reggie's texts. But she kept her voice steady, professional. "This is archaeology in real-time, folks. Sometimes the most significant discoveries come not from planned excavations, but from nature's own excavating force."

She glanced at the clock — twenty minutes left in the session. She decided to fill the time with a short Q&A, which usually spurred deeper thinking. But as the first student raised a hand to ask about "weapons trade," Sarah felt a pang of dread at the word "weapons," so close to what Reggie had described: gunshots, violence, everything she'd wanted to keep far from her world. She answered, hoping her voice stayed steady.

A soft knock on the door broke her mid-sentence. The department's administrative assistant, Carla, slipped in, wearing a slightly apologetic smile. "Sorry to interrupt, Dr. Lindgren. Just letting you know there's a scheduling update for your next session."

Sarah nodded, grateful for an excuse to redirect her swirling thoughts. She excused herself from the students for a moment and stepped into the hallway with Carla. The corridor was quieter now, most morning classes already in progress.

"Everything all right?" Carla asked, handing over a printed schedule. "You seem... distracted."

Sarah forced a casual shrug. "Late night. Working on new research leads." It wasn't entirely a lie. "Anything major with the schedule?"

Carla shook her head. "Just that your next session's moved to a smaller room on the third floor, room 308. Some maintenance issue in your usual space."

"No problem. Thanks, Carla." Sarah forced a polite smile. Carla gave a short wave and headed off.

Returning to the lecture hall, Sarah found the students in an almost festive mood — maybe relieved that class was nearly over. She asked if there were any final queries about early Caribbean trade or settlement patterns. She fielded a few basic ones, scribbled a note or two on the white-board, then closed out the session with a gentle reminder about the upcoming reading. The class dismissed, and they trickled out in small chatty groups.

She managed a smile with each "bye, Dr. Lindgren," but inside she felt hollow. She collected her notes in silence, stacking them neatly, a reflex of habit. The moment the last student left, she grabbed her phone. No new messages from Reggie. A sigh of mixed relief and frustration slid past her lips.

She locked up her laptop, glancing around the now-empty room. The overhead lights flickered faintly — this old building had such unreliable fixtures. For a second, the image of that fisherman's murder Reggie had described rose unbidden in her mind, an echo of violence in stark contrast to her peaceful lecture environment. She shook it off.

All she wanted was to catch a bus or hop in her car and drive to wherever Reggie and Ben were hiding, make sure they were truly okay. But that was impossible at the moment; she still had departmental obligations, another class to teach. And Reggie had insisted on handling it. *We're not alone,* he'd said. *We'll figure it out.* She wondered if he was just trying to reassure her.

She typed a new text to him anyway:

I'm out of my lecture. Call me when you can?

She debated sending it, fretted for a half-second that she was being too clingy. Then decided *to hell with it* and hit Send. The message vanished into the ether, and she could only hope he'd respond.

The hallway outside was cool and quiet. She stepped into it, hugging her notes against her chest. Another professor emerged from a nearby office and gave her a polite greeting. Sarah nodded back, but her mind was drifting to the possibilities of what Reggie and Ben might face next — who was this Syndicate, really? How dangerous? The fisherman's dying words implied something bigger than a few petty smugglers.

Her phone still showed no new notifications. She sighed, tapping it to black. *Focus on the next class, Sarah. You can't unravel a criminal ring from campus.* But the pit in her stomach refused to ease. She swallowed, steeling herself for the next hour. Then, if Reggie still hadn't called or texted, she'd consider making a few phone calls of her own — perhaps to local contacts, or even a colleague in law enforcement who occasionally consulted on heritage-site theft.

She started toward the stairs, the soles of her shoes clicking on the polished floor. Outside the windows, sunlight glowed on the campus lawns. A gentle breeze swayed the branches of a flamboyant tree — vivid red-orange blossoms shining in the morning sun. Normally, she'd take comfort in that pastoral view. But all she could do was imagine Reggie in some bleak moment, overshadowed by criminals. She inhaled. *He said they'd be careful.* She had to believe him.

"Dr. Lindgren?" a voice called. One of her graduate TAs, carrying a box of library books, rushed over. "We just got these references you requested on Saladoid trade patterns. Want me to bring them to your office?"

She forced a bright nod. "Yes, please. That'd be perfect. Thank you."

As they walked together down the corridor, Sarah tried to slip back into her academic persona. But in the corner of her mind, she pictured Reggie's last text. *All good here.* Maybe he was telling the truth.

Maybe.

She clung to that small hope, repeating it like a mantra. But her heart pounded with a lingering sense of dread that refused to fade, no matter how many facts or references she stacked in her arms.

CHAPTER 32

BEN

BEN STOOD at the end of a rickety wooden pier, squinting against the pale orange glow of dawn. The tropical night had surrendered to morning, and a few seabirds screeched overhead, slicing through the cool air with graceful sweeps of their wings. The water beyond the pier was startlingly calm, its surface reflecting the early sunlight in broad swaths of muted gold.

He exhaled slowly, wishing the calm ocean mirrored his own mood.

So much for a quiet vacation.

A day ago, he and Reggie had been minding their own business, trying to enjoy the laid-back charm of Culebra, Puerto Rico. Now they were caught up in a lethal puzzle involving sunken wrecks, a murdered fisherman, and the rumor of a ruthless syndicate.

Behind him, Reggie paced along the dock, running a hand over the brim of his ball cap. "She'll be here," he muttered for the third time, glancing down at his phone. "Said first light, right?"

"Yeah," Ben replied, scanning the horizon. *Isla Torres. Our diving guide.* She'd been recommended by a local contact who owed Reggie a favor.

Or maybe Reggie just found her name by hounding the morning dockworkers. The story changed with each retelling, but either way,

Reggie had found her, and Isla had grudgingly agreed to take them out to the infamous reef.

That was, *if* she decided to show up.

Ben looked out across the harbor. A handful of fishing boats bobbed at anchor, their outlines hazy in the dawn light. A small charter catamaran had just left, presumably ferrying early tourists to some scuba spot. Aside from a few dockhands moving crates, the place was nearly deserted. Most people in this part of the world preferred a later start.

"Think she changed her mind?" Reggie asked, halting his restless pacing.

Before Ben could respond, the low rumble of an engine drew their attention. A modest blue-and-white boat chugged around a rocky outcropping, heading straight for the pier. At the helm stood a woman with short, curly hair pulled back in a bandana, her expression set in a steely mask of concentration. She wore a faded tank top, board shorts, and sturdy sandals. The boat itself looked serviceable, though not fancy: scuffed paint, a salt-stained windshield, and a small covered area at the back for gear storage.

"That must be her," Ben said under his breath. He hefted a backpack filled with what little gear they had — mostly personal items, plus some of the extra cash they'd brought. Hiring Isla hadn't been cheap, especially when she discovered they wanted to go to *that* reef.

The boat slowed as it approached the pier, engine gurgling. Isla maneuvered with deft skill, cutting power at the right moment so the hull slid gently against the tires fastened along the dock's edge. She looped a rope around a cleat, then glanced up at them.

"You two better not be as stupid as you look," she called, her voice crisp but low. Ben detected a faint accent — Puerto Rican Spanish with an edge he couldn't quite place. "Because that place you're asking me to take you? It's not for amateurs."

Reggie forced a grin, stepping forward. "Good morning to you too, Isla." He crouched to help her tie off the boat. "We're not amateurs, promise."

She gave Reggie a once-over, unimpressed. "could have fooled me. You got the money?"

Reggie patted a pocket on his cargo shorts. "Yeah. Same amount we agreed on. Extra if we run into trouble."

Isla's eyes narrowed, flicking to Ben. "I expect trouble," she said.

Ben felt a flicker of annoyance but stifled it. He carefully stepped aboard the boat, noticing how sturdy it felt underfoot despite its worn appearance. "Name's Harvey Bennett," he offered, extending a hand.

Isla hesitated, then shook it firmly. "I know who you are. Or at least I know you're the 'gringos' stirring up talk around the docks. Asking about some murder in a bar, something about *El Cementerio de los Contrabandistas*." Her expression turned wary. "This is not a good idea, you know."

Ben shrugged. "Probably not. But a fisherman was killed last night, and we'd like answers."

"We were his last hope," Reggie interjected, stepping aboard after paying a startled dockhand a tip to push them off. "At least, that's how it felt. He died believing we might do something. So, here we are."

Isla snorted, started the engine, and guided the boat away from the pier with a gentle throttle. "Then you are fools with a conscience. Dangerous combination."

Ben frowned, glancing back at the receding shoreline. He could see the pastel buildings of Culebra's main strip waking under the early sun. "We'll take that risk," he said, gripping the railing as the boat picked up speed.

CHAPTER 33

REGGIE

REGGIE HOPPED up next to Isla, peppering her with questions about the route, the distance, the depth of the reef. She answered in terse mono-syllables at first but eventually offered more detail.

"Part of the reef is shallow," Isla explained, resting a hand on the steering console. "A graveyard of old ships. You can see them from the surface if the light's right — pirate galleons, or so they say. Other sections drop off to deeper water. Some people think that's where the bigger wrecks lie — drug boats, maybe even submarines." She shrugged, eyes flicking over the gentle swells. "Local fishermen avoid it. Too many accidents."

"Accidents?" Ben asked, stepping up on Reggie's other side. The two of them exchanged a silent look, a confirmation of the caution both already felt.

Isla cut the throttle, letting the boat ease through the gentle swells. Salt spray misted across them in the sudden lull. Reggie watched a few droplets catch the sunlight, turning the air into a shimmering haze.

"Claro. Boats sink out there," Isla said, her gaze on the horizon. "People go diving and never come back. Last year, three sport fishermen disappeared. Police found their boat two days later, empty." One of her hands brushed a small silver pendant at her neck, an unconscious gesture of unease. "The coast guard claimed they got drunk and fell overboard. But their gear was still on board, perfectly stowed."

She gave Ben a pointed glance. "But you knew about this place already, no? You mentioned the murdered fisherman."

Ben nodded. "*El Cementerio de los Contrabandistas.* Something about being cursed? His brother found something out here — something 'older than the Spanish.'"

Reggie noticed how Isla's mouth drew into a tight line at those words. Her grip on the wheel tightened as she studied Ben's face. From Reggie's vantage, it looked as though she was balancing skepticism with genuine concern. She made a small adjustment on the boat's control panel, the light morning breeze ruffling her hair.

"Rumors, maybe," she said. "Ghost stories to scare away tourists. Or maybe something else. If there's a curse out here, it's man-made."

"What do you mean?" Reggie asked. He could feel the tension climb in his chest, mirroring the hush that had settled over the boat.

"Smugglers," Isla said. "Gangsters. The Black Coral Syndicate." She spat the words as if they left a bitter taste. "They use these waters for their business — moving drugs, weapons, whatever pays. They don't like witnesses." Her knuckles whitened around the throttle control. "Two months ago, I saw three black Zodiacs cutting through the dawn fog. The men aboard wore tactical gear, carried assault rifles. Not the kind of sight you want to attract."

"You reported it?" Ben asked.

Isla laughed harshly. "To who? Local police are bought. Coast Guard can't be everywhere." A weary resignation underlined her voice. "Out here, it's better to keep your head down and your mouth shut. Whatever your fisherman's brother found... maybe it should stay lost."

"Trust me, we don't want to attract them either," Reggie said, exchanging a worried glance with Ben. Both recalled the old man's warning, the fisherman who'd died hoping they might do something. "We just want to confirm a story."

Isla studied Reggie and Ben for a moment, her expression unreadable. Finally, she sighed and revved the engine again, sending the boat surging forward across the calm ocean. The sun had climbed a bit higher, brightening the gentle waves. Reggie felt the humidity rising, though it was still mercifully mild compared to midday. He breathed deeply, letting the salt air fill his lungs.

They cruised for nearly an hour, passing occasional fishing skiffs and one tourist catamaran whose passengers waved cheerfully. Isla kept them on a course that veered away from the usual dive spots, heading toward an isolated stretch of reef. Reggie tried making small talk, but Isla seemed preoccupied with navigating. Meanwhile, Ben leaned against the side rail, scanning the horizon in that watchful way he always did.

As they neared the reef, Reggie noticed a shift in the water color: it turned a crystalline turquoise, hinting at shallower depths. Beneath the surface, blurred shapes of coral formations came into view. Farther off, a flock of seabirds circled, perhaps trailing a school of fish. The entire area looked picturesque to an outsider, but Reggie remembered the fisherman's dire warning. Beauty sometimes masked real danger.

Eventually, Isla cut the engine to idle, the boat drifting in a hush broken only by the lap of water on the hull. She scanned the open sea. "This is close," she said. "We can go a bit farther inside, but I want to check the currents first. We'll see what's there. But be warned: if I sense trouble, we leave — no arguments."

Reggie shot a sidelong look at Ben, who simply nodded. None of them wanted a repeat of the violence they'd already witnessed. "Fine by me," Ben said.

Isla steered them into a labyrinth of partially submerged coral heads, their skeletal shapes jutting from the clear water. Reggie felt a chill prickle along his neck. The clarity of the water allowed glimpses of twisted timbers and corroded hulls only a few meters below the surface. Some protruded above, barnacle-encrusted relics of some old tragedy. Others lay deeper, their outlines ghostly suggestions of past voyages gone wrong.

"Look at that," Reggie breathed, letting out a low whistle. "Must be half a dozen wrecks in this one spot."

His eyes flicked across a steel hull angled on the reef slope, half-rusted holes revealing a decaying interior. Next to it lay a crumbling wooden structure, so overtaken by sea growth that it was barely recognizable as a ship. He exchanged a grim glance with Ben, recalling the fisherman's story of murders and sabotage out here. So many secrets, he thought, an involuntary chill creeping along his neck.

Isla guided the boat meticulously between coral outcroppings, the hull scraping occasionally with a cringe-inducing squeal. "There's a channel ahead," she said. "Deeper water. Fishermen say that's the heart of the Graveyard." Her voice dropped, laden with caution. "If your fisherman's brother found anything, it'd be in there."

Reggie glanced at Ben again. The old man's desperate warnings about curses and stolen relics echoed in his mind. They might truly be walking into the same trap that claimed those other divers. But neither Reggie nor Ben spoke against it — there was an unspoken agreement that they had to see this through.

They navigated into a region where the water darkened, revealing a sudden plunge in depth. Isla tossed a small anchor over, letting the boat settle with a gentle lurch. "All right," she said, switching off the engine so they drifted. "We're here."

Reggie exhaled, scanning the surroundings. Nothing moved except for a faint swirl of current. No sign of black Zodiacs or patrolling smugglers. Yet everything about this place felt... unsettled.

Ben, face set, stepped forward to gather the dive gear they'd stowed. Reggie joined him, strapping on a lightweight vest. Isla had provided flippers, masks, and an underwater flashlight. A tangle of adrenaline sparked in Reggie's stomach — he'd snorkeled plenty, but diving in a cursed reef rumored to hold old wrecks and criminals was far from a breezy tourist outing.

As Ben adjusted his gear, Reggie forced a confident grin. "Ready?"

Ben gave him a faintly exasperated look. "As I'll ever be."

Isla watched them from the helm, arms folded. "I meant it: be careful. The reef can be unforgiving. If anything's off, come up." Her voice took on a softness that hinted at real concern. "No one will blame you if you decide it's not worth it."

Reggie tried a small, reassuring grin back. "We'll be careful," he promised, though inside, he braced for the unknown. He heard the hum of tension in Ben's posture as well. They would do this because the fisherman's dying request had sunk into them: find out the truth, maybe avenge the old man, maybe stop more deaths. But a part of Reggie still hated the risk.

After a few more gear checks, Reggie and Ben stepped to the boat's edge. Reggie ran a quick mental list: mask secure, fins ready, small first-aid kit within arm's reach. The water was bright turquoise near the surface, shading to a darker blue where the reef dropped off. He let out a breath and slid into the warm sea, feeling an immediate rush of buoyancy. The salt content was pleasant, the temperature mild.

Ben joined him, and together they tested their masks, giving Isla a thumbs-up. They'd snorkel first, gauge the reef's layout before deciding on anything deeper. Reggie's heart pounded with a mix of dread and excitement — cursed or not, this was still an extraordinary sight. He turned to check on Ben, who nodded once. Then they started forward, gliding across the surface, letting the sunlit water reveal the reef beneath them.

Reggie couldn't help a final glance at Isla, who watched them with narrowed eyes. She nodded, as if giving them silent permission to proceed. Even from a distance, Reggie sensed her skepticism. He hoped their rumor-based coordinates would at least lead them to some clue. Then he submerged his face, peering into the shimmering world below, trying to ignore the fisherman's final warnings rattling at the back of his mind.

They were truly doing it. Chasing the rumor of a cursed wreck, in waters claimed by smugglers. Part of him wanted the thrill of it.

Another part of him dreaded what they might find.

CHAPTER 34

RAMÓN

RAMÓN MENDOZA STOOD at the water's edge, scanning the pale morning sky with a gaze that had grown accustomed to spotting threats where others saw only open waves. The sun was still low, its bright shape glinting over the horizon and sending reflections dancing on the surface. The air felt fresh in that early hour, though the promise of heat clung to the breeze. Around him, the island's small cove lay mostly silent, save for the gentle lapping of ripples against the rubber sides of his black Zodiac. He could hear the quiet hum of the outboard's idle behind him, a sound that steadied his nerves as much as it reminded him how quickly he might need to move.

He caught a breath, inhaling the mix of salt and faint diesel. The events of the previous night still weighed on him. Shooting José Ortega in a busy bar had been a desperate measure — too public, too messy. The Syndicate liked its kills to be clean, leaving no ripples. Now they had to be even more watchful. If anyone else showed up in these waters, it meant only one thing: they'd learned something about El Cemetario de Bandistas and the rumor of older-than-Spanish wrecks. That was exactly the scenario Valeria Cruz feared the most, and precisely why Ramón and his men had been ordered to patrol at first light.

He stepped onto the Zodiac's bow, black windbreaker unzipped enough to let a faint breath of cooler morning air in. The sky was a gentle shade of blue, the sun's rays angled in such a way that the water shone with pastel turquoise along the shallows, shifting to deeper blues farther out. He tried to appreciate the beauty for half a second — how the scattered rocks and reefs created small pockets of sparkling light — but the weight of the Syndicate's mission drove that appreciation away. He could not relax here. Not yet.

Ortiz stood at the helm, one hand on the outboard's tiller, the other resting near the concealed pistol under his jacket. Lopez and Castellanos lingered near the stern, quietly discussing the morning's instructions. All of them understood the gravity: if a suspicious boat turned up, they were to strike with lethal speed. No more half measures. The boss had made that clear after Ortega's final words in the bar hinted too strongly at something hidden in these waters.

Ramón climbed in, giving a short nod to Ortiz. The men settled in with the ease of a unit that had done this often: a small-scale maritime patrol, scanning the labyrinth of reefs and islets that surrounded this corner of the archipelago near Culebrita. The plan was to stay in these channels, watch for signs of any incoming craft, and relay updates back to the Syndicate's cave on the hidden island. If no one showed, they'd keep watch until midday. If someone did show, they'd intercept and destroy as needed.

He keyed the radio clipped to his belt, calling the cave to confirm they were moving out. The cave's watch officer answered, telling them to remain alert because sunrise flights had spotted a small boat heading in their general direction. The man's voice crackled through static, but the message was clear: a vessel no one recognized was cutting across the distance beyond Culebrita. They wanted Ramón to see if it was just a fisherman or if it looked more deliberate.

With that, the Zodiac pulled away from the cove, the engine humming at low throttle. The morning light cast spidery reflections on the water's surface, and the boat made a gentle wake behind them. Ramón set a course around the eastern edge of a small islet, using the landmass as partial cover. Once they cleared it, the open sea beyond would be easier to survey. He trusted Ortiz to keep a steady hand on the controls — neither too fast nor too slow. They needed to remain inconspicuous until they spotted the target.

Lopez crouched by the bow, a pair of binoculars ready. He peered across the shimmering distance where the water met the sky. Castellanos, near the stern, clutched his rifle under a cloth to keep it out of sight from any passing planes or chance observers. The boat, black and unmarked, looked unassuming enough unless someone peered closely at the men's gear.

As they rounded a rocky outcrop, the morning sun rose a bit higher, splashing the boat in a golden hue. Ramón felt the temperature begin to climb, the tropical humidity merging with the intangible weight of tension. They'd been at sea for maybe twenty minutes when the radio came to life again — one crisp burst of static. The cave's watch officer repeated coordinates that matched a reef zone near the southwestern corner of the rumored wreck site. The suspicious boat was apparently heading that way.

Ramón's pulse throbbed a little faster. So the men at the cave were right. If a random boat were just out for a scenic trip, they'd avoid that nest of reefs. Only someone determined — or very foolish — would push into that area. After acknowledging, he turned to the others and relayed the location. Lopez used his binoculars again, scanning the horizon's luminous haze. It took him a moment, but then he paused, breath catching.

"There it is," Lopez said, pointing.

Ramón followed his gesture, narrowing his eyes at a faint speck drifting off to the west. The sun glinted off what looked like a small cabin or console. From this distance, it was just a shape, but definitely a boat. He let Ortiz slow their engine, not wanting the suspects to see them too soon. The gentle rise and fall of the ocean provided rhythmic cover for their low craft.

Ramón took the binoculars from Lopez, pressing them to his own eyes.

What he saw confirmed their suspicion: a modest-sized craft, single engine, with at least a couple of people aboard. One appeared to be a woman, her silhouette was clear against the bright backdrop. The other was a man.

He watched as another — also clearly male, as they were large, tall, and broad-shouldered — stood up, then the two men fell backwards overboard, prepped and commencing a dive.

Three on board, Ramón thought, taking mental notes.

He pulled the binoculars down for a moment, frowning. *They seem to be...*

Yes.

He was sure of it. These were the same two men who had been at the bar the prior night. The same two men who Jose Ortega had stumbled into, just before his team had shot him.

He was now positive they were dealing with meddlers in the Syndicate's affairs — that they had arrived in this exact location was no mere coincidence. And they had come here at first light, delivered by a woman who must be a local guide or fisher.

Unfortunately for her, she would not live to pilot her vessel home.

The other boat was holding position near an outlying reef, as if examining something in the water. No local fisherman would dally there — too many hidden corals ready to shred a hull. No diving charters typically ventured there, either. The entire place was known for dangerous currents. Again, proof that they were there on purpose.

Looking for something.

Ramón felt that coil of dread tighten. Last night's fiasco was *exactly* about preventing outsiders from uncovering these secrets. Now, less than a day later, this boat was creeping in. He lowered the binoculars, turning to his men. They read the determination in his face.

"They're heading straight for that southwestern channel," he said quietly. "No tourist or fisherman goes there by accident. They must know something." He glanced over at Ortiz. "You heard the boss's orders. We intercept, we shoot first. No time for questions."

Ortiz gave a curt nod, though the seriousness in his eyes showed he understood the stakes. Castellanos adjusted his hidden rifle, lips pressed tight. Lopez checked his own gear again, then peered anxiously at the boat on the horizon. None of them relished opening fire on unsuspecting people, but the Syndicate was resolute: no one was allowed to poke around the rumored site of that ancient wreck. If these newcomers had gleaned details from José or anyone else, they had to be silenced.

CHAPTER 35

BEN

BEN EASED into the water first, surprised by its warmth. He took a moment to adjust his mask, breathing through the snorkel. Reggie joined him, giving a thumbs-up. The sunlit surface shimmered above them, turning the world into a kaleidoscope of blues. Beneath, the reef came into sharper focus, revealing a maze of corals, sponges, and fish darting in flashes of color.

They began a slow swim downward, scanning for any sign of the fisherman's story — *a struggle, broken gear.* The deeper they went, the cooler and darker it became, though the morning sun still provided decent visibility. Coral towers loomed on either side, riddled with cracks and tunnels that smaller fish used like highways. Ben's breath echoed in his ears, a steady rhythm of inhalation and exhalation.

This is beautiful, he thought, momentarily awed by the vibrant life around him. A school of bright-blue tang fish zipped past, unconcerned by human intruders. But just when he felt the pull of wonder, a darker shape caught his eye. He nudged Reggie and pointed.

A few meters away lay the rotting hull of what might have been a smuggling boat. The once-white paint had peeled away, revealing corroded metal. Tangled netting and some sort of harness hung from a rusted cleat. As Ben approached, his pulse quickened — *this must be one of the more recent wrecks.* He scanned the immediate area, heart thudding. *Where's the sign of struggle?*

He spotted something half-buried in the sand: a broken dive fin. Its bright color was nearly lost under a layer of silt, but it was definitely modern. Reggie swam over and picked it up, turning it over in his hands. He raised an eyebrow, as if to say, *Might be relevant.* Ben nodded, feeling a cold dread settle in his gut. *Someone was down here recently.*

They continued searching. Rounding a coral outcropping, Ben noticed a suspiciously shiny object caught on a jagged piece of metal — an air tank, partially wedged in the wreck's collapsed cabin. The harness straps were tangled, as though torn free in a hurry. As he reached out to touch it, a swirl of sediment dislodged, revealing a faint red stain. Ben's stomach clenched. *Blood, maybe.* Even in water, some things didn't just vanish.

He gestured for Reggie to keep watch. The tank was battered, the regulator missing. More troubling was the presence of a severed hose drifting near the wreck. *This can't be good.* He felt a surge of sorrow for whoever had been diving with this gear.

Then he saw it: a dive weight belt still attached to a patch of coral, the belt twisted unnaturally. Ben's mind conjured an image of a diver struggling, perhaps pinned, or forcibly removed from the harness. *This is definitely a scene of violence,* he thought, heart pounding.

As they swam farther along, a subtle current carried them toward a deeper section. A shape loomed beneath, half-buried in sand — massive and wooden, distinct from the modern hulls around it. Reggie tapped Ben's shoulder excitedly, pointing. Even from a few meters away, the lines of the structure looked... wrong for anything Spanish or modern. The timbers were large, worn smooth by centuries, but the style was different. *Could this be the rumored pre-Columbian wreck?*

Ben's pulse quickened. *If so, then the fisherman's story was true.* Reggie moved closer, shining a small underwater flashlight across the ancient timbers. Strange carvings, barely visible, covered some sections. Age and coral growth obscured most details, but the lines that remained hinted at symbols or possibly glyphs.

He signaled for Reggie to approach carefully. They circled the hull, searching for any clue as to how large the ship might be. Judging by the partial shape, it had been enormous once, far bigger than any canoe or typical fishing boat from pre-colonial times. Ben felt a jolt of astonishment. *What civilization could have built this?*

He spotted a small section of the deck that had collapsed inward. From the hole, a swirl of silt drifted upward, hinting at a recent disturbance. *Could the diver — Carlos or his partner — have been in there? Searching?* The possibility made Ben's skin crawl. This was no normal tourist dive site. It was a watery grave that might hold secrets the world had never seen.

Reggie signaled him, wide-eyed behind the mask. *We found it.* Ben nodded, though excitement warred with dread inside him. *Let's go up and tell Isla.* But as he turned to ascend, he felt Reggie's arm on his shoulder again. Reggie pointed toward a small mound in the sand near the hull. Something glinted there, a shape half-buried like a piece of sunken treasure.

They kicked over slowly. The swirling silt parted enough for Ben to see a chunk of metal or stone carved with symbols, reminiscent of some archaic script. He reached out, hesitant, but Reggie shook his head vigorously — *no time.* Right. They needed to get out of the water. The memory of last night's gunfire flickered in Ben's mind. If someone was protecting this site, they might not appreciate interlopers.

Ben gave one last glance at the battered hull. *The fisherman was right.* He felt a pang of sadness, recalling the man's plea for help. *We have to get out of here, let the authorities or someone else handle this.* But he knew in his gut that the local authorities might be in the syndicate's pocket. *We'll have to handle it ourselves, somehow.*

Together, they ascended, mindful of their air consumption. The sunlit surface shimmered overhead, a beacon of safety. *At least for now,* Ben thought grimly. *Wait till we tell Isla.* Reggie's strokes were hurried, as if spurred by the same sense of urgency.

They broke the surface, gasping the warm air, blinking in the sudden brightness. The boat drifted a few yards away, with Isla leaning over the side. She waved them over. "Find anything?" she called.

"Yeah," Reggie replied between breaths. "Plenty."

Ben spat out his mouthpiece. "We'll tell you on deck." He noticed the tension in her posture. Her gaze kept flicking to the horizon, as though she was expecting unwelcome company.

They climbed aboard, removing their gear. Ben sank onto a bench near the boat's modest console, wiping droplets from his face. "We found dive equipment," he said. "Broken tank, belt, signs of a struggle... and a massive wooden hull that looks pre-Columbian, half-buried in the sand."

Isla's eyes widened. For a second, she looked genuinely rattled. Then she schooled her features into careful neutrality. "So the rumors are true? That the hurricane revealed some ancient wrecks?"

Reggie nodded. "I think so. This place is a graveyard, all right. We found modern wrecks too, likely from smugglers."

Isla's jaw tightened. "And you want me to take you deeper? Because that's what you're about to ask, yes?"

Ben shook his head, scrubbing a hand over his hair. "We've seen enough for now. The fisherman's story checks out. If these divers were murdered for a relic or something, it's got to be down there. We —"

He never finished the sentence. A sharp buzz from Isla's radio crackled to life, spitting static and a few urgent words in Spanish. Isla cursed under her breath and snatched the device, listening.

"Una lancha negra..." she whispered. "They're coming."

Ben and Reggie shared a sharp look. *Black Coral Syndicate,* Ben thought, dread curling in his gut.

They're coming.

AFTER RADIOING THEIR PLAN, Ramón started the engine again, angling the Zodiac so that they'd approach from behind a cluster of outcroppings. The idea was to keep line-of-sight minimal until the last moment. The morning sun above cast the water in a rich aqua near the shallows, turning darker farther out. They cut through the gentle chop, the boat's bow rising slightly with each crest. Ramón's adrenaline spiked. The entire scenario felt too similar to how so many episodes of violence began: an unknown boat, the Syndicate's lethal response.

He guided them around another islet, careful to stay out of direct line of sight from the suspicious craft. The men readied themselves, tucking windbreakers aside to free up movement for a quick draw. The plan was simple: close to within range, gun them down. If they attempted to run, the black Zodiac would outpace them, or the men's rifles would handle that. The only concern was if these intruders were armed and prepared, but Ramón doubted it. People rarely expected to be attacked at dawn in a seemingly idyllic sea.

They eased forward, weaving between coral heads, the engine throttled low enough not to roar. The morning light glinted off the water, sending bright flecks dancing over the hull. Ramón's senses sharpened. One miscalculation, and they might run aground or lose the element of surprise. The men kept quiet, scanning the horizon. Each wave that parted offered glimpses of that small boat, still idling in the same general zone. Ramón found it odd that the intruders remained there, as if deliberately searching the reef's perimeter.

He tried to push aside the memory of Ortega's dying words: older than the Spanish, the mention of some secret or relic. If these people were investigating that rumor, the result would be the same: they wouldn't leave here alive. A pang of regret flitted through him, but he buried it. The Syndicate's secrecy was absolute.

At last, they crept into a position from which they could see the boat more clearly. Maybe two hundred yards separated them from the target, the morning sun on their right side. Ramón killed the engine again, letting momentum carry them. He used the binoculars to confirm there were still three people on deck — the two men had returned from their short dive.

He couldn't see any obvious weapons. Another sign that they might be clueless or poorly defended. Tourists who had just gotten wrapped up in the old man's story the night before, and were now looking for a bit of innocent thrill.

Perfect.

He handed the binoculars back to Lopez, then gave a silent signal: they'd approach, open fire as soon as the intruders reacted. If they tried to run, they'd be cut down. If they tried to surrender, well, the Syndicate had no reason to accept. The boss wanted no possibility of new witnesses. Ramón's stomach knotted, but he kept his expression stony. This was the life he was chosen to lead.

He flicked the ignition, the engine rumbled low, and the boat moved in a final beeline toward the unsuspecting target.

They closed the distance swiftly, the gentle morning breeze carrying the scent of seaweed and salt. Ortiz knelt beside the center console, one hand on a pistol under his jacket. Castellanos and Lopez braced with rifles. Ramón kept them angled behind the other boat's stern, hoping to remain out of the occupants' peripheral vision until it was too late. The water was calm enough that they could accelerate without too much rocking.

A sudden hush seemed to fall over the ocean, as though the entire world held its breath. The sun brightened, reflecting off the calm sea in dazzling rays, but Ramón hardly noticed the beauty. His focus centered on that boat, on its unsuspecting crew. One more second, two more, and they'd be in range for a lethal volley. He forced any leftover moral doubt from his head. The Syndicate demanded loyalty, demanded that no more secrets leak out.

He wasn't about to second-guess the boss's will.

They roared in, slipping from the partial cover of a rock spur. Instantly, the small craft's occupants noticed them, heads whipping around. One seemed to point, perhaps shouting a warning. Ramón glimpsed a flash of alarm on their faces.

Good. They had only seconds to realize they'd made a fatal choice in coming here.

He jammed the throttle forward, and the Zodiac surged, water spraying in an arc behind them. Ortiz raised his pistol, eyes narrowing. Castellanos hoisted the rifle, lips forming a grim line. Lopez steadied himself near the bow, adrenaline etched into every line of his posture. No words needed: they'd open fire the moment Ramón gave the nod, or if the other boat so much as tried to flee.

Everything seemed suspended in time. The men and woman on the other boat scrambled, possibly reaching for gear or trying to start their engine in a panic.

Ramón steeled himself for the shots that would follow. Another day, another kill, all to guard the secrets lurking beneath the waves. He told himself it was necessary. Valeria Cruz demanded it, and the fisherman's final gasp in that bar had proven the threat was real. If these strangers knew about the old wreck, that knowledge *had* to die out here on the open sea.

CHAPTER 37

REGGIE

REGGIE FELT his spine stiffen the instant Isla's expression went from confused to alarmed. Only a moment ago, she had been clutching the radio to her ear, straining to catch the broken bursts of static that crackled over the speaker. The transmission was fragmentary — just a smattering of words, half-lost in the hiss of poor reception — but it was enough for her to mutter a low curse in Spanish.

He stood a few feet away, trying to glean any sense from the clipped, garbled phrases. Something about another boat... moving in... ready to intercept.

Then the signal cut out, leaving only white noise. "Damn," she breathed, dropping the radio onto the small bench near the console. "That's not good." She shot Reggie a look that he read instantly: they had trouble coming, and it was coming fast.

Before he could ask more, Isla lunged for the helm and cranked the throttle, sending the boat surging forward. The boat's engine roared in a jarring contrast to the calm morning air that had surrounded them just moments earlier. Reggie stumbled, grabbing the gunwale to keep from pitching forward. Across the deck, Ben did the same, eyes wide with surprise. Salt spray flung into the air, dappled sunlight catching the droplets until they sparkled like shattered glass around them.

"Get ready," Isla snapped, her tone vibrating with tense urgency. "They're coming after us." She didn't specify who "they" were, but Reggie needed no explanation. The mention of an approaching vessel alone was enough for him to understand. He and Ben had been bracing themselves for a Syndicate response ever since they got wind of these waters being a no-go zone. Now it looked like they had found exactly the trouble they feared.

"Hang on!" she shouted, yanking the wheel. The boat veered dangerously close to a half-submerged reef, the hull scraping with a shriek that made Reggie's heart skid in his chest. Another yard or two, and they might have cracked the hull wide open. It was only Isla's honed instincts that kept them afloat. She mumbled something about them being idiots for even coming out here, but Reggie couldn't quite make it out over the engine's roar and the pounding blood in his ears.

He shot a quick glance behind them, just in time to see Ben pivot, scanning the horizon. There it was — a sleek black Zodiac, rounding a rocky point and gunning straight for them at a lethal clip. Sunlight grazed the black hull, showing shapes crouched low, men in dark clothes that spelled trouble. Reggie's gut twisted. If this was the Syndicate, they weren't pulling any punches. They would have come armed.

He ducked instinctively as the first burst of gunfire ripped through the serene morning air. The staccato blasts felt surreal, like fireworks where they didn't belong. Bullets pinged off the metal frame near the stern, each ricochet sending fragments of fiberglass into the air.

His mind spun. *This is actually happening. We're being shot at.* The realization clamped around his chest.

"Down!" Reggie yelled, voice straining over the engine's roar. He dropped to his knees on the slippery deck. From the corner of his eye, he saw Ben flatten himself as well. The boat shuddered from the impact of bullets against its surface. Smoke or dust puffed out from the hits, leaving behind raw holes. His skin prickled with the awareness of how close those shots were.

One inch of difference, and we'd be done.

Isla cursed, voice laced with fury, then jammed the throttle. The boat lurched forward in a blur of motion, salt spray drenching them. As Reggie struggled to keep hold of the rail, he felt the deck tilt beneath him. They were going too fast for these precarious waters. The reef-littered channels had looked forbidding even at a cautious speed, and now they were screaming through them like a bullet. He caught a glimpse of bright coral just inches below the surface, ready to tear their hull to shreds if Isla's reflexes faltered.

A volley of gunfire hissed overhead again. Reggie heard the horrifying metallic whine of bullets raking the boat's canopy. Bits of plastic or fiberglass showered down. Somewhere behind him, Ben let out a breathless curse, presumably trying to stay as low as possible.

Another bullet cracked a small gauge on the console, drawing a shout from Isla.

"They want us dead!" she barked, wrestling the wheel from side to side to avoid the countless coral heads that thrust up from the shallow water. Her voice had an edge somewhere between frustration and raw panic. Still, Reggie noticed her quick, efficient movements. Even with bullets singing past her ears, she handled the boat like it was second nature.

Reggie tried to steal a look behind them, ignoring the swirl of fear in his gut. He glimpsed the black Zodiac in fierce pursuit, albeit slowed by the same coral formations. At least their pursuers had to navigate these hazards too, giving Isla a chance to put some distance between them. But the men aboard that Zodiac clearly knew how to aim; Reggie could see muzzle flashes from time to time, flickers of orange in the bright morning.

Another burst struck near the stern, a few rounds hitting the water with plumes of spray. He bit his tongue to keep from crying out. They had no weapons on board, no immediate means of returning fire. Just their wits and Isla's recklessness. Reggie's heart galloped.

If we lose the engine, if we snag the reef, if these men get just one lucky shot, it's over.

CHAPTER 38

BEN

BEN SHOUTED to no one in particular, "Isn't there a gun in here?" as he rummaged under the boat's bench seat. Through soaked hair plastered to his forehead, he yanked open a storage compartment. All he found was a tangle of rope, some old flippers, and a battered snorkel mask — nothing that would help. "Damn it," he spat, slamming it closed. Even a flare gun would have felt like something, but they had none.

He peeked over the edge, body pressed flat. "They're still right behind us," he said, voice tense. "They're not giving up."

"I can see that," Isla snapped, jerking the wheel so violently that Reggie almost lost his grip. The boat nearly sideswiped a coral pillar that jutted up from the sea like a bony finger. The hull let out a shriek, but they cleared it. Ben felt an adrenaline-laden gratitude for Isla's skill.

Another bullet pinged off the boat's flank. Reggie winced. How many more hits could the hull take before something critical blew?

Spray blinded Ben for a second as the boat slammed into a small crest of water, and then they were bouncing over a shallow ridge, leaving white foam behind. The black Zodiac roared into view again, near enough that he thought he could see the intensity in the driver's stance. They'd clipped a coral outcrop, from the look of it, because he heard shouts over the engine noise. One man was waving his arms, trying to keep the boat steady, but their pursuit didn't falter.

Isla cursed again, each breath ragged. "If they get a clear shot at our engine, we're done." She swerved around a rocky spur, nearly tossing Reggie off his feet. The sting of salt water in Ben's eyes was unrelenting. Another round of bullets hissed overhead. He clenched his teeth, forcing himself not to think about the possibility of a direct hit to his body. The rational side of his brain pointed out that they were outmanned, outgunned, but not necessarily outsmarted. Isla's knowledge of these reefs might be their only advantage.

He risked a glance to the right. A series of coral heads rose in a half-circle, creating what looked like a natural alleyway. If they threaded the boat just so, they might force the pursuers to maneuver carefully, losing speed. Isla seemed to read his mind. She angled the boat that way, ignoring the hair-raising closeness of the coral ridges. Each swerve unleashed a new squeal of fiberglass scraping against calcified edges.

They careened through that narrow pass, water churning into milky froth behind them. From the corner of his eye, Ben saw the Syndicate's Zodiac hesitate for a fraction of a second, the men presumably shouting at their driver to slow so they wouldn't rip open the bottom of their hull. That gave Isla an extra couple of heartbeats to widen the gap.

He found himself sucking in breath after breath, mind reeling. That radio call had been just a scrap of intel — chatter from the Zodiac to its handler — but it had been enough for Isla to suspect that a Syndicate boat was on its way. He wanted to scream at the men chasing them, ask them why they were so desperate to kill, but he knew full well why. The cursed wreck, the rumor of ancient relics — it was enough to bring out lethal protectiveness from criminals who thrived on secrecy. And now he, Reggie, and Isla were inadvertently in their crosshairs.

Another bullet whipped across the deck, too close for comfort. Ben clenched his fists, fear — driven by the recognition that he had no control over his fate — sizzling in his veins.

Isla coaxed the boat around another tight bend, the passage so narrow that Ben worried they'd wedge themselves. A chunk of coral tore at the hull's side with a grinding sound that rattled his teeth, but the boat remained afloat, speed unbroken. He clung to the seat's edge, watching the swirl of turquoise water that threatened to shred them at any moment. Gunfire erupted once more, muzzle flashes strobing. Rounds pinged off a rock face near them, sparking chips of stone into the air. The men behind them were persistent. They must truly want them gone, to keep some secret from being uncovered.

Ben's lungs burned, as if he'd been sprinting. The morning sun climbed higher, intensifying the glare on the water. He wiped the back of his hand across his eyes, blinking away salt and sweat. Another swerve nearly sent him sprawling. The boat hammered through a small wave, each jolt spiking adrenaline through his system. They were still going, though. That had to count for something.

"Still behind us?" Reggie managed to shout, risking an occasional glance over the stern.

Ben nodded, face drawn. "They definitely clipped something, but they're still coming."

A fresh wave of panic soared through him. He cursed under his breath, scanning for any alternative route. He spotted a patch of open water ahead — clearer, deeper — but if they emerged there, they'd be in the open. No reefs to shield them. The men in the Zodiac would have a perfect line of fire. Another wave of bullets hissed overhead, reminding him the chase wasn't over.

CHAPTER 39

REGGIE

"WE CAN'T KEEP WEAVING FOREVER!" Reggie shouted. "One wrong move, and we're done."

"No choice," Isla snapped, voice hoarse. "We find a route through the reef that they can't follow."

Ben hunched low. "No sign of weapons on our boat?"

Reggie shook his head, a fresh wave of hopelessness threatening to swallow him. "Nothing." He found it absurdly ironic that they were pinned down by heavy fire while afloat on some battered boat with zero armaments. They should have known better than to come unprepared.

Isla angled them again. The hull scraped with a nails-on-chalkboard screech that made Reggie's spine prickle. The engine coughed, but mercifully it kept going. With a roar, they burst past a last chunk of coral, slicing into a new stretch of open water. The morning light dazzled off the waves, momentarily blinding Reggie.

He blinked, heart pounding.

Behind them, the black Zodiac tried to follow. Reggie heard a loud metallic crunch, then frantic yelling. He chanced a look: the Syndicate men had rammed or snagged on a jagged outcrop of rock Isla had narrowly missed, and the wave caused by their rapid pass must have temporarily hidden it from view.

The zodiac was still afloat, but the driver had to wrestle the boat free. That gave Isla a chance to throttle up, racing away from the reef labyrinth into safer, deeper waters. Reggie felt a surge of relief so intense it almost made him dizzy.

Ben let out a ragged breath, one hand on the side rail, the other pressed to his forehead. "They clipped the reef," he gasped, eyes scanning. "We might have a head start."

Isla now pushed the engine to its limit, the boat's hull skimming across waves with a hammering motion that rattled Reggie's teeth. Spray whipped across them, some of it washing away the sweat and fear, but not all. They shot forward at a breakneck pace, the morning sun shining relentlessly overhead.

Reggie braced for more gunfire, but none came. A glance back showed that the black Zodiac was still out of commission, or at least delayed.

For a solid minute, none of them spoke. The roaring engine and the slapping water filled the air. Every sense in Reggie's body was on high alert, adrenaline still surging, chest too tight to breathe easily. Slowly, as the reef receded behind them, he realized they had put enough distance to be out of immediate range. Isla kept them going, face grim, jaws clenched. She didn't slow until they reached a safer channel near open water, a place with fewer coral heads. Only then did she ease off the throttle and let the engine settle into a lower roar.

Reggie, trembling, sank onto the nearest seat, running a hand through his damp hair. His heart battered his ribs. They were alive. The black Zodiac, for now, was left behind in the labyrinth. "Are we clear?" he asked no one in particular, voice coming out shaky.

Ben peered behind them, hands still shaky. "No sign of them," he said. Then, after a pause, he breathed, "We did it. We're out."

Isla cut the power further, letting them drift. Her shoulders heaved in silent anger or maybe relief. The morning sun shone on her face, revealing the tension lines around her eyes. "Idiots," she muttered. "They didn't care about the reef or about shooting in broad daylight."

Reggie swallowed, scanning the horizon. No black hull crested the waves, no muzzle flashes. Just the glittering ocean, full of deceptive serenity. He let his gaze wander to the brightening sky, noticing how late it had become. Another day, another narrow escape. That seemed to be the pattern since they'd started chasing the rumor of that cursed wreck.

"We're safe… for now," Isla said, though her tone suggested that safety might be short-lived. "But I doubt they'll give up. We need to figure out our next move fast."

Ben slumped beside Reggie, both of them soaked and battered. Reggie tried to think of a plan: the Syndicate men were behind them, possibly forced to limp back for repairs. They had a chance to get away, find safer harbor, or even run. But would it be enough? The ocean was vast, yet these criminals had resources, could track them at sea. He felt the weight of it in his chest.

He found himself wishing the half-baked radio call they'd overheard had included more details — some hint of where the Syndicate's base was, or how many men they had on the water. Instead, Isla had only caught enough fragments to know trouble was inbound.

Now that trouble had escalated into a full-blown chase and firefight.

Still panting, Reggie leaned back against the boat's side. With a final, shaky breath, he forced himself to regroup. They were alive, the morning sky was open above them, and the black Zodiac was out of sight. They'd figure out the rest. The murmur of the engine and the hush of the waves anchored him in the present. For a moment, the memory of bullets slicing the air played on loop in his mind, and he had to exhale slowly to calm the ragged pace of his heart.

Glancing at Ben, he saw the same haunted relief in his friend's eyes. They were both thinking the same thing: This was too close. Again. Another testament to how lethal these waters had become, thanks to the rumored relic or the Syndicate's obsession. Reggie thought about the fisherman's warning, about the cursed nature of this place, and his pulse gave another stutter. Maybe it wasn't curses. Maybe it was just man-made terror.

Either way, they'd barely survived.

Isla revved the engine gently, turning them away from the reef and toward what she hoped would be open ocean. The boat moved less frantically now, skimming at a moderate speed. "We'll head southeast," she announced, her voice as steady as she could manage. "Put distance between us and them. Once we're sure they're not following, we can decide where to go next." She shot Reggie a quick, flickering look. "I hope you realize how close that was."

Reggie nodded, throat too dry to speak. He tried a small smile, laced with jittery relief. "Yeah," he croaked, voice unsteady. "Close is an understatement."

Ben stared at the horizon, silent but alive with tension, his mind obviously churning. Reggie guessed they'd discuss it all soon enough, but for now, they'd let the boat and the ocean carry them away from immediate peril. The bright morning sun continued to climb, pouring hot light over the water, as if oblivious to the chaos that had just erupted. And Reggie let himself breathe in that salty air with every intention of staying alert, because if there was one thing he'd learned, it was that the Syndicate never gave up easily. He could only hope that, for this day at least, they'd slip through the cracks and keep their battered boat afloat for a little while longer.

CHAPTER 40

BEN

ISLA EASED off the throttle once they were a safe distance away, letting the boat plane over calmer seas. She wiped sweat from her forehead, her hands trembling on the wheel.

"You... you see now?" she asked. "This is what they do. They guard this place. They don't want you or anyone near that wreck."

"Yeah," Reggie said, panting. He slumped against the cabin wall, his shirt soaked through with seawater and sweat. "We got the message loud and clear."

Ben walked the length of the boat, taking stock of the damage. A line of bullet holes peppered the stern like angry stars, and the canopy hung in tatters where rounds had torn through the fabric. Water sloshed around his feet from a small leak near the transom. But the engines still hummed, the hull still cut through the waves — all thanks to Isla's quick thinking and steady hands at the helm. He made his way back to the cockpit. "Thank you."

She waved him off with one hand, her chest still heaving from the chase. "I only did it because I want the extra money you promised." The words came out harsh, but her expression softened, betraying the relief she felt at their escape. She glanced over her shoulder, scanning the horizon.

"Look, we have to get back to port, fix this damage. The Syndicate might have more boats out searching."

Ben caught Reggie's eye across the cabin. His partner gave a sharp nod, and Ben turned back to Isla. "We're with you. Let's go."

Isla didn't hesitate. She revved the engine, setting a course back toward Culebra. The morning sun had risen higher, bathing the sea in brilliant light as though mocking the violence they'd just survived. *So much for calm waters,* Ben thought grimly, adrenaline still thumping through his veins. *Vacation's over.*

He leaned against the railing, letting the ocean wind blast his face. His shirt, still damp, clung to his skin as the boat cut through the waves. In the distance, the reef that held so many secrets vanished from view. But the knowledge of what lay beneath it clung to him like a wet shroud.

The half-buried hull flashed through his mind — weathered wood and metal, a ghost ship telling tales of death. He couldn't shake the image of those odd carvings, or the way the silt had swirled around the deck. Someone had been there recently. The signs of struggle were everywhere.

Reggie sidled up next to him, his usual wisecracks nowhere to be found. "That fisherman wasn't exaggerating, was he?"

Ben shook his head, gaze fixed on the horizon where blue met blue. "No. He wasn't." The evidence played on repeat in his head — blood stains dark against the dive belt, the battered air tank tossed aside like garbage. It all screamed murder. The Black Coral Syndicate had killed a diver for whatever relic they'd found down there. And now they'd tried to kill *them* just for looking.

We're in deep, he thought.

Reggie let out a low whistle. "The question is, what now?"

Ben's jaw tightened as he searched for an answer, his mind racing through their dwindling options. "We regroup. Figure out how to expose this. Or stop them. Because if we back off, they'll come after us anyway."

Reggie nodded, chewing his lip as he considered their next move. His fingers drummed against the gunwale, a nervous rhythm that matched the churning seas. "We could find that Manny Delgado guy. He might know more about this. But we need to watch our backs."

"You know Manny Delgado?" Isla asked, cutting into the conversation as she drove.

Ben chewed his lip for a moment, hesitating. "Why? Who is he to you?"

She snorted in laughter. "Easy, big guy," she said. "He's harmless. Everyone knows Manny. Well, *locals* know him. I'm just surprised two... *out-of-towners* like you know him."

"We don't," he answered. "But we were told he might be able to, uh, help us."

"If we got bored," Reggie added.

At this, Isla threw her head back and laughed. "*Bored*. Right. Yes, Manny is a good cure for boredom. And actually, I don't think it's a terrible idea. If anyone knows anything about anything, it's Manny. He's well-connected, but not corrupt."

"You trust him?"

She shrugged. "As much as I trust anyone, sure."

Ben didn't speak, but his silent agreement hung in the salt-heavy air. No turning back now. The fisherman's words hammered in his mind like a drumbeat, reminding him of the unstoppable tide pulling them deeper into this mess. Each passing wave seemed to drag them further from the simple life they'd known just days ago.

The boat pushed forward through the swells, its hull creaking in protest. From her position at the helm, Isla kept scanning the horizon, her eyes darting between the sea ahead and the wake behind them. Every few minutes, she'd sweep the waters for the telltale black shapes of Zodiac boats. But the ocean remained empty except for the occasional seabird.

By the time they spotted Culebra's harbor in the distance, the morning had ripened into full day. The sun blazed overhead in an empty blue sky, turning the water into a sheet of hammered brass.

Ben knew better than to think they'd found anything more than temporary shelter.

CHAPTER 41

BEN

AT THE PIER, Isla navigated carefully, wincing at the bullet holes in her hull. As she tied off, she glared at Ben and Reggie. "You both owe me more than cash for this," she said. "My boat... it's my livelihood, understand?"

Reggie dug into his bag, pulling out extra bills. "We've got money," and we can get more. We'll pay for the repairs," he said quietly, pressing the wad of cash into her hand.

She closed her fingers around the money, but her scowl lingered. "Money is money, but I don't want more trouble, got it?" She aimed a pointed look at Ben. "Those men won't stop. They'll kill anyone who pokes around that wreck. You go talk to Manny Delgado, but leave me out of it."

Ben sighed, stepping onto the dock. His legs felt shaky, the rush of near-death chasing him. "We'll be careful."

She scoffed, retrieving a coil of rope. "*Careful*? You're naive. There's no careful with them."

"Then we'll watch our backs," Reggie said softly, glancing at Ben. "But we're not going to stop here. We can't let them get away with murder."

Isla said nothing more, focusing on securing her damaged boat. Ben's mind churned as he gathered his gear and stepped onto solid ground.

We learned what we came for, he thought. *The fisherman's story was real, the wreck is real, and the Syndicate protects it fiercely.*

The question now was how to proceed without getting themselves killed.

He glanced at Reggie, who hefted a soggy backpack in one hand and ran the other through his hair. "So," Reggie said, "how about we find Manny Delgado or someone else who can fill in the blanks?"

Ben nodded, noticing the set of Reggie's jaw. *We're beyond the point of no return.* He looked back at Isla, who was now examining bullet holes along the port side, muttering curses under her breath. "Thank you," he told her again, wanting to show genuine gratitude. "You saved our skins out there."

She shot him a wary glance, then sighed. "Just... don't come back to me if you want another ride to that place. I won't do it again." She folded her arms, the money from Reggie still clutched tightly. "Unless... unless things change. But it'll cost you double."

Ben gave a half-smile, though he didn't blame her for wanting to stay out of the line of fire. "Understood."

As they walked away from the pier and Isla, still muttering about her wounded vessel, the bustle of morning activity surrounded them — fishermen unloading the day's catch, small trucks rumbling past with supplies, a tourist or two snapping photos of the colorful boats. No one paid special attention to Ben and Reggie, which was a relief. *The Syndicate might have eyes everywhere.*

They found an out-of-the-way spot near a cluster of palm trees, setting their gear down on a bench. Ben gulped fresh air, trying to process the last hour. "We nearly got shot out there," he muttered. "Over some ancient relic."

Reggie dropped onto the bench, wiping sweat from his brow. "That's the reality. Whatever's in that wreck, the Black Coral Syndicate wants it secret."

Ben thought of the carved hull, the possible significance of an unknown civilization. "If it's truly pre-Columbian, it might be priceless — either historically or monetarily. The Syndicate could sell it on the black market for a fortune." He felt a surge of anger. *History shouldn't be trafficked like this.* "That diver died for it. The fisherman died. And they tried to kill us just for looking."

Reggie stared at the harbor, where Isla's boat was dwarfed by a tour catamaran pulling in. "So Manny Delgado is our next stop, right? Sarah mentioned he's an old smuggler turned historian. He might know how to handle these guys or at least how to keep the local cops from burying this."

Ben nodded. "Yeah. We track him down, ask him what he knows about the Graveyard and the Black Coral Syndicate." He paused, glancing at his phone. No new messages.

"All right," Reggie said, standing, "let's find Manny."

Ben took a last look at the tranquil water. *It looks so peaceful, but we know better.* He picked up his gear and followed Reggie. Their footsteps crunched on gravel as they left the harbor behind. Despite the sun's warmth, a chill refused to leave Ben's bones. *We've confirmed the fisherman's story, all right. Now the real danger begins.*

They wove through the narrow streets of Culebra, searching for any lead on Manny Delgado's whereabouts. Along the way, locals bustled with their morning routines — unloading trucks, haggling over fresh-caught fish, children in uniforms scampering to a small schoolhouse. Life went on, seemingly oblivious to the lethal drama lurking in the region's waters.

Ben felt the dryness in his mouth, a reminder of the tension from the boat chase. As they passed a small café, Reggie ducked in to buy bottles of water. They resumed their walk, sipping in silence. Questions buzzed in Ben's mind: *What if Manny won't talk? What if the Syndicate finds us first?* But he forced them aside, focusing on each step. He needed a clear head.

"Word is Manny has a shack near the old docks," Reggie said, pointing down a side street. "Some folks said he's been lying low since he had a run-in with the Syndicate months ago."

Ben grimaced, not relishing the idea of a confrontation. But they had few options. They reached the end of the street, where the paved road gave way to dirt and rubble. A series of dilapidated huts lined the water's edge, each one more forlorn than the last. The smell of rotting seaweed and stale beer made Ben's nose wrinkle. A couple of stray dogs slunk between garbage piles.

"Home sweet home," Reggie mumbled. "Let's hope Manny's here."

They approached a small shack that looked as though it might collapse if someone slammed the door too hard. The roof was patched with corrugated metal, and the single window was boarded up. An old fishing net hung from a nail, draped across the wall. A battered sign read "No Trespassing," scrawled in Spanish. Ben exchanged a look with Reggie, who shrugged.

"Worth a shot," Reggie said. He rapped on the door. No answer. He knocked again, louder. The door rattled in its frame.

Finally, they heard shuffling inside. The door opened a crack, revealing a chain latch. Through the gap, a single eye glared at them. "Qué quieres?" came a gravelly voice.

Reggie lifted his hands, palms out. "We're looking for Manny Delgado. We have questions about *El Cementerio de los Contrabandistas.*"

The eye narrowed. A moment passed, then the door shut. Ben tensed, exchanging a worried glance with Reggie. *Maybe he's telling us to go away.* But after a few metallic clicks, the door opened again, this time fully. A short, wiry man with iron-gray hair and a leathery face stared them down. He wore stained cargo pants and a ragged T-shirt. A faint scar ran across his temple.

"Why are you looking for Manny Delgado?" the man demanded, voice thick with suspicion.

Reggie answered slowly. "Because we almost got killed looking for a wreck out there. We heard Manny might know how to handle the Syndicate, or at least explain what we're dealing with."

The man studied them, then huffed. "Maybe Manny's done dealing with strangers. Especially strangers who bring trouble."

Ben took a small step forward. "A fisherman was murdered last night, trying to warn us about that place. We found evidence that others have been killed, too. We need Manny's help to stop it." He hesitated, then added, "We can pay if that's an issue."

The man's eyes flicked between them, weighing their words. Eventually, he exhaled, stepping back. "Fine. Come in. But keep it quick."

CHAPTER 42

REGGIE

REGGIE HELD BACK near the doorway as they entered Manny's shack, letting his eyes adjust to the dim interior. The place reeked of stale tobacco and rotting wood. A weather-beaten chair slouched in one corner — the only real furniture besides a rickety table overflowing with books, charts, and what looked like well-used diving equipment.

His gaze swept the room, noting escape routes out of habit. A single grimy window. The door they'd come through. The walls were lined with bookshelves that had seen better days, crammed with an eclectic mix of texts — maritime logs with cracked spines, dog-eared Spanish dictionaries, and notebooks so stuffed with loose papers they looked ready to explode.

"Manny Delgado," their host announced, dropping into the chair with a grunt that suggested old injuries. "That's me. Now talk."

Ben took point on the explanation, which was fine by Reggie. His partner had always been better at reading people, knowing how much detail to share. He watched Manny's face as Ben walked through their story — the vacation gone wrong, finding the dead fisherman, their dive to the wreck that shouldn't exist. With each new detail, the old smuggler's expression grew darker, his eyes harder.

Reggie kept his hand near his hip, where his dive knife was still sheathed. Just in case. But something in Manny's reaction told him this man knew exactly what kind of danger they were describing. He'd seen it himself.

Manny's spit hit the floorboards with a wet smack. "Idiots, the lot of you," he snarled, his weathered face twisting into a scowl. "You've stepped into a snake pit here. The Syndicate owns these waters, and they don't play nice. Cross them, and you're shark food."

Reggie watched the old man's eyes darken as he spoke. There was real fear there, buried under layers of gruffness and bravado. The kind of fear that comes from seeing too much death.

"We figured that out when they tried to kill us," Reggie said, unable to keep the edge from his voice. He shifted against the wall, feeling the reassuring weight of his dive knife. "But what's got them so trigger-happy? The fisherman swore this wreck was ancient — older than anything known in these waters."

A change came over Manny's face. His eyes drifted to a battered trunk in the corner, its metal bands orange with rust. Something about that trunk made Reggie's skin crawl. Like it held secrets better left buried.

"Ancient doesn't begin to cover it," Manny said finally. "We're talking pre-Spanish. Hell, some say it outdates even the Taíno by hundreds of years. The kind of find that could flip history on its head." He leaned forward, voice dropping to barely above a whisper. "But there's more. Stories passed down, warnings about a curse. Whatever that ship carried was bad news — so bad that whole civilizations worked to keep it hidden." His eyes locked onto Reggie's. "The Syndicate doesn't care about curses. They see dollar signs. And they'll stack bodies like cordwood to keep their prize."

The words hung in the stale air of the shack as Ben voiced the question. "So you believe it's real?"

Manny's eyes went distant, like he was seeing ghosts. His fingers traced unconsciously over a deep scar on his forearm. "I dived there once, long ago." The grimace that followed told its own story. "Lost a friend. Even before the recent hurricane, we found fragments down there, stone carvings, glyphs. None of it made sense — hell, none of it should have even *existed*. But we knew something was wrong. *Dead* wrong." He shook his head. "Then this Syndicate came out of nowhere, guns blazing. I barely made it. My friend..." His voice trailed off.

Reggie felt his muscles tighten as memories of their own encounter flashed through his mind. The black Zodiac emerging from the mist, the thunder of gunfire, Isla's desperate maneuvers. "We saw them too," he said, his voice hard. "Those bastards nearly killed us this morning."

"And they won't stop trying," Manny shot back. His weathered face twisted with a deeper anger now, something personal. "The Syndicate's got their hooks in everything — cartels, officials, whole police departments. Rich collectors throw money at them for artifacts, no questions asked." He leaned forward, jabbing a finger at them. "But this wreck? If they can prove it's something nobody's ever seen before? They'll be untouchable. And they'll kill anyone who might expose their operation."

Ben swallowed, remembering the fisherman's broken body. "So how do we stop them?" His voice cracked, raw with exhaustion and something deeper — fear, maybe, or rage at what they'd witnessed.

Manny let out a sharp, humorless laugh that made Reggie's skin crawl. "Stop them? Ha. You can't. Not alone." The old smuggler's eyes went hard as steel. "Maybe if you had international authorities, real scientists, a legal case. But local cops?" He spat on the floor. "Useless. The Syndicate owns half of them."

Reggie caught Ben's eye across the dim room. His partner's face mirrored what he felt — that sinking feeling when your worst fears prove true. But running wasn't an option, not after what they'd seen. Ben cleared his throat. "Is there any way to gather proof? Enough to get outside help — someone who can't be bought?"

The silence stretched as Manny worked his jaw, one hand absently tracing the raised scar on his temple. Reggie watched him think, noting how the old man's eyes kept drifting to that rusted trunk in the corner. Finally, Manny leaned forward, dropping his voice so low they had to strain to hear. "If you had indisputable evidence — photos, video, samples from that hull — something you could show to, I don't know, media or reputable archaeologists. Or maybe the Coast Guard." He paused, weighing each word. "*Then* the Syndicate's hold on it might break. International eyes on them might force them to back off."

Ben inhaled sharply, and Reggie watched his partner's face tighten as the implications sank in. They both knew what gathering evidence meant — another dive into those deadly waters.

"That means diving again," Ben said quietly, his voice barely above a whisper. "We'd have to get close, gather images... maybe retrieve a piece of that hull or a carved artifact."

Manny's lips twisted in a half-smile that held no warmth. "Suicidal, yes. But it might be the only way to blow this thing open." He leaned back, shoulders tense. "If you want me to help... well, I'm not cheap, and I'm not eager to die. But maybe together we stand a chance. We'd need a bigger boat, better gear, a plan to avoid the Syndicate's watchers." His eyes moved between them, measuring their resolve. "All stuff I can get. But... you sure you want to go down that path?"

Reggie's mind raced through possibilities. Sarah. She'd know what to do with evidence like this. As an anthropologist with solid academic credentials, she'd have connections — maybe even someone at the Smithsonian or National Geographic. The kind of backing that could shine a spotlight too bright for the Syndicate to shoot out.

His jaw set as the plan started taking shape. "A fisherman asked for our help. Good men died. We can't walk away." He looked at Ben, hoping his partner would back his play. They'd need every advantage they could get, and Sarah's expertise might mean the difference between exposing the truth and ending up as fish food.

Reggie watched his partner's face, seeing the storm of emotions play across it. Fear, anger, determination — all warring for control. He knew exactly what Ben was thinking. But they'd seen too much blood spilled to walk away now. Whatever they'd stumbled into, they were neck-deep.

"We're in," Ben said, his voice steady despite everything.

Manny pushed himself up from the chair with a creak of old joints and older wood. His face had hardened into something fierce, like a man preparing for war. "All right, then. We'll talk details." He crossed to a shelf, pulling down what looked like maritime charts. "But understand this — from the moment we do this, the Syndicate will come at us hard."

"We'll be ready." Reggie heard himself say the words, flashing what he hoped was a confident smile. But his mind flashed back to that morning — the black Zodiac appearing like a shark through the mist, the way bullets had torn through Isla's canopy like angry wasps.

Ben's throat worked as he swallowed hard. Reggie knew his friend was replaying the same scene, hearing those shots crack across the water. Neither of them said it out loud, but the thought hung between them like smoke:

We better be ready.

They left Manny's home and Reggie pulled his phone from his pocket. Once again in the realm of cell connectivity, he tapped on the screen to call his girlfriend.

He owed her at least a check-in, but he dreaded hearing her reaction to their little escapade. With luck, she'd be out at dinner with a colleague, and he wouldn't have to dish everything just yet.

He took a breath and pulled the phone up to his ear as it started ringing.

CHAPTER 43

SARAH

SARAH SHOVED HER PLATE AWAY, the remnants of an unsatisfying dinner untouched. The sound of the microwave beeping had barely faded when her phone buzzed with Reggie's name lighting up the screen. Her heart skipped, a mix of excitement and unease swelling in her chest.

"Hey," she answered, a smile creeping onto her face, though she could sense an edge in his tone.

"Hey, Sarah. Sorry it took a bit to call back. Things got... complicated."

His voice held a strain that sent alarm bells ringing in her mind. "Complicated how? What happened?" She leaned against the counter and forced herself to breathe evenly, unable to help but imagine the worst.

"I don't want to freak you out," he said, but the way he hesitated sent a chill running down her spine. She was used to his usual bravado, the fearless Reggie who leapt at every adventure. This version of him felt weighed down, as if he'd already seen too much.

"Reggie, just — spit it out," she urged, her patience fraying.

"Okay." He took a breath, and she could almost envision him running a hand through his hair — a tell that he was stressed. *"So, Ben and I found a wreck."* There was a pause. *"An old one, older than anything anyone's claimed to find around here. But... it hasn't been easy."*

Her instincts kicked in, and she remained calm. "You guys went diving?"

He chuckled, but it wasn't lighthearted. *"Yeah. Let's just say it didn't go as planned. We ran into trouble — some serious trouble. That Black Coral Syndicate's involved."*

A lump lodged in her throat. She gripped the edge of the counter to steady herself. "It's a cartel, right? Or something like that?"

"Yeah, and they're definitely not messing around. They think they own the waters we were in, and they didn't take too kindly to us poking around. They're already onto us, Sarah. It's a mess."

She shook her head, fighting back a rush of anger and fear. "Why didn't you tell me sooner?"

"We were out on the boat, and... I... I didn't want to worry you." His voice softened, but that only irritated her more. *"We're fine for now, but..."*

"But," she echoed, "you're planning to dive again?"

"Only if —"

"I'm coming over," she interrupted, the decision flying from her mouth before she could second-guess it.

"What?" He sounded genuinely shocked. *"No, Sarah, you can't —"*

"I'm cutting my class short, and I only have one afternoon talk tomorrow anyway. I can't sit here while you're down there playing hero. I need to be there."

"Sarah —"

"Reggie," she said firmly. "Nothing you say will change my mind. You need support, and I can help. You know I am good under pressure."

Silence hung over the line, thick and tight. She could hear the wheels turning in his head, weighing the risks.

"Okay," he finally relented, but she could sense his reluctance. *"Honestly... we could use the help. This stuff might be related to some ancient culture somehow. These guys are after artifacts, we think. Just... be careful, alright? I don't want you in any more danger than you already are."*

"Don't worry about me," she replied, a spark of determination igniting in her gut. Travel's easy. Small enough airport that I can just walk in tomorrow morning and grab a quick flight, or there are ferries. You and Ben do what you need to until I get there, but *do not* do anything stupid."

"God, I hate that you're going to be involved in this."

"It's not an option," she shot back. "I'll handle the history — you handle these Syndicate guys."

He chuckled weakly. *"Fine. Just make sure to stay out of sight. The Syndicate won't hesitate to take you out if they know you're with us."*

"I'll see you soon, okay?"

"Soon," he agreed, but the words carried an unspoken weight.

After hanging up, Sarah stared at her reflection in the grimy bathroom mirror, her mind racing. She had a few hours to figure out logistics: flights, gear, diving procedures, before she'd need to get some sleep. She threw a few essential clothes into a backpack, her mind churning with thoughts of what awaited her on the other side of the narrow gap of ocean separating Puerto Rico from its neighboring island.

CHAPTER 44

BEN

A RUMBLE of distant thunder punctuated the silence as Ben trudged up the narrow beach path, eyes fixed on the looming storm clouds that gathered over the horizon. The late afternoon light had taken on a grayish cast, shadows stretching long across the sand. He could feel the atmosphere shift, a crackling tension that matched his own sense of dread.

Finding Isla hadn't been easy. After their meeting with Manny, they'd tracked her down at a dive shop two beaches over, where she'd been restocking air tanks. Ben had watched her tense up when she spotted them, but Reggie's quick mention of their successful meeting with Manny had kept her from bolting.

That, and the thick stack of bills Ben had pulled from his pocket, after visiting a local bank branch just before closing.

But he'd decided to lay it on thick and play to her ego as well. "Look," he'd told her, "we need someone who knows these waters. The currents, the coves, the places the Syndicate might not expect. We've already seen you in action; there's no one else who can help us like you." He'd seen the flicker of interest in her eyes at that. "Manny agreed. He says you're the best boat handler on this stretch of coast."

She'd sized them up for a long moment, arms crossed. "Manny's got a big mouth." But she'd taken the money, stuffing it into her pocket before adding, "The Syndicate's got eyes everywhere. You'll need someone who knows their blind spots."

Now, trudging back to his and Reggie's bungalow, Ben couldn't shake the feeling they'd made the right call bringing her in. *We've poked the hornet's nest,* he thought, recalling their near-fatal run-in with the Black Coral Syndicate out on the reef. Every step felt heavier as the three of them walked. Sand clung to Ben's damp shoes, and a stiff breeze carried the scent of rain.

"Storm's coming," Isla muttered, glancing skyward. "Fitting."

Reggie brushed aside a low-hanging palm frond. "Yeah, a literal storm *and* a figurative one."

The three of them stepped onto the short gravel road that led to the beach rentals, the ocean's roar behind them growing muted as the land rose slightly. The place looked different under the brooding sky — less like paradise, more like a staging ground for something dangerous.

Ben wiped a trickle of sweat from his brow. The day's heat hadn't broken yet, but the humidity was oppressive, weighing on him like a soggy blanket. *All I wanted was to relax in the sun for a week,* he lamented silently. *Instead, we're fighting a crime syndicate.* At this point, he was beyond exhaustion. His muscles ached from diving, and his nerves were raw from dodging bullets.

They paused at a bend in the road, near a small grove of palm trees. Isla tugged off her bandana and shook out her short, curly hair. "I owe you an explanation," she said, glancing between the men. "You paid me to take you to the reef, and I tried to warn you. But maybe you deserve more than just a warning."

Ben arched a brow. "We're listening."

She exhaled, folding the bandana in her hands. "You already suspect that the Black Coral Syndicate is behind these murders — and judging by today, for good reason. They control a lot more than just artifact smuggling. Drugs, weapons, even human trafficking. They have connections all the way up the chain — police, politicians, maybe even the coast guard."

Ben remembered what Manny had said, about possibly getting the Coast Guard involved. *Maybe even he doesn't know how far this goes...*

"Like a cartel?" Reggie asked.

Isla shrugged. "A cartel by another name, sure. But they're clever — focusing on high-value contraband, not just drugs. Things that will make a profit, but is far easier to hide from prying eyes. And they've taken special interest in that wreck. They've been monitoring it for months. If you saw divers murdered out there, it's because the Syndicate deemed them a threat."

Ben clenched his jaw. *Great. So it's worse than we thought.* "Why are you telling us this now?"

She met his gaze, her eyes hard. "Because you're in too deep to get out. If you try to leave, they *will* track you. You said it yourself — you saw too much." She let her voice go quiet. "I've seen this play out before."

Reggie exchanged a look with Ben, then turned to Isla. "Why do you care?"

Something flickered in her expression. "Let's say I lost someone to these bastards once. I don't want them ruling these waters forever."

Ben's chest tightened at the thought of someone else losing their life to the Syndicate. "I'm sorry."

Isla gave a curt nod, lips pressed thin. "Don't be. Just be smart, or they'll kill you too."

They continued along the gravel road in tense silence until they reached the cluster of pastel-painted bungalows near the beach. The wind had picked up, carrying the briny smell of seaweed and the first hints of oncoming rain. Gulls wheeled overhead, squawking as they sought shelter from the brewing storm.

When they turned the final corner, Ben froze in his tracks. Even from a distance, he could see the front door of their rental bungalow standing wide open. *We locked that...* Dread stabbed through him.

"Ben," Reggie said in a low voice. "You see that?"

"I see it." Ben's heart hammered. He dropped the bag he was carrying and reached for the phone in his pocket — a useless gesture, since he knew calling the police might not help. *But I might need to call Sarah... or Manny...*

Isla swore under her breath. "You think it's them?"

Ben set his jaw. "Only one way to find out." *Though I'm not thrilled about it.* He moved cautiously, scanning the bungalow's windows. The place was eerily quiet, no sign of movement inside. *If the Syndicate is in there, they might be waiting.* But the door stood ajar, banging softly against the frame with each gust of wind.

They crept up the steps to the porch. Reggie gestured for Ben to wait, then stepped forward to push the door fully open. It squeaked on its hinges. The interior was dim, the lights off. Ben's pulse thudded in his ears.

Please let this be a simple burglary. But he knew better.

Reggie slipped inside, scanning left and right. Ben followed, with Isla behind them. The first thing that struck Ben was the stench of stale ocean air mixed with something acrid — maybe spilled food or chemicals. The second thing was the chaos: cushions torn apart, furniture overturned, shards of broken glass scattered across the floor.

The bungalow looked like a hurricane had passed through. The small kitchenette was a wreck, plates smashed, drawers yanked out, silverware scattered. The lamp they'd left on earlier was knocked over, bulbs shattered. The entire place screamed *forced entry*. Or, more accurately, *deliberate sabotage.*

Ben's stomach clenched when he noticed a large smear of black paint scrawled on the nearest wall. He moved closer to read the words:

STAY OUT OF THE WATER.

CHAPTER 45

RAMÓN

RAMÓN WATCHED his men secure their weapons, tucking them beneath canvas covers as they entered the hidden cove. The Zodiac's wake dissolved into gentle ripples behind them, erasing any trace of their passage. His fingers drummed against the wheel housing. The morning's failed operation gnawed at him like a shark that wouldn't let go. Those three targets had slipped away too easily, vanishing into the maze of reefs before his team could get within range.

An amateur mistake — *his* amateur mistake.

The cave entrance yawned ahead, a dark maw in the limestone cliff face. Ramón had made this approach hundreds of times, but something about today made the passageway feel more oppressive. Maybe it was the weight of failure riding his shoulders, or maybe it was how the morning's salt air gave way to the dank breath of earth and stone.

Generations of smugglers had carved this sanctuary, or so Valeria liked to tell new recruits. The truth, as Ramón had pieced together over his relatively short time contracted with the Syndicate, was less romantic. Sure, pirates may have used these hollows centuries ago, but the modern amenities — the reinforced dock supports, the ventilation system, the backup generators — those came from Swiss bank accounts and shell companies.

Valeria Cruz might dress up their operation in historical charm, but her organization was pure twenty-first century efficiency, backed by serious money.

Water dripped from stalactites, each drop echoing in the growing darkness. The sound tracked Ramón's descent into the cave like nature's metronome, counting down to his inevitable report. He'd seen how Valeria decorated her private "office" — a squarish chamber deeper in the sprawling cave — with colonial-era maps and replicas of old Spanish weapons — all part of the carefully curated image she maintained. The reality was fiber optic cables running through these ancient walls, satellite uplinks disguised as rock formations, and enough computing power to run a small country.

The Syndicate could have operated from anywhere — a high-rise in Miami, a compound in the Caymans. But Valeria insisted on this theatrical base of operations, as if trying to channel the spirits of long-dead privateers. Ramón supposed everyone needed their illusions.

His was that he could fail her and walk away unscathed.

He cut the engine, letting momentum carry them toward the dock, where his men tied off and headed into the shadowy interior. He followed shortly after a quick gear check. The familiar smell of salt and stone wrapped around him as he entered the cave.

Near the planning table, illuminated by strings of LED work lights, Ramón glimpsed Valeria's silhouette. She stood bent over what looked like charts, her posture rigid with purpose. His jaw clenched hard enough to ache. She'd want answers, and he had none worth giving.

"Local muscle already paid your targets a visit," she said without looking up as he approached. Her finger traced something on a faded nautical map while her other hand swiped across a tablet showing satellite imagery. The blue glow from the screen cast harsh shadows across her face. "Two men, from America. With a local woman named Isla Torres."

Ramón waited.

"Left them a message they won't miss."

"A *message*?" Ramón shifted his weight, already hating where this was going. He'd lost three high-value targets today, and now she was talking about leaving notes like some schoolyard bully.

"They trashed the place." She zoomed in on the satellite feed, marking coordinates with quick, precise movements. "Writing 'STAY OUT OF THE WATER' on a wall or something. Big enough to read from the street, I'm told."

Ramón snorted and shook his head. The cave's dampness seemed to crawl under his skin. "'Stay out of the water?' Sending a cute message? That's your play?" He planted his hands on the table's edge, studying her composed features. His fingers left wet marks on the map's corners. "These guys went *straight* for the wreck site. They're not some lost tourists you can scare off with property damage."

"We escalate as needed." Her voice cut through the cave's dampness like a knife. She finally looked up, her dark eyes meeting his across the planning table. The cave's shadows played across her face, turning her features to stone. "But we keep this quiet." The last word fell between them with the weight of an anchor.

"Quiet?" Ramón straightened, blood rushing to his face. His fists clenched at his sides, years of discipline barely holding back the explosion building in his chest. The morning's failure had already left him raw, and now this — painting walls like street thugs while their targets slipped closer to whatever lay beneath those waters.

"You ordered me to protect that site," he pressed on, knowing he was pushing too far but past caring. His voice echoed off the cave walls, sending ripples through the pools of standing water. "But while we're painting threats on walls, they're out there pushing closer." He leaned forward, invading her space. "What's on that wreck, Valeria? What's got you running scared?"

Valeria's shoulders stiffened at his use of her first name, and the temperature around her seemed to drop ten degrees. Her fingers stopped their movement across the tablet, freezing mid-gesture like a predator spotting prey.

Her eyes finally met his, dark and unreadable. The cave's dim light caught the silver at her temples, earned through years of maintaining the Syndicate's iron grip. For a moment, only the lap of water against stone filled the silence.

She tapped a spot on the chart. "You wouldn't believe me if I told you. That wreck? It's tied to something *ancient*. Something beyond just monetary value. We *must* control..." She let the words hang.

Ramón studied her face, searching for cracks in her composure. He'd spent long enough doing the Syndicate's wet work, no questions asked. But that type of work had been sporadic — now men were dying every day, and the ocean held secrets that made Valeria Cruz nervous. That scared him more than any threat.

"They won't back down," he said finally. "So we hit harder."Ramón fell silent, watching Valeria's face for any sign of approval or rejection. The cave seemed to hold its breath.

She gave a single, sharp nod. "Do what needs to be done."

He turned to his waiting team, their shadows stretching long against the cave walls. These weren't the kind of men who needed detailed instructions — they'd worked together long enough to read between the lines. "Miguel, get the night vision gear prepped. Carlos, I want our gear checked and rechecked. We're not going back in unprepared in any way." He paused, letting his next words carry weight. "And get a few more men."

The men's faces hardened with understanding. No more playing games. No more warnings. When their targets surfaced again, they'd find something far worse than graffiti waiting for them.

CHAPTER 46

BEN

THUNDER RUMBLED AGAIN, this time closer. It felt like the storm outside had found its counterpart in here, a surge of violent intent. Ben exhaled shakily. *So they're sending a message.*

"Damn," Reggie muttered, glancing around. "These people don't mess around."

Isla hovered at the threshold, her expression grim. "I told you. They murder witnesses, sabotage anything that threatens their control. Consider yourself threatened."

Ben ran a hand through his hair. *This is too much.* He bent to pick up a photo that had fallen from the nightstand. The family who owned the bungalow, he guessed, now lying face-down on the floor, frame cracked. *They messed with everything.* A flash of anger seared him — how dare they invade this space, handle his family photo?

Reggie kicked aside a broken lamp. "Anyone else get the feeling we should bail?"

At the same time, Isla said, "They'll find you wherever you go. Better to face them here." Her voice rang hollow in the gutted room.

Ben stared at the message on the wall again — STAY OUT OF THE WATER. *They're practically daring us to leave.* He ground his teeth. "I'm done with this," he snapped, turning to Reggie. "We should call Sarah, pack up, and get the hell out of here before we end up like that fisherman."

Reggie let out a slow breath, stepping over the debris. "We can't just walk away, Ben."

"Watch me," Ben said, hearing the anger in his own voice. *I have a family, a life. I didn't come here to die.* He paced through the living area, noticing how the Syndicate thugs had left no corner unturned. The pillows were slashed, the couch cushions gutted. A sense of violation churned in his stomach. *They want us scared. They want us to run.*

Isla's gaze flicked between them. "Ben, if you run, they'll hunt you. They'll assume you have enough knowledge to be a threat, so they won't let you slip away."

Ben clenched a fist, staring at the broken shards of a vase. "So you're saying we have to stay?"

Her jaw tightened. "Or you vanish so thoroughly they can't find you, which isn't easy with a group like this. They have eyes everywhere on this island — and beyond."

Reggie stepped closer to Ben. "Look, man, I know it's terrifying. But the fisherman who died in that bar, the diver who died out on the reef — they deserve justice. And if we leave, no one else will step up."

Ben's heartbeat thundered. The words *they deserve justice* struck a chord. *It's the same reason we stayed involved in so many other nightmares,* he thought. *But it's different now. I have a baby girl at home.* He closed his eyes, imagining Julie's disapproval if he got himself killed trying to fight Caribbean smugglers.

It reminded him to call her, but that was the last thing he wanted to do. It would only stress her out — she couldn't make it there in less than two days, minimum, and besides, she couldn't leave Hope, either.

He decided he'd rather take the heat of not checking in with his wife rather than stress her out now — *and* take the heat for it.

A flash of lightning illuminated the sky outside, followed by a crack of thunder. The shadows in the bungalow flickered ominously. *We're in a real storm now,* he thought, feeling the humidity shift as a gust of wind rattled the windows. Rain pattered against the glass, intensifying by the second.

Reggie gently clasped his shoulder. "I know you're worried about Julie and Hope," he said quietly. "But the Syndicate could probably track you back to them if you run, especially if they find out who we really are. Chances are they're in bed with any number of groups we've bested over the years. And I'd be willing to bet if they knew we were the CSO guys who beat up their friends, we'd have even more of a problem than we do now. Better to stand our ground and finish this."

Ben swallowed hard. He hated that Reggie was right. If they slunk away now, the Black Coral Syndicate might interpret that as a loose end — and loose ends got tied up violently. *Damned if we do, damned if we don't.*

Finally, he turned, scanning the wrecked living space. "All right," he muttered, voice thick. "Let's think this through. We have Manny Delgado on our side now — sort of. We know the wreck is real, and the Syndicate's protecting it, likely because it somehow means a massive payday for them. They clearly don't want us anywhere near the water."

"Guess we're not going fishing anytime soon."

Reggie scoffed. "Yeah, I'm sure they meant 'don't go near that area you guys were in today,' but I wonder how wide that circle is?"

"I don't think I want to find out," Ben answered. He gestured at the painted threat on the wall. "But we do need more intel."

Isla nodded. "You *also* need a place to stay, because this one," she waved a hand at the trashed bungalow, "is compromised."

"You live around here?" Reggie asked.

She eyed him with a perfect mix of curiosity and hesitation. "You inviting yourself over, big guy?"

A smile grew ear-to-ear across his face. "I'm in a relationship, but thanks for asking."

"*Okay,*" Ben said quickly. "Back on track. Isla — we're not inviting ourselves over, *but...* you do have a point."

"So you *are* inviting yourselves to my place?" She asked. She paused, then added, "sorry. Just trying to lighten the mood a bit. Look, I *do* have a place. But it won't work. I share it with my sister and her kids, and it's a closet, anyway. Maybe if I tell her —"

"No," Ben said abruptly. "Absolutely not. Not if there are kids."

Isla and Reggie nodded solemnly. "Still," Reggie said with a grimace. "We can't sleep here tonight."

Ben's anger flared at the reality of being uprooted like this. *But we have no choice.* He forced himself to breathe steadily. "Maybe Manny can put us up, or we can find another rental under the radar. Reggie, give him a call, see if he can meet us somewhere later. But first, we clean up this mess."

"Why bother?" Isla asked, perplexed.

"I don't want to leave any personal stuff behind," Ben said.

Reggie hefted a small duffel onto an overturned chair, checking if anything remained inside. "They rummaged through everything. If we had anything valuable, it's gone."

Ben sighed, taking a moment to collect what was salvageable — mainly clothes, a spare phone charger, some leftover snacks. The rest lay in ruins on the floor. *It's just stuff,* he told himself. *We're lucky they weren't waiting to shoot us.* The thought made his chest tighten again.

Once they gathered what they could, they regrouped by the doorway. Rain drummed on the bungalow's roof, creating a dull roar that underscored the tension in the air. The message on the wall — STAY OUT OF THE WATER — loomed like a grim warning.

CHAPTER 47

VALERIA

THE CAVE SWALLOWED the last sounds of Ramón's boots as he and his men disappeared into the lower levels. Valeria Cruz remained motionless beside the operations table, one hand resting on the cold steel, her eyes tracing the nautical chart splayed before her.

She waited until she heard the far door seal shut, then moved to the reinforced cabinet behind her private workstation. A satphone lay inside — separate from the networked systems, hardwired to nothing.

She dialed. One ring.

Halim's voice crackled through, smooth as polished glass. *"Yes?"*

"It's handled," she said. "Our team made contact. No casualties. Targets escaped, but we've reestablished perimeter control."

"You let them escape?"

She kept her tone steady. "We weren't deployed in full strength yet. They moved earlier than expected. But no damage to the site. They didn't see anything."

A brief pause. Then, *"good."*

She heard the rustle of fabric, maybe the clink of ice in a glass on his end. He was never rushed, never raised his voice. A man who measured success in silence.

"I assume no unnecessary attention was drawn?" he asked.

"No. Quiet, just like we wanted. No police chatter, no civilian noise."

"Then we're still on track."

Valeria nodded slightly to herself. "Your engineers will have a clean slate to work from. No protests, no headlines."

"Any progress on the recovery efforts?"

"We've secured new scans of the reef floor. Still combing the sediment. There's more buried than we expected, but we'll have it cleared before your team arrives."

"Good," Halim said again. *"The board is growing... eager."*

There was something in the way he said that. Not pressure. Not even a warning. Just a signal. The Syndicate wasn't just protecting the perimeter — they were on trial.

"I understand," Valeria replied. "I've doubled our patrol rotations. Added redundant suppression routes. No one gets within two kilometers without my knowing."

"Do they suspect?"

"Not the full picture. Maybe not even half." She tapped a fingernail against the satphone's metal casing. "They think we're chasing artifacts to resell. That's all. Just another raid. Standard black-market excavation."

A pause. Then Halim chuckled — a rare, thin sound. *"You haven't corrected them?"*

Valeria smiled faintly. "No. Let them believe I'm just hoarding history. It's simpler."

"Smart," he said. *"Let everyone stay in their lanes."*

That told her everything. He *liked* the misdirection. Probably encouraged it. If anyone ever traced the Syndicate's movements, they'd find only black-market shadows. Nothing corporate. Nothing infrastructural. Nothing pointing to the real plan.

"How soon do you need the site cleared?" she asked.

There was another small pause. *"We're moving up the window."*

Her stomach clenched. "How far?"

"My board wants to start site preparation and construction in ninety days. Maybe less. You said you were almost ready to clear the site, so we need

that done in 24 hours. We'll be flying in observers. Quiet ones. The Saudis want proof of control. Real, enforceable control. Before the full buy-in."

So that was it. Not a rollout. *A test.*

"And if they like what they see?"

"If I *like what I see, then you get the contract,"* Halim said. *"Your people become the permanent solution. For Culebra... and elsewhere. But again — we need this done* tomorrow, *at the latest."*

Valeria let that sink in. This wasn't just about guarding a reef. This was legacy. The Syndicate as the sanctioned sword of a global initiative. Floating cities. Unregulated zones. No extradition. No oversight.

She forced her voice to stay calm. "Understood."

"You built this organization for jobs like this," Halim said. *"If you can keep it clean, quiet, and invisible —"*

"I will."

There was silence for a moment. "I know you will."

He ended the call.

Valeria stared at the satphone for a long moment before setting it down.

She crossed the room to the wide steel desk and opened the top drawer. Inside was a rolled dossier, bound in twine. She unwrapped it slowly, revealing a map of the Culebra reef system, dotted with red annotations. Beneath it, a separate sheet — a list of names.

Locals. Divers. Researchers. One of them had circled back. *Isla Torres.*

Valeria tapped her pen on the name, eyes narrowing.

This wasn't just about control of a location. It was about *controlling the story.* Suppress the history, sanitize the site, and no one would ever know what lay beneath the reef — or what was lost to make way for progress.

Ninety days.

She could do it.

But it would mean crossing every name off that list.

One by one.

CHAPTER 48

BEN

THE FLICKERING NEON sign outside the cantina glowed sickly pink, casting warped reflections across the rain-slick cobblestones. Harvey Bennett pulled up the hood of his windbreaker and took in the narrow alleyway. A single streetlamp buzzed overhead, revealing chipped plaster walls that seemed to sweat in the humid night air. The distant roll of thunder spoke of another storm gathering over the ocean.

Where does Manny find these places? Ben wondered, stepping carefully over a puddle. *It's like he prefers to do business where no one can see or hear.* He glanced back at Reggie and Isla Torres, who trailed behind him. Both looked uneasy, which was rare for Reggie.

"Sure this is the right spot?" Reggie asked, flipping up the collar of his jacket. He eyed a couple of locals loitering by the wall, cigarettes glowing red in the gloom.

Ben nodded. "He said 'the seedy cantina with a pink sign, near the old docks.' To be fair, that could be any number of places on this island. But this one seems... *extra* seedy. This must be it." He squinted at the neon letters, half-burned out, that read *Cantina Estrella*. A battered rowboat propped against the wall further marked the place as Manny's territory — he'd told them to look for it.

They exchanged a look of mutual apprehension and pushed open the warped wooden door. A wave of stale air, cigarettes, and old liquor hit them like a slap. Inside, the cantina was dimly lit by a few tarnished sconces and a single flickering neon sign behind the bar. A battered jukebox squatted in a corner, playing a soft salsa tune that crackled with static. A handful of patrons hunched over rickety tables, giving the newcomers suspicious once-overs.

A row of plastic nets, old buoys, and fishing memorabilia hung from the rafters, along with a tattered pirate flag that might have been meant as a kitschy decoration — though in this part of the Caribbean, it felt more ominous than playful. The entire vibe screamed *keep your head down and don't ask questions.*

Ben stepped deeper into the cantina, scanning for Manuel "Manny" Delgado. Eventually, he spotted the wiry, gray-haired man seated at a corner table, nursing a glass of rum. Manny's eyes flicked up, and he lifted a hand in greeting.

"This place is charming," Reggie muttered under his breath, lips quirking into a half-grin. "Better than the storm outside, I guess."

Isla just shook her head. "Manny has a knack for choosing holes in the wall." She smoothed back her short curls, which were damp from the perpetual drizzle.

They wove between tables toward Manny. Locals gave them hostile or curious stares, and Ben felt a flash of paranoia. *Any one of these people could be connected to the Black Coral Syndicate.* He shook off the thought, focusing on Manny's neutral expression.

"Hola," Manny said quietly as they approached. He gestured for them to sit on the rickety chairs around his table. A flickering candle illuminated a half-empty bottle of rum and several mismatched glasses. "You're late."

Isla slid into a seat first, crossing her arms on the table. "We had to go the long way around. Syndicate watchers near the old highway."

Manny grunted. "Figured. They've been on high alert since your little expedition to the reef. Word travels fast on this island."

Reggie took a seat next to Ben, resting his elbows on the table. "*Rumors* travel fast."

Manny clicked his tongue, swirling the rum in his glass. "Rumor or not, they think you found *something* out there. And I've heard enough stories to piece together a bigger picture." He paused, glancing around warily. Then he leaned forward, voice dropping. "But be warned: some things are best left buried."

Ben suppressed a shiver. *He's talking about that cursed ship.*

Reggie tapped his fingers, impatience evident. "We want to know the truth. If that wreck is as old as the fisherman claimed — older than the Spanish — it could change history. And if the Syndicate's protecting it, there's a reason, right?"

A bitter smile twisted Manny's lips. "You're like me, back when I thought finding the next big treasure would solve all my problems. Let me tell you: sometimes treasure only creates more nightmares." He raised his glass to his lips but didn't drink yet, as though savoring the moment. "My boat was called *La Ventura*. A real beauty. Lost it thanks to those bastards. Lost a good friend too."

Isla watched him carefully. "You said you used to hunt deep-sea wrecks. Did you ever try for this one — this rumored ship that's older than anything in the region?"

Manny exhaled, eyes distant. "I did. Years ago, when I first heard the whispers of a lost ship that predated Columbus. It was supposed to be impossible to find, buried too deep under the sand that piles up underwater against the reef. Hell, people even said it was cursed, that the *taínos* and even the pirates avoided it. But I was arrogant, *sure* I could outsmart any curse, and find it, even under all that sand."

Ben exchanged a quick glance with Reggie. The mention of a curse made his skepticism flare. *But after everything we've seen... maybe it's not just superstition.*

Manny's gaze dropped to the rum in his glass. He finally drank, swallowing hard before continuing. "But that was before the last big hurricane came through. The sands covering everything were deeper then. After the hurricane, my friend Rosario and I dove near the reef anyway, tried to find proof that the old rumors were true... " He trailed off, eyes haunted.

"What happened out there?" Ben prompted when Manny fell silent.

Manny let out a long breath. "That night, a storm raged so fierce it nearly capsized *La Ventura*. We couldn't get out in time. Rosario vanished, lost overboard." He closed his eyes. "Never found his body."

CHAPTER 49

BEN

ISLA'S BROW FURROWED. "You think it was just a storm, or do you believe in that... curse?"

Manny's laugh was short and devoid of mirth. "I don't know what I believe. But that wreck has only brought bad luck. A week later, the Black Coral Syndicate showed up, demanding anything I found. They shot up my boat for good measure. *La Ventura* sank a week later, thanks to the damage. I barely got out alive."

Reggie frowned. "Did you two find anything down there?"

Manny nodded, hate etched in every line of his face. "A trinket. I gave it to the Syndicate, who sold it on the black market, I heard. Some private collector in Europe. Meanwhile, the rumors of the wreck kept circulating: a vessel older than any known civilization in these waters, loaded with something more dangerous than gold. They say it's called *The Devil's Cut* because it carried a cargo so foul that even pirates steered clear. They believed the ship was cursed to doom anyone who claimed it."

Ben's gut twisted at Manny's tone. *This is madness.* He recalled the fisherman's final words about an older-than-Spanish relic. "Wait, you're saying the ship's name is *The Devil's Cut*?" he asked quietly.

"That's one name," Manny conceded. "A modern one, of course. Locals have others, some lost to time. But *The Devil's Cut* is the popular one, referencing an old pirate legend. They claimed it ferried cargo from a civilization that vanished overnight... or so the story goes."

Isla shook her head slowly. "That's insane. How would a pre-Columbian ship exist like that? No records. No references in the history books."

Manny shrugged. "Exactly. It shouldn't exist. But if it does, it would rewrite what we know about exploration of the New World. Maybe it's from another unknown group, older than the Taíno. Maybe it's all superstition." He gave Ben and Reggie a pointed look. "But you've seen the wreck's timbers, right? Doesn't look Spanish, does it?"

Ben shuddered at the memory of that half-buried hull in the reef. *The lines, the carvings... they were definitely not European.* "No," he admitted, glancing at Reggie. "We saw carvings that looked completely alien."

Reggie, far from discouraged, leaned forward eagerly. "This is *huge*, Manny. If we could prove that wreck's existence, we'd blow the Syndicate's operation wide open. They can't stave off everyone, forever. If we get this out — get it big enough — we might have a chance at seizing control. They're hoarding something the world needs to see."

Manny's grim chuckle returned. "And you think the world *wants* to see it? Some do, sure — archaeologists, maybe. But all the Syndicate sees is money, power. Private collectors pay fortunes for lost artifacts, especially if there's a whiff of the supernatural."

Isla took the bottle of rum, poured herself a measure, and tossed it back. "Supernatural or not, the world *doesn't* know about it yet. The Syndicate has a vice grip on the entire reed. And they kill anyone who gets too close. Why risk it?"

A heavy silence reigned. Rain drummed on the cantina's corrugated roof, and the jukebox crackled, switching to a melancholic bolero. One of the local patrons eyed them from a distance but seemed uninterested in approaching.

Reggie finally broke the hush. "Because if we *don't* stop them, more people will die. They'll keep using that wreck to funnel contraband, or they'll keep searching for more relics to sell. People like that fisherman, or Manny's friend, or the divers who stumbled on it — lost for no reason."

Ben suppressed a groan, pressing his palms to his temples. *He's not wrong, but I can't shake the sense of dread.* "Reggie, you heard Manny's story. He literally lost a friend and his boat. And we've seen how deadly the Syndicate is."

Reggie nodded. "I know. But we can't just walk away."

Manny watched the exchange, swirling his rum again. "This wreck is not just any treasure. Some call it *The Devil's Cut*, others call it *La Maldición Antigua*. But all the stories say the same: it carried something that brought ruin to whoever possessed it. Pirates, smugglers, explorers... none survived intact."

Ben locked eyes with Manny. "So you're telling us it's... cursed." He tried to keep the sarcasm out of his voice, but weariness frayed his patience.

Manny raised a brow. "You think curses are just stories, maybe. But you can't deny the bodies piling up around this thing."

Isla cleared her throat. "All right, so assume it's real, assume it's cursed. The Syndicate has control of it. What does that mean for us? We want them exposed, or at least stopped, but how?"

Manny set his glass down. The candlelight flickered across his weathered face. "What you need is *proof*. Enough evidence that the Syndicate *can't* bury it. Photos, video, physical artifacts. Then you get that into the hands of someone who can't be bought — international media, a big university, maybe a museum with a reputation." He shrugged. "Easier said than done."

Reggie's gaze flicked to Ben. "We can do that. We get in, document the wreck, maybe retrieve a small piece of that carving. Sarah can help guide us to someone who can authenticate it."

Ben felt a rush of conflicting emotions. *Going back to that reef is suicidal.* "We already almost got killed once," he growled, frustration leaking through. "Remember the black Zodiac and those dudes with assault rifles?"

Manny lifted his rum glass in a toast of grim agreement. "And you'd face worse than them, if the stories are true."

A knot formed in Ben's chest. *Damned if we do, damned if we don't.*

He hated feeling cornered. "So, Manny," he said, voice tight, "what's your advice? If it's so dangerous, why even consider going back?"

Manny's lips thinned. "Because you asked me for a solution that ends the Syndicate's hold on that wreck. This is the only solution I see." He leaned forward, eyes gleaming with a strange intensity. "Find the artifact, the most irrefutable piece of evidence in *The Devil's Cut*. Bring it to light. It's the only play."

Ben stared at him. *He's basically telling us to walk into the lion's den.* He bristled, but Reggie spoke first.

Manny suddenly pulled a half-empty bottle of rum from under the table — he must have had it in his lap — and poured a round into mismatched glasses as they sat. "Drink," he said tersely. "Warms you up."

Ben took the glass, uncertain. *I'm not sure I want to dull my senses with alcohol right now.* But Manny's glare left little room for debate. He sipped, the rum burning a path down his throat.

Manny tossed back his own shot, then wiped his mouth. "So. Your bungalow was hit?"

"Trashed," Reggie confirmed. "Message on the wall telling us to 'stay out of the water.'"

"Figures." Manny grimaced. "They want you to run scared. Or die. Either one works for them. A storm's rolling in, so it's a perfect time for them to tighten the net. Tourists won't be out. Fewer witnesses."

Ben bristled. "So what's next? We can't go back to our place, we can't do much in this storm, and by now everyone on this island knows what we look like."

Manny set his glass down, leaning forward. "I talked to a friend right after you called me. He has a... 'safehouse' a few miles inland. His words, not mine."

Ben frowned. "It's not safe?"

Manny chuckled. "It's not a *house*. It's ramshackle, but the Syndicate rarely checks that part of the island. You can lie low there, regroup."

Isla folded her arms. "And how do we know *he's* not Syndicate?"

"He hates them," Manny said simply. "He lost his son to their drug trade. Trust me, if there's one place they won't easily find you, it's his property."

Ben exchanged a glance with Reggie. "We'll go. Thanks, Manny."

"I'll take you," Manny continued. "Then I'll try to secure more intel — maybe equipment for a proper search of the wreck, or at least a better boat than yours," he added to Isla, who scowled at him.

"You have a death wish," Isla muttered.

Manny shrugged. "I have *reasons*. Besides, you're the ones stirring the pot." He stood, pulling his slicker's hood up. "Now, let's get you moving before the Syndicate notices you here."

CHAPTER 50

BEN

THEY DOWNED the rest of their rum — Ben grimaced at the taste — and followed Manny out into the raging storm. Wind whipped across the pub's tattered awning, sending a torrent of rain against their faces. Manny led them to a beat-up truck waiting by the side alley. It looked ancient, rust streaking the sides, but when Manny turned the key, the engine rumbled to life.

"Get in," Manny ordered. Isla took the passenger seat before the two six-foot-plus men could argue, so Ben and Reggie climbed into the cramped back seat, gear piled under their feet. The interior smelled of mildew, salt, and old leather. Manny gripped the steering wheel, peering through the streaked windshield. "Let's go," he muttered.

They lurched onto the slick road, wipers struggling to keep pace with the downpour. Visibility was minimal, headlights reflecting off the water-slick pavement. Ben tensed, scanning the street for any sign of Syndicate vehicles. He wasn't sure what, exactly, a 'Syndicate vehicle' would look like, but he kept his eyes open. Possibly black SUVs or sedans? Or would that be too obvious?

No, these weren't government grunts — no need for unmarked, shiny black vehicles. Besides, this was a tiny island of Puerto Rico. Vehicles like that would stand out even more than just a run-of-the-mill *new* vehicle.

He had to accept the fact that if the Syndicate was watching from one of the relatively few cars on the road, he'd have no idea.

Lightning flashed overhead, illuminating the run-down buildings and shuttered shops. *No one else is crazy enough to be out in this storm; we stand out like a sore thumb.*

They drove in tense silence, Manny weaving through narrow back streets to avoid main roads. Occasionally, they spotted a figure peering from a window or a stray dog dashing for cover. Otherwise, the town felt deserted, as if everyone had boarded up for the night.

Eventually, Manny navigated out of the main district, following a winding road that led into the island's interior. The terrain rose gently, thick with dense foliage on either side. The truck's headlights revealed overgrown vines and palm trunks bending under the storm's fury. Water gushed across the road in spots, forcing Manny to slow.

After about twenty minutes, Manny turned onto a gravel path barely visible in the swirling rain. "Not far now," he said, voice tight.

They bounced along the uneven ground, wheels churning mud. The wind howled, rattling the truck's frame. Ben gripped the door, bracing himself. *If we get stuck out here...*

At last, a small farmhouse came into view — a single light glowing over its porch. The structure looked old but sturdy, with walls made of cinder blocks and a tin roof. Manny pulled up, the engine coughing as he parked near a dilapidated shed. "This is it," he announced.

A gaunt figure emerged from the farmhouse, shining a flashlight and the unmistakable outline of a shotgun. Manny rolled down the window, exchanging words in rapid Spanish. Ben only caught fragments — *amigos, refugio, Syndicato.* The figure nodded, stepped aside, and Manny gestured for Ben and Reggie to exit.

They bolted from the truck, hunched against the rain as they ran for the porch. Isla followed, cursing under her breath about the downpour. Manny stayed in the driver's seat, leaning out the window.

"I'll be in touch," he said, his voice nearly drowned by thunder. "Stay here, keep your heads low. I'll contact you once I have more info. Remember, the Syndicate is not invincible, but they *are* deadly."

"Got it," Reggie shouted back, wiping water from his eyes.

Ben forced a nod. *Again, we're stuck waiting, reliant on Manny's goodwill.* But what choice did they have?

Manny raised a hand in farewell, then reversed the truck, headlights soon disappearing into the darkness. The man with the flashlight, presumably Manny's friend, motioned them inside. *At least we have shelter,* Ben told himself.

Inside, the farmhouse was dim and smelled of damp wood, but it was relatively dry. The man introduced himself as Esteban, speaking broken English. He showed them a small living area with two worn couches and a cot. "Stay as long as you need," he said. "Mi casa es su casa."

Ben thanked him, mustering a tired smile. Esteban retreated to another part of the house, leaving them to settle in. Reggie and Isla plopped onto the couches, exhausted. Ben walked to a small window, peering through the streaks of rain into the night. Lightning illuminated the yard, revealing overgrown shrubs and a couple of chickens huddled under an awning. The storm raged on, matching his internal turmoil.

So here we are, half fugitives, half vigilantes. He clenched his fists, recalling the fisherman's last words, the bullet holes in Isla's boat, the scrawled warning in their bungalow. He didn't want this fight, but it seemed they had no choice.

He turned to see Isla rummaging for a blanket, Reggie stripping off his soaked shirt. They looked weary, battered by more than just the weather. *We're in this together.* The realization grounded him somewhat.

"Tomorrow," he said quietly, "we'll figure out our next steps. Maybe Sarah arrives by then. Manny might have a lead. One way or another, we have to keep going."

Reggie nodded, leaning his head back against the couch. Isla muttered a soft *sí*. Outside, thunder cracked again, making the walls tremble.

Ben stared at the shadows dancing across the floor. *We can't stop now, even if we want to.* A part of him longed for Alaska's cold clarity, where he could hide in his cabin with Julie and Hope. But that was a world away. Here, the storm raged, and the Black Coral Syndicate roamed the dark.

He exhaled, a note of determination building in his chest. *We'll face them here.* The fisherman's death wouldn't be in vain, nor would the diver's, or anyone else who suffered under the Syndicate's brutal reign. *Even if it costs us everything, we have to try.*

As the storm raged outside, the farmhouse offered a fragile shelter. Ben settled onto a wicker chair in the corner, mind spinning with possibilities. They were deep in dangerous territory, but for the moment, they had a roof and relative safety. For the moment, they could breathe.

Thunder boomed again, rattling the tin roof. With each flash of lightning, Ben pictured the Syndicate's threat. Ironically, it was too late to heed any warning. They were already submerged in a conflict that threatened to pull them under.

And we're definitely in too deep to just swim away.

CHAPTER 51

RAMÓN

RAMÓN MENDOZA CROUCHED beside the rain-slicked hood of the Hilux truck, fingers curled tight around the suppressed pistol resting in his lap. Water streamed from the brim of his ball cap, soaked through his black windbreaker, and pooled around his boots in the churned mud. The jungle around the farmhouse churned and breathed with the storm — leaves whipping, trees groaning, wind hissing like a serpent.

He didn't care.

He glanced over his shoulder at his team — Ortiz, Lopez, and Castellanos — silhouetted in the dark beneath the canopy. All three wore matching gear: black tactical vests, thigh holsters, low-profile radios. Faces painted in dark streaks. Efficient. Silent.

Deadly.

And ready to finally finish this wild goose chase.

He'd scoped the place for an hour, after word came down from one of their watchers in town: the trio had left the bar with Manny Delgado during the storm and never returned. A contact had followed them just far enough to see the truck disappear down a dirt road leading out toward the interior. Thankfully there were only a few homes dotting the sides of the road, so the trio and Delgado had already helped narrow it to down.

A few phone calls, a quick bribe, and the farmhouse was confirmed.

This was it. Their hidey-hole.

Ramón turned his eyes back to the farmhouse fifty meters ahead, its windows glowing faintly behind rain-streaked glass. A single porch light illuminated the entrance and part of the front yard, painting silver outlines across the overgrown shrubs and the battered truck out front. It cast a dark shadow over the *other* structure nearby — a single, dilapidated shed.

That's where they're hiding, Ramón knew. He'd been told the owner of the farmhouse had loose ties to Manny Delgado, the same well-known local who'd taken the trio to this place. But the farmhouse was too obvious, too... *open*.

No, they'd be hiding in the dark little shed barely hidden behind the gravel drive.

A chicken darted through the light, wings flapping, then vanished into the dark.

Ramón didn't want another ambush. No more warning shots. No more screwups.

He wanted them dead.

All three.

"Move in silent," he whispered into his comm. "No light. We go hard on my mark."

Ortiz clicked in response. Castellanos nodded silently. Lopez was already adjusting the stock on his rifle.

Ramón slipped forward, his steps half-swallowed by the wind and the squelch of mud. The others moved with him, a phalanx of shadows gliding through the dark. They crept along a natural path in the underbrush, the angle of approach taking them around the shed and toward the rear of the house. No dogs barking. No signs of movement in the windows.

But then —

He froze.

A soft voice cut through the static of rain.

Female.

Ramón ducked, motioned the others down. He shifted closer,

squinting between leaves. On the porch, just outside the front door, stood Isla Torres.

Alone.

She wore a windbreaker over her tank top, her hair pulled into a wet braid. One hand held a cell phone to her ear. She paced just inside the range of the porch light, moving back and forth near the edge of the overhang, where the storm lashed down just inches from her feet.

"Sí," she said, her voice raised above the wind. "I told you. We're safe for now, but it's getting worse. I don't know how long this place will hold."

Pause.

"No. Manny's gone. Said he'll check back in the morning."

Pause.

"I don't know. We're tired. Reggie's sleeping, I think. Ben's still up. We're all rattled."

Reggie and Ben, he thought. *The two men she's with.*

Another pause. She sighed, rubbed her forehead. "I can't leave them. Not now."

She turned slightly, and for a moment, her face was fully illuminated. There was no fear in her eyes. Not yet.

Ramón's heart pounded. This was it.

He could signal the kill now. Take her out from this range, then storm the house. Quick, violent. All three would be dead in less than twenty seconds.

But a beat later, she lowered the phone.

And screamed.

She had seen Castellanos — just a flicker of movement between trees — and her instincts kicked in. She dropped the phone, turned to bolt back toward the door.

Shit. It was too late for surprise. Even if they killed her, the two men — the real threat, he figured — would be coming to, ready to fight.

"Go!" Ramón barked.

The four men surged forward.

Lopez vaulted the porch railing, catching Isla by the arm before she could reach the door. She fought like hell, swinging an elbow, screaming again. Her foot connected with the edge of a bucket and sent it flying across the boards.

Ramón grabbed her other arm. "Shut her up — don't kill her!"

Ortiz darted forward with a cloth and vial of chloroform, the sedative ready. Isla thrashed, nearly broke free, but Castellanos looped an arm around her waist and dragged her back toward the edge of the porch.

Inside the farmhouse to his right, something stirred. A shadow passed across the window.

"Now!" Ramón hissed.

It took all three of his men, but they were able to get her sedated and still, and together they stumbled back toward their parked vehicle.

They were shuffling out the gate by the time one of the men — the one she'd called Ben, perhaps? — yanked open the front door and stepped into the storm. A flash of lightning split the sky — and Ramón saw his face, wide-eyed, hair matted to his forehead, mouth open mid-shout.

Too late.

Ramón and his team vanished into the jungle, Isla limp in their grip.

They reached the truck, already mud-splattered and idling. The back doors were open. Castellanos and Lopez climbed in with her, locking her arms in place.

Ramón slammed the passenger door. Ortiz gunned the engine.

They peeled away from the farmhouse, tires kicking up mud and shredded leaves. Behind them, voices rose in alarm — Ben and Reggie shouting, maybe chasing for a moment — but the storm swallowed it all.

Ramón didn't look back.

He sat in the passenger seat, breathing hard, adrenaline still humming in his chest.

"Dammit," Ortiz muttered, adjusting his grip on the wheel. "You see her fight? She nearly broke my nose."

Ramón didn't reply.

He was already thinking ahead — what would Cruz say? Would she care that he hadn't killed the others? Would she reprimand him for letting Isla see them before the grab?

He didn't think so. Not now.

The men were compromised. They would go to the cops — of course they would. And if they did, the Syndicate's allies in the precinct would step in. Detain them, question them. Perhaps even hand them over.

And if they didn't? Well, now the Syndicate had leverage.

Ramón turned in his seat, watching Isla's unconscious form in the dim red glow of the taillights.

What do you know? he thought.

And how much are you going to tell us when you wake up?

CHAPTER 52

RAMÓN

THE TRUCK BUCKED over a washout in the gravel road, throwing Ramón's hand against the window frame. He barely registered the pain. His gaze stayed fixed on the dark swath of jungle behind them, his thoughts locked in a loop, churning like the storm overhead.

Raindrops beat the cab's roof in rapid-fire bursts, a staccato rhythm that mirrored the blood in his veins. Lightning flared again, white-hot and sudden, illuminating the massive leaves and drooping vines crowding the roadside like walls closing in. The jungle felt alive, breathing around them, bearing silent witness to what they'd just done.

He turned slightly, stealing a glance at Isla Torres.

She slumped unconscious in the rear seat between Lopez and Castellanos. Her head lolled against the window, one cheek pressed to the cold glass. Her braid, soaked through, stuck to her collarbone, and her hands were bound tight with zip ties at the wrists. Lopez had looped a length of paracord around her waist, tethering her to the center seatbelt.

Good. She wouldn't be able to run, even if she came to. Not right away.

Ramón stared at her for a few long seconds, taking in the bruised line across her temple where she'd hit the porch railing in the scuffle. Her legs were smeared with mud, one sandal missing. She looked small, even fragile.

But he knew better.

He'd seen it in her eyes before they'd closed: fury, not fear.

This one's not just a local dive guide, he thought. *She knows more than she let on. A hell of a lot more.*

Still, her scream had changed everything. The plan — Cruz's loosely framed directive to "fix it" — had always meant execution. Clean and clinical. The two men, the woman, Isla — all of them silenced.

But Isla had wandered outside. Her mistake. Or maybe fate's nudge.

She'd exposed herself. And that had given Ramón an opportunity.

They didn't have to go in, guns blazing. Didn't have to risk killing a woman with local ties and a face half the town recognized. That kind of noise brought attention. Journalists. Law enforcement not on their payroll. Tourists sniffing around. And worse: whispers. Rumors. Stories.

Cruz hated stories.

So no, the abduction had been the smarter move in the moment. Less blood. More options.

But still...

"We should have finished it," he muttered.

Ortiz glanced at him. "What?"

Ramón didn't answer. He pressed two fingers to his radio earpiece and spoke low into the encrypted channel. "Marquez, this is Sierra-Two. Confirm fallback site is ready for secure hold. ETA ten minutes."

Static, then a reply. *"Copy. Entry clear. No tails. You... bringing in just her?"*

Ramón's jaw ticked. "Affirmative."

Another pause.

"Understood. No visual markers outside. We'll be waiting."

Ramón let go of the mic and looked back out the window. The road curved left, climbing into a ridge, the truck's engine groaning as it powered through muddy incline.

He felt Ortiz studying him again.

"What?" Ramón finally said.

Ortiz hesitated. "You think Cruz is going to be okay with this? Leaving the gringos alive?"

Ramón's lips thinned. He didn't answer immediately.

"They were out of reach," he said eventually. "Inside. Lights on. We had seconds."

"But we had eyes on them, didn't we?"

"We had a woman screaming on the porch and a thunderstorm lighting up the sky like a prison yard. You want to shoot through windows? Start a gunfight in front of a witness? In front of the farmer? Maybe his kids? Besides, I'm starting to think these gringos are trained. Ex-military. I don't know."

Ortiz said nothing.

Ramón continued. "They could have been waiting for us, expecting us to come for them. Perhaps even used the woman as bait."

At this, Ortiz nodded. "Then we made the right call. Get in, get out, make them chase us."

Ramón looked back again at their kidnapping victim. Still out. Rain streaked down the window behind her like tears. He turned back, focusing on the road.

A few minutes later, Castellanos shifted in the back seat, muttering something under his breath. Lopez elbowed him and grunted. "She's coming to."

Ramón turned in his seat again.

Isla stirred, her shoulders shifting. She mumbled something, brow creasing as she blinked herself toward consciousness.

Lopez reached into his vest and pulled out a damp cloth, wadding it in his hand in case she tried to scream again. Castellanos angled slightly, free hand resting on the handle of his sidearm.

Isla's head rolled. She blinked again, this time managing to focus. Her eyes locked on Ramón. Then on Lopez. Her jaw clenched.

She didn't speak, but the hatred in her stare was unmistakable.

"Welcome back," Ramón said, his voice dry.

She shifted, trying to sit up straighter, but the paracord held her tight. Her eyes narrowed.

"Where...?" she rasped.

Ramón shook his head. "No questions. Not yet."

Isla spat a wad of blood onto the floor mat. "You picked the wrong people to mess with."

Ramón raised an eyebrow. "That right?"

"You don't know who they are — Ben, Reggie. What you've done... you're not just poking at tourists."

"We know *exactly* who they are," Ramón lied, hoping his show of confidence would invite her to tell him more about these two men. "And if they're dumb enough to come after you, they'll meet the same fate."

She didn't answer. Just glared. Her knuckles whitened where her hands were bound.

A moment later, the truck crested the ridge. Ahead, a narrow road veered off the main track, nearly swallowed by palm fronds. Ortiz slowed and eased into the overgrown path. Ramón leaned forward, checking for markers in the dark.

Two small stones, stacked just beside a fallen tree trunk — barely visible, even in the headlights.

"There," he said.

The truck crawled forward, tires crunching over loose gravel. The foliage thickened, branches scraping the windows as they moved deeper into the hidden trail.

Then the cave mouth appeared — barely a wound in the hillside, ringed by jagged rock and a rusted piece of corrugated metal acting as a crude awning.

Two men stepped out of the shadows.

Marquez and Salas. Two men he'd worked with only a few times. They were newer recruits, zealots for the cause and dedicated to winning Cruz' favor. To Ramón, men like them were often useful cannon fodder, crazed fools who would happily run into to a firefight with the hopes of earning respect and reward from their queen.

But Ramón tried to keep his distance. Of the two small mercenary units Cruz employed as protection, and the dozen or so local thugs like Marquez and Salas she kept loyal by tossing a few scraps their way, the

Syndicate was more like a small-time gang that had found luck in recent endeavors. Cruz acted like her organization was the largest blackmarket operation on the planet, but in truth it was just a well-funded, well-resourced club of misfits bound together by a somehow charismatic matriarch.

Ramón was making great money, but he would be glad when this little tour was over. He'd take the operation bonus, thank Cruz through gritted teeth, and move on. He was a journeyman, a merc-for-hire with a skillset that would keep him employed until he was no longer functional, and there were plenty of Cruz-like gang operators around the globe.

But first, he had to play nice with these blackmarket arms dealer cosplayers.

Marquez wore a rain-slick poncho, his rifle slung over one shoulder. He raised a hand, then dropped it quickly once he saw Isla in the back seat.

"About damn time," he muttered as they parked. "Thought you'd bring more bodies."

Ramón opened the passenger door and stepped into the rain. "Open the hatch."

Salas jogged toward the metal sheet covering the cave. In direct sunlight, the metal would reflect, becoming a beacon. But covered in foliage, rusted, and hidden from view from the road, it was almost impossible to see, even when looking directly at it.

Salas unlocked the sheet metal's padlock and swung the thin door open, revealing the cave behind it.

Cruz really loves her caves, Ramón thought. He hadn't been here before, but he knew Cruz kept places like this around the islands, staffing them only when necessary with the same sort of low-level employees as Salas and Marquez.

Inside, the cave was dry, the air smelling of stone, salt, and metal. The power generator hummed in the distance, casting a faint vibration through the rock.

He turned back to the truck.

"Bring her."

Lopez and Castellanos climbed out and yanked Isla with them. She twisted, fought, tried to throw an elbow again. They were lucky she wasn't still fully lucid or they might have to knock her out again. Castellanos muttered a curse and shoved her forward. She stumbled but didn't fall.

Marquez raised an eyebrow. "And this was smarter than just dropping her and two others?"

"She's leverage," Ramón said. "She'll be the key to getting the other two."

He meant it. But it still tasted like rationalization.

CHAPTER 53

BEN

A ROLL of distant thunder broke the hush as Harvey Bennett stood on the deck of *El Rescate*, a small fishing trawler Manny had procured for them under the radar. The boat rocked gently in the black water, which extended in every direction like a void. Clouds blotted out the moon, rendering the night impossibly dark. Even the stars were hidden, leaving only the faint glow of the boat's navigation lights. Ben's stomach churned with anticipation, a cold dread creeping into his bones despite the warm Caribbean breeze.

We shouldn't be out here again, he thought, gazing down toward the invisible reef. *Not in the middle of the night.* Yet here they were, anchored near *El Cementerio de los Contrabandistas* once more. This time, Manny wasn't with them — he'd stayed behind to coordinate possible backup or an escape route. Tonight, it was just Ben, Reggie, and a single deckhand Manny had arranged, a quiet local man named Rodrigo who kept mostly to himself.

Of course, they were missing one crucial ally: Isla Torres. She'd been kidnapped hours ago, right from under their noses.

At the 'safe' house, Ben scoffed.

Then came the message. They'd somehow gotten Reggie's phone number — not a difficult task, considering the corrupt state of affairs on the island. Easy enough to do, since Reggie had had to leave a working number when they'd checked in at the beach house, as well as when they'd first landed on the shores of Culebra. They had come here as tourists, expecting a break from this sort of thing.

Now, they were in it, and the message Reggie had gotten from the Black Coral Syndicate confirmed.

We have the girl. Meet us at 0900 or she dies.

There were coordinates underneath, which Reggie had discovered led to one of the innumerable tiny, rocky islands near Culebra.

Neither man could sleep, and neither wanted to try. They'd contacted Manny immediately after, planning to set sail as early as possible after midnight.

Manny had tried persuading them otherwise — they would be ocean-bound under the worst possible conditions. *A moonless night, a reef full of hidden shoals, and Syndicate mercenaries waiting in the shadows.*

But there was no turning back now. Ben and Reggie were convinced that the best way forward was to continue down the same path they'd decided upon with Isla and Manny the night before: they'd head to the reef, looking for the famed wreck.

Only this time, rather than looking for mere *proof*, they were looking for a bargaining chip.

If they found something valuable, they might be able to trade it with the Syndicate for Isla's life. It was a long shot, but it was their *only* shot. Far better than showing up empty-handed and hoping the Syndicate had mercy.

Reggie, standing at Ben's side, finished checking over their gear: oxygen tanks, wetsuits, flashlights, spear guns.

And *real* guns. Nothing crazy — Manny couldn't get them fully outfitted in so little time, so they each had a pistol from his own collection. Both were Glocks, to their pleasant surprise, and he'd given them enough 9mm rounds to start a small war.

Still, the Syndicate was packing a lot more heat — the last thing Ben wanted was to get into an open firefight against a team of bloodthirsty mercenaries who had the range and firepower advantage against two guys with handguns.

"All set," he said, voice grim. The usual excitement that flickered in Reggie's eyes before an adrenaline-fueled operation was dulled now. "We go in with *something* that will convince them we have leverage. Then we exchange it for Isla."

Simple.

Ben exhaled, glancing at the lumps of diving equipment that looked sinister in the red glow of the boat's night-lights. "Still, we have to assume they'll be expecting this. If they're smart, they won't just wait around at those coordinates, hoping we'll show up to plead for Isla's life. They're probably waiting to ambush us at the reef the moment we dive. We're playing right into their hands."

Reggie nodded slowly. "Yeah. But do we have a choice? Isla's life is on the line. We can't trust the cops, and —" he paused a moment —"I'm still not sure we can trust Manny."

Ben sighed. This was what he had been worried about as well. It was true that the island of Culebra was small, word got around quickly, and the Syndicate mercenaries could have just followed them to the safe house.

But it was *also* true that Manny could have just led the Syndicate right to their doorstep. He had admitted to them that he'd given an artifact — a trinket, as he'd called it — to them once before.

Has he been working with them this whole time?

Still, Ben wasn't sure they had another play. If they tried to call the Syndicate's bluff and simply wait them out, he was sure Isla would die. If they tried to get the authorities involved, they might be setting themselves up for an even larger and more intricate trap.

He shifted his weight, checking the water's surface. *El Rescate* was drifting quietly, engine idling at minimal throttle. The deckhand, Rodrigo, lurked near the helm, occasionally glancing at them with worried eyes.

Lightning flickered far away, illuminating jagged clouds on the horizon. Ben's pulse hammered. "All right," he said, forcing steel into his voice. "We go down. We find anything we can lift, bring it up as proof. Then we figure out how to trade it for Isla."

Reggie's jaw tightened. "And pray we live long enough for that trade."

Pray indeed, Ben thought, and goosebumps prickled his arms.

"All right," Ben muttered, stepping to the small bench where their dive bags waited. "Let's suit up."

Fifteen minutes later, they were poised at the trawler's stern, fully geared. Rodrigo offered them a wan smile, face drawn in the faint glow of the boat's running lights. "Suerte," he said quietly, stepping back.

Ben pulled on his dive mask, adjusting the straps and exhaling a few test breaths through the regulator. Reggie tested his flashlight, the beam slicing through the darkness to reveal only the boat's railing and swirling sea mist. Then he nodded at Ben.

Ben clenched his fists, stepping to the edge of the deck. *Here goes everything.* "Okay," he breathed. "On three... "

They counted silently and dropped over the side, plunging into the water with muffled splashes. The ocean closed around Ben like a damp shroud, its temperature eerily warm against his skin. He took a moment to orient himself, inhaling steadily through his regulator. *It's so dark.* Beneath the surface, any lingering glow from the boat vanished. The blackness was near-total, broken only by the narrow beams of their flashlights.

Reggie tapped his shoulder, gesturing forward. They'd agreed to anchor just outside the reef's perimeter, in deeper water, to try to avoid alerting any watchers. Rodrigo had run without any lights, and they'd done all they could to ease toward the reef quietly.

Now they had to swim the rest of the way toward the labyrinth of wrecks. *At least the sea is calmer this morning,* Ben consoled himself, though a faint current tugged at them.

Together, they kicked into motion, flashlights bobbing like ghostly wands in the void. Almost immediately, the environment shifted from an open undersea plane to a chaotic maze of coral outcroppings and submerged debris.

If the Syndicate's waiting for us, they could be anywhere. Far from the open-ocean, flat underwater plains they'd swam above to get here, the reef was a near-solid wall of sharp, craggy spires. It was like moving over an expansive desert toward an urban metropolis. Skyscrapers of coral jutting up and out, in every direction.

Plenty of places for the Syndicate to hide.

An underwater firefight — just what we need.

They pressed on, trying to maintain stealth. Reggie occasionally flicked off his flashlight to minimize detection, using Ben's beam to navigate. Drifting lumps came into focus: the broken hull of a modern speedboat, half-submerged in silt and already mostly consumed by pops of bright-pink coral; a cluster of barrels or crates from who-knew-what illicit cargo. Each shape seemed to loom out of the darkness like a predator waiting to strike.

Stay calm. Ben's breath rasped in his ears, echoing inside the mask. The rhythmic hiss of his regulator was the only constant. He wasn't afraid of diving, per se, but he wasn't terribly experienced at it. Reggie had done it plenty of times before, and he tried to borrow his friend's confidence as they swam.

Focus on the objective. Manny had indicated that the Syndicate believed the real treasures would be hidden in the deeper portion of the wreck — the part that couldn't be easily salvaged. Whatever had been loose in the hull as the ship had gone down would have tumbled deeper, and the constant barrage of current pressing it deeper into the sand meant that the wreck's biggest secrets wouldn't be an easy find.

That meant descending into the labyrinth's darkest recesses, toward the half-exposed wooden hull that might be pre-Columbian or older, and going inside.

They swam deeper still, using the reef's contours to shield them from possible watchers above. The water around them glowed faintly in places with bioluminescent plankton, swirling in eddies whenever they moved. It gave the impression of luminous dust motes in a pitch-black tunnel, disorienting yet mesmerizing.

Beautiful, if not for how terrifying it is.

CHAPTER 54

RAMÓN

THE CAVE SMELLED like wet dog and rusted metal.

Ramón sat on the edge of the folding cot shoved into the back corner, knees spread wide, elbows on thighs. His rifle was propped against the wall beside him, but he didn't feel any safer for it. The cave's ceiling dripped occasionally, fat droplets plinking into a rusted tin bucket someone had forgotten to empty days ago. The entire place had the energy of a halfway house for ghosts and gunrunners. Maybe it was both.

Across the open cavern, Marquez and Salas were still arguing. Whispering, technically — but in that aggressive way men do when they're trying not to raise voices while also clearly attempting to dominate a conversation.

Ramón didn't care what it was about. Probably something idiotic. Whether or not they should have gagged Isla. How to split their next payment. Whose turn it was to handle the generator fuel run. Shit that didn't matter.

He leaned back against the damp stone wall, trying to will his body to rest, to maybe catch an hour or two before the next round of chaos. But his thoughts wouldn't stop spiraling. The jungle had soaked into his clothes, his skin, his mind. He could still smell the rain, still feel the rush of adrenaline when Isla screamed.

He should have killed all three of them.

He knew it.

He could dress it up however she wanted — leverage, discretion, public scrutiny — but at the end of the day, live witnesses were dangerous. Especially ones like those two gringos. They didn't flinch. They didn't freeze. And now they were pissed, and had reason to be on edge.

"You hear me?" Salas asked suddenly, his voice cutting through the cavern.

Ramón opened one eye.

"I'm not your supervisor," he muttered. "You want to complain, call HR."

Salas snorted and went back to his whispered rant with Marquez.

He waited another fifteen minutes, finally finding respite from the two thugs' incessant arguing, but one of them soon began snoring — loudly, too. He groaned, turning onto his side, knowing he would be fine but wishing for just a bit of shut-eye.

An hour flew by with no sleep. Near the front of the cave, the makeshift steel door groaned against its hinges as the wind howled outside. The storm hadn't fully passed — just taken a breath. Lightning flickered somewhere out at sea, throwing long shadows across the cave floor. In that brief light, Ramón could just make out Castellanos sitting by the interior wall, arms crossed, chin dipped toward his chest.

He was on shift. Watching Isla.

Or supposed to be.

Ramón tilted his head to get a better view.

The candle near the back was still burning low, but it wasn't much — just a dull orange glow that danced on the walls. He squinted.

The cot beside Castellanos was empty.

His blood turned cold.

He sat up straighter, every sense suddenly sharpened. That shadow — had it just moved? Or was it a trick of the candlelight?

Ramón reached slowly for his sidearm.

Another gust of wind howled down the corridor, rattling the old steel at the cave's mouth. The candle guttered and threatened to go out.

Ramón rose silently and crossed the cave in three strides. Castellanos didn't move. The dumb bastard was asleep, chin slumped to chest, breathing through his mouth like a kid with a stuffy nose.

Ramón grabbed his shirt and yanked him upright. "Where is she?"

Castellanos blinked, confused and groggy. "What — ?"

Ramón shoved him aside and rounded the small outcropping where the prisoner cot had been set up. Nothing.

No Isla.

No rope. No zip ties.

Gone.

"*Damnit!*" he barked, spinning back toward the others. "She's gone!"

Castellanos scrambled to his feet, panic now surging into his face.

"What the hell do you mean she's *gone*?" Salas shouted, already reaching for his weapon.

Marquez was next to him, ducking around an overturned crate. "Where did she — ?"

Ramón raised a hand for silence.

A distant sound. Outside.

A click. Then a low, sputtering cough. *An engine.*

Ramón's eyes widened.

"She's taking the truck."

He didn't wait. He sprinted back toward his cot, grabbing his rifle and then diving for his pack, shoving gear out of the way in the dim light, hands scrambling for his sidearm, his flashlight, his keys.

Outside, the sputtering engine turned over, once, twice —

Then caught.

"Move!" Ramón yelled. "She's taking the damn truck!"

They poured out of the cave like hornets from a kicked nest. Ramón was first through the rusted steel door, rifle slung, flashlight in hand. The jungle roared with wind and leftover rain, palm fronds whipping wildly in the dark.

Down the muddy track, he caught the flash of brake lights — red eyes in the darkness.

Then taillights flaring as the truck bounced once over a rut in the trail and accelerated.

"Shit!"

He raised the rifle, sighting along the rail.

Too far. Too much cover.

And no clean shot — he'd risk killing her.

Not that he cared about her safety — but he needed her now. She was leverage, and that leverage was only good to them if it were *alive*.

He lowered the rifle, breathing hard.

Marquez appeared beside him, panting. "What now?"

Salas swore under his breath. "We let her go?"

"No," Ramón said.

He turned slowly, mind already adjusting, recalibrating.

"She'll go to them," he said. "That was the whole point. She's going to lead us right to the gringos."

Marquez frowned. "But we already know where they are."

"No," Ramón snapped. "We know where they *were*. But they're not going to stay in that farmhouse, not after what happened. But she knows where they'll go next. She knows what they'll be doing."

Castellanos growled. "You sent them a message already — meet at 0900. You think that will change?"

Ramón shook his head.

"No. They'll meet. I'm confident of that. But now we have an opportunity to find out what they're planning *before* they meet up later. So we let her run, but we stay close. We'll track her every move. And when she leads them to wherever they're headed next, we cut them off."

The others exchanged glances.

Marquez said, "Cruz is going to want an update."

"She'll get one," Ramón said. "*After* we have all three of them hogtied in the back of that truck."

Then, under his breath, as he turned back to the jungle:

"Or dead."

CHAPTER 55

BEN

A METALLIC CLANG STARTLED BEN. He spun, flashlight flaring. Reggie's eyes shone wide behind his mask. They scanned the gloom — no sign of an attacker. Possibly a piece of debris knocked loose by a fish, or maybe the subtle shifting of a sunken hull. *Or a Syndicate diver.* The sense of claustrophobia soared, the dark pressing in from all angles.

They advanced cautiously, shining lights across twisted beams and rusted railings. Ben recognized the remains of the same modern boat they'd seen days before — where they'd found the broken tank and dive belt.

They could be watching us right now.

Reggie pointed downward, urging them deeper. Ben nodded, exhaling a shaky bubble. The silence down here was immense, each bubble roar feeling like a klaxon in a library. They kicked downward along a coral-encrusted slope. At the edge of their flashlight beams, a massive shape loomed — a series of old timbers partially buried in sand. *This must be it.* The ancient wreck Manny claimed was older than anything else in the Caribbean.

Reggie signaled him to circle around. They parted slightly, scanning for signs of an artifact. The hull was covered in thick growth, patches of algae and coral forming bizarre patterns. As Ben swept his beam across a particularly overgrown section, the water seemed to swirl ominously.

And then he felt it — a sudden chill enveloping him. Despite the warm sea, goosebumps rose on his skin. *What the... ?* He held his breath, shining the flashlight deeper into a gap between two broken timbers. The darkness within was absolute, like a wound in the seafloor.

It's so cold here, he realized, an irrational prickle of fear slithering down his spine.

Ben held himself still, floating in the water column above the sand-swept remains of the ancient wreck. His breath rasped loudly inside his mask, each exhale a tremble of silver bubbles ascending toward the dim surface. The water here, deeper than the reef shelf they'd crossed earlier, pressed in around him like a second skin — thicker, darker, and somehow expectant.

This wasn't just the cold of depth or shadow. It felt older than that, as if the water had memory — one it didn't like to share.

He turned slowly in place, sweeping his flashlight across the broken hull beneath him. The beam revealed more of the warped and buried remains of what must have once been a formidable vessel. Wooden ribs jutted from the silt like skeletal fingers, draped in a shroud of sea growth. Coral had colonized everything. In places, it looked less like wreckage and more like part of the reef itself.

A startled fish darted past, vanishing into a crevice. Something shifted in Ben's gut.

We're not supposed to be here.

He kicked downward, careful not to stir too much silt. That was easy to do at a site this old — one fin stroke and visibility would vanish in a muddy cloud. They'd come here looking for evidence — just that. Proof that this submerged graveyard of ships held more than just colonial-era wrecks. The fisherman had mentioned something ancient, something that predated the Spanish.

Something that was, hopefully, valuable enough to exchange for a human life.

So far, all Ben could see were planks and rot. The real history was buried under centuries of detritus, and they had no map, no markings, no guide. Only rumor.

Reggie appeared on his right flank, illuminating the edge of a partially collapsed deck structure. It looked like it had once been a cabin or hold. His beam caught something — what looked like a length of weathered rope, but upon closer inspection, had the faint square pattern of carved fiber. Maybe a woven cord? Ancient fishing gear? He pointed, and Ben nodded, taking mental note. Nothing definitive, but odd.

He swam a little farther around the wreck's perimeter, careful to keep the wreckage within sight. The gloom thickened to his left — something massive loomed there, part of the original hull, now coated in shadow. He followed its edge.

His hand brushed a carved beam. Not just shaped by tools — etched. He stopped.

Holding the flashlight steady, he traced the faint grooves in the water-worn timber. It was covered in shallow spiral patterns, like concentric waves or suns — each about the size of a hand. Glyphs? Decoration?

He'd seen pictures of Taíno petroglyphs carved into stones at ceremonial sites back in mainland Puerto Rico. These looked similar — but more flowing. More... purposeful.

Ben angled his body lower, running the light along the entire beam. The pattern repeated at irregular intervals, some glyphs clearer than others, as if whoever carved them had run out of time or strength. The edges of the plank were scorched, oddly enough. Fire? Before it sank?

His breath caught.

Whatever this was, it definitely wasn't Spanish.

Another few feet ahead, half-buried in sand, rested something smooth and rounded. He hesitated. Moved closer.

It was a bowl — he was almost certain of it. Made of something dark and porous, like volcanic rock, with scalloped edges. He swept the silt away gently with a gloved hand, revealing more. A crude design along the lip. Spirals again. He took a breath.

This wasn't the ornate cargo of a European trade ship. This was something native. Pre-contact.

He flashed his light back toward Reggie and gestured, trying to signal what he'd found. But Reggie had already moved on, deeper into the wreck.

Ben followed.

The wreckage deepened here, the ribs of the ship arching like cathedral supports above him. He ducked under one and paused.

Here, the seabed had a slight drop — just a few feet — but enough to form a basin in the sand. Detritus had collected here: broken wood, a half-collapsed mast, something that looked like a shattered barrel. Ben was about to turn away when he saw it.

Bones.

Not fish, not turtle — human. Unmistakably.

At least, what looked like a section of rib cage and spine, now laced with marine growth. It could have been anything, centuries old and jumbled in with the debris. But it was placed oddly — curled, fetal. *Purposeful.*

A burial?

He felt a chill entirely separate from the cold water.

Movement above. Reggie, looping around from the other side.

Ben flicked his light up and caught his attention, pointing down at the bones. Reggie hesitated, then dropped lower, cautious.

As Reggie drifted closer, Ben turned to scan the surrounding debris once more. Coral. Planks. The broken mast. A shimmer in the silt.

He moved toward it. Something cylindrical protruded slightly from the sand. Not natural. Not wood.

Stone?

He angled the beam and brushed the silt away slowly.

A curve emerged, then a ridge. Patterns. Glyphs.

Something statue-like.

That's when Reggie's beam cut across from the opposite side.

He waved for Ben's attention, pointing to a shape half-buried in the silt. It looked like a carved stone pillar or statue — something cylindrical, but with protrusions suggesting arms or a face.

Ben's scalp prickled.

He swam closer.

CHAPTER 56

RAMÓN

RAMÓN STOOD ankle-deep in the mud, arms crossed as he stared at the truck.

It was theirs — no question. Parked haphazardly in a shallow pull-off on the overgrown path just off the main road, the front wheels angled as if they'd swerved at the last second. No damage. No signs of a struggle. But the driver's door was hanging open, and the engine was stone cold. She'd been gone a while.

He walked slowly around the truck, eyes scanning the jungle fringe beyond. Mosquitos buzzed in thick clouds, and the beginnings of morning mist was already starting to cling to the canopy. The sun wouldn't be up for a while, but already birds chattered overhead.

"Clear," Salas called, stepping back from the treeline, rifle slung. "No tracks, but the ground's too soaked. Could have gone anywhere."

Marquez crouched beside the truck's front tire, tapping the hood. "Still warm?"

Ramón shook his head. "Long gone."

He moved to the passenger side and yanked the door open. The glove box had been rifled through. A water bottle still laying in the footwell. Muddy footprints on the floor mats — smaller than theirs. He squatted and examined one closely.

"Someone else was with her."

"Another pickup?" Salas asked.

"Maybe. Maybe not." Ramón stood, wiping his hand on his pants. "The timing doesn't make sense. This isn't where we lost her."

Lopez stepped around the truck, squinting toward the narrow road beyond. "You thinking she met up with someone?"

Ramón didn't answer at first. He stepped past them and followed the line of the road a few paces north. It curved along the edge of a mangrove cluster before dipping again toward the coast. A smattering of footprints — some fresh, some not — dotted the muddy shoulder. But it was the generator hum that drew his attention.

He paused, listening.

"That sound," he said, nodding toward the trees. "Someone's nearby."

Marquez joined him, tilting his head.

The group moved together, quiet now. They followed the sound through a thin break in the trees until the outline of a small structure emerged — half lean-to, half shack. A tin roof sagged over the porch, and ropes hung from hooks driven into the eaves. Nets. Dive gear. Buckets.

"Manny Delgado," Lopez muttered.

Ramón raised a brow. "That old fisherman?"

"Lives alone not far from here, but I think he also owns this little shack and the dock. Deals in gear for dive outfits, mostly. Keeps to himself. Apparently deals in antiquities every now and then, too."

Ramón's ears perked up.

"Yeah, he sold something to the Syndicate a while ago. Didn't end well for his partner, I'm told. I think he's had a bone to pick with us ever since."

Ramón crouched at the edge of the trees. From this angle, he could see the rear of the shack — an old panga boat bobbed gently against a rickety wooden dock on the water, tethered with a frayed rope. The opposite slip was empty, but there were telltale signs that it had recently been evacuated.

He scanned the scene, noticing the buoy gently smacking against the dock. He confirmed — a line was hanging over the edge of the dock, not touching the water, but still dripping. A second line had been haphazardly tossed onto the dock.

"His boat," Ramón said. "That's why the truck's here. She drove to Manny, asked for help."

"You think he did?" Salas asked. "He might have before, too. Could have been their hookup for that safe house place you nabbed her at."

Ramón didn't answer. Instead, he stood and walked forward, boots squelching in the muck. He reached the dock and knelt, brushing his fingers along the edge of the rope.

Lopez grunted. "So she's out on the water now. Great."

Ramón stared out toward the horizon. Clouds loomed low, dark and fast-moving — remnants of last night's storm still prowling the sky.

"But we know where she's heading," he said flatly. "She'll be heading for the reef. That's where she'll find the other two."

Lopez glanced toward the shack. "You want me to check inside?"

"No time. He helped Isla, either way. And we'll pay him a visit later."

CHAPTER 57

BEN

BEN HOVERED inches above the sand, the carved surface of the idol emerging slowly under his gloved fingertips. It wasn't just decorative — this thing had been shaped with intent. The spirals and ridges gave way to faint humanoid features: a flattened face with hollowed sockets, arms pulled in close to the torso, and faint geometric symbols incised into the sides.

Not Spanish. Not African. Something older.

He turned his head toward Reggie, who had drifted closer now, his flashlight playing over the same form. Reggie's expression behind the mask was unreadable, but he didn't move to touch it. Just stared.

Ben flicked his wrist in a quick signal — *you see this?*

Reggie gave a slow nod. Then he pointed behind him, toward a section of the wreck they hadn't explored. A broad gesture: *Keep looking.*

Ben hesitated, then gave a small *okay*, and let the idol be. For now.

They fanned out again, the beams of their lights dancing through the darkness like ghostly fingers. A low rumble pulsed through the water — distant thunder, muted by the sea but still distinct. *Storm's still building,* Ben thought. *We don't have much time.*

Above them, the last traces of surface light had vanished into deep blue. Even at this depth, the occasional flicker of lightning from the surface bled through, like veins of silver cracking the water. It was eerie and disorienting, and beautiful in a way that made Ben's gut clench.

A cloud of tiny fish parted as he drifted into a new chamber formed by collapsed timbers. Reggie had gone silent again, somewhere to the left. This part of the wreck was more intact. The beams were charred on one side — scorch marks frozen in time, now blackened and calcified. There were signs of fire here, sure, but what kind of ship burned and didn't sink until later?

Ben's light landed on what looked like a piece of pottery, wedged between two crossbeams. A bowl or jar, half-shattered, rim etched with those same swirling motifs. Nearby, a slat of wood bore a line of carvings — shallow, hand-cut marks that ran horizontally like a sentence in a language no one spoke anymore.

He swept closer. There was something... *ritualistic* about the whole scene. Not just debris, not the random chaos of shipwreck. These items felt placed. Even though the ship had gone down and things were in disarray, the shifting sands and coral life strewing things about, everything remaining had an oddly proper quality to it.

Behind him, Reggie let out a short, sharp grunt of air — half a shout, half a gasp, warped by the regulator. Ben turned sharply and swam toward him.

Reggie hovered near the stern. He'd found what looked like a once-sealed compartment — barely large enough for one man. Inside, behind a collapsed wall of ribs and coral-crusted beams, sat an array of objects: woven fiber, a small pile of polished stones, and a carved mask, resting upright as though watching them.

Ben's breath caught.

The mask was different — elongated, with a prominent brow and deeply grooved lines trailing from the eyes like tears. Around it, small objects sat arranged in a loose ring. Offerings? Tools? None of them looked European.

He motioned to Reggie. *We have to get this documented,* he thought, uselessly, then shook his head. There was nothing they could do but choose what to bring home. They had no camera, no equipment. And he couldn't exactly pull a pencil and piece of paper out of his dive suit and draw a picture to commemorate the moment.

Reggie nodded anyway, as if understanding. Ben hovered, scanning the compartment.

Something about this space — this wasn't cargo. It was a shrine.

Or a grave.

More thunder rolled overhead, deeper now. Louder, punctuating through the water even at this depth.

Ben's mind drifted back to Isla, still missing, still in danger. The weight of it thudded in his chest like a heartbeat. They'd come here hoping to trade something ancient for something irreplaceable. And now, staring at the mask and the stone idol behind them, he finally felt the weight of that exchange.

We're grave robbing, he thought bitterly. *That's what this is.*

But what choice do we have?

By not pillaging this grave, they would be digging Isla's.

The mask would be interesting, but he wasn't sure if there was monetary worth to it. He swam back toward the idol. Reggie followed without needing a signal. They hovered together, just above the sand, staring down at the carved stone figure.

Ben didn't want to be the one to move first.

Reggie did.

He reached down and placed both hands around the idol's midsection, feeling for a grip. A swirl of silt rose, obscuring the lower half of the figure. The thing was heavier than it looked. Reggie strained, shifting its weight to one side. The sand sucked at it, reluctant to release.

Ben moved in and helped, bracing from the other side. Together, they pried it loose, inch by inch. When it came free, it did so with a soft thunk, like a bone pulled from wet clay.

The water around them immediately darkened as the disturbed silt ballooned upward.

Ben clutched the idol to his chest. Even through his gloves, the stone felt cold, almost slick with something that wasn't just water. He tried not to think about it.

Reggie made a signal — ascend. They had what they came for.

Ben nodded, adjusting his grip on the artifact. He kicked upward, cutting through the silt cloud like smoke, the wreck fading beneath him.

The lightning above had grown more frequent now — every few seconds a bright flare lit the upper water column, throwing strange shadows across the reef.

As they broke into open water, the wreck beneath them disappeared into the murk. The sea felt bigger now, vaster — and less welcoming.

Reggie kept glancing behind them, checking for movement. Syndicate divers hadn't shown themselves yet, but that didn't mean they weren't watching. Or waiting.

Ben clutched the idol tighter.

This better be worth it.

CHAPTER 58

BEN

BEN'S HEART hammered as he clutched the heavy idol, struggling to maintain buoyancy. The thing weighed more than he expected. He signaled Reggie: *Let's get out of here.* Reggie nodded vigorously.

Then, from the corner of his eye, Ben saw movement — shadows that didn't align with their own. He whirled, flashlight slicing the water, revealing murky outlines. Two, maybe three divers, hugging the reef's contours, advanced with purposeful stealth.

The Syndicate. His pulse skyrocketed. He tapped Reggie's shoulder, pointing. Reggie instantly raised the spear gun strapped to his vest, his expression behind the mask deadly serious. The nearest shadow froze, then darted behind a protruding chunk of wreckage.

A flurry of motion followed. The second diver lunged forward, brandishing what looked like an underwater firearm. Reggie fired his own spear, the projectile slicing through the water. The attacker twisted aside just in time, the spear glancing off the wreck with a metallic clink.

He imagined Reggie cursing behind his mask — the spear gun, while deadly, was slow to reload, and Reggie only had three rounds. Bubbles erupted from the Syndicate diver's gear as he triggered his own weapon. Ben watched muzzle flashes strobe in the water, muted pops that reverberated in his skull.

He yanked the idol close and kicked backward, heart pounding. Bullets or flechettes whizzed past, stirring up sediment. Reggie reloaded with shaking hands, eyes furious. *We have to get out.*

The idol's weight threatened to drag Ben down, but letting it go wasn't an option. *Isla's life depends on this thing,* he reminded himself, adrenaline surging.

Another muzzle flash lit the gloom. Reggie swerved, narrowly missing the far more powerful underwater rifle's round. The underwater corridor devolved into chaos — clouds of silt, flickering beams of light, muzzle bursts like ghostly fireworks. The reef transformed into a war zone.

Who fights underwater at night?

He glimpsed a third Syndicate diver emerging from behind a coral outcrop, heading straight for him. The diver brandished a long knife, apparently wanting to avoid shooting the idol. Apparently they'd already assessed what it was Ben was carrying, and decided it was something of value.

They want it intact. That gave Ben a sliver of advantage.

He kicked upward, hugging the idol to his chest. The diver lunged, slashing at his shoulder. Pain flashed as the tip of the blade nicked Ben's wetsuit, cutting shallowly.

No choice. Ben angled the idol as a makeshift shield, bracing it between them. The diver slammed into it, momentum stalled. With his free hand, Ben groped for the shorter diving knife strapped to his thigh. He yanked it free and slashed wildly. The diver jerked back, trailing a swirl of blood. But the diver wasn't finished — he kicked forward again, more cautious now.

Meanwhile, Reggie fired another spear at the diver with the gun. This time, a muffled grunt signaled a hit. Bubbles poured from the man's regulator as he clutched his side. Then he drifted, either wounded or stunned. The third diver seized the moment, darting in to help his comrade.

Reggie was near the spot where his first spear had landed, and he yanked it out of the sandy rise it had fallen into, then reloaded.

Ben's chest constricted. *We can't keep this up.* The idol was a dead weight in his arms, limiting his maneuverability. He tried signaling Reggie to retreat, but Reggie was busy reloading. Another bullet hissed overhead, narrowly missing them. The reef's corroded edges cast eerie shadows, flickering with each muzzle flash.

Gathering his courage, Ben kicked upward, deciding to break away from the wreck's deeper zone. If they could reach open water, maybe they could outrun or outmaneuver these divers. Clutching the idol, he ascended a few yards. Reggie followed, occasionally turning back and aiming with the spear gun to keep the Syndicate at bay.

The divers, however, seemed determined. The one with just a knife pursued, ignoring the blood seeping from his arm. Another emerged from behind a rusted hull, raising a short harpoon. The surprise strangled Ben's breath. *We can't handle so many.* Every sense was heightened, the darkness pressing in, the fear of drowning or being shot swirling in his mind.

Suddenly, a new burst of light flared from behind them — a second flashlight, shining with frantic motion. Ben's heart plummeted, expecting more reinforcements for the Syndicate. But as the figure drew closer, he realized it wasn't wearing the Syndicate's black gear. The beam angled onto the second attacker, and a loud pop reverberated. The attacker jerked, releasing a stream of bubbles, then sank out of sight. *What the — ?*

The newcomer's flashlight turned momentarily on Ben and Reggie, revealing glimpses of a familiar face behind the mask.

Isla.

Ben's chest constricted in relief and confusion. *How is she here?*

Isla gestured wildly, a sign for them to ascend now. Ben caught a fleeting glimpse of the fear in her eyes. *We can't stay here.*

Ben nodded, hauling the idol upward. Reggie exchanged a shocked look with him — Isla was alive, armed, and somehow assisting them.

The next thing he realized was even more of a surprise.

Isla wasn't alone.

CHAPTER 59

SARAH

SARAH DIDN'T EVEN GET a moment to breathe before Reggie turned and threw his arms around her, the wet thud of his dive gear pressing cold and sharp against her chest. He pulled back, eyes wide, saltwater dripping from his lashes.

"Sarah? What the hell... how — ?"

Ben was on the deck behind him, still clutching the stone idol to his chest like a life preserver. His face was pale, his eyes locked on her as if he was trying to confirm she was real. Isla, already at the helm, was wrenching her gear off with practiced haste, the muscles in her arms trembling with exertion. She didn't even look back.

"No time for a reunion," Isla barked. "We need to move. Now."

Sarah nodded and stepped around Reggie. "We're not alone out here."

"Yeah, we noticed," Ben said.

Isla didn't answer, but she shoved the throttle forward, and the boat jolted under their feet, lurching into motion. Waves slapped the hull, the sea angry and restless under the rising wind. Lightning flared in the distance — just enough to silhouette the black Zodiacs closing in from the edge of the reef.

"They're still nearby," Isla said tightly. "Their boats were to the southwest of yours. I think they were mid-dive when you showed up."

Reggie grunted. "We saw them underwater. Three of them at least."

"I counted four on the boat," Isla said. "Maybe more below. Doesn't matter now — hold on."

The boat surged forward, carving a sharp turn away from the reef. Spray kicked up in sheets, and Sarah grabbed the nearest rail, knuckles white. She didn't ask how Isla knew how to handle the boat — she just silently thanked whatever force of luck had put her in the driver's seat.

Ben sat beside the idol, arms wrapped around it, shivering.

Reggie turned back to Sarah, voice ragged. "Okay, seriously — how did you find us?"

Sarah's jaw clenched. "You left your phone on, dumbass."

Reggie blinked. "I what?"

"Location sharing," she said, brushing her soaked hair back. "Remember two weeks ago, you needed me to find your laptop at the gym?"

He stared. "You've been tracking me this whole time?"

"Yeah, up until now." She gave him a look. "You left it on your boat, and we sent your driver back already. But whatever — it paid off."

Ben was listening now, head tilted. "You came all the way here from Puerto Rico?"

"I was still in San Juan, finishing the conference," she said, nodding. "When I saw Reggie's phone ping from a beach near Culebra, I thought, no way. Not unless you suddenly took up surfing."

"I'm not a surfer," Reggie mumbled.

"No kidding. And based on our last conversation..." She paused. "I figured getting here sooner would be better."

Isla's voice cut through the reunion. "I was at Manny's already when she found me. I saw her pulling up and figured, what the hell — another person looking for you two."

Ben finally spoke. "Wait — how did you get away? Last time we saw you —"

"I was tied up in one of their spots up in the jungle," Isla said without turning. "They were on shifts, with one guy guarding me. He fell asleep. *I* didn't."

Sarah gave her a sideways glance. "How'd you get all the way to the docks?"

Isla just smiled — sharp and humorless. "I stole their truck."

Reggie blinked. "Their truck?"

"I didn't really have time to call an Uber," she said with a shrug. "Manny was on the way to prep his dive boat for another run. I caught him before he left his house."

Sarah leaned on the rail beside her. "So you just... grabbed gear and drove straight to the reef?"

"He keeps his boat ready to go. But I didn't even have a full plan," Isla admitted. "Just that I needed to find these two. I was hoping the Syndicate hadn't found you first." She paused, then looked Reggie up and down. She made a disgusted face.

Reggie scowled. "What's wrong?"

"Your wetsuit. It's neon green," Isla said. "You look like an avocado."

Ben let out a dry chuckle.

The tension eased slightly — but only slightly. Behind them, the ocean was still black and angry, though the sun was trying to poke out from the horizon. The Syndicate's Zodiacs were now mere pinpricks on the horizon, their searchlights struggling to pierce the darkness. But they weren't gone.

"How long until they catch up?" Sarah asked, her voice lower now.

Isla's hands gripped the wheel tighter. "Depends how bad they want that thing." She nodded toward the idol. "And I think they want it bad."

Ben still hadn't let go of it. The carved stone was slick with seawater and covered in strange glyphs. Every time Sarah's eyes skimmed it, she felt... unsettled. Like the shapes were wriggling slightly, like her brain was doing backflips trying to decode a language no one was ever meant to read.

"What is it?" she asked, more to herself than anyone.

Ben shook his head slowly. "If anyone can figure it out, it's you. But it was in the wreck. Deep. And they were down there with us. Armed."

"They definitely want it intact," Reggie added. "One of them came at us with a knife instead of shooting."

"Makes sense," Isla muttered. "No point in destroying what you came to steal."

The boat continued east, away from the reef, toward the open waters separating them from the island. Lightning flared again. The wind was picking up.

Sarah turned to Isla. "Do we have a plan?"

"Well, our plan *was* to use this thing to get Isla back," Reggie said. "Not sure if there needs to be a new plan now."

Isla exhaled through her nose. "Yeah. Get to shore. Lay low. And figure out what the hell we're going to do with that rock."

"I can hold onto it for a while," Reggie offered. "Give Ben a break."

Ben didn't answer at first. Then, slowly, he nodded and handed it off. Reggie cradled it like it was a chunk of uranium.

The boat sliced through the dark water. Behind them, the Syndicate's boats remained just visible. But Isla knew how to navigate the islands better than most, and she was already angling them through a natural barrier of rocks that would slow any pursuit.

"I'd like to pay these guys a visit," Reggie said finally. "We've got Isla back *and* a bargaining chip. We've been running from them all along. I think it's time we end this for good."

CHAPTER 60

BEN

THE FIRST RAYS of dawn painted the horizon in streaks of amber and blood-red. Ben squinted through the salt-crusted binoculars, tracking the distant shapes of three Syndicate boats cutting northwest through the morning chop. His hands were still shaking from the dive, and the constant spray of seawater made it hard to keep the lenses clean. But he couldn't afford to miss anything now.

The boats ahead were sleek black Zodiacs, their twin engines throwing up white roostertails as they carved through the water. Professional gear, military-grade — not the kind of thing you'd find at the local marina.

"They're moving fast," he said, lowering the binoculars to wipe them again. "Like they know exactly where they're going."

Isla leaned over the rail beside him, her wet hair plastered to her neck. She'd been scanning the coastline, marking features on a wrinkled chart spread across the deck. "They do. There's a place up the coast — locals talk about it in whispers. Hidden cove, carved right into the cliffs. Ex-military types started using it maybe fifteen years ago. Now it's... something else."

"Smugglers?" Sarah asked from her position near the stern. She hadn't taken her eyes off the idol since they'd loaded it aboard, watching it like it might sprout legs and crawl away. The stone seemed to drink in the dawn light, its carved surfaces throwing back strange reflections.

"Worse." Isla's mouth tightened, and she traced a line on the chart with one finger. "The kind of people who need somewhere to hide things that shouldn't exist. Things like what you just pulled up from that wreck."

Sarah sat behind the driver's seat, hands loosely gripping the setback. "So we're following them straight to their base? That's the plan? After barely getting away from them twice?"

"You got a better one?" Ben lowered the binoculars and turned to face him. "They've got resources, weapons, probably answers about that idol. Time to stop running and find out what we're really dealing with."

The morning sun caught Reggie's face, highlighting the fresh cuts and bruises from their underwater fight. He looked exhausted, but there was something else in his eyes now — a hardness that hadn't been there before the reef.

"Cut the engines," Reggie said suddenly, straightening up. "They're scanning. We need to drift."

Isla killed the power immediately. The boat's rumble died to silence, leaving only the slap of waves against the hull. They glided between two moss-draped islands, using the morning shadows for cover. The volcanic rock rose from the water like ancient sentinels, draped in thick jungle vegetation that hung almost to the waterline.

Ben raised the binoculars again, tracking the Syndicate boats through gaps in the island chain. Hundreds more rocky outcrops dotted the coastline ahead — a maze of stone and jungle perfect for staying invisible. Or perfect for an ambush.

"Keep them just in sight," he said. "But stay in the cover of these islands. We follow them home, then figure out our next move."

Sarah moved to stand beside him, her voice low. "And what exactly is our move once we find their base? We're not exactly equipped for a frontal assault."

"We'll figure something out," Ben said, but his tone wasn't convincing even to himself. "Right now we need intelligence. Layout, numbers, defenses. Then we can make a real plan."

"The cove should be up here somewhere." Isla pointed toward a section of coastline where the cliff face jutted out into the sea. "Natural formation, but they've modified it. Reinforced the walls, added docks, maybe more."

"How do you know all this?" Reggie asked, drifting them carefully behind another island.

"I hear things," Isla said flatly. "When you're in this part of the world, you learn which places to avoid. That cove's always at the top of the list."

The Syndicate boats maintained their heading, cutting through the morning swells with military precision. They were running in a loose triangle formation, the lead boat slightly ahead and to port. Professional. Trained.

Clearly the same guys who attacked us underwater, Ben thought.

Ben lowered the binoculars and rubbed his eyes. The adrenaline from the dive was wearing off, leaving him drained. But they couldn't rest — not yet. The idol sat wrapped in a towel near his feet, and he could swear he felt it humming, like a tuning fork struck against stone.

"We need to be ready," he said. "Once we find this place, things are going to move fast. No more running. No more reacting. We take the fight to them."

Sarah gave him a sharp look. "That's not like you, Ben. Usually *you're* the voice of caution."

"*Usually* I'm not dealing with ancient artifacts and paramilitary groups trying to kill us," he replied.

Reggie looked over at him, then smiled, his huge grin causing Ben's stoic expression to crack.

"Okay, fine," Ben said, "I guess we usually *are* dealing with exactly that. But whatever. Sometimes caution gets you killed just as fast as reck-lessness, and these guys are done pissing me off."

Isla made a sound of agreement. "He's right. We're past the point of playing it safe. These guys are the big fish in a small pond, and I've had enough of it. I was skeptical of you guys at first, but you seem to all have a knack for getting out of things alive. That's good enough for me. What-ever this thing is —" she nodded at the wrapped idol —"they want it bad enough to kill for it. Which means we need to know why."

Dawn turned to a hot morning as they shadowed the Syndicate boats, staying just within visual range. The sun climbed higher, burning away the last of the storm clouds. Heat began to shimmer off the water, and the jungle-covered islands threw back the calls of waking birds.

Isla handled the borrowed boat like she'd been born on it, reading the currents and keeping them hidden in the island chain's shadows. Every time the Syndicate boats seemed to scan the horizon, they were safely tucked behind volcanic rock or thick mangroves.

"They're slowing down," Ben said finally, an hour later. "Starting to angle toward the coast."

The others gathered at the rail, watching as the Zodiacs reduced speed and began a more careful approach to the shoreline. The cliffs here rose straight from the water, their faces scarred by centuries of storms.

"This is it," Isla said quietly. "Their home base."

The Syndicate boats pressed on, unaware of the shadow on their tail. Behind them, the storm clouds that had chased them from the reef were finally breaking apart, revealing a sky blue and empty. It would have been beautiful if they weren't all thinking about what waited ahead — what kind of fortress they were about to find, and what they'd have to do to get inside it.

CHAPTER 61

BEN

BEN HELD his breath as the lead Zodiac vanished into what looked like solid rock. One moment it was there, slicing through the morning swells — the next, gone. The other boats followed, threading through a gap he couldn't even see from this angle. The maneuver was practiced, fluid — they'd done this dozens of times before.

"Jesus," Reggie whispered. "If you didn't know it was there..."

"You'd sail right past," Isla finished, pulling out an old leather-bound journal from the compartment next to the boat's wheel. "That's the point." Her fingers drummed against the rail, a nervous tick Ben hadn't seen from her before. "Took me three years of running in these waters before I even heard whispers about this place. Most locals think it's just another section of dead cliff."

He watched as she opened the journal, finding an empty page near the end. Judging by the chicken-scratch numbers and equations lining dated pages, it appeared to be a notebook Manny kept on board for calculating dive times, oxygen levels, or whatever else the old guy felt he needed to keep track of during one of his excursions.

Isla started sketching something, and Ben saw that it took the shape of the coastline of Culebra. She even drew in the main towns and villages dotting the shore nearby.

They'd killed the engine again, drifting behind a curtain of mangrove roots half a mile out. The massive root systems formed a natural screen, their twisted shapes casting strange shadows on the water. The cliffs beyond towered above them, a natural wall of volcanic stone draped in vines and creepers. Nothing about it suggested a hidden base — which made it perfect. *Nature's camouflage*, Ben thought. *Better than anything man-made.*

The morning sun had risen higher now, burning away the last wisps of fog that clung to the water. Heat rippled off the dark stone faces, distorting the air and making the cliff seem to writhe and shift. It was disorienting — probably by design.

Sarah had commandeered the binoculars, scanning methodically. Her hands were steady despite the boat's gentle roll. "Got movement on the upper ledges. Two... no, three guards. Assault rifles." She shifted position slightly. "They're moving like military. Obviously mercenaries — these guys have serious training, or they really like playing soldier."

"What else?" Ben asked, squinting at the cliff face. Without magnification, all he could see was an endless wall of stone and vegetation.

"Supply crates near what looks like a loading dock. Modern security cameras disguised behind rock formations." She adjusted the focus, the lenses clicking softly. "There are likely a hundred little places more of them could be hiding, since there are that many islets and sandbars around us. Whoever designed this place knew what they were doing."

"They've been busy," Isla muttered. "More fortified than the last time I heard about it. Used to be just a smuggler's hideout — now it seems like it's a fortress."

Ben studied the cliff face, trying to spot the entrance. From this angle, it was invisible — just another fold in the rock. But he could see how the Zodiacs had disappeared now, through a narrow channel that curved away from the main cliff wall. The entrance must dogleg to the right, he realized, hiding the interior from any passing boats.

Reggie moved up beside him, still wearing the borrowed wetsuit. It squeaked slightly as he walked. "We can't just waltz in there," he said.

"That'd be suicide. Those guards up top have perfect firing positions — they'd cut us down before we got within a hundred yards."

"No kidding." Ben rubbed his jaw, feeling the salt crust on his skin. The stubble beneath was rough — how long had it been since he'd shaved? Days seemed to blur together now. "But there might be another way. These islands — they're all connected underwater, right? Part of the same volcanic formation?"

Isla caught his meaning immediately, her eyes lighting up. "Right, there could be caves. Natural tunnels they could use, if they're above the water line. They'd be idiots not to use them for emergency exits."

She pulled the boat left a bit to keep them out of sight. "There were always rumors about a whole network down there — smugglers used to talk about moving product without ever surfacing."

"Or supply runs," Sarah added, still scanning. "Wait — movement on that smaller island to the north. Looks like a patrol route." She tracked something through the binoculars. "Two men, regular intervals. They're probably making a circle around the island, probably every fifteen minutes or so."

"Maybe they keep a generator? They'd need those for a base this size."

The boat drifted slightly, forcing Isla to adjust their position with a quick burst from the engines. The mangroves closed around them again, their gnarled roots creaking in the swells. A fish jumped nearby, its scales flashing silver in the morning light.

"Then that's where we start," Ben said. "We find their patrol patterns, maybe nab some equipment, if we can find any. I'd love to not have to go in with just a pistol, and I'd especially love to not have to find an underwater entrance."

He shuddered. He *hated* caves, and though he'd had quite a bit of 'exposure therapy' in recent years, adding an underwater cave dive to this already impossible mission was not something he was looking forward to.

"Intel first, then we make a real plan." He traced the coastline with his finger. "There have to be blind spots in their security — no one can watch everything all the time."

Reggie nodded slowly, considering. "I like it better than a frontal assault, since the power's going to be concentrated in wherever their main base of operations is. But we need to move fast — those guards are definitely going to notice an idle boat if we hang around too long." He glanced at the towel-wrapped object. "And *that* thing... I swear it's getting heavier. Like it wants to be found."

Ben knew what he meant. The idol sat wrapped in canvas between them, silent but somehow watching. He could feel it like a weight in his chest, pulling him toward... whatever way might be considered *forward*. It gave him pause, but at the same time he realized it also meant he couldn't just walk away, couldn't just leave this place to the Syndicate.

For better or worse, this was his mission now. He thought of Hope and Julie back home, wondered if Julie would be surprised at this latest twist of fate.

No, probably not.

She'd likely scold him for his lack of ability to stay out of trouble, but she wouldn't be surprised that he'd found it.

He also knew a part of her would love to be here right now, fighting alongside him and Reggie and Sarah. She'd be useful, too — her sharp wit and analytical mind, combined with Sarah's expertise and knowledge of these cultures and traditions, would make short work of deciphering the idol's cryptic meaning.

He looked down at it now, saw some of the symbols peeking through the open flap of the towel.

The carved symbols beneath the fabric seemed to pulse with each wave that rocked the boat. But whatever answers waited in there, it wasn't their mission to decipher them.

No, this piece was a bargaining chip. A way to convince the Syndicate leader — whoever they were — to stop their pillaging and plundering of the ancient offshore site.

"How many spare tanks do we have?" Sarah asked suddenly. "If we have to look for underwater caves, we'll need air."

Isla moved to check the equipment lockers. "Manny's got four full tanks here, plus what's left in the two you had from the reef dive. Maybe... three hours of bottom time total — if we're careful." She pulled out a depth gauge, checking its readings. "Water's shallow here, too — thirty, forty feet max, but I'd suspect anything we're looking for will be much shallower. We can make it work."

"I'm really hoping they didn't plan on having to gear up and train their troops for an emergency dive as their main exit strategy," Ben said. "In other words, I'm hoping this cave entrance to their main lair is *above* the waterline."

"What are we looking for, then?" Isla asked.

"First we scout that island," Ben said firmly. "No diving until we know exactly what we're dealing with up top, because if we're able to find any useful gear, I'd rather not have to lug it with us underwater. Sarah, keep watching their patrol patterns. Isla, see if you can edge us closer using these mangroves for cover. Also..." he paused. "You think you remember enough about this place to draw us a rough layout?"

She was already sketching. "Working on it. And no, it's not going to be perfect — I really haven't been over here in a long time. But Ben — whatever we find in there... I don't think we're ready for it. The rumors, the way they've fortified this place... something bigger is happening here. At least bigger than a boatload of disgruntled visitors is ready for."

Ben looked at Reggie, then at Sarah. He had no doubt his best friend was ready for whatever they'd find. Sarah was a bit more of a wildcard, but he trusted her judgement implicitly.

And the look on her face told him she was more than ready.

"I know," he said quietly. "But we're out of options. And out of time."

The morning wore on as they studied the cliffs, looking for any hidden entrance. Birds called from the jungle above, their cries echoing off the stone.

"Alright," Ben said finally, decision made. "Let's go island hopping."

CHAPTER 62

BEN

THE 'ISLAND' was barely more than a bump of sand and rock jutting from the water, its highest point maybe fifteen feet above the waves. A single twisted palm tree clung to the crown, providing meager shade for the two figures sprawled beneath it. Their rifles lay propped against the trunk, forgotten toys in the late morning heat.

"Amateurs," Isla whispered, peering through the dense mangrove screen. "They're not even scanning the water."

Ben watched the two guards through the binoculars. Young guys, probably local muscle rather than the hardcore mercenaries they'd seen at the main base. One was actually dozing, his cap pulled low over his eyes. The other played with his phone, completely absorbed in whatever was on the screen.

Their Zodiac was tied off at a crude wooden pile of rubble on the far side, its black hull reflecting the sun like obsidian. Supply crates were stacked near the waterline, partially covered by camouflage netting that had started to slip in the breeze.

"If they're guarding those crates," Ben said quietly. "And they're worth storing away from their main base, it means there's probably something in them they don't want the cops to find if the you-know-what hits the fan.

Reggie, you and Isla take point. Sarah and I will cover you from here. Quick and clean — we need them alive for intel."

Reggie swallowed hard but nodded. The hesitation in his eyes was clear, but his jaw was set. Isla was already stripping down to her swimsuit, checking the dive knife strapped to her calf.

"Follow my lead," she told Reggie. "And don't overthink it."

They slipped into the water without a splash, two shadows gliding beneath the surface. Ben tracked their progress through the binoculars as they split up, circling the tiny island from opposite directions. The guards never looked up from their distractions.

Isla surfaced first, silent as a shark, water streaming from her hair. She pulled herself onto the sand behind a pile of weathered coral, moving like a shadow. Reggie emerged moments later on the opposite side, his borrowed avocado-colored wetsuit dark against the pale sand.

The guard with the phone never saw them coming. Isla's arm locked around his throat as Reggie tackled the sleeping one, driving him face-first into the sand. There was a brief struggle — then stillness. No shots fired. No alarms raised.

Ben let out the breath he'd been holding. "Bring us in," he told Sarah. "Nice and easy."

They ghosted the boat up to the islet, bumping gently against the Zodiac and the wooden pilings the pair of thugs had used as a makeshift dock. By the time Ben and Sarah jumped off, Isla had already tied the guards using some cord they'd had on their belt, and was going through their pockets. Reggie stood watch, holding one of the abandoned rifles with white-knuckled hands.

"You good?" Ben asked him quietly as they stepped onto the sand.

Reggie nodded stiffly. "Yeah. Just... hits different when it's up close, and I'm a bit out of practice. Easier to shoot at someone than choke them out."

"They're not dead," Ben said.

"Still."

"Get used to it," Isla called over her shoulder. "Because look what our friends were guarding." She yanked aside the camo netting, revealing more than just supply crates. Rack after rack of military hardware gleamed in the sun — assault rifles, pistols, crates of grenades. And underneath it all, hardened cases stamped with communications symbols.

"Radio gear," Sarah said, kneeling to examine one case. "High-end stuff too. Encrypted channels, signal boosters..." She popped a case open. "These aren't cheap walkies from the local surplus store."

Ben studied the arsenal laid out before them. "They're gearing up for something big, or they've got a major order coming in they want to protect. You don't stockpile hardware like this unless you're planning to use it, sell it, or trade it."

"Let's hope it's one of the two latter options," Reggie said. "But still, I wouldn't be surprised if they're also *quite* capable of protecting all this stuff."

"Plus, knowing that you and I are out here, operating in their territory," Ben added. "Since Isla escaped, they're going to be on edge. And that little underwater skirmish at the wreck — they'll know we're still alive, and still around. We can expect them to be expecting us."

One of the guards groaned, starting to come around. Isla knelt beside him, speaking rapid Spanish in a low, dangerous voice. The man's eyes went wide with fear.

"Says there's more stuff inside the main base," she reported, switching back to English. "And that it is, in fact, in one of the larger caves, just a few islets away. They use this one as little backup armory and monitoring station." She smiled grimly. "He wouldn't tell me exactly where it is, and I'm not sure I have the fortitude to... extract that information."

Reggie shook his head. "Not worth it, anyway," he said. "They're close, and we're not here to kill everyone in sight. These guys are just local thugs — kids wrapped up in the mess. No need to do anything like that."

The morning sun beat down as they stripped the tiny islet of anything useful. Weapons, ammo, communications gear — all of it disappeared into their boat. The guards were secured in the patrol boat's cabin, tied up but alive.

"What about them?" Isla asked, nodding toward the prisoners.

"We leave them," Ben said. "Someone will find them eventually. But we'll take their boat — no sense leaving them an easy way to raise the alarm. Let's tie it behind ours for now; we're just trolling slowly, so it shouldn't be a problem back there."

"I've got another idea," Reggie said suddenly. All eyes turned to him. "Let's take their, uh, *clothes*, too."

Isla looked him up an down, a sickened expression on her face.

He rolled his eyes. "I ain't some weirdo, Isla. I've got my vices, but stripping down passed-out mercenaries isn't one of them." He paused, incredulous that he had to actually spell it out. "We can use their *uniforms*. These guys might all know each other. But they also might not. Either way, from a distance we'll just look like a couple of their own. Might be able to get even closer that way."

No one argued, and Ben knew it was a good idea. They worked quickly, efficiently, like they'd all been a team for years. When they finally pushed off from the dock, Manny's boat rode lower in the water, heavy with stolen gear. The island slowly receded behind them, its secrets stripped bare.

Sarah was already setting up the radio equipment, her fingers dancing over unfamiliar controls. "Give me an hour with these," she said. "I'll have their channels mapped and monitored."

"Good." Ben checked his watch. "Because we're running out of time. Whatever this group is preparing for — besides us — it's imminent."

The stolen arsenal gleamed dully under the tarp they'd thrown over it. Tools for the job ahead. But as Ben glanced at the wrapped idol, he wondered if any amount of firepower would be enough for what waited in that hidden cove.

CHAPTER 63

REGGIE

THE ARSENAL LAY SPREAD across the deck like lethal puzzle pieces. Reggie checked each weapon methodically, muscle memory from his military days taking over. Magazine capacity. Safety mechanisms. Firing modes. The familiar routines helped steady his still-trembling hands, though his fingers kept catching on the unfamiliar wear patterns of these stolen weapons.

He lifted each rifle, checking the sights, testing the actions. Some were well-maintained, others showed signs of neglect – scratched barrels, stiff triggers, rust starting to bloom in the hard-to-reach spots. Not surprising for weapons stashed on a humid island outpost. But they'd fire, and right now that's all that mattered.

"Three M4s, four Glocks, handful of flashbangs," he reported, laying everything out in neat rows. "Plus whatever fancy toys are in those radio cases Sarah's playing with." He paused, checking another crate. "Found some spare magazines too. About two hundred rounds total."

"Having fun?" Ben asked without looking up from Isla's rough sketch of the cove layout. He'd been studying it for twenty minutes straight, as if staring at the hastily-drawn lines would somehow reveal their secrets.

"Like Christmas morning." Reggie tried to smile but it felt forced. The weight of what they were planning settled in his gut like lead. "Just wish

Santa brought body armor instead of grenades. These guys were prepared for a fight, but I guess they weren't expecting to need protection out here on their little vacation island."

He picked up one of the rifles again, stripped it down to its components with practiced ease. The parts spread across an old towel – buffer spring, bolt carrier group, charging handle. Each piece told its own story. These weren't cheap knockoffs – they were military-grade weapons, probably "disappeared" from some government armory. The Syndicate had connections, that much was clear.

The idol sat wrapped in canvas between them, but Reggie swore he could feel it watching. Sarah kept darting glances at it while she worked with the comm gear, her hands moving over the equipment with growing confidence. Even through the fabric, something about the artifact made his skin crawl. The air around it felt wrong somehow – heavier, charged with something he couldn't name.

"Got their frequencies mapped," Sarah announced, not looking up from the equipment. Her fingers flew over the unfamiliar controls with surprising skill. "They're running encrypted channels but the cipher's pretty basic. Amateur hour, really. I can monitor their chatter, maybe even spoof their comms if we need to." She adjusted something, and static-filled voices emerged from the speaker, speaking rapid Spanish.

Isla hunched over her phone, thumbs tapping furiously. "No signal out here," she muttered. "Trying to get word to Manny about what we found. He needs to know we might need a quick exit. But these islands might as well be in the middle of the ocean for all the coverage we're getting."

"If we can get a message through," Ben said, finally looking up from the map, "tell him to stay well back until we call. Last thing we need is another boat and unarmed civilian to worry about. We're stretched thin enough as it is."

They drifted in the shadow of yet another tiny island, one of dozens dotting this stretch of coast. Through gaps in the mangroves, they kept the main cove entrance in sight – that nearly invisible crack in the cliff face that had swallowed the Syndicate boats earlier. The assumption was that the largest cove hid a larger island that was the Syndicate's main operating base, and they planned to make concentric circles around the area until they were sure their base was nowhere else. The last thing they wanted was to accidentally sound the alarm and have the Syndicate spread out in every direction, effectively to the wind.

The morning had grown hot and sticky, the kind of heat that made everything feel slightly unreal. Sweat beaded on Reggie's neck as he reassembled the rifle, each piece clicking home with satisfying precision.

The boat rocked gently in the swells, making the weapons slide slightly on their towels. Above them, seabirds wheeled and cried, oblivious to the tension below. Every few minutes, they'd hear the distant sound of boat engines – regular patrols, searching for them. But Isla had chosen their hiding spot well, tucked into a natural blind spot between three smaller islands.

"So what's the play?" Reggie asked finally, unable to bear the waiting any longer. "We can't just walk in the front door. Even with their gear, we'll stick out the moment anyone takes a close look."

"We don't," Isla said. She'd given up on the phone and moved to help Sarah with the radio equipment. "You and I go in first, use their own gear against them. We know the patrols now, we've got their weapons. We create a gap, then Ben and Sarah slip through behind us. Quick, clean, professional."

"Classic two-team breach," Reggie nodded, but his expression was troubled. "But we need an exit strategy. *Multiple* exit strategies. This isn't like hitting a warehouse or office building – we're talking about a natural fortress with who knows how many defenders inside."

Sarah finally looked up from the radio equipment, her face pale despite the heat. "I can coordinate from here, run comms. Keep you updated on their movements. It makes more sense than all of us going in blind."

"No." Ben's voice was firm, brooking no argument. "As much as I want you back here, staying safe, we need to stay together. We've seen what these people can do — splitting up more than necessary is asking for trouble. They've already proven they're willing to kill. And whatever's in that base, whatever they're protecting..." He glanced at the wrapped idol. "It's worth dying for, to them at least."

Reggie chambered a round, let the familiar click-snap settle his nerves. The sound echoed slightly off the water. "Then we move fast, hit hard, find what we need and get out. No hesitation. No trying to be heroes." He looked at each of them in turn. "We go in together, we come out together. That's the only way this works."

"Right." Isla's phone screen went dark one final time — still no signal. She tossed it aside in frustration. "Because whatever's waiting in there, whatever this is all about..." She gestured at the wrapped idol, careful not to touch it directly. "It has to be more than just weapons smuggling — this idol is something they'll want. And they're not going to just hand over answers."

The boat rocked gently in the swells, water lapping at the hull in an almost soothing rhythm. Around them, the islands kept their secrets, walls of green and stone hiding who knew what else. But soon, Reggie knew, they'd breach those stone walls and find the truth — or die trying.

He finished his weapons check, laying everything out in precise order. Clean, loaded, ready. Sarah continued monitoring the radio traffic, while Ben and Isla refined their entry plan. The sun climbed higher, turning the water into hammered silver. Somewhere in that maze of rock and jungle, answers waited. Along with who knew how many armed defenders, traps, and other surprises.

Reggie pulled out the spare magazines, began loading them one round at a time. The repetitive motion was calming, familiar. But his hands still shook slightly, and not just from the morning's exertion. He couldn't shake the feeling that they were about to step into something ancient and dangerous – something that had been waiting for them all along.

He just hoped they were ready for what waited inside. Somehow, he doubted anyone could truly be ready for what they were about to find.

CHAPTER 64
SARAH

THE RADIO CRACKLED, spitting bursts of static-laced Spanish through the humid air. The voices were garbled, distant, but something in their tone made her pulse quicken. She'd heard that kind of urgency before — the sound of plans changing, of deadlines crashing forward.

"Hold up," she said, throwing up a hand to silence the others. "Something's happening."

The boat drifted in the lee of a small island, hidden from prying eyes by a thick curtain of mangroves. Water lapped quietly against the hull. Sarah cranked up the gain, fighting to pull coherent words from the static. Two male voices emerged, their words clipped and tense:

"...demo teams need another day minimum..."

"No time. Cruz wants the site prepped before the client walkthrough tonight."

"But the supports aren't —"

"Just get it done. Contract starts as soon as they confirm clearing of the site. Initial inspections start as soon as Halim arrives."

Sarah's stomach clenched. She motioned to Isla, who handed her the sketched map and the pen she'd been using. Sarah turned it over and started scribbling on the back. She listened on as the voices continued their heated exchange:

"What about the artifacts?"

"Take what's easily retrievable. Leave the rest, and focus on the structural test areas."

"But —"

"Those are Cruz's orders. Move your ass."

The transmission died in a burst of white noise. Sarah looked up to find three pairs of eyes fixed on her — Ben leaning forward from his position near the bow, Reggie's hand unconsciously tightening on his rifle, Isla's face unreadable in the gathering shadows.

"They're not just stealing artifacts," Sarah said, her voice barely above a whisper. "They're preparing the site for something else. Something big."

Ben shifted closer, water dripping from his borrowed tactical gear. "What kind of preparation?"

"Demo teams. Structural tests." Sarah tapped her notes with the pen. Seawater had made the ink run slightly, but the words were still legible. "They keep mentioning Monday inspections and some kind of contract. Whatever they're planning, it's happening fast."

"Demo teams?" Reggie's expression darkened, his military experience clearly painting pictures in his mind. "They're going to blow the place?"

"Maybe." Sarah ran a hand through her salt-crusted hair, mind racing. "But why rush it? Why risk —"

"Cruz," Isla cut in. The name seemed to freeze the very air around them. Sarah turned to find Isla's face had gone chalk-white beneath her tan. "You said Cruz was giving orders?"

Sarah nodded slowly. "Yeah, someone named Cruz. Seems to be calling the shots."

"Valeria Cruz." Isla spat the name like it was poison on her tongue. Her hands clenched the edge of the console. "I should have known. This has her fingerprints all over it."

"You know her?" Ben asked.

"Know *of* her." Isla's laugh was sharp and bitter. "Everyone in certain circles does. She runs a private security firm that specializes in... well, they're pirates. I didn't realize she might actually be running the Syndicate, but it makes sense. She's said to be driven, stubborn, and charismatic.

The perfect person to build the disparate groups of local gangs into an organized force."

Ben and Reggie nodded.

"If it's the Syndicate that's been after us," Isla continued, "and this Valeria person is at its helm, we need to expect a *very* prepared force here. She's not going to let ego make her complacent. But it does confirm our suspicions — she's getting nervous. Probably because we're close to figuring out what it is she's really doing here. We've already guessed this isn't about black market artifacts or treasure hunting."

"What's it really about, then?"

Isla shrugged. "She's probably just the muscle. The Syndicate's got numbers, but not brains. She's smart, but probably is working with someone else. Someone wanting to... do something with the land around the reef."

"But why go to these lengths?" Ben asked. "Why not just file permits, do it legally?"

"Because they can't," Sarah said, the pieces clicking into place. "The idol we found — it *proves* this whole area is historically significant. Protected. If word got out about what's down there..." She trailed off, the implications settling like lead in her stomach.

"Oh, my God," Isla said. "That's *exactly* what it is. They're collecting what they can, but destroying all the rest. Cruz and the Syndicate have a *client*, and that client wants to make sure their interests aren't tied up with governmental oversight, heritage organizations, local murmuring."

"They're going to destroy ancient history," Sarah continued quietly. "What they can't sell off on the black market, they'll just rebury. The caves, the artifacts, all of it. Bury it under sand and sediment before anyone can document what was out there. And this place, too. Their base of operations is clearly a temporary home, put here to be close to the reef, so they can keep an eye on it. But if they successfully destroy the reef and rebury whatever's out there, they'll do the same thing to this place, and then move on."

"And they're blowing the reef tonight." Reggie checked his watch, the luminous display casting a ghost-light on his face. "Which means we're out of time."

The boat rocked gently in the swells, creaking softly. Through gaps in the mangroves, Sarah could see the cove entrance – that dark crack in the cliff face that somehow held the key to everything. Lightning flickered on the horizon, promising another storm. The air felt charged, heavy with more than just approaching rain.

She turned back to the radio, adjusting frequencies with trembling fingers. More voices filtered through — patrol reports, equipment requests, mundane chatter. But beneath it all ran an current of urgency, of preparation. They needed more intel, more time. But the voices were clear – by tomorrow, it would all be gone.

Unless they stopped it now.

"We need to move," Isla said, already checking her weapon. "If Cruz is involved, this just got a lot more dangerous. Her people aren't all thugs or hired guns — some are professionals, which I suspect you guys have figured out by now. Ex-military, mostly. And they don't leave witnesses."

"How many are we talking about?" Reggie asked.

"No idea. Probably a dozen or more. Plus support staff, technical experts." Isla's expression was grim. "And they'll have the home field advantage."

Sarah studied the rough map they'd sketched of the cove and surrounding islands. "We still have surprise on our side. They know we're coming, but they don't know when or how."

"No," Ben said quietly. "But they're rushing the timeline, tightening the noose." He looked at each of them in turn. "We go in now, we're walking into a hornet's nest. They'll be on edge, trigger-happy."

"Doesn't matter," Sarah said. She was surprised by the steel in her own voice. "Whatever's down there — whatever they're trying to erase — it's important. We *can't* let them destroy it."

The others nodded slowly. They'd come too far to back down now.

"All right," Reggie said, checking his ammunition one last time. "But we do this smart. Isla and I will go in, quick and quiet, in and out. Document what we can, then try make sure word gets out before they can bury it all. Ben, Sarah — you stay back and patrol. Stay quiet and be ready in case we need a quick exit. You guys have your phones?"

Isla held hers up. "No service, though. And I don't suspect they'll have free WIFI in there."

Reggie smiled. "We just need pictures. Proof. Get whatever you can."

"And don't leave your phone on someone else's boat," Ben added, looking at Reggie.

"Hey, I didn't know we were going to be boat-hopping, too. Who knew these two would come back for us?"

Isla smirked. "I've still got my phone, and I'm happy to save your asses. Again."

CHAPTER 65

REGGIE

REGGIE PEERED toward a tall spire jutting out of the rocks, tracking another sloppy patrol change along the cove's edge. Two guards, barely old enough to shave, fumbled a handoff of their rifles before splitting up. One nearly dropped his weapon, catching it awkwardly against his chest. The other laughed, then quickly looked around to make sure no one had seen.

Amateur hour.

The sun was already starting its crawl toward the horizon, painting the water in deep oranges and reds. Perfect timing — as bright as it still was, the changing light would work in their favor, making identification harder as shadows lengthened across the cove. Reggie could make out at least six Syndicate guards visible from his vantage point, but their movements suggested no real coordination or professional training.

"They're green," he whispered to Isla, who was zipping up her borrowed uniform jacket beside him. The fabric made a soft rasping sound in the quiet air. "Half of them look like they learned to handle weapons from video games. Look at that one — he's got his sling adjusted all wrong."

"Don't underestimate desperate kids with guns," she replied, adjusting the stolen shoulder holster until it sat right. Her movements were precise, practiced. "Sometimes they're the most dangerous kind. They've got something to prove and no experience to tell them when to back down."

He studied the base entrance again. It was a cave, one that had been reinforced with concrete, cleverly disguised with local vegetation but obvious once you knew what to look for. The patrols were erratic, uncoordinated — clear signs of a rushed operation being run by inexperienced troops.

Good for getting in, bad for predicting what might happen once they were inside.

"Your uniform fit okay?" he asked, tugging at his own tight collar. The previous owner had been shorter, broader across the shoulders. The fabric pulled uncomfortably across his back every time he moved. At least the boots fit — small mercies.

Isla yanked her sleeves straight, smoothing out the wrinkles. "It'll do. At least until someone looks too close." She adjusted the name tag they'd stolen along with the rest of the gear. "Garcia" it read — hopefully no one would notice she wasn't the original owner.

Behind them, partially hidden by a thick screen of mangroves, Manny's boat bobbed gently in the inlet. The small craft represented their backup ride now, their escape route if things went sideways. Which, given their track record so far, seemed more likely than not. The thought made Reggie's prosthetic arm twitch — phantom pain from a previous close call.

The radio Sarah had been monitoring crackled softly. She adjusted the volume down, not wanting the sound to carry across the water. The chatter had been increasing over the last hour — mostly routine stuff, but with an underlying current of nervousness that hadn't been there before.

"Ben," Reggie called softly. "You see any pattern to the tower rotations?"

Ben was positioned twenty yards to their left, where the elevation gave him a better view of the guard towers flanking the entrance. He'd been making verbal notes, trying to piece together the schedule.

"Not really. Seems like they're supposed to swap every thirty minutes, but some are staying longer, others cutting out early." Ben shook his head.

"They're scrambling, trying to cover gaps. I've seen the same guy make three different positions in the last hour."

Sarah's voice filled them in on the talk on the Syndicate channel. "More chatter about missing personnel. They're starting to ask questions about that patrol we took down. Someone named Ramón is doing head counts."

Reggie checked his watch. The golden hour was approaching — when the light would be at its most deceptive, creating deep shadows and false shapes across the water. Perfect cover for their approach, but they needed to move soon.

"Ready?" he asked Isla.

She pulled her black cap low, obscuring her face. The shade cast by the brim would make facial recognition — if they had it — harder in the failing light. "Born ready. Just remember — act like we belong there. Walk straight, look bored, and don't make eye contact unless you have to. These guys are scared enough to shoot first and ask questions later."

"Right. Just two more grunts, heading in for shift change. Nothing to see here."

"And if someone asks questions?"

Reggie smiled grimly. "Then we'll give them something else to think about." His prosthetic arm flexed unconsciously. It was state-of-the-art, paid for by their benefactor at the CSO, and even had the ability to receive over-the-air firmware updates. He hadn't needed to update anything in a while, but the arm was still quite capable. Stronger than his original appendage, he could control each finger and the wrist independently, almost as dexterously as he could the one that had been taken from him.

He remembered that moment as if it were yesterday, and he could still see the face of the man who had put him in that position.

The face of the man who was now *dead*.

He wondered if the leader of the Syndicate, Valeria Cruz, was anything like that man. If she were hell-bent not just on getting her way, but on making those standing in her way suffer.

He glanced back at Sarah — the woman he'd loved almost from the moment he'd met her. *What I wouldn't do for her.*

They did one final gear check — weapons secured but accessible, backup magazines distributed between them.

The mangroves around them rustled in the breeze, providing natural cover as they slipped down to their ride. The Zodiac had been carefully positioned to avoid detection — its dark hull blending with the shadows under the overhanging vegetation. Ben and Sarah would maintain their observation position from Manny's boat, monitoring radio traffic and providing what coverage they could from outside, while Reggie and Isla took the Zodiac in.

Reggie settled into the pilot's position of the Zodiac while Isla took up watch in the bow. The engine was loud, but dampened by the foliage as they pulled away from the mangroves. The water ahead was calm, mirror-smooth in the protected inlet. Beyond lay the narrow entrance to what might be the most heavily-guarded cove in the Caribbean.

And possibly their last chance to stop whatever Cruz was planning.

CHAPTER 66

REGGIE

THE ZODIAC CUT through the water with barely a ripple, its dark hull merging with the lengthening shadows. Isla gripped the bow line, scanning the narrow gap in the cliffs ahead. Her knuckles whitened against the rough rope as she fought to keep her movements controlled, measured. The entrance was tight — maybe thirty feet across at most. Just wide enough for a decent-sized boat, if you knew what you were doing. And they had to know what they were doing, or this would end before it began.

"They'll ask questions," she said, keeping her voice low enough that it wouldn't carry across the water. The sound of waves lapping against the cliffs nearly drowned her out.

"Then we lie well." Reggie's hand was steady on the tiller, guiding them through the natural bottleneck. His prosthetic arm whirred softly as he made micro-adjustments, compensating for the current that tried to push them toward the rocks.

The sunlight played tricks with depth perception, making the gap seem to shrink and expand with each passing wave. Isla counted the seconds between swells, timing their approach. Too fast and they'd draw attention. Too slow and they'd lose control in the current.

The cove opened up like a mouth, revealing a hidden half-moon of protected water. Rock walls rose nearly vertical on all sides, creating a natural fortress. Concrete platforms studded the cliff faces, jerry-rigged docking spots covered in camouflage netting that had seen better days. Shallow caves dotted the walls, some natural, others clearly carved out by human hands.

A guard lounged against a metal drum on the nearest platform, cigarette dangling from his lips. His rifle hung loose across his back — more decoration than weapon. His boots were untied, laces trailing on the wet concrete. The kind of sloppiness that got people killed in real operations.

He straightened slightly as they approached, raising a lazy hand to wave them down. The cigarette bobbed as he spoke. Reggie cut the motor, letting them drift toward the dock. The sudden silence felt heavy, broken only by water slapping against the hull.

"¡Identifíquense!" the guard called out, voice rough with smoke. He made no move to properly shoulder his weapon, but his free hand did drift toward the radio at his belt.

Reggie's Spanish came out deliberately mangled, the way someone might speak after learning from training manuals rather than actual conversation: "Unit nueve. Orders from Cruz. Transmission problemas." He kept his face neutral, bored — just another grunt following orders.

The guard's eyes narrowed, suddenly more alert. The casual posture stiffened. "¿Cruz? ¿Qué unidad?" His fingers wrapped around the radio now, thumb hovering over the call button.

Isla stepped in before the situation could deteriorate, her Spanish crisp and authoritative. The kind of tone that expected — demanded — immediate compliance. "We're coming from the outer islands. Our clearance is time-sensitive. *La señora* expects confirmation of our findings *before* sundown." She let irritation color her words, as if explaining simple things to simple people was beneath her.

She saw the guard's posture shift at the mention of Cruz — a mix of wariness and uncertainty. The name carried weight, cast shadows. Everyone in the compound knew crossing Cruz meant consequences. Isla pressed harder, playing on that fear: "She will not be happy if this gets delayed."

The guard chewed his lip, clearly weighing his options. The radio crackled with routine chatter — position checks, status reports. Normal sounds that could turn dangerous in seconds. Isla leaned forward, dropping her voice to a threatening whisper. "Want to call her and explain why her asset didn't make it inside before the client arrives?"

That hit home. The guard's face went slack for a moment before he recovered. He muttered into his radio, something quick and coded about checking credentials. His eyes never left them as he waited for a response. Reggie's hand drifted toward the dry bag hiding their backup weapon, movements casual but ready. Isla watched the radio, muscles coiled tight beneath her borrowed uniform.

Static crackled, then a garbled response — words too distorted to make out clearly, but the tone was affirmative. The guard's shoulders slumped slightly — relief or resignation, hard to tell which. Either way, the moment of crisis passed.

"Stay clear of the private office tunnel," he growled, jerking his head toward a dark opening in the cliff face. "She's down there." The warning carried an edge of genuine concern, as if he was doing them a favor.

Isla nodded, already memorizing the tunnel's location for later. "Wouldn't dream of it." The lie came easily, wrapped in just enough truth to sound sincere.

They powered past him, deeper into the complex. The boat's wake bounced off the rock walls, creating complex patterns in the darkening water. Other boats dotted the protected harbor — patrol craft with mounted guns, sleek speed boats built for quick escapes, even a cigarette boat that probably cost more than most houses. Each vessel told its own story about Cruz's operation — money, firepower, contingency plans.

Isla counted cameras as they moved, noting blind spots and coverage zones. Most were professional setups, but a few looked hastily added, suggesting recent security upgrades. She logged it all away — useful intelligence if they needed another way out.

"That's one wall down," she whispered as they approached an empty berth. The concrete was newer here, less weathered than the surrounding structures.

"Just a few dozen more to go." Reggie killed the engine, letting them bump gently against the dock. The sound echoed briefly before being swallowed by the constant drip of water from the cliff faces. Time to see if their borrowed uniforms would hold up under closer scrutiny.

The guard above hadn't been their biggest hurdle — he was just the first filter, designed to catch obvious threats. The real challenges lay ahead, past the initial security layers where people actually knew each other, where borrowed uniforms and fake credentials wouldn't stand up to familiar faces and shared histories.

Isla secured the bow line while Reggie handled the stern, their movements practiced despite never having worked together before. Everything had to look routine, unremarkable. In places like this, standing out meant dying — usually quickly, always painfully.

Above them, the sky continued its slow fade from orange to purple, creating new shadows with each passing minute. Soon the compound would shift to night operations — different guards, different protocols, different expectations. They needed to be well inside before that transition began, established enough that no one would question their presence when the shifts changed.

The next few minutes would determine everything. Either their preparations would hold up, or they'd find out exactly how many guards Cruz kept hidden in those cliff-side caves. Isla adjusted her holster, making sure the weapon would clear smoothly.

Then they stepped onto the dock, becoming just two more soldiers in a fortress full of killers. The real infiltration was about to begin.

CHAPTER 67

RAMÓN

THE DIVE COMPUTER beeped as Ramón checked his depth — perfect trim at fifteen meters. Through his mask, he watched the last charge settle into position against the coral. The small device looked harmless, like a child's toy lost at sea, but he knew better. When triggered, it would turn this peaceful reef into ground zero. His team had placed twenty similar charges in the last hour, each one precisely positioned to maximize the blast radius.

He watched bubbles spiral up from his exhale, distorting the shafts of afternoon sunlight that pierced the water. Fish darted between the coral branches, oblivious to the destruction waiting to be unleashed. A green sea turtle glided past, regarding him with ancient eyes before disappearing into the blue. In twelve hours, this entire ecosystem would be nothing but rubble.

His radio crackled. *"Ramón."* Valeria's voice, tight with tension. *"Surface. Now."*

He signaled his team and began his ascent, careful to follow proper decompression protocols. Whatever had Valeria spooked could wait three minutes. He'd seen too many cowboys get bent rushing ascents. He'd watched a hotshot diver convulse and foam at the mouth last year after skipping his safety stop. The guy lived, but his diving days were done.

Ortiz and Castellanos fell in behind him, their tanks gleaming in the filtered light. They'd worked together long enough to move like a single unit, even underwater. Each knew their role, executed their tasks with military precision. No questions asked, no hesitation. That's why he had handpicked them for this operation.

The boat's ladder creaked as he hauled himself aboard, stripping off his mask. Salt water streamed from his wetsuit as he grabbed the tablet mounted near the helm. Valeria's face filled the screen, her expression stormy. Dark eyes that usually sparkled with calculated charm now burned with barely contained rage.

"We've got ghosts," she said without preamble. *"Two guards missing from C-sector. Someone's snooping our frequencies."*

Ramón peeled off his wetsuit top, letting the tropical breeze dry his skin. His mind raced through possibilities, but one name kept surfacing. "Manny Delgado?"

"Has to be. He's been too quiet, and no one has seen him anywhere." She looked off-screen, barking orders to someone. The sound of rapid footsteps echoed behind her. *"I need you to prep a response team. Fast."*

"The charges-"

"Are set. Priority shift." Her eyes narrowed. *"There's more. Another vessel was spotted off the eastern marker. Low profile, running dark."*

Ramón grabbed his binoculars, scanning the horizon. Castellanos and Ortiz emerged from below deck, already changed and armed. They knew the drill — when Valeria's tone changed like this, things were about to get messy.

There — a shadow against shadows, barely visible in the growing dusk. If they were trying to be stealthy, they'd picked the wrong time of day. Silhouettes stood out like neon signs at sunset. The boat was maybe forty feet, stripped down for speed. No fishing gear, no dive flags. Not tourists, not local fishermen.

Not the same boat Ramón thought Manny owned, either. No matter — there were countless boats on Culebra and the surrounding islands, and Manny knew plenty of their owners. He'd probably borrowed one for this.

"I see it."

"Intercept. Now." Valeria's voice could have frozen hell. *"They're coming for the wreck. For us. Stop them."*

Ramón was already moving, signaling his team. The watertight weapons locker beneath the back seat in the bow opened with a satisfying click. Inside, their arsenal waited — MP5s modified for maritime ops, suppressed sidearms, flash-bangs designed to work underwater.

Tools for wet work, carefully maintained and ready.

Ortiz grabbed extra magazines while Castellanos prepped the second zodiac they had tied to this one. Ortiz had the engine on and was idling before Castellanos had finished.

Lopez was behind the wheel of his and Ramón's vessel, guiding it around the reef. They moved with practiced efficiency, no wasted motion. Each man checked his partner's gear — a habit that had saved their lives more than once. The small boat slapped against the waves as they loaded it, eager to hunt.

"Valeria," he said, checking his magazine. The rounds gleamed like copper teeth. "If it is Manny..."

"Then you get to prove your worth." Her smile was razor-sharp. *"They're coming. I want them dead before nightfall. Before the client arrives."*

Ramón ended the call, shouldering his rifle. The weight felt good, familiar. Like greeting an old friend. Memories of betrayal burned fresh in his mind. Not Manny's — he didn't know the man from Adam — but betrayals like this, nonetheless. The ambush in Caracas, good men dead because a snake he thought he'd trusted had sold him out. He'd waited two years for payback before giving up.

Men like Manny Delgado were meddlers. Men who just wanted to get ahead, and didn't care about which side they played. Ramón, on the other hand, was a professional. His side was the side that paid him.

The sun hung low and bloody on the horizon. Perfect hunting conditions. Waves chopped the water into obsidian shards, hiding their approach. Their zodiacs' black hulls would blend with the darkening sea, silent under its electric motor. They'd come in from the west, using the setting sun to mask their silhouette.

Lopez gunned the zodiac's motor, sending him and Castellanos skimming away from them, across the low waves. Ramón felt the old familiar tension coil in his gut — the hunter's anticipation, the predator's patience. He saw Castellanos chamber a round.

The mystery boat they believed Manny Delgado was on grew larger as they closed the distance. No lights, no radio chatter. Professional. But not professional enough. They'd made the amateur's mistake of thinking darkness alone would hide them. Ramón smiled behind his tactical mask. The sea was his territory, his killing ground. These intruders were about to learn why Valeria kept him on retainer.

The charges waited below, their timers counting down. Soon the wreck and its secrets would vanish forever, buried under tons of coral and rock. But first, he had a debt to collect. The zodiac knifed through the waves, carrying death on its black hull. Somewhere ahead, Manny Delgado waited. The sun sank lower, painting the sky in shades of fire and blood.

Perfect hunting conditions, indeed.

CHAPTER 68

REGGIE

THE FLUORESCENT LIGHTS hummed overhead as Isla and Reggie moved through the main corridor, their boots echoing off wet concrete. The cave system had been transformed into something between a military bunker and a construction site. Temporary power cables snaked along the walls like black vipers, zip-tied in messy bundles. The air hung heavy with diesel fumes and salt spray, making each breath taste like corroded metal.

Reggie's prosthetic arm whirred softly as they walked, the servos adjusting to keep his movements natural. He'd insisted the sound wasn't noticeable, but in the hollow tunnel, every tiny noise seemed amplified. Their footsteps bounced off the rock walls despite their best efforts to step quietly. Water dripped somewhere in the darkness, a steady metronome counting down their remaining time.

"Check your six," Reggie muttered, barely moving his lips. A pair of guards passed, deep in conversation about soccer scores. One gestured animatedly, arguing about a controversial penalty kick while his companion shook his head in disgust. Neither spared them a second glance — just two more uniforms in a sea of identical outfits.

Reggie could tell Isla fought the urge to watch them go by. He was glad she didn't. Amateur moves got you caught. Instead, she kept her pace steady, shoulders relaxed, like she'd walked these tunnels a hundred times before.

The borrowed uniform itched at his neck where the previous owner had spilled something sticky. He resisted scratching it.

They rounded a corner into what had to be the command center. The temperature dropped several degrees, courtesy of industrial-grade cooling units fighting the heat from dozens of servers. The machines lined one wall in neat racks, cooling fans whirring in synchronized harmony. Blue status lights blinked in systematic patterns, reflecting off the polished concrete floor.

Multiple screens dotted the walls, showing security feeds from around the complex. Guards at checkpoints, empty corridors, the dock where they'd entered — all under constant surveillance. And there, on a laptop left carelessly open, Reggie spotted familiar coral formations. The underwater feed showed their wreck site, lonely and exposed on the seafloor. Delicate branches of coral swayed in the current, unaware they were being watched.

"Found something," Isla whispered, angling her body to block the screen from view. She grabbed a clipboard from a nearby desk, pretending to check inventory lists while studying the footage. A ROV drifted through the frame, its mechanical arms probing the wreck with scientific precision. Its cameras scanned methodically, documenting every inch. "They've got eyes on the site."

"That's not all they've got." Reggie had drifted toward a massive whiteboard covering one wall. The surface was a maze of technical drawings and notations. "Look at this."

The blueprints were professional grade — no amateur hour here. Precise annotations marked structural points throughout the cave system, each accompanied by timestamps and load calculations. Red dots clustered around key junctions like deadly constellations. But it was the second overlay that made Reggie's blood run cold — a detailed bathymetric map of the reef shelf, with the wreck site dead center in a grid marked for "systematic clearance."

He studied the diagrams, his mind racing to process the implications.

The engineering was impressive in its thoroughness — every variable accounted for, every outcome predicted. This wasn't a rush job thrown together by amateurs. Someone had spent serious time planning this.

"Jesus," she breathed, next to him. "They're going to collapse it. All of it." The clinical language couldn't hide the intent — every trace of the wreck, every piece of evidence, buried under tons of coral and rock. The destruction would be total, irreversible. Centuries of history wiped away in minutes.

"Phase One and Phase Two," Reggie confirmed, his prosthetic hand clenching with a subtle whir of servos. The metal fingers flexed unconsciously, mirroring the tension in his voice. "Inside out. They're covering their tracks permanently. They've got this place and the wreck wired to blow. But they don't have the wreck and reef fused yet, so that will likely be their next move. They'll have to have boats out there so they can wire it manually."

"What does that mean?" Isla asked.

"It means we need to focus on the wreck site," he said. "This place is likely ready to blow, but they're waiting to do it all at the same time. The wreck, the reef, here — probably to put on a show for their visiting dignitaries."

"So we've got the proof," Isla said, "now we just need to get to the wreck before they can wire up the explosives."

"Right," Reggie said, hesitating. "But this isn't a roadrunner and coyote cartoon."

Isla cocked her head, obviously not understanding the reference.

"There's no actual *wiring* out on the reef," he explained. "It's not like there's going to be a detonator box with a big cartoony handle they push down. It will be a wireless, waterproof system, with a virtual 'fuse.' Basically, they'll have to be in range of the fuse, but out of range of the actual underwater explosions."

"In other words, we have less time than we thought," she said. "We need to get back out there and warn Ben and Sarah. If we can stop their boats from getting within range of the explosives they've planted, we can maybe stop it."

Reggie nodded, but noise captured his attention before he could respond.

Footsteps approached from the corridor — the sharp click of boots on concrete. Reggie smoothly pulled out his radio, pretending to check frequencies while a technician hurried past. The man carried an armload of det-cord, the explosive line coiled like deadly snakes around his shoulders. He kept his eyes on the radio's display, looking bored and occupied.

The explosive supplies were everywhere now that he looked — stacked in corners, lined up against walls. Crated charges waited in neat rows, their warning labels stark against olive drab metal. Blasting caps filled specialized cases, each one carefully cushioned. Reggie counted enough firepower to reshape the seafloor, to erase any trace that anything had ever existed down there.

"Sarah needs to see this," he said once they were alone again, his voice barely above a whisper. The technician's footsteps had faded, but others would come soon. This place was too busy to stay empty long. "The whole operation — it's not about stealing artifacts. It's about making them disappear completely."

Isla nodded grimly.

Reggie moved his prosthetic arm lifted slightly, the embedded camera capturing high-resolution images of the demolition plans. Stored on a micro SD card inserted into the prosthetic's wrist area, he could store hours of HD video and countless high-resolution images by pointing the camera — in the tip of his middle finger — and pressing his thumb and forefinger together. There was no shutter sound, as it was all digital, but a slight clicking noise as the aperture moved was lost in the ambient noise of servers and air conditioning. Each photo might be crucial later, if they survived to use them.

"Cruz is erasing history," he said, his organic hand running through his hair. "Question is — what's so important about that wreck that it's worth going nuclear?"

The answer lay somewhere in those depths, he knew. Something valuable enough to justify this level of destruction. Something worth killing for, worth destroying priceless historical sites to keep hidden. The wreck held secrets — deadly ones.

Before Isla could answer, an alarm blared through the complex. The sound bounced off concrete and steel, multiplying until it seemed to come from everywhere at once. Red warning lights began to strobe, casting bloody shadows across the command center's equipment.

They locked eyes for a fraction of a second. No words needed — time to move. Whatever they'd stumbled into was indeed bigger than they'd imagined, and now the clock was really ticking. Every second they stayed increased their chances of discovery. And in a place like this, discovery meant death.

Reggie's hand drifted to his borrowed sidearm, confirming it was still accessible. They had the intel they needed — now they just had to get it, and themselves, back out alive.

The alarm continued its electronic scream as they slipped back into the corridor, becoming two more shadows in a complex full of secrets. Whatever Cruz was hiding, they were now part of it. The only question was whether they'd live long enough to expose it.

CHAPTER 69

RAMÓN

THE SKIFF DANCED like a drunk across the reef line, veering too close to the shallows. Ramón gritted his teeth, watching through his scope as the boat zigzagged through the maze of coral heads.

Manny Delgado.

It had to be — who else was just connected enough to help the Americans, gather the support of locals, and field a rescue operation, no matter how janky and unorganized?

He knew the old man had a bone to pick with the Syndicate. The motive was there, and it was clear this would be his last stand.

The erratic movements weren't random — they were calculated, precise despite appearing chaotic. *Who else would be dumb enough to bait a trained kill team?*

Only someone who knew these waters like they knew their own heartbeat.

"He's playing us," Lopez muttered from his position at the helm.

He's buying the others time.

Ramón didn't respond aloud. He didn't need to. They'd all seen this game before — a target trying to draw pursuers into dangerous territory. Sometimes it worked.

Usually it got them killed faster.

The setting sun painted the water in shades of amber, making depth impossible to judge. Another boat lurched across their bow, running dark — Castellanos and Ortiz, moving to cut off escape routes.

Good. They had protocols for situations like this, patterns practiced until they became instinct. Box them in. Force them to ground. Clean up the mess.

It was a perfect place for it, too. No one knew the reefs and channels cut through it like a local, but the zodiacs were much easier to maneuver through them. Their engines didn't drop quite as far into the water as a standard fishing boat motor, nor did the hull dip as deeply.

A wrong move on a standard-fare boat meant slamming full-speed into coral or rock. A zodiac would have to severely miscalculate to have the same effect.

A warning flare streaked across the darkening sky, burning white-hot against purple clouds. Castellanos signaling the flank was in position. The net was closing. Even Manny had to see that now.

"Cut him off. He's forcing us into the rocks," Ramón barked into his comm, keeping his voice low despite the engine noise. Sound carried strange over water, bounced off waves in unpredictable ways. The coral maze below was treacherous — sharp reef teeth waiting to gut their hull — but as he'd suspected, Manny navigated it like he was born to it.

Ramón didn't know these waters, couldn't predict the hidden channels and deadly shoals. While he'd trained here and tried his best to memorize the landscape, he was the outsider now.

And that pissed him off.

He'd learned early that knowledge was power in this business. Know the terrain. Know the target. Know the angles. Right now, Manny had that advantage. The man was local, had probably fished these reefs since childhood. Every coral head was a landmark, every channel a potential escape route.

The distance between boats shrank. Twenty meters. Fifteen. Ramón could see Manny clearly now, hands steady on the wheel despite the violent maneuvers. He was alone on the boat. No sign of panic. No desperate glances over his shoulder. Just calm, focused determination.

Wrong attitude for a man about to die.

Ten meters. Ramón shifted his grip on his rifle, compensating for the Zodiac's bounce across the waves. One clean shot would end this chase. But something held him back — instinct, maybe. The nagging sense that this was too easy.

Five meters. Manny's boat suddenly slowed, as if surrendering. Ramón's finger tightened on the trigger.

Then everything went sideways.

The skiff's engine roared to full power again, turning hard into them. Ramón had a split-second glimpse of Manny's face — not afraid, not desperate, but grimly satisfied — before the boats collided with a sick crunch of fiberglass and metal.

The impact launched Ramón off his feet. His back slammed against the console seat, driving the air from his lungs in an explosive grunt. The rifle clattered away somewhere in the chaos. Everything tilted sideways as the boats ground together, screaming in protest.

His training kicked in before his brain could fully process what happened. *Roll. Get up. Find weapon. Assess threat.* Basic stuff, drilled into muscle memory through years of operations. He came up in a fighter's crouch, sidearm already drawn.

Manny was trying to crawl upright in his own boat, movements jerky and uncoordinated. Blood ran freely from a gash at his temple, matting his hair. The way he favored his left side suggested broken ribs. No weapon visible. No radio. Just a man who'd sacrificed his boat to buy... what? Time?

Ramón stepped across the mangled bow, boots crunching on shattered fiberglass. His pistol found Manny's forehead. The other man's breathing was ragged, wet-sounding. Internal injuries, probably. The collision had done its work.

"*That* was your move?" Ramón asked. "You think this stall bought them time?" His genuine curiosity was mixed with professional assessment. It was always interesting to see how people faced their final moments.

Some begged. Some cursed. Some tried to bargain.

Manny just coughed, spitting blood and seawater onto the deck. His silence was answer enough.

The radio on Ramón's hip crackled to life, breaking the moment. Static hissed, then cleared: *"...Manny, we're coming! Don't do anything stupid!"*

A man's voice — obviously one of the Americans — faint but clear through the interference. Ramón smiled. So *that* was the play — sacrifice the knight to protect the king. Noble, in a futile sort of way.

Manny's lips curled up at the sound, revealing bloodstained teeth. It wasn't fear in his eyes, or even defiance really. It was satisfaction. The look of a man who'd accomplished his mission, whatever the cost.

Ramón had seen that expression before. In Venezuela, when a wounded operative had held off his team long enough for valuable intel to be evacuated. In Colombia, when a local guide had led them into an ambush to protect his village. The smile of someone who knew they were dead but had achieved their goal anyway.

He hated that smile.

The pistol barked once, the sound sharp across the water. Manny's body slumped, the satisfaction frozen on his lifeless face. The waves lapped at the joined boats, slowly washing red stains into the darkening sea.

Ramón keyed his radio. "Target eliminated. Still have inbound hostiles." He paused, looking toward the deeper water where Ben's voice had come from. "Orders?"

Valeria's response was immediate, cold: *"Find them. End this. The client arrives in three hours, and I want the wreck and the evidence here smoldering. I'm standing by — once you've taken care of this, say the word and I'll blow it all."*

"Understood." He switched channels. "Castellanos, you heard her. Form up. We're hunting."

The sun dipped lower, painting the sky in deeper shades of purple and red. Somewhere out there, Ben and his ragtag team was racing toward a dead man. Racing toward their own end, though they didn't know it yet.

Ramón reloaded his pistol, muscles already anticipating the night's work ahead. The sea would claim more bodies before dawn. He would make sure of it.

Manny's boat shifted beneath his feet, settling lower in the water. Soon it would sink, taking its captain to the depths. Just another secret for the reef to keep.

Ramón stepped back to his own vessel, mind already plotting intercept courses.

CHAPTER 70

BEN

THROUGH SALT-STUNG EYES, standing on Manny's tiny fishing boat, Ben tracked the two boats knifing across the water. The lead Zodiac skimmed the waves like a thrown stone, its bow lifting with each swell. A man crouched at the helm while another — muscled, tactical vest, rifle at the ready — balanced beside him. The second boat followed in their wake, two more armed men aboard, creating a pincer movement toward the main cave.

"We're too late," Sarah whispered, prone beside him on the rocky outcrop. Her borrowed rifle stayed trained on the lead boat.

"Maybe for Manny, but not for the others." Ben checked the magazine of the rifle he'd pilfered from the downed guards — half full. Not great, but it would have to do. "He bought us time. Now we use it."

They'd heard the gunshot echo across the water minutes ago. Neither spoke about what it meant. They couldn't afford to think about Manny now.

The boats were closing fast, heading directly toward the cave entrance. Ben steadied his breathing, found his sight picture. "On my mark."

Sarah's only response was to shift her weight slightly, settling into a better firing position. They'd worked together enough that words weren't needed. Not for this.

She might be an anthropologist by trade, but she was dating Gareth Red. Ben smiled as he imagined it. She'd been well-trained by Reggie.

"Mark."

Their rifles cracked in unison. Water exploded in white plumes around the lead boat as rounds stitched across its path. The helmsman swerved hard, trying to dodge the incoming fire. It was the wrong move. At that speed, the sudden turn sent them straight into a hidden sandbar.

The Zodiac's bow hit first, launching up like a breaching whale. Equipment and men catapulted through the air as the boat flipped completely over. The second vessel veered away, but Sarah was ready. Her rifle chattered, forcing them wide and away from their fallen comrades.

One of the men from the crashed boat was struggling to his feet in the knee-deep water — the one who'd been standing, the fighter. He'd managed to hold onto his knife. Blood ran from a cut above his eye, but his movements were focused, deliberate. Dangerous.

Ben jumped over the edge of Manny's boat, swam a few paces until the ground reached his feet, and hit the sandbar running. Sand and water sprayed behind him. He hadn't taken the rifle, not trusting it to the water and needing his arms to swim.

The armed man saw him coming, recovered much quicker than Ben would have guessed, and shifted stance, blade ready. Professional. Trained. This wasn't some tourist with a pocket knife — this was someone who killed for a living.

They met in the surf like colliding waves. Ben dropped his shoulder for a tackle, but the man side-stepped, slashing in a tight arc. Fire bloomed across Ben's forearm as the blade found flesh. He trapped the knife hand, threw an elbow that caught mostly air. They grappled, feet struggling for purchase in the shifting sand while waves crashed around their legs.

The man was good — better than Ben. Each movement flowed into the next, every strike setting up another. But Ben had desperation on his side, and he knew that often it was enough.

He reeled back, then drove his forehead into the bridge of the man's nose, feeling cartilage crunch. The grip on the knife loosened just enough.

Ben hooked a leg behind his opponent's knee and drove forward.

They went down together in a spray of saltwater and blood. The knife disappeared somewhere in the chaos. Ben's hand found something solid in the surf — a piece of driftwood, worn smooth by the sea. He swung it before conscious thought could intervene.

The wood connected with a dull thunk. The man's eyes rolled back, body going slack. Ben rolled away, gasping. His arm throbbed where the knife had opened it, but the cut wasn't deep. He'd had worse.

"Ben!" Sarah's voice cut through the ringing in his ears. She was racing down the beach, rifle slung across her back. A hard-shell case bounced against her hip as she ran. "Found something!"

She dropped to her knees in the wet sand beside him, already working the latches on the case. Inside, nestled in foam padding, sat what looked like a tablet computer. Sarah's fingers flew across its casing, popping it open to reveal a mess of circuits and antennas.

"Receiver unit," she said, eyes scanning the components. "Has to be for the charges they planted. See these transmitters? They're designed for underwater detonation. Military grade stuff."

Ben glanced at the unconscious man beside them. "You think Valeria's really planning to bring down the entire reef and wreck site?"

"Why not? It's what I'd do in her position. Destroy the evidence, bury the wreck forever." She traced a finger along one of the circuit boards, pointing at a tiny red LED. "This is still broadcasting. Must still in range of the charges."

Their radio crackled to life, making them both jump. Isla's voice came through breathless and desperate: *"Ben — we're still inside — Reggie found a detonator."*

Before Ben could respond, Reggie cut in: *"It'll take out the caves... and the wreck, all at the same time. The charges here have been set, but the systems are tied together. You've got to break the link or we lose everything, and the Syndicate wins. We're running out of time."*

As if to emphasize his point, alarms began wailing across the cove. Red lights flashed from the Syndicate compound, reflecting off the darkening water. Guard stations high above on the rocks came alive with searchlights, sweeping across the beaches and numerous sandbars.

"How long?" Ben demanded, already gathering Sarah's computer case.

"No idea. Minutes maybe," Reggie answered. *"The timer's counting down, though. I can try to —"* Static swallowed the rest.

Ben grabbed Sarah's arm. "Can you disable it?"

She was already shaking her head. "Not in time. This is just the receiver and a signal booster. It'll receive the signal from the base, then amplify it and send it out again to detonate the charges out by the reef."

"Can you just turn it off?" Ben asked. "Like... toss it overboard?"

Sarah shook her head. "Believe it or not, they've thought of that. It'll be watertight, at least for a certain amount of hours. And this area's not nearly deep enough that we could sink it to force it lose connection with the signal source."

"So we have to figure out how to sever the connection another way," he said.

She nodded. "The actual detonator must be with Valeria. But maybe..." She bit her lip, thinking. "Maybe we can jam it. Create enough interference that the signal can't reach the charges."

"Do it." Ben checked his rifle, then the unconscious man's pulse. Still steady. He zip-tied the man's hands behind his back, just in case. "What do you need?"

Sarah was pulling components from the case, working with swift precision. "Cover. Time. And..." She yanked a fistful of wires free. "The boat's battery. I can use the one from this zodiac, as long as it didn't get completely destroyed. If I can boost the signal enough, flood the right frequency..."

The second boat was still out there, circling just beyond effective rifle range. As if reading his thoughts, a burst of automatic fire kicked up sand near their position. Ben grabbed Sarah's shoulder, pushing her behind a pile of wreckage from the zodiac.

"Okay, on it. Stay here and work fast." He checked his magazine again — four rounds left. Not enough. He grabbed the unconscious man's rifle, checking the action. Full magazine. "I'll keep them busy."

Sarah caught his arm. "Ben. If this doesn't work..."

"It'll work." He managed a grin he didn't feel. "You're the smart one, remember?"

More gunfire peppered their position. The boat was closing in, using the growing darkness for cover. Soon they'd flank around the sandbar and surrounding isles, catching them in a crossfire.

Unless...

Ben chambered a round, sighted on the boat's searchlight, and began his own countdown. Sometimes victory came down to simple math — how many bullets you had, how many seconds remained, how many chances you got to make it right.

Three seconds of darkness. Four rounds in the magazine. One chance to make it count.

The light swept away. Ben smiled into the fading light and squeezed the trigger.

The fate of the reef, the wreck, and everyone he cared about now balanced on the edge of a knife. Or more accurately, on Sarah's ability to jam a signal before Valeria could send it. The next few minutes would determine everything.

Ben hoped they were fast enough. Smart enough. Lucky enough.

The dusk skyline erupted in gunfire and searching beams of light. Somewhere in the chaos, a timer continued its relentless countdown toward zero.

CHAPTER 71

REGGIE

GUNFIRE RICOCHETED off the metal crates, sending sparks flying. Reggie yanked Isla behind a stack of supply boxes as another burst peppered their position. The acrid smell of cordite filled his nostrils as brass clinked against concrete. He checked his borrowed weapon — half a mag left.

Not great odds, but he'd worked with less.

The gun felt wrong in his hands — Soviet-made, probably black market. The previous owner's blood still stained the grip. He'd taken it off the guard during their initial firefight, when everything went sideways. Now it was just another tool to keep them alive.

But the tablet detonator he'd found and was holding in his other hand felt worse. He knew with a button press he could rain down absolute terror — and instant death — on all of them.

Come on, Ben, he thought. *Get it done.*

"Exit's that way," he said, jerking his chin toward the corridor. Three Syndicate gunmen blocked their path, methodically advancing behind cover.

Professional. Organized. Bad news.

Dammit, he thought, *why couldn't we get a few of those idiot kids from outside instead?* These guys weren't rent-a-cops — their movements spoke of serious training. Ex-military, perhaps. The kind who shot first and never bothered asking questions.

The alarm's wail drilled into his skull. Red emergency lights strobed through gun smoke, turning the cave into some kind of hellish disco. The effect was disorienting, making depth perception tricky. More boots thundered past in the adjacent tunnel — personnel evacuating topside.

This place was about to become a tomb.

Reggie's artificial fingers flexed unconsciously, the servos adjusting to his stress levels. The prosthetic was state-of-the-art, but even cutting-edge tech had limits. He could already feel the battery running low after their earlier acrobatics. Usually he charged it overnight, but he'd not been able to. Twenty minutes left, maybe less. After that, it would be dead weight.

"Cruz is clearing everyone out," Isla said, reading his thoughts. She pressed closer as bullets chewed the crate above them. "She'll blow it as soon as she's clear."

"Then we better move." Reggie popped up, squeezed off two rounds. The first went wide, but the second found its mark. One of the gunmen cursed, ducking back with blood streaming from his shoulder. "Sarah needs time to kill that signal."

They'd lost radio contact minutes ago — too much rock between them and the surface. The cave system's natural geometry played hell with communications. No way to know if Sarah had managed to jam the detonator frequency. No way to know anything except that the clock was running down.

Isla checked her own weapon — a 9mm she'd lifted from the command center. "Four rounds."

"Make them count." Reggie scanned their surroundings, mind racing through scenarios. The supply crates offered decent cover, but they were trapped here. The longer they waited, the worse their odds got.

A metallic clink caught his attention. A grenade bounced off the wall, rolling toward them. Time stretched as his combat training — and instincts for self-preservation — kicked in.

Reggie's hand shot out, snatching it mid-tumble. He hurled it back the way it came. He'd used his prosthetic, so the throw was faster than human, but it was still close. The explosion rattled his teeth, but the screams told him it had found its mark.

"Now!" He grabbed Isla's arm, yanking her up. They sprinted through the smoke together, borrowed boots sliding on shell casings. The corridor ahead was a shooting gallery — fifty meters of exposed space. His fingers found another grenade on his belt — his last one. He didn't look as he threw it behind them, letting the sound of pursuit guide his aim.

The blast bought them precious seconds. Reggie heard cursing in at least three languages as their pursuers scrambled for cover.

Good. Let them think twice about following too close.

They rounded a corner at full tilt, nearly colliding with an abandoned tool cart. Medical supplies spilled across the floor — bandages, trauma kits, morphine. Someone had been prepping for casualties. Apparently, Cruz's people knew this wouldn't end clean.

They'd taken a different way back, but he had memorized where they were — since the Syndicate had used the relatively small cave's existing tunnels as their base, there weren't a lot of ways to get back to the main cave entrance and exit.

Two corridors until the exit. Then up the main shaft. Assuming it wasn't already collapsed. Assuming Cruz hadn't changed her mind about waiting. Assuming a lot of things that could get them killed. The math wasn't great, but it was all they had.

His prosthetic arm twinged — battery dropping faster now. The advanced sensors were power-hungry, and he'd been pushing the servos hard. After it died, he'd be down to flesh and bone. Not ideal in their current situation.

More gunfire erupted ahead — different weapons, different shooters. The reports were sharper, more disciplined. Isla skidded to a stop, pressing against the wall. "Company!"

"Good." Reggie checked his mag again. *Three rounds.* Hardly enough to sneeze at, but beggars couldn't be choosers. "I was getting bored."

He tried not to think about the tons of rock above them, wired with enough explosives to reshape geography. Tried not to calculate blast radii and structural collapse patterns. Those thoughts led nowhere good.

The alarm screamed on, counting down their remaining time. Some-where deeper in the cave, Cruz's finger hovered over a button that would bury them all. Obviously, she wasn't planning to blow it yet — if she was still inside when the explosives detonated, she'd be signing her own death sentence.

But the fact it was imminent meant that she had a plan to get out just in time. Perhaps she was already on the way out, and they only had seconds left.

The smart play would be to cut their losses, find another way out. But smart wasn't always right. Sarah needed more time to work her technical magic, and every second they kept Cruz's people busy was another second she had to shut down the repeater signal that would take out the reef.

He glanced at Isla. Her face was streaked with grime and blood — none of it hers, thankfully. Reggie flashed her a grin, cold and sharp as a knife's edge. "Ready to make some noise?"

She matched his smile, equally fierce. "Always."

Heavy boots approached from both directions now. Cruz's people were done playing games. Soon they'd be caught in a crossfire, with nowhere to run and nothing left to lose. But sometimes that's when the best plans came together — when your back was against the wall and all the smart options were gone.

You should never corner someone with nothing left to lose.

CHAPTER 72

VALERIA

VALERIA CRUZ TAPPED her manicured nails against the steel desk, watching the security feeds with cold satisfaction. Her private office — more of a bunker, really — offered the perfect vantage point to orchestrate the endgame. The monitors showed chaos above: gunfire, explosions, her people engaging the intruders on multiple fronts.

Let them fight. It wouldn't matter soon.

She turned to the sleek laptop centered on her desk. The detonation program waited for her command — elegant in its simplicity. One button to erase all evidence, bury her enemies, and ensure the Syndicate maintained control. Ramón had confirmed the charges were set at the wreck site hours ago. Everything was ready.

"Quite the show up there," she murmured, switching between camera feeds. The angle from the guard tower caught her attention — muzzle flashes lighting up the beach like fireflies. Her people had the Americans pinned down near a boat. *Good. Let them watch helplessly as I bury their precious discovery.*

The red emergency lights cast a bloody glow across her office's polished surfaces. She'd designed this space for moments like this — when hard decisions needed to be made in comfort. The leather chair cradled her perfectly. The air conditioning hummed at exactly 72 degrees. Even the lighting was calibrated to reduce eye strain.

Besides the rough-hewn stone walls, carved out by millennia of gentle dripping water, it had all the comforts of home.

Details mattered. *Control* mattered more.

She picked up her coffee — still hot, the ceramic warmed by the built-in heater in her desk. The rich aroma of Brazilian beans filled her nose as she savored a sip. No reason this had to be unpleasant.

The radio on her hip crackled with updates from her security teams. She switched it off. She needed focus now, needed to time this perfectly. The automated sequence would give her exactly twenty seconds to reach the escape tunnel — more than enough time at a casual walk. But she wanted to wait, to ensure maximum impact.

Her people were *technically* expendable, yes, but needlessly wasting assets was poor business. Better to give them time to clear out. And if Halim happened to be watching when she brought down the mountain and wreck site... well, that was just good theater.

Cruz pulled up the demolition schematics on a second monitor. The charges had been placed with surgical precision — shaped explosives that would collapse the cave system in a controlled sequence. The wreck's charges would detonate simultaneously, leaving nothing but rubble under thousands of tons of coral.

"Let's check one last time," she said to herself, fingers dancing across the keyboard. The program responded instantly, displaying status read-outs from each charge. *All green. All perfect.*

She allowed herself a small smile. Even without the radio, she could imagine the frustration in the Americans' voice right now. The desperation. The dawning realization that he'd failed. That everything they'd fought for would disappear forever.

The thought pleased her immensely.

Movement on the security feed caught her eye. Two figures sprinting across the compound — the girl and the one-armed man. She watched them dodge gunfire, making for the tree line. Their desperation was almost admirable.

"Run all you want," Cruz murmured. "It changes nothing."

She opened her desk drawer, removed a small case. Inside, nestled in foam padding, sat her insurance policy — a detonator, independent of the main system. Simple. Analog. Unhackable. If something went wrong with the automated sequence, she could still trigger everything manually from her tablet, or elsewhere in the base.

The case went into her jacket pocket. She wouldn't need it, but she hadn't survived this long by leaving things to chance.

Cruz checked her watch — a Patek Philippe worth more than most people's homes. The second hand swept smoothly across the face, marking time with Swiss precision.

The cameras showed more of her people evacuating topside. *Good.* She reached for the laptop, fingers hovering over the keyboard. The program was elegant in its simplicity — three keystrokes to start the countdown.

Three keystrokes to end it all.

Cruz allowed herself another sip of coffee, savoring the moment. These Americans had been thornier than expected, she had to admit. Lesser opponents would have broken after the ambush. But they'd proven remarkably resilient.

Like cockroaches, really. Scuttling from shadow to shadow, refusing to die.

No matter. Cockroaches could still be crushed.

She set down her cup, perfectly centering it on its coaster. The motion reminded her of placing chess pieces — each move calculated, each position exact. The game was ending now, and she held all the winning moves.

The security feeds showed increasing chaos above. More gunfire, more explosions. Her teams were pushing hard, pressing the advantage.

Cruz straightened in her chair, smoothing nonexistent wrinkles from her silk blouse. The weight of the manual detonator pressed against her ribs, comforting in its solidity. She'd planned this moment carefully, coordinating each element like a symphony conductor.

The charges would cascade through the cave system in precise sequence. First, the support pillars in the main shaft would shatter. Then the secondary tunnels would fold inward as strategically placed explosives compromised key structural points. Finally, the main cavern housing would implode, crushing everything beneath millions of tons of coral and limestone.

Poetry in demolition.

Her fingers moved to the keyboard. The program responded instantly, cursor blinking in anticipation.

She input the first command. Green text scrolled across the screen, confirming activation. Warning messages flashed — standard safety protocols that she dismissed. The system hummed to life, power cycling through redundant circuits.

Second keystroke. More confirmations, more warnings. The program was quite insistent about verifying the user's intent. As if she hadn't planned this moment for weeks, hadn't calculated every variable.

Her finger hovered over the final key. Through the cameras, she watched her remaining personnel clear the upper levels. They moved with professional efficiency, executing their evacuation protocols perfectly. She'd trained them well.

The American team was still fighting, still trying to salvage their doomed mission. Such determination. Such futility. They reminded her of ants trying to stop a tsunami — admirable perhaps, but ultimately meaningless.

Cruz pressed the final key.

The screen flared to life with cascading data. Status indicators turned amber, then red. A countdown appeared in the center display: *20:00*. Then *19:59*. Then *19:58*.

The symphony was beginning.

She stood smoothly, adjusting her jacket over her blouse. The manual detonator shifted against her side as she moved. It was redundant, but redundancy was useful. The weight felt good — reassuring.

Control, after all, was everything.

Her shoes clicked against smoothed stone as she crossed to the hidden door. It opened silently on pneumatic hinges, revealing her private escape tunnel. The passage had been a considerable expense — requiring specialist engineers and absolute secrecy — but moments like this made it worthwhile.

She paused in the doorway, looking back at her office one final time. The monitors still showed chaos above. The countdown continued its relentless march toward zero. Everything was proceeding exactly as planned.

Cruz smiled. It wasn't often that reality matched one's expectations so perfectly. She would savor this victory, she decided. Perhaps celebrate with a bottle of '82 *Lafite* when she reached the offshore yacht they'd purchased as a floating safe house. Good wine appreciated properly marked the difference between mere success and true triumph.

Or even better, an aged tequila.

The door sealed behind her with a soft hiss. Emergency lights illuminated the tunnel ahead — a straight shot to freedom. She began walking, unhurried. No need to rush. After all, she had twenty minutes until her masterpiece's first movement began.

More than enough time for a perfect exit.

CHAPTER 73

REGGIE

THE GUARD never saw the bullet coming. His arm was cocked back, grenade ready to throw, when Reggie's last round caught him in the chest. The man's grip went slack as he fell, fingers releasing the pin.

"Down!" Reggie tackled Isla as the grenade dropped. The explosion rocked the tunnel, showering them with debris. His ears rang, but training kept him moving. He rolled to his feet, pulling Isla up with his good arm.

Through the smoke, he saw their opportunity. The blast had collapsed part of the tunnel ceiling, crushing two more guards beneath rubble. The third was struggling to stand, dazed from the concussion.

Isla's pistol cracked once. The guard dropped.

"Exit's clear," she said, already moving. "For now."

They sprinted past the bodies, boots crunching on fallen rock. Reggie's lungs burned — too much smoke, too much running. But stopping meant dying, so he pushed through it. The emergency lights still strobed, painting everything in hellish red pulses.

The main shaft loomed ahead — their last obstacle. Fifty feet straight up to the surface. Metal rungs bolted into concrete led the way, disappearing into darkness above. It would be slow going one-handed — he needed to preserve as much battery in his prosthetic as possible — but there was no choice.

"Ladies first." Reggie gestured to the ladder. "I'll cover."

Isla was already climbing, moving fast despite exhaustion. *Smart girl. Don't waste time arguing when seconds count.* Reggie backed toward the ladder, scanning for pursuit. The tunnel behind them stayed quiet — maybe the collapse had bought them more time than expected.

His arm trembled as he grabbed the first rung. The prosthetic hung useless, throwing off his balance. Each movement was an exercise in careful positioning, making sure he had solid grip before reaching for the next hold. Isla was already twenty feet up, moving like a spider in the darkness.

Boots echoed below — someone had found a way around the cave-in. Reggie climbed faster, muscles screaming in protest. A bullet pinged off the wall near his head. Then another. He didn't look down, didn't think about the fall. Just kept moving.

Thirty feet up. His palm was slick with sweat, making each grip precarious. More shots rang out, the sound amplified by the shaft's acoustics. But the shooters were firing blind now, barely visible shapes in the red-tinged darkness below.

Isla reached the top first, disappearing over the rim. Seconds later, her hand appeared, reaching down. Reggie grabbed it with his good arm, letting her help haul him up the final few rungs. They collapsed together on solid ground, gasping.

"That was fun," he managed between breaths. "Let's never do it again."

Any reply Isla might have made died in her throat as they took in their surroundings. The cove had transformed into a war zone. Searchlights swept across the water from guard towers, cutting through the growing darkness. The beams found whitecaps and coral heads, searching for targets.

Two Zodiac boats circled near the reef line, their crews scanning with rifle-mounted optics. Red emergency strobes pulsed from the Syndicate compound, matching the rhythm of alarms still wailing from below. The whole scene felt surreal, like something from a Michael Bay movie.

"There!" Isla pointed toward the beach. Muzzle flashes sparked from behind an outcropping of rocks — Ben and Sarah's position. Return fire from the boats kicked up sand around them. "They're pinned down."

Reggie did a quick ammo check — three rounds in Isla's pistol, nothing else. His near-dead prosthetic meant he couldn't even shoot straight if they *had* more guns. Not great odds for a rescue attempt.

A radio squawked nearby, making them both jump. A guard lay sprawled beside the shaft entrance, neck twisted at an unnatural angle. Must have met the wrong end of Isla's fighting skills during their earlier escape. His tactical vest still held equipment — including spare magazines.

"Christmas came early." Reggie grabbed what he could with one hand while Isla reloaded her pistol. The guard's rifle was a bonus — identical to the one he'd lost below. Same Soviet knockoff, same ergonomics. He could work this one-handed if needed.

More guards were shouting orders across the compound. Soon they'd have company up here too. But the high ground gave them options — clear fields of fire, good cover behind ventilation equipment. They might just survive this.

"Ben's trying to draw fire," Isla said, studying the firefight out on the water. "Keeping them busy while Sarah works."

Reggie nodded. Classic Ben — maximum chaos, minimum subtlety. "Then let's help. You got a shot on that rear boat?"

Isla's answer was a single crack from her pistol. One of the Zodiac's crew pitched backward, splashing into dark water. The boat swerved, nearly colliding with its partner. Confusion was always good in a firefight — made people sloppy, made them rush decisions.

Reggie braced the rifle against a vent housing. The boats were regrouping, trying to coordinate. Bad mistake. Bunching up just made them easier targets. He put two rounds through the nearest engine housing. Black smoke began pouring from the cowling.

The disabled boat wallowed, crew scrambling to restart their dead motor. The other Zodiac moved to assist, leaving Ben's position momentarily clear. Reggie saw him sprint from cover. He was making for the tree line, away from the beach.

Smart. Change the battlefield. Make the enemy come to you.

"Moving!" Isla was already up, keeping low as she circled the shaft housing. Reggie followed, rifle ready. They needed to reach the trees before-

The world exploded.

Gunfire ripped through the air as the working Zodiac spotted them. Bullets sparked off metal, forcing them flat against the ground. Reggie rolled behind a generator, off balance. More rounds punched holes through the thin metal inches from his head.

"Left side!" he shouted to Isla. She was pinned down behind another generator twenty feet away. The boat's gunner had them zeroed — any movement would draw instant fire.

Isla answered by blind-firing two rounds over the generator. The shots went wide but forced the gunner to duck. Reggie used the moment to pop up and squeeze off a burst. His one-handed grip made the rifle jump, but he caught one of the crew in the shoulder. The man dropped his weapon, clutching at the wound.

"Run! I'll cover!" Reggie emptied his magazine toward the boat. The sustained fire kept their heads down long enough for Isla to sprint toward the tree line. His rifle clicked empty just as she reached the first row of palms.

The boat gunner recovered fast, stitching a line of bullets that walked closer to Reggie's position. He was out of ammo, out of options, and running out of cover. The generators wouldn't stop their rounds much longer.

CHAPTER 74
BEN

BEN'S LUNGS burned as he dove behind the Zodiac's hull. Bullets peppered the rubber sides, the impacts feeling like punches through the material. He rolled, came up shooting, dropped another guard rushing their position.

"How much longer?" he shouted over his shoulder.

Sarah didn't look up from her work. Tools and wires spread around her like mechanical entrails, connecting the receiver unit to the boat's battery. "Two minutes. Maybe less."

"We don't have two minutes." Ben popped up, fired twice, ducked back as return fire kicked up sand. "They're flanking right."

The night had turned into a shooting gallery. Searchlights swept the beach while guards advanced in teams, using the rocks and vegetation for cover. They'd lost the element of surprise, and now it was just a matter of time before the Syndicate got restless and started closing the trap.

Sarah cursed as something sparked. The smell of burning insulation mixed with gasoline fumes — she'd emptied the boat's fuel tank across the deck, a last-resort backup plan. If the signal hack failed, Ben realized, they'd blow the receiver the old-fashioned way. It wasn't exactly a *scientific* solution, but it was better than nothing. With luck, the repeater device was programmed to send multiple signals over a set time period, to cause the explosives at the wreck site to blow at different times. By destroying it completely, it may not completely kill the outbound signal, but maybe they could at least save a portion of the site.

Hopefully it was just an unneeded failsafe, and Sarah's MacGyvering would be enough.

"The amperage is wrong," she muttered, stripping more wires. "Need to boost it without frying everything."

Ben took down another guard trying to circle wide. His magazine ran dry — last one. He grabbed a fallen MP5 from the sand, checked the action. Half a mag left. Better than nothing.

"Company!" he warned as more shapes emerged from the darkness. Three men, moving fast between cover. *They're not even on a boat.* Apparently the Syndicate had had enough — this group had parked nearby, hoping to sneak up on them over the sandbar. Their rifles thundered, forcing Ben lower behind the boat. One round punched through the hull near his head, missing by inches.

He felt Sarah tense behind him. "Don't stop," he said. "I got this."

Ben waited for a pause in the shooting, then rolled right, away from the boat. His sudden movement drew their fire — exactly what he wanted. He came up running, zigzagging between palm trees and boulders as bullets chewed bark around him.

The guards shifted to track him, exposing their flanks to the boat. *Rookie mistake.* Sarah's pistol cracked twice. One man went down clutching his leg. The others scattered, losing their coordinated advance.

Ben used the confusion to close distance. He slid behind a boulder, popped up firing. The MP5 bucked in his hands as he emptied the magazine. One guard took three rounds center mass, falling backward into the surf. The other dove for cover, but Ben was already moving.

He hit the man like a freight train, driving him into the sand. They grappled, rolling in the shallow water. The guard was strong, trained in close combat. But Ben had more desperation and sheer will on his side. He'd been in plenty of scrapes like this, and his size, grit, and resilience often won the day, even against superior opponents.

Plus, he'd been training for moments exactly like this back at the CSO headquarters and his home.

He let the man pull him in, giving him the brief illusion he'd won. Then, continuing the motion and speeding up, he slammed his forehead into the man's nose, feeling cartilage crack. Blood sprayed as the guard's grip loosened more.

Ben grabbed the man's head and drove it into the packed sand. Once, twice, until he went limp. The whole fight lasted seconds.

"Ben!" Sarah's voice carried across the beach. "It's ready!"

He sprinted back toward the boat, staying low. More guards were pushing forward, using suppressing fire to cover their advance. The night lit up with muzzle flashes and searching beams. They were running out of time.

Sarah had the receiver unit balanced on the boat's console, a rat's nest of wires connecting it to the battery. The deck around her feet sloshed with spilled gasoline. She looked up as Ben vaulted over the side, her face streaked with grease and sweat.

"I boosted the power," she said, hands still working. "When I throw this switch, it'll pump enough juice through to hopefully overload their detonator frequency." She paused. "Or... it might explode."

"Lovely options." Ben scanned the beach. More shapes moving in the darkness. "How big an explosion?"

"With all this gas? Big enough." She stripped the last wire. "That's why you need to get clear."

"*We* need to get clear."

She shook her head. "Someone has to throw the switch. The timing has to be perfect — right when Reggie sends the detonate signal. Too early and she'll notice something's wrong, and might be able to stop it. Too late and..." She gestured at the cave entrance.

Ben grabbed her arm. "No. We do this together or-"

Gunfire forced them both down as rounds punched through the boat. Water began seeping through the holes. They had minutes before the Zodiac became useless.

Sarah met his eyes. In the strobing emergency lights, he saw the determination there. The certainty. "Ben. Please."

"You pull this off," he said, "I'm making Reggie take you out somewhere *really* nice."

"And really expensive," she added with a smile.

He sighed. He wanted to argue. Wanted to find another way. But she was right — someone *had* to stay. And she was the only one who could time it perfectly.

His radio crackled. Reggie's voice came through, tight with tension. *"Ben, we're in position. Cruz is moving. It's now or never."*

Sarah pressed her pistol into his hands. "Go. I got this."

Ben vaulted over the side as more bullets struck the boat. He sprinted for the tree line, drawing their fire. Behind him, Sarah hunched over the receiver, hands hovering over the jury-rigged switch.

"Reggie," Ben shouted into his radio. "Get ready with that detonator!"

"Copy. Radio chatter says Cruz has left her personal quarters, after initiating an automated countdown sequence. It will obviously give her enough time to get out. I'd guess thirty seconds or less before she's out of the caves and safe."

Ben reached the palms, turned back toward the beach. Guards were closing on the boat from three sides. Sarah remained focused on her work, ignoring the incoming fire. The gasoline sloshed around her feet with each impact.

"Twenty seconds," Reggie updated.

A bullet struck the receiver unit, sending sparks flying. Sarah ducked, but kept working. The guards were twenty yards out now. *Fifteen.* Their rifles lit up the night.

"Ten seconds!"

Ben raised his pistol, trying to buy her more time. But there were too many. The boat was being shredded, taking dozens of hits. Water poured in through the holes. Any second now it would sink, taking their last chance with it.

"Five seconds!"

"Sarah!" Ben screamed. "Now!"

She threw the switch.

The night turned to day as electricity arced between wires. The receiver glowed white-hot, smoking. For a horrible moment, nothing else happened.

Then the gasoline caught.

THE TABLET in her hand displayed scrolling status indicators, all green. Each explosive charge checked in sequence, ready to perform its role in the coming symphony. She'd spent weeks planning the demolition, ensuring the cave system would collapse inward with mathematical precision, leaving nothing for salvage crews to find. The wreck site charges would detonate simultaneously, leaving nothing but rubble under tons of coral, and that under tons of sand.

Just the way it had been before the hurricane had almost undone her work.

The Syndicate stood to make a lot of money, and she wasn't going to let anyone stop her.

She walked further down the cave's hall toward the escape tunnel. The sound echoed off stone walls — sharp, authoritative. The weight of the tablet pressed against her ribs.

The tablet chirped.

Cruz glanced down, irritation flickering across her perfectly composed features. She hadn't activated any audible alerts. The screen flickered, went dark, then flashed back to life. Numbers appeared:

5...

Her breath caught. This wasn't right. She'd programmed twenty minutes — enough time for a dignified exit, and then some. She'd planned to get well away from the cave, and possibly out to where Halim's boat might be waiting, so they could watch it together and raise a glass to the next phase of their partnership.

But she couldn't think of that now. Her fingers flew across the interface, muscle memory executing override commands. *Nothing* responded. The system remained locked, running its fatal countdown. She'd designed it that way herself — no stopping the sequence once initiated. The manual detonators like this one were only intended to *restart* the countdown if there was a software or hardware failure.

4...

The escape tunnel stretched ahead, harsh shadows making distances deceptive. The ladder waited at the far end, maybe thirty feet away. *Too far.* Her heart slammed against her ribs as reality crystallized. She'd been played. All her careful planning, all her contingencies, turned against her.

3...

Cruz ran. Her shoes betrayed her, throwing her off balance. She kicked them off mid-stride, expensive leather skidding across concrete. Her bare feet slapped against the cold floor as she sprinted. The ladder seemed to stretch further away with each step, mocking her efforts.

The tablet's screen pulsed with artificial heartbeats, counting down her remaining moments. She could imagine them above — the one-armed man, the girl, the two other Americans — watching and waiting. They'd beaten her at her own game, turned her perfect plan into the perfect trap.

But how?

2...

She couldn't stop it. Couldn't outrun it. Didn't have enough time to even consider how they'd done it. The tablet pressed against her side like a burning brand, useless now. The charges would cascade through the cave system, each explosion triggering the next in a chain reaction of destruction. Her masterpiece of demolition would become her tomb.

Sweat ran down her spine, soaking silk and fear into her skin. The ladder was still too far. The tunnel much too long. Physics and fate had conspired against her, reducing all her careful plans to dust.

1...

"No..."

The word was lost in thunder as the charges detonated. The shock wave hit like a freight train, hurling her forward. Her shoulder slammed into concrete as the world turned sideways. Steel support beams screamed in protest as precisely placed explosives shattered their integrity.

The ceiling came down in chunks, millions of tons of coral and limestone following ancient gravity toward the earth. Emergency lights strobed crazily, painting the chaos in stuttering snapshots of destruction. The perfect bunker became a perfect coffin.

Cruz tried to roll, to find some pocket of safety in the collapsing tunnel. But there was nowhere to go. No escape route left. The dust cloud rushed toward her like an apocalyptic tide, carrying pulverized stone and shattered dreams.

Her last conscious thought was of control — how she'd built her empire on it, lived by it, died for it. In the end, it had been nothing but illusion. A fantasy as fragile as the walls now crumbling around her.

Then darkness took everything, and Valeria Cruz's carefully ordered world disappeared beneath the mountain she'd tried to master.

The rubble settled. The dust slowly cleared. But in the silence that followed, only the soft drip of ancient water marked the passage of time, patient and eternal as it had been for millennia before human ambition dared to challenge its domain.

Control, in the end, was always an illusion.

CHAPTER 76

BEN

THE EXPLOSION LIFTED the boat three feet out of the water. Guards went flying as the shockwave hit them. The fireball rose into the darkness, reflecting off the waves. The receiver unit disappeared in the inferno.

"Reggie!" Ben was already running back toward the beach, still shouting into the radio. "Hit it! Hit it now!"

Static answered. Had it worked? Had Sarah's sacrifice been enough?

Then the cave entrance collapsed in a thunderous roar. Concrete and rock rained down as the charges detonated. The controlled demolition sealed the entrance.

He watched the horizon in the other direction, where the wreck site was. There would be some telltale sign of the underwater explosion — light against the darkness, a white-capped rogue wave, something.

But there was nothing but the calm stillness of the post-storm seas.

They'd won. But the victory felt hollow as Ben reached the burning wreckage. He waded into the surf, searching desperately.

"Sarah!" His voice was raw. "Sarah!"

Movement in the water caught his eye. A dark head broke the surface thirty feet out. Sarah gasped for air, coughing.

Ben swam to her, grabbed her arm. She was singed but alive — she'd jumped clear at the last second, diving deep to escape the blast.

"Did it work?" she managed between coughs.

Ben pulled her close, feeling her heart hammer against his chest. "Yeah. It worked. You did it."

She sagged against him, exhausted. "Good. Because I'm never doing that again."

"Agreed." He helped her toward shore, eyes watching for any Syndicate members or silent zodiac boats still creeping toward them. "How about that dinner instead?"

Sarah managed a weak laugh. "Somewhere very expensive. With *lots* of wine. And he's buying me the whole bottle."

CHAPTER 77

REGGIE

REGGIE GUNNED the Zodiac's engine, the twin Mercury outboards screaming as they carved through the choppy water. Isla crouched beside him, rifle ready, scanning the shoreline through her scope. The explosion had lit up the night like a second sun, and now thick black smoke billowed where Cruz's mountain fortress had stood.

"There!" Isla shouted over the engines, pointing toward flickering flames near the beach. "By that burning boat!"

He spotted them — two figures in the surf, one supporting the other. Ben and Sarah. Still alive, thank God. But not for long if the remaining Syndicate guards regrouped.

"Hold on!" Reggie cranked the wheel hard, sending the Zodiac into a tight turn. Salt spray whipped across the bow as they carved toward shore. Behind them, the mountain continued its slow collapse, great chunks of rock and coral tumbling into the sea. The sound was like distant thunder, a constant rumble that seemed to shake the very air.

Most of Cruz's people had stopped shooting, transfixed by their base literally falling into the earth. But not all of them. Bullets kicked up white spots in the water around the boat. Isla returned fire, her rifle cracking sharply.

"Two on the ridge!" she called out. "Another team by the palms!"

"I see them." Reggie kept the boat moving in an erratic pattern, making them harder to hit. The shore rushed closer, black sand gleaming in the firelight. "Ben! Sarah! Get ready to move!"

Ben waved acknowledgment, pulling Sarah toward deeper water. They were both soaked, covered in soot and blood. Sarah looked barely conscious, leaning heavily on Ben's shoulder.

Reggie cut power, letting momentum carry them the last few yards. Isla provided cover fire, forcing the guards to duck behind what little protection remained. The mountain's collapse had scattered debris across the entire cove, leaving nowhere truly safe.

"Come on!" Reggie reached out as Ben half-carried Sarah to the boat. "We need to go *now*!"

More shots rang out — closer this time. A round pinged off the hull near Reggie's head. He ducked instinctively, but kept his hand extended. Ben practically threw Sarah aboard, then scrambled up himself. They both collapsed in the bottom of the boat, gasping.

"Hit it!" Isla shouted. "More incoming!"

Reggie didn't need to be told twice. He threw the throttles forward, and the Zodiacs's bow lifted as they accelerated away from shore. Behind them, guards rushed the beach, firing wildly. But they were too late.

"Everyone okay?" Reggie called over his shoulder, keeping his eyes fixed on the dark water ahead. Rocks and coral heads lurked just beneath the surface, waiting to tear out their bottom if he wasn't careful.

"Been better," Sarah managed between coughs. She was curled against Ben's chest, shivering despite the warm night. "But alive."

"Cruz?" Ben asked.

"Still inside when it went," Isla reported, finally lowering her rifle. "No way she made it out. That whole mountain came down right on top of her escape tunnel."

Reggie smiled grimly. "Couldn't have happened to a nicer person."

They cleared the cove's mouth, entering open water. The swells were larger here, making the Zodiac buck and slam. But Reggie kept the power on, wanting as much distance as possible between them and any pursuit.

Behind them, the last of the mountain collapsed with a final thunderous roar. Dust and debris fountained into the sky, briefly obscuring the stars. When it cleared, there was nothing left but a massive pile of rubble where Cruz's base had stood.

"The wreck site?" Isla asked quietly.

Ben nodded. "Still there. We didn't see any explosions from here."

"Good." Sarah's voice was barely audible over the engines.

Isla moved to check her over. "You're burned," she said, examining Sarah's arms. "And these cuts need cleaning. We should get you to a doctor."

"Later." Sarah managed a weak smile. "Right now I just want to get far away from here."

"Working on it," Reggie assured her. He adjusted their course slightly, aiming for the distant lights of civilization on the shores of Culebra. They had no safe house arranged, but they could easily source medical supplies, fresh clothes, and food. Most importantly, they could get back to a place with no Syndicate presence.

The night settled around them as they put distance between themselves and the destruction. The temperature dropped slightly, and Sarah shivered again.

"Hey Reggie?" she called suddenly.

"Yeah?"

"You owe me dinner. Somewhere *really* expensive."

Reggie laughed, feeling tension drain from his shoulders. "Fair enough. Actually, you recommended a place — best steaks on the island. I think I'd rather go with you than Ben, anyway. Plus, they've got a wine cellar that would make Valeria Cruz jealous." He paused. Everyone looked at him. "Because, you know, it's *buried underground* — like her."

Sarah closed her eyes, groaning, then let out a sigh, finally letting exhaustion take over. "Wake me when we get there."

Reggie caught Ben's eye and nodded silent thanks.

Reggie turned back to his navigation, checking their heading, keeping far away from the dangerous shallow reef area. The Zodiac's engines hummed steadily, eating up the miles between them and safety. Soon they'd be able to rest, to heal, to plan their next move.

But for now, he concentrated on the simple act of guiding them home through the darkness, while behind them, Cruz's empire crumbled into the sea.

CHAPTER 78

BEN

THE LIGHTS of Culebra's main strip winked through the palm trees as Ben pulled their rental car into the lot of a clinic. The clock on the dashboard read 2:17 AM, but Isla had worked her magic — the small medical facility's windows glowed warm and welcoming.

"I'm fine, really," Sarah protested as Isla helped her from the backseat. Her salt-crusted hair had dried in twisted ropes, and angry red welts marked her arms where burning debris had found its mark.

"Humor me," Isla said, keeping a steady hand on Sarah's elbow. "Besides, Miguel owes me about fifty favors."

Inside, the doctor — a weathered man in his sixties — worked efficiently, cleaning Sarah's burns and applying antibiotic cream while pepper-firing questions at Isla in rapid Spanish. Ben caught maybe one word in ten, but the doctor's expression grew increasingly grave.

"He wants to know if we're reporting this," Isla translated.

"We are," Ben said firmly. "All of it."

In the waiting room, Reggie had commandeered a corner table, spreading out Isla's laptop. His fingers flew across the keyboard as he downloaded the night's photos he'd taken with the appendage camera on his prosthetic — dozens of shots documenting the Syndicate's operation, the documentation they'd found, writing about the explosion that had nearly killed them all.

"These are gold," he muttered, zooming in on a crystal-clear image of the schematics of the cave system's Syndicate base. "Between these and the GPS coordinates of their operation, we've got them dead to rights."

Ben pulled up a chair, wincing at his own collection of scrapes and bruises. "We need to be strategic about this. The wrong people get hold of this first, it all disappears."

"Already on it." Reggie turned his laptop screen. "I'm uploading everything to three separate secure clouds. And I've got a contact at the Miami Herald who owes us. Once this hits the press, it'll be too big to bury."

Sarah emerged from the exam room with fresh bandages and a prescription for antibiotics. She made a beeline for Reggie's impromptu command center.

"Let me see the wreck photos," she said, pulling up a chair. Despite her exhaustion, her eyes sparked with academic fire. "We need to document the site before anyone else gets down there."

"You think the university will bite?" Ben asked.

"Are you kidding? A previously undocumented wreck, predating the Spanish? And later wrecks, possibly connected to the Spanish treasure fleet?" Sarah's fingers traced the outline of the ship's remains on Reggie's screen. "They'll have a full archaeological team assembled before I finish the email."

"Good," Ben said. "The more official eyes on that site, the harder it'll be for anyone else to exploit it."

Isla joined them, phone pressed to her ear. She'd been making calls non-stop since they'd gotten back, leveraging her network of contacts across the islands. "Yes, Sergeant Martinez. Yes, I understand it's late. But you'll want to see this now."

She hung up and addressed the group. "Local police will be here in twenty minutes. Hopefully just the clean ones," she added. "But either way, we've cut the head off the snake, and more authorities than just the local cops know about this, so they'll have to play along. They'll take our preliminary statements tonight, full interviews tomorrow. I've also got calls in to the FBI field office in San Juan and the DEA."

"What about Manny's family?" Ben asked quietly.

Reggie's typing slowed. "I found his sister's online profile, and a way to contact her. I reached out just so she'd hear about it before the local news. She... she knew something was wrong when he wouldn't answer his phone. Apparently he was supposed to meet her earlier. I promised her answers." He swallowed hard. "I'm just glad we can give them to her."

Sarah squeezed his shoulder. "We can give her justice."

Ben stood, stretching muscles that were already starting to stiffen. "I need coffee. Real coffee, not that waiting room sludge. Anyone else?"

A chorus of exhausted agreements followed him. As he headed for an all-night restaurant across the street, Ben glanced back through the clinic's windows. His unlikely team of treasure hunters had transformed into something else entirely — investigators, witnesses, advocates for the truth. The weight of what they'd discovered, what they'd survived, settled across his shoulders like an all-too-familiar load.

This was just the beginning. There would be statements to give, evidence to process, bureaucratic battles to fight. Even without a de facto leader, the Syndicate's tentacles likely reached deep, and they wouldn't go down without a fight. But looking at his companions — Sarah bent over the laptop with academic intensity, Reggie methodically organizing his damning photos, Isla working her phone like a weapon — Ben knew they'd see it through.

The night air carried the salt-tang of the Caribbean as Ben crossed the street. Behind him, the first hints of dawn began to lighten the eastern sky. A new day was coming, and with it, the real work would begin.

Back in the clinic, he distributed coffee as Reggie's laptop chimed with another incoming email.

"FBI," he announced. "They want everything we've got, and they want it now."

"Then let's give it to them," Ben said, pulling up a chair. "Start from the beginning. Don't leave anything out."

Sarah opened a new document and began to type: "Report regarding criminal activities of the Caribbean Syndicate and the death of Manuel Delgado..."

The words flowed onto the screen as the sky outside grew lighter. They had promises to keep — to Manny's family, to history itself, to the truth. The story had to be told, and they were the ones to tell it.

Isla's phone buzzed again. "DEA's sending a team. They'll be here by noon."

"Perfect," Ben said. "That gives us time to get everything in order." He turned to Sarah. "How long before the university can get a team down here?"

"Once they see these photos?" She smiled grimly. "They'll move heaven and earth. I'd give it a week, tops. We'll need permits fast-tracked, but with law enforcement involved..."

"I know someone at the Puerto Rican Heritage Commission," Isla offered. "They can expedite things."

Reggie looked up from his photo editing. "We should reach out to some journalists I trust. Not with everything, not yet, but enough to put the story on record. Make it harder to disappear."

Ben nodded. They were building a web of accountability, spreading the truth so wide it couldn't be contained. It was what Manny would have wanted.

Hours slipped by as they worked, piecing together their testimony from photos, notes, and memory. Outside, Culebra stirred to life, another tourist day beginning. But inside the clinic, history was being written, justice was being served, and the truth was finally coming to light.

When Sergeant Martinez arrived with his team, they were ready. The story would be told, the wreck would be preserved, and the Syndicate would face what they'd done. It wasn't the treasure they'd set out to find, but it was worth more than all the gold in the Caribbean.

VALERIA

THE WORLD WAS GONE.

At least, the part of it that had mattered to her.

Her breath rasped in the blackness, each inhale pulling the sharp taste of dust deep into her lungs. Every attempt to exhale slowly caught midway, as though her body knew what her mind had only begun to accept. She couldn't move her legs. She couldn't even feel them anymore.

When she had first regained consciousness, she had tried. She had pushed until her spine screamed and white-hot knives of pain lanced up through her hips. Something deep inside her had given way then, and she'd known: both were broken. Probably worse. The arm was bad too. The way it was pinned at that unnatural angle, throbbing in sick rhythm with her heartbeat — yes, that was gone.

The boulder held her in place like the fist of God. She could tilt her head just enough to see the jagged edge of rock an inch from her cheek. Beyond that — nothing. Just black. The kind of black that swallowed the very idea of light before it could form.

She wasn't sure how long she'd been there. Hours, at least. Her watch was gone, her phone somewhere beneath a thousand tons of stone. Time had shrunk to the slow, steady drip of water somewhere out in the collapsed darkness. Drip. Drip. Drip.

Then, eventually, one of those drops landed on her lips. Cold, mineral-rich — pure spring water. She jerked slightly at the shock of it, the reflexive way her tongue darted out to taste it. Her body didn't care where it came from.

Another drop followed. Then another. Soon, the rhythm was maddening. Her throat, raw from dust, ached for more. She pressed her lips together, trying to resist. If she didn't drink, dehydration would take her quicker. That would be a mercy.

But her body betrayed her. Each time the water touched her mouth, her tongue stole it. The reflex was ancient, unstoppable. Every swallow bought her more time she didn't want — more hours in the dark, trapped with her thoughts and the grinding ache of her shattered bones.

Every so often, there was another sound — a tiny crack, a pebble skittering down, the deep groan of rock settling into its new shape. Sometimes the sounds came from directly above her. Those were the moments her breath went shallow, waiting for the next shift to be the one that ended it.

She had always thought she wasn't afraid of death. Too many close calls, too many orders sending others into theirs, to believe otherwise. But this — this was different. Death in a gunfight was fast, clean. This was slow. This was knowing.

It was cold. The damp gnawed into her skin and crept toward her bones. Hypothermia would come long before thirst finished her — unless the damn dripping kept her alive just long enough to truly understand what dying in a place like this felt like.

Her thoughts drifted to Halim. He would never see the reef destroyed now. He would never know why she'd failed him. Maybe he'd think she had betrayed him, or simply gotten sloppy. Maybe that was better than the truth — that she had been beaten. That she was dying alone in the dark, and no one would ever find her.

Drip. Drink. Drip. Drink.

She hated herself for every swallow.

Her lips trembled, and for the first time in years, she whispered a prayer she didn't believe in.

Drip. Drip. Drip.
She closed her eyes, but it made no difference at all.

AFTERWORD

If you liked this book (or even if you hated it…) write a review or rate it. You might not think it makes a difference, but it does.

Besides *actual* currency (money), the currency of today's writing world is *reviews*. Reviews, good or bad, tell other people that an author is worth reading.

As an "indie" author, I need all the help I can get. I'm hoping that since you made it this far into my book, you have some sort of opinion on it.

Would you mind sharing that opinion? It only takes a second.

Nick Thacker

BOOKS BY NICK THACKER

Six Assassins Thrillers

Primary Target (Book 1)

Subtle Target (Book 2)

Unstable Target (Book 3)

Captive Target (Book 4)

Vendetta Target (Book 5)

Final Target (Book 6)

Mason Dixon Thrillers

Mark for Blood (Book 1)

Death Mark (Book 2)

Mark My Words (Book 3)

Harvey Bennett Mysteries

The Enigma Strain (Book 1)

The Amazon Code (Book 2)

The Ice Chasm (Book 3)

The Jefferson Legacy (Book 4)

The Paradise Key (Book 5)

The Atlantis Artifact (Book 6)

The Book of Bones (Book 7)

The Cain Conspiracy (Book 8)

The Mendel Paradox (Book 9)

The Minoan Manifest (Book 10)

The Napoleon Job (Book 11)

The Embers of Siwa (Book 12)

The Epsilon Event (Book 13)

The Cerberus Protocol (Book 14)

The Russian Betrayal (Book 15)

The Eye of Odin (Book 16)

The Polaris Cycle (Book 17)

The Devil's Cut (Book 18)

Harvey Bennett Mysteries - Books 1-3

Harvey Bennett Mysteries - Books 4-6

Harvey Bennett Mysteries - Books 7-9

Harvey Bennett Prequels

The Icarus Effect (written with MP MacDougall)

The Severed Pines (written with Jim Heskett)

The Lethal Bones (written with Jim Heskett)

Gareth Red Thrillers

Seeing Red

Chasing Red (written with Kevin Ikenberry)

The Lucid

The Lucid: Episode One (written with Kevin Tumlinson)

The Lucid: Episode Two (written with Kevin Tumlinson)

The Lucid: Episode Three (written with Kevin Tumlinson

❦

Standalone Thrillers

The Atlantis Stone

The Depths

Relics: A Post-Apocalyptic Technothriller

Killer Thrillers (3-Book Box Set)

Short Stories

I, Sergeant

Instinct

The Gray Picture of Dorian

Uncanny Divide (written with Kevin Tumlinson and Will Flora)

ABOUT THE AUTHOR

Nick Thacker is a thriller author from Texas who lives in Hawaii and Colorado. In his free time, he enjoys reading in a hammock on the beach, skiing, drinking whiskey, and hanging out with his beautiful wife, two dogs, and two daughters.

For more information and a list of Nick's other work, visit Nick online:
www.nickthacker.com